MW00745577

SECRET COMBINATIONS

To Steven

secret
COMBINATIONS

Enjoy!

GORDON COPE

TouchWood
Editions

TouchWood Editions
www.touchwoodeditions.com

Canadian Cataloguing in Publication information
is available from Library and Archives Canada

Editor: Linda Richards
Proofreader: Lenore Hietkamp
Design: Pete Kohut
Cover image: Linda Steward, istockphoto.com
Author photo: Bob Blakey

We gratefully acknowledge the financial support for our publishing activities
from the Government of Canada through the Canada Book Fund, Canada
Council for the Arts, and the province of British Columbia through the
British Columbia Arts Council and the Book Publishing Tax Credit.

The interior pages of this book have been printed on 100% post-consumer
recycled paper, processed chlorine free, and printed with vegetable-based inks.

1 2 3 4 5 15 14 13 12 11

PRINTED IN CANADA

This book is lovingly dedicated to my mother and father, Rose and Syd Cope.

One

His stomach growled. It was after three, and he hadn't had a bite to eat all day. Not only was he hungry, but the afternoon sun was turning the inside of the FBI surveillance van into a furnace. He peeled off his jacket and tucked the pistol into the back of his jeans, where the Sig Sauer 9mm fit nicely, and removed his shoulder holster. He stood up, his long, lanky frame bent to avoid banging his head. Squeezing between the jumble of equipment, he peered out the back window.

The van was parked on a side street beside a run-down tourist hotel on the south edge of downtown. The sidewalk was deserted; most tourists were down on the waterfront, taking in the Independence Day weekend festivities.

As he watched, a dark grey sedan parked behind the van, and a young African American woman got out of the driver's seat. She was dressed in form-fitting blue jeans and an emerald-colored blouse. After removing a casserole dish from the passenger side of her car, she approached the van.

"Sorry I had to haul you away from your family picnic, Jasmine," he said as he opened the side panel door. Jasmine Leroi had been Jack Kenyon's partner for two years, ever since she had arrived at the FBI's San Francisco office as a rookie.

"No problem, Jack," she said as she climbed into the van. "Uncle Vince was playing his ABBA records again."

"Hey, something smells great," Kenyon said, his nose twitching.

Leroi handed him the casserole dish. "I brought you some of mama's ribs."

Kenyon eagerly peeled the tinfoil from the top of the dish and pulled out a succulent honey and garlic treat. "Man, I love her ribs."

"I don't know why I waste money on perfume," said Leroi. "I should just wear some of those ribs around my neck." She sat down at the main surveillance console and glanced at the screens. "What have we got?"

Kenyon, his hands full, turned to expose a folded sheet of white paper sticking out of the left rear pocket in his jeans. "Have a look."

Leroi pulled the paper out and held it up to a patch of light. It was a print-out of an e-mail addressed to Kenyon. She read aloud: "Simon is selling a Nebula Labs program code-named Cyberworm at four this afternoon in room 313 at the San Francisco Deluxe." She glanced up. "Anonymous tip?"

"Got it this morning at my apartment," Kenyon said. "I called Nebula and spoke to their security man. When he heard 'Cyberworm,' he hit the roof."

Leroi handed the paper back. "What's Cyberworm?"

"Some software program. They wouldn't tell me what it does. Nebula handles a lot of work for the military, so it could be anything."

"And they're missing this Cyberworm?"

"Yeah. Nebula ran a check on their internal computer monitor system; Simon came in Saturday morning and loaded it onto a memory stick."

"I take it he's the double agent?" asked Leroi.

"Yup." Kenyon licked his fingers and pulled a thick, leather-bound notebook from the right rear pocket of his jeans. Taking a photo from the notebook, he handed it to Leroi. It was a standard employee mug shot; a clean-shaven Caucasian man with receding hair and thick glasses stared at the camera. "Matthew Q. Simon's a mid-level software engineer. He was passed over for a promotion last year. Management says he's pals with Captain Morgan."

"What?" Leroi said.

"You know," Kenyon said, miming a drinking motion with his free hand. "Plus he's going through a messy divorce, wife got the house and kids, he's living in a rental in Palo Alto."

Leroi nodded. "I'm thinking he needs a little spare cash."

"That's my guess," agreed Kenyon.

"Who's buying?"

"You'll never believe it." Kenyon pointed to a color print-out sitting on the console. "I pulled this off the hotel's security monitor." The print-out showed a tall, clean-shaven man with close-cropped blond hair and a broken nose. He was standing in front of a hotel check-in desk, picking up a keycard.

Leroi whistled. "Charlie Dahg."

"When Marge heard we had bad boy number one in our sights, she gave me the go-ahead to mount surveillance."

"I thought he was into selling Sarin to the North Koreans," said Leroi. "What's he doing in software?"

"Maybe he got tired of wearing a gasmask," Kenyon said chewing on another rib.

Leroi unpacked a digital camera with a high-powered lens from its aluminum case. "Who do you think he's contracted with?"

"Depends on what the software does. The Chinese military would pay big time for the latest missile-guidance stuff. With any luck, Dahg's working for them. We've been trying to close those boys down for a year."

Leroi mounted the camera on a tripod. "Where is he now?"

"Room 313. He checked in about two hours ago."

"We got video in the room?"

Kenyon smiled as he tapped a monitor marked #4. It showed a grainy, black and white image of a hotel room. Dahg was lying on the bed, idly flipping TV channels with the remote. "We dressed Liz Parker up in a maid's outfit. She dropped off some towels and a remote hidden in a roll of toilet paper."

Leroi tipped her head in approval. "Let's just hope he doesn't get the trots."

While Leroi dug out the camera, Kenyon positioned the tripod so that it sighted out the front window of the van. The side of the three-story, run-down hotel was visible across the street. The view included the entrance to the underground garage. A half-block further south, the downtown access ramp for the 101 freeway cast its shadow toward the hotel.

"Who's inside?" asked Leroi.

"We've got Cravitz and Low down the hall in room 326. They went in half an hour ago with the honeymoon luggage." The FBI's SWAT team kept a special kit of bullet-proof vests, a heavy sledge, monitoring equipment, and assault weapons packed into tourist suitcases. "I've got Akita behind the front desk."

"Where's Simon?"

"Been home all day. Benn is tailing him."

Just then, a voice came on the radio. "Benn to Kenyon."

Kenyon picked up the radio mike. "Jack here, over."

"Jasper's on the move. Red Toyota sedan, license plate C-O-D-E."

Kenyon glanced at his watch; it was 3:35 PM—twenty-five minutes to go to the arranged meeting time. "Roger, Benn, we copy. Out." Kenyon punched the radio button for all-frequencies. "Jasper is approaching lair. ETA is twenty-five minutes. Status check."

The radio hissed; Akita behind the desk came in. "Big Dog's on point."

A second call from room 326. "Welcome Wagon ready to roll."

Leroi glanced up from the camera equipment. "All set here."

A few seconds later, Benn radioed in his status report. "We're on the 101."

"Okay, Benn. Let us know when you hit the off-ramp." Kenyon signed off and stared out the window, a lopsided smile of satisfaction on his face. Everything was falling into place. Marge Gonelli, the special agent in charge of San Francisco, had been riding him hard to get a big case against the espionage rings that infiltrated the Bay area. With any luck, they would be able to record the drop, then follow Dahg back to his masters.

His thoughts were interrupted by a rap on the sidewalk side of the van.

Leroi glanced up. "You expecting anyone?" she whispered.

"No." Kenyon drew his Sig Sauer.

The side door opened, and the balding head of Will Deaver poked into the van. "Don't shoot!" he warned. "It's me!" The assistant US attorney for the judicial district of San Francisco was a small, wiry man in his forties. He was dressed in casual slacks and a golf shirt.

"What are you *doing* here?" Kenyon whispered hoarsely. "You trying to blow our cover?"

Deaver ignored the remark as he climbed into the van. "Hope I'm not too late."

Kenyon glanced out of the corner of his eye at Leroi. "No, the more the merrier." He flipped the video camera case on its side and tucked it against the back door. "Sit on this and stay out of the way."

Deaver continued to ignore him. "Hey, what's that great smell?" He dug a rib out of the casserole dish.

"You still haven't told us why you're here," said Kenyon.

"I hear you've got Charlie Dahg in your sights," said Deaver.

"Where'd you hear that?"

Deaver grinned over the rib. "I have my sources."

The agent didn't doubt it. Deaver was only an assistant attorney, but he had a rich wife and an ambitious streak as wide as San Francisco Bay; he was openly touted as the next Republican candidate for state governor. Somebody looking to join the bandwagon must have tipped him off.

Deaver craned his neck to peer at the video monitor. "When's the guy with the stolen goods supposed to show up?"

"We estimate inside of twenty minutes."

"Good. We take them down as soon as he enters the room."

Kenyon cursed under his breath. A political hot dog like Deaver was only interested in getting himself a nice, front page story. "Our plan is to follow Dahg to see who's paying him," he said. "We want the entire ring."

"No way," replied Deaver, putting down his rib. "The chances are too great he'll slip away."

"We have no probable cause for entering room 313," countered Kenyon. "We don't even know if Simon has the stolen property on him. If we bust in and they're clean, we have a major liability."

Deaver faced him square. "If you don't take them down, Kenyon, you're going to have a major liability, and it's going to be me."

Deaver was not, on paper, Kenyon's superior, but the FBI agent had no delusions about the problems the other man could stir up. He glanced at Leroi who was studiously keeping her attention focused on the video camera.

"We do it my way," said Kenyon.

Deaver stared hard at the agent, but Kenyon didn't blink and he was forced to turn his attention to the console. "Is that Dahg?" he asked, pointing to monitor #4.

Leroi glanced up. "Yeah, that's him,"

Deaver turned back to Kenyon. "If you see Simon pass anything to Dahg, we got probable cause, right?"

Damn, thought Kenyon. "Right."

A smile broke out on Deaver's face. "Then you go in the moment we see the exchange."

You little piece of shit, thought Kenyon. "It's your funeral," he finally said.

Deaver smiled. "I knew you'd see it my way."

Kenyon turned to the radio and called the tail car. "Benn? This is Jack. What is your status?"

"Just passing over Army Street, heading north. Traffic is clear. ETA ten minutes. Over."

Kenyon turned to all-frequencies. "This is Jack. ETA is ten minutes. There's been a change of plan. I want take-down after Jasper enters the room. Assume extreme counter-force. Do you copy?"

"We copy," said Cravitz from the surveillance room.

"Ditto," came Akita's reply from behind the desk.

Kenyon pulled the keys from the ignition and opened a footlocker behind the driver's seat. He lifted out two lightweight armored vests with large yellow FBI letters on the back and handed one to Leroi. After donning his vest, Kenyon pulled out a pump-action shotgun and a handful of shells. He loaded five rounds into the 12-gauge and handed the gun to Leroi. She racked a shell into the chamber and propped it beside the radio.

Kenyon turned to Deaver. "No matter what happens, stay inside the van unless I say otherwise; you got me?"

Surprisingly, Deaver merely nodded.

The radio crackled. "This is Benn. Jasper exiting at Mission."

Kenyon grabbed the mike and crouched at the rear window. A few seconds later, a red Toyota sedan turned the corner. "I have visual contact." The car slowed, then turned into the underground garage. "Jasper has just entered the parkade. Akita, stand by on visual."

Kenyon licked his lips. Thirty seconds passed, then a minute, and still no response from Akita at the desk. Kenyon clicked on the mike. "Akita, do you have a visual?"

The response from the front desk came through clearly. "Nothing yet."

Kenyon tapped the mike against the van wall; it was taking too long for Simon to get up to the reception area. Did he have a change of heart? Was he sitting in his car, frozen by indecision? Something was wrong. Kenyon stripped off his vest and opened the side door of the van. He glanced up and down the street, but no one was on the sidewalk. He turned back toward Leroi. "I'm going into the garage. Keep everyone on stand-by until I return."

Kenyon hopped out of the vehicle and crossed the street toward the entrance to the underground parkade. Just as he reached the ramp, a blue commercial van pulled out of the garage. The agent jumped to one side as the vehicle rushed past, then he ran down the ramp, into the darkness.

It took a second for his eyes to adjust to the gloom. He looked around, but there was nobody moving in the garage. He scouted the rows of cars until he spotted Simon's red Toyota. It was parked, the motor turned off. As far as Kenyon could tell, there was nobody in or around the car. Good, thought Kenyon, he's headed up. He relaxed as he approached the rear of the vehicle.

As the agent crossed over to the driver's side, however, he spotted two feet sticking out along the ground. A man lay on his back, his eyes staring at the cement ceiling. Kenyon pulled his gun and chambered a round, simultaneously glancing left and right. Seeing no one, he advanced cautiously toward the prone man. It was Simon, a large, dark stain on the chest of his white shirt. He was alive, his breath ragged and labored.

Kenyon turned and ran for the garage entrance. He pulled out his cell phone and dialed 911 as he galloped up the ramp, calling for an ambulance as he ran. He sprinted across the road and reached the open door of the command van. "Simon's down!" He shoved the cell phone into Deaver's hand. "I got emergency on the line; guide 'em in."

Kenyon scrambled inside and grabbed the mike. "Cravitz! Bust in now! Do you hear me? Now!"

"We copy," responded Cravitz.

Suddenly, Kenyon remembered the other vehicle. He turned to Deaver, hunched by the door, the cell phone pressed to his ear. "Which way did the van go?"

Deaver looked at him in confusion. "What van?"

"A blue van came out of the garage when I was going in. Which way did it go, dammit?"

Deaver stared up and down the street. "I don't know."

Leroi leaned forward. "I saw it out the back window. It went down the street and turned left."

Kenyon grabbed Deaver by the shoulder. "Gimme your keys."

"Why?"

"Gimme your keys!"

Deaver dug in his pocket and pulled out the keys to his car. Kenyon turned to Leroi as he stepped out of the van. "I'm heading south on Valencia. Tell SFPD to keep a look-out for a blue plumbing van. It says 'Al's' or something on the side."

Kenyon jumped into Deaver's car. He pulled a U-turn, crashing over the curb, then sped down to the end of the side street and turned left onto Valencia and roared down the block. There was a red light ahead but the oncoming lane was empty and he zigged into it. He squealed to a halt at the intersection and glanced on the floorboards, but there was no cherry. Goddamn civilian car. He nosed the hood out into the intersection, then zipped through a break in traffic.

Valencia ran through a bustling Latino neighborhood. People crowded the sidewalks, ordering food at take-outs and drinking beer on the curb. Kenyon tried to imagine how long it had been since he saw the blue van; one minute? Three minutes? He glanced nervously down side roads as he passed; he had no idea if the van had turned off the street. Too much time, he thought. Too much time.

Then Kenyon saw the van. It was sitting in the left lane at an intersection, three cars back from the stoplight. The light turned green, and the van pulled slowly away. Kenyon didn't figure he'd been spotted. The agent swung over to the right lane into the driver's blind spot, following at a safe distance.

Time to call for back-up. Kenyon felt in his pocket for his cell phone, remembering as he did so that he'd left it with Deaver. He scanned the interior of the sedan, but there was no phone or radio hook-up. Shit. He would have to follow the van until it stopped, then call for back-up.

The vehicle continued south until it reached a commercial district. Still moving sedately, it turned onto a side street. Kenyon waited for a few seconds, then followed.

The side street was lined with run-down warehouses and boarded up factories. He eased in behind a parked car and watched from a distance as the blue van pulled over to the curb.

It stopped in front of a high steel gate. The driver, wearing a baseball cap, black sunglasses, and gloves, got out of the van and opened the barrier, then got back in and drove into the yard, disappearing around the far side of a building.

Kenyon looked around the street. There were no payphones nearby. The van might reappear at any time; he couldn't risk going to find a phone. Just then, a brown coupe came around the far corner and drove toward Kenyon. The FBI agent jumped out of Deaver's car, flipped open his ID, and stepped in front of the coupe, forcing it to stop. "I'm with the Federal Bureau of Investigation," he said. "I need your help."

The driver was an older Latino man. He rolled his window down a fraction of an inch. "What's wrong?"

"You got a cell phone?"

"Yeah."

Kenyon pulled out a card from his ID wallet. "I need you to call this number."

The man took the card through the slit at the top of the window. He glanced at it briefly. "What should I say?"

Kenyon turned and read the faded sign over the warehouse door. "Agent Kenyon is at the Salmon King fish packers, just off Army Street. Send reinforcements."

As the man drove off, Kenyon entered the gate and ran across the yard to the front of the warehouse. He peered around the corner. The blue van sat fifty feet ahead, beside a door. The motor was turned off.

Kenyon pulled out his automatic and advanced on the van, trying to keep out of view. He reached the rear window and glanced inside. The vehicle was empty and there was no sign of the driver.

Kenyon checked the warehouse door. It was unlocked. As quietly as he could, he opened the door and eased inside. The interior of the warehouse was lit by sunlight pouring through small windows high on the walls. Long zinc-metal tables covered the concrete floor. He listened for sounds of movement. Except for the dripping of water somewhere, all was quiet.

Glancing down, Kenyon could see a fresh set of footprints receding in the dust.

He advanced slowly, following the footprints to a set of wooden stairs that led up to an office that overlooked the warehouse floor. The windows to the office were shuttered.

Kenyon sniffed the air, detecting the aroma of fresh cigar smoke. The driver was up top. He tested the stairs. The wood was old, but solid. He eased his way up, placing his weight on the side of the steps where they met the riser. He kept his gun pointed at the door to the office, the trigger cocked.

When he reached the top of the stairs he found the door to the office closed, but the smell of cigar smoke was very strong. He braced himself on the top step, then rushed against the door, bursting it open. "Freeze!" he shouted. "FBI!"

A shadow darted from behind a desk. Kenyon lunged to the left to cut off his retreat.

Suddenly, there was no floor. Kenyon's foot shot into a gap and he pitched forward onto his face, his gun clattering across the room. He tried to rise, but his boot was stuck in the joists. While he struggled to free himself he heard the crack of a gun. It felt as if he had been punched in the back with a sledgehammer. The floor rose up in slow motion, and a wave of blackness engulfed him.

Two

Monday, July 4

Kenyon dreamed he was back in Montana, riding the horse that Cyrus and Daisy had given him as a birthday present when he was ten. The young boy he had been climbed through the pine-scented forest to a ridge that overlooked Eden Valley ranch. Below him, tucked into a sheltered valley, were the fields and barns and stables that Cyrus' father had built in the shadow of the Rocky Mountains. Above him, a hawk circled the sun, a tiny dot in the immense blue sky.

A ringing phone awoke him and he stared around, momentarily disoriented.

He was lying in a narrow bed with protective chrome rails, propped on his side with an orthopedic pillow. The curtain that surrounded the bed had been pulled back. The walls of the room were white, and the floor was finished in beige Formica tiles. A tag sewn on the bed cover said "San Francisco General Hospital."

With a start, a jumble of memories came pouring back. Flashing red lights, a rush to the hospital, the brilliant white glare of an operating room.

Kenyon stared irritably at the bedside phone, but it continued to ring. He finally reached over and picked it up.

"What?" he croaked, his voice hoarse and phlegmy.

"It's me," said Leroi. "How you doing?"

There was a plastic bottle with a straw resting on a table beside the phone. Kenyon took a sip of water. "Somebody tried to cut me a new asshole. It hurts like hell."

"Good. That means you're too mean to kill. You get the flowers from the guys?"

Kenyon looked over at a table covered with several bouquets. He couldn't read any of the tags from where he lay. "Yeah, I got 'em."

"How long you in for?"

"I don't know. The doc hasn't come in yet. They wanted me to get some sleep."

"Sorry about waking you, but I wanted to talk before the posse arrives. You alone?"

"Yeah," replied Kenyon.

"Good. What happened?"

"You first," said Kenyon.

"Okay," said Leroi. "After you took off, I went in and covered Simon."

"How is he?"

"Real bad, last I heard."

"What happened to Dahg?"

"The SWAT team took him down, no problem. Cravitz says his eyes just about popped out of his head when they crashed the door. I guess the last thing he expected was a bust."

Kenyon briefly explained to Leroi how he tailed the killer south to the warehouse. "I was worried he might escape, so I tried to take him solo. I screwed up."

"Hey, shit happens," said Leroi. "Mama says you get better real quick. Talk to you later."

Kenyon hung up the phone and took another sip of water. He was relieved that his squad had arrested Dahg without incident, but there was no masking the operation as anything but a fiasco. His head hurt, and his guts were filled with a queasy feeling.

There was a knock on the door, and a young, attractive Asian woman in a white lab coat entered. "I'm Doctor Lui," she introduced herself. "I did the surgery on you last night. How do you feel this morning?"

"I'm fine," he replied. "How's Simon?"

Lui sat down on the edge of the bed, facing Kenyon. "He suffered a lung puncture and a lacerated aorta. We tried to repair the damage, but he lost too much blood. He didn't make it."

"He's dead?"

The doctor nodded. "Yes. I'm sorry."

Kenyon felt numb; the death of Simon weighed heavily on his heart.

"You want to know how you're doing?" asked the doctor.

Kenyon turned back to her. "What? Yeah, sure."

Lui lifted Kenyon's hospital gown and listened to his chest with the stethoscope. She then examined the wound to his backside. "You were lucky," she finally said. "The bullet was deflected by the notebook you had in your back pocket. You got a bad bruise and ten stitches in your butt."

"Can I go home?"

Lui stood up. "I want to let the swelling go down and check it again this afternoon." She gave him a wink as she was leaving. "If it still looks as good as it did last night, I'll cut you loose."

Kenyon blushed, but also breathed a sigh of relief. The last thing he wanted was to get stuck in San Francisco General for several days. Ever since he had watched Daisy die in a cancer ward, Kenyon hated hospitals.

The doctor left the door open, and Kenyon glanced out into the hallway. An agent stood to one side, guarding his door. Kenyon wondered if that was for his own protection, or to keep everyone out until the official investigation. The agents had a name for all the second-guessers who swarmed over a botched assignment: the rear-admirals. He wondered which rear-admiral would be in first.

He didn't have long to wait. There was a rap on the door post, and Will Deaver entered, a brittle smile on his face. "How are we this morning?" he asked cheerfully.

"*We'd* be a lot better if our ass didn't resemble swiss cheese."

Deaver glanced briefly at the prone FBI agent, then turned his attention to the flowers. Kenyon almost expected him to go over and check to see if there were any from celebrities, but Deaver reached into his pocket and pulled out Kenyon's cell phone, instead. "I just wanted to return this to you," he said. "I got the ambulance there in record time."

"I'm sure Simon would be pleased if he weren't still dead."

Deaver turned red. "I hardly think that's an appropriate comment."

"Oh, it's appropriate, Deaver. If we had done what I wanted to do, maybe Simon would be alive."

Deaver pointed his finger at Kenyon. "He'd have been just as dead with your plan. Don't you try to pin your fuck-up on *my* chest, mister."

Someone spoke from behind him. "He'd have to find it first."

Deaver turned. A short woman in her mid-fifties with permed grey hair and cats-eye glasses stood in the doorway. She clutched a large leather purse in her hands. Except for the unlit cigar butt in her mouth, she looked just like someone's granny.

"Oh, hi Marge," replied Deaver. "I was just leaving."

"No, you ain't," she replied in a nasal, New York accent. "Not until you listen to what I got to say." She marched right up to Deaver and poked him in the ribs with a short finger. "You stuck your nose where it don't belong yesterday and that pisses me off big time."

Deaver backed up. "Marge, I was just trying to . . ."

"I know what you was trying to do. The next time you screw up one of my operations, I am going to shoot you right between your beady little eyes. Now get out of my sight."

Deaver made a show of straightening his tie and brushing his lapels until Marge opened her purse and reached inside. Deaver lunged out of the room.

"That's better," said Marge, slamming the door shut behind him. She turned to Kenyon. "You feel good enough to talk, sweetie?"

Kenyon patted the side of the bed. "Yeah, sure, Marge."

Marge Gonelli was the special agent in charge of the San Francisco office. She was one of the most talented recruits ever to be appointed as a field agent. She had risen to her current station as SAC after a long and illustrious career, and her treatment of agents under her wing had earned her their unqualified respect.

Gonelli sat down on the bed and reached into her bag. "Hey, I got something for you." She pulled out a card and present.

"You shouldn't have," said Kenyon. "Happy 33rd Birthday" was written across the top of the card. The illustration showed a young man in a red convertible. He opened the card and read "To my favorite agent. Marge."

Gonelli handed him the present. "Go on, open it. I made 'em myself. Oops! Spoiled the surprise."

Kenyon unwrapped the box; it held two dozen brownies. "My favorites," he said, taking a bite. "These are great, Marge."

Actually, they smelled like gun oil, but then, everything in Gonelli's purse did. Several years ago, a bank robber had entered her branch while she was picking up a new debit card. She reached into her purse and fired her .38 Smith & Wesson through the bottom of the bag, knocking the big toe right off his left foot.

As Kenyon ate his brownie, a nurse entered the room with a glass of juice. She stopped short and stared at Gonelli. "I'm sorry, Ma'am, but you'll have to put out that cigar; this is a no-smoking environment."

"I ain't smokin' it, honey," Gonelli replied, holding up the inert stogie. "Any rules against eatin' it?"

The nurse looked at Gonelli askance; she put down the juice on Kenyon's bedside table and quickly retreated.

"I think she's sweet on you," said Gonelli, after the nurse had left. "You should ask her out."

"Yeah. I'll offer to show her my circumcision scar."

"Cute. Keep up the wise talk and you'll never find a nice girl."

Just to change the subject, Kenyon recounted the botched stake-out. He left nothing out; the most embarrassing part was explaining how he had fallen through the floorboards, letting the perp get away.

"What were you packin'?" asked Gonelli.

"My Sig Sauer. Did they find it?"

"Yeah. One bullet fired. Did you hit him?"

Kenyon shook his head. "I didn't fire it."

"You didn't?"

"No. I dropped it when I fell."

"So, he capped your tuckus with your own gun," said Marge.

Kenyon was mortified. "Marge, please, don't tell anyone."

Gonelli shook her finger. "I gotta. Besides, it lets you off a discharged-firearm review. All that leaves is Simon."

Kenyon grimaced. "You know, Marge, if I had just ignored that asshole Deaver, he might be okay."

"Rule number one in this business, never second-guess," replied Gonelli.

"Deaver's going to be looking for a scapegoat."

"Let me worry about him. I wanna go over some stuff with you." Gonelli pulled out a file from her purse and adjusted her glasses. "We think Simon was carrying a coded memory stick containing a software program called Cyberworm."

"Is it a secret military program?" asked Kenyon.

"Yeah," said Gonelli. "We're working to get clearance."

"What about Dahg?" asked Kenyon. "Is he talking?"

"Nope," Gonelli said, glancing back at her notes. "He checked into the Raphael Hotel under an assumed name last week. We got a warrant and found fifty thousand dollars in cash under his pillow. Phone records for the hotel shows he called Simon at home. We'll sweat him with conspiracy in the murder of Simon."

"Can we make it stick?"

Gonelli shook her head, no. "My guess is, he's a mule hired to make the pickup and delivery."

Kenyon scratched his chin. He hadn't shaved since Sunday morning, and a day's worth of dark stubble was growing in. "What about the guy in the blue van?"

"The van was stolen the day before. The plates were pinched from a second car. It was abandoned at the fish plant; he musta had a back-up car. We got no prints in the vehicle. We're gathering hairs and fibers, but don't hold your breath."

"And the warehouse?"

Gonelli pulled the cigar butt from her mouth and squinted at it. "The company that used to own it is bankrupt. It's been abandoned for about ten years. All we found was some footprints and cigar ash."

Kenyon nodded. "I remember smelling it."

Gonelli leaned back. "So, we got a dead double agent, a spook who ain't talkin', and a wise guy who can't shoot worth beans. Ya' know what's buggin' me most, though?

"What?"

Gonelli pushed her glasses up the bridge of her nose. "Who tipped us off?"

Kenyon shrugged. "Maybe it was another gang. They couldn't do the deal, so they spoiled it."

"If I were a rival gang that knew the time and place of the pass, I would have just gone in and ripped off Simon when he was at home," said Gonelli. "No, there's more to it than that."

Kenyon thought for a moment. "How about a double-cross? Whoever hired Dahg planned all along to cut Simon off at the underground garage and steal the stuff there, then head back to their rat hole. They leave Dahg holding the bag."

Gonelli pondered his idea. "Better, but it still don't scan."

"Anything on the e-mail itself?" asked Kenyon.

"It came from a java joint wi-fi near Haight and Ashbury. The clerks in there are baked. Maybe if we take your description down, we can luck out."

Kenyon shook his head. "I never got a clear look at him."

Gonelli crossed a note off in her file. "Well, that burns that bridge."

"I think our best bet is to look at who stands to gain from the theft," said Kenyon. "Once I find out what kind of program this Cyberworm is, I should be able to narrow down the possible suspects."

Gonelli rolled the cigar butt in her mouth. "No."

"Why not?"

"You ain't on the case."

Kenyon stared at the blanket. "You think I screwed up?"

"No. You're not on the case because you're taking a personal leave of absence."

"Hey, it's only a few stitches," argued Kenyon. "The doc says I can go home today."

Gonelli looked down at the back of her hands. "This is a different kind of personal leave," she said. "I got a call from some lady lawyer in London. She told me Lydia Kenyon was dead."

Kenyon's expression was blank, until he made the connection. "You mean, my *Aunt* Lydia?"

"Yeah. I'm sorry, Jack. Lydia was killed in a car accident."

For a moment Kenyon stared at the ceiling, trying to decide what to say. "I hardly knew her, Marge."

"She's your relative."

"She was the daughter of my foster parents, Cyrus and Daisy."

"That still makes her family."

Kenyon rubbed his face with his hands. "She had already grown up and left home when I was born. I never met her in my entire life."

"So?"

"Look, I'm sorry she's dead and all, but I don't see why I need a personal leave of absence."

Gonelli reached into her purse and pulled out another file. "'Cause, you've been appointed executor in her will." She handed the slim file to Kenyon. "There's papers and stuff you have to sign."

Kenyon rubbed his eyes wearily. "Does Cyrus know?"

Gonelli nodded. "I phoned his ranch in Montana. He already got a call."

Kenyon thought about his foster father, sitting alone in Eden Valley. Cyrus the Tyrant, Kenyon had called him; they hadn't spoken in years. The straight-laced old man had a way of driving his children out of his home. He never even knew what the feud that had alienated Lydia was about.

"Marge, you know I'm the computers guy. You need me here."

Gonelli patted the blanket over his knee. "I'll call you every day."

Kenyon tried one last time. "They can handle all that stuff in London without me. I have more important things to do here."

Gonelli stood up and headed for the door. "No you don't, sweetie. You gotta go to England."

Kenyon leaned back in the bed and crossed his arms. "Marge, there's no way I'm going."

Three

Friday, July 8. London

The overnight flight from San Francisco touched down at Heathrow Airport a little after one in the afternoon. Kenyon pulled his carry-on bag from the overhead bin and slowly shuffled down the aisle.

"Have a nice visit to London," said the stewardess as he exited the plane.

"Nice and short is what I'm looking forward to," he replied.

The landing gate was almost a quarter mile from the central hub, but Kenyon was glad for the opportunity to walk. The swelling had gone down considerably in the five days since he had been shot, but the last ten hours crammed into an economy seat had left him feeling stiff and sore.

By the time Kenyon reached immigration, a long line had formed behind the three officers checking passports. He groaned and took his place in line, but a man in a blue uniform stepped forward and tapped him on the shoulder. "Mr. Kenyon? I'm wondering if you wouldn't mind coming with me."

Kenyon accompanied the immigration officer to an adjacent office, where he was met by the FBI's legal attaché, Stan Fairmont.

"Jack!" exclaimed Fairmont, in a booming, midwestern voice. "How was the trip?"

Kenyon shook Fairmont's extended hand. It was big and meaty, like the man. "I feel like I've been riding in a cattle car all night."

Fairmont laughed and slapped him on the back. "Marge called and warned me that you were coming. I'm glad I had time to see you before I head out. I'm flying to Belfast in about twenty minutes."

"Trouble?" asked Kenyon.

"Nope," replied Fairmont. "Ambassador Stewart's flying over in two weeks and I have to spend a few days going over security with the Royal Ulster Constabulary."

Kenyon nodded. There had been another flare-up of sectarian violence by a break-away group of the IRA. The US ambassador to the United Nations was flying in to chair a new round of peace talks. Part of Fairmont's official duties in Britain was to protect American politicians abroad.

The immigration officer returned Kenyon's passport. "That's all, sir. Enjoy your stay in the UK."

Kenyon was about to leave, but Fairmont held up his hand. "One last thing: you know you're not allowed to carry here."

"Yeah, Marge warned me." Kenyon felt naked without his Sig Sauer 9mm, but unless they were traveling on official business, British regulations strictly prohibited international law officers from carrying firearms in the UK.

Fairmont nodded. "Okay, let's go."

Customs waved Kenyon through after giving him a cursory glance, and he was soon following Fairmont down the main concourse of the airport.

"Sorry to hear about your aunt," Fairmont said. "The ambassador tells me she was a fine woman."

"Thanks," said Kenyon. "I didn't really know her, myself."

Fairmont stopped abruptly in front of an exit and glanced at his watch. "I've only got a few minutes before I have to run, but here's the drill. I know you're here in an unofficial capacity, but if you need any help, anything at all, I want you to call my guy at Scotland Yard."

Fairmont pulled a card from his wallet and handed it to Kenyon. It read "Detective Inspector Humphrey Arundel, Metropolitan Police." "He's an odd duck, but don't take him lightly," said Fairmont. "He's connected."

Kenyon tucked the card in his pocket and shook Fairmont's hand.

"Thanks for taking time to greet me, Stan, but I can see you're busy, so I'll just grab a cab . . ."

"Hey, don't even think of it," said Fairmont. "I brought you some wheels." The legal attaché led Kenyon outside, where a black Lincoln town car rested by the curb.

"Compliments of the ambassador," said Fairmont. "When he heard you took one in the ass for your country, he coughed up a free limo ride."

A Marine sergeant hopped out of the driver's seat, saluted Kenyon, and grabbed his carry-on bag. Kenyon eased into the back seat and turned his attention to the interior of the car, but Fairmont tapped on the window. The agent found the button and lowered the smoked glass.

"Remember, anything comes up, you call Arundel, got me?"

Kenyon smiled. "Got you."

Fairmont nodded to the driver, then disappeared back into the terminal.

The marine climbed back into the car. "Where to, sir?" he asked.

Kenyon handed him the address, then leaned back into the plush upholstery as the driver wheeled onto the main highway.

It was a hot, sunny day, and traffic moved briskly down the left-hand side of the road. Kenyon shook his head; he was still on San Francisco time and it felt like the middle of the night. Having all the traffic reversed added to his sense of unreality.

The driver was engrossed in his task, giving Kenyon the opportunity to sit back and observe the city as it rolled past. The streets were wide and lined with row houses of red brick and white stone. Many of the buildings rose up to a height of five stories, with impressive entrances flanked by columns of carved marble. They passed several palaces and landscaped parks, and an immense monument dedicated to Wellington's victory at Waterloo.

After almost an hour's ride the cab drove under a limestone arch inscribed "New Square." The square was a large, rectangular park carpeted in green lawn and fringed by a ring of four-story, brown brick buildings. Men and women dressed in long black gowns and white wigs walked along the perimeter of the square. Several of them stared at the limo as it passed, trying to see through the tinted glass windows.

The large automobile pulled up to the curb about halfway around the square. "This is it, sir," said the marine. "Shall I wait for you?"

"No thanks," said Kenyon, glad to be out of the big, ostentatious car. "I'll grab a cab when I'm done."

The marine removed Kenyon's luggage from the trunk and, after one final salute, drove away.

Kenyon double-checked the address before advancing up the walkway. An unpolished brass plate on an ancient oak door proclaimed this to be "Burnham Sharpley & Co. Law Firm." The door was open and Kenyon entered.

The interior of the building was dark and gloomy and looked to be several hundred years old. Kenyon took a moment to let his eyes adjust to the low light of the reception room.

A male clerk sat at a desk, pecking away at a grimy keyboard. He looked up irritably. "What is it?" he demanded.

"My name is Kenyon. I'm here to see Miss Tanya O'Neill."

"Just a moment." The clerk picked up a phone that would have looked right at home with a hand crank on the side of it, and dialed a number. "Yes, a Mr. Kenyon to see you." He hung up the phone and arched an eyebrow. "She'll be right out." The clerk went back to his typing.

Kenyon looked around the room. The only free seat was greasy and worn, and he didn't want to risk staining his suit. The whole office looked cheap and run down. Is this all that Lydia could afford? He wondered if they had buried his aunt in Beggar's Row.

A small woman in her late twenties appeared at the door. She extended her hand in greeting and the cuff of a turquoise blouse peeked from beneath her dark solicitor's robes. "Good afternoon, Mr. Kenyon," she said, in a soft Irish brogue. "I'm Tanya O'Neill."

Kenyon shook her hand solemnly. "Pleased to meet you, ma'am."

O'Neill turned and pointed down the hall. "Would you care to join me in my chambers?"

Kenyon smiled as he followed her into the inner recesses of the office. Her dark red hair, cut in a page boy style, bounced from side to side as she walked.

The dark corridor doglegged several times. Kenyon had to take care not to bang his head on the low, exposed beams. They finally turned into a small office, and O'Neill closed the door behind them.

Kenyon glanced around the room. The lawyer's desk was made of ancient, heavily scarred wood. A large computer screen rested in the center, and a decorative alabaster vase sat on one corner. The remainder of the surface was almost completely covered with legal files.

The rest of the room was as fashionable as the desk. The carpet was dull brown and needed cleaning. Except for a small lead-paned window that opened onto a tiny courtyard, the walls were covered with shelves of legal texts.

The only decoration in the room was an oil painting, propped against the wall beneath the window. It was a portrait of a nude woman, framed in a thick, burgundy-colored wood. It looked distinctly out of place.

"Care to sit down?" O'Neill motioned her visitor to a wooden chair as she took her place behind her desk.

Kenyon eased himself down onto the hard chair and grimaced at the pain.

O'Neill, not noticing his discomfort, picked up a folder marked "Kenyon." She opened it, and began to read. "I, Lydia Kenyon, of 61 Herringbone Gardens, London, hereby revoke all wills and testamentary dispositions made by me and declare this to be my last will, which I make this 29th day of June."

O'Neill flipped the first page over and was about to begin reading the contents of the will when she noticed Kenyon's pained expression. "Is there something amiss?" she asked.

Kenyon squirmed in the hard wooden seat. "It's nothing—I got shot in the backside a few days ago, and this chair is a little uncomfortable."

O'Neill blinked in surprise. "Oh, dear. Let me see if I can find you a cushion." The solicitor stood up from behind her desk and exited the room.

O'Neill was gone for several minutes and Kenyon took the opportunity to stand up and take a closer look at the painting. The nude was reclining in a settee beside a large bay window. Her slim body was angled to one side, but her gaze was turned directly toward the viewer. Her blond hair was cropped short, and there was something about the way she cradled her breasts in her left arm that was sensuous, yet vulnerable. Her lips were curled up in a sly, mysterious smile. She appeared to be in her mid-fifties, a little old for Kenyon, but he still found her very attractive.

O'Neill came back into the office holding a thick, bright-orange cushion. "Will this do?"

Kenyon placed the cushion on his chair and gingerly lowered himself down. It was surprisingly comfortable. "That's great," he announced.

Satisfied, O'Neill returned to her chair behind the desk, and resumed her reading of the will. "On behalf of Mrs. Ilsa Ingoldsby-Legrand, of Ingoldsby Manor, Surrey, I give a donation of ten thousand pounds to the Daughters of Mercy charity."

"Who's that?" asked Kenyon.

O'Neill glanced up. "I beg your pardon?"

"Sorry to interrupt, but I was wondering who Mrs. Ilsa whatever is."

"Mrs. Ilsa Ingoldsby-Legrand," repeated O'Neill. "She is a patron of the arts and charity."

"She must have been a friend of Lydia's, then."

O'Neill paused for a moment. "I wouldn't say that, no."

Kenyon raised an eyebrow. "Lydia gave ten thousand to someone she didn't like?"

"Lydia held the Daughters of Mercy charity very close to her heart," said O'Neill. "In fact, I have a recording of the charity auction that Lydia organized." She dug in a drawer of her desk and pulled out a

DVD, handing it across the desk to Kenyon. "The production company just sent it to me yesterday."

"Thanks." Kenyon put it in his suit pocket.

The solicitor cleared her throat, then continued. "In recognition of his long friendship, I give Mr. Raymond Legrand of Ingoldsby Manor, Surrey, a Louis Vuitton briefcase, stored at 61 Herringbone Gardens, London."

Kenyon interrupted again. "Is Legrand connected to Ilsa?"

"Mr. Legrand is Ilsa's husband." O'Neill wet her finger and quickly flipped a page in the document. "Finally, I give all my remaining property and assets, both real and personal, movable and immovable, to Mr. Jack Kenyon, of San Francisco, California." She picked up a small folder and handed it to Kenyon across the desk.

The FBI agent flipped it open. "What's this?"

"It is a tabulation of Lydia's property, prepared by her last month."

Kenyon whistled. According to the list, he was now the proud owner of a home in the borough of Kensington and Chelsea, an art gallery in Mayfair, and a vineyard somewhere in France. There was also an extensive list of furniture, artwork, silverware, and other valuables. Kenyon's eyes grew wide as he flipped through page after page. "Man, she had a ton of stuff."

"Lydia was an affluent woman," agreed O'Neill. "You have quite a bit of work ahead of you."

Kenyon's pleased expression immediately dissolved, and he looked up in alarm. "Whoa, what do you mean: 'quite a bit of work'?"

O'Neill pointed to the list. "The will has not been fully probated yet. As executor, you must value Lydia's estate, pay out the inheritance taxes, then finalize all behests."

"How long is all that going to take?"

O'Neill thought for a moment. "Assuming that the list is correct, and you can find and account for everything, it shouldn't take more than a few months."

"A few months!" cried Kenyon. "I don't have months, I gotta get back to San Francisco as soon as possible!" Kenyon pictured the mess the Cyberworm investigation would be in if he didn't get home within the week. "Can't you speed things up?"

O'Neill stared down at the will. "I'm sorry, Mr. Kenyon. I'm trying to move ahead as quickly as possible, but you must understand, it was only two days ago that we, we . . ." The solicitor didn't finish her sentence. Her shoulders began to shake, then she began to cry, softly.

Kenyon stared at the lawyer for a moment, unsure what to do. He finally dug into his jacket pocket and found a paper napkin left over from the airplane meal. He stood up and limped around the desk. "Here, use this," he said.

O'Neill took it and dabbed at her eyes. "Thank you," she replied. "I'll be all right."

"Was it something I said?" Kenyon asked.

"No, I was just thinking about Lydia," replied O'Neill. "Her memorial service was two days ago. It was very beautiful. I'm sorry you couldn't be there."

"Yeah, well," Kenyon pointed to his posterior, "I was in the hospital."

O'Neill nodded, wiping her nose. She offered the napkin back, but Kenyon motioned to her to keep it. "I take it you were good friends with Lydia?"

"She was a wonderful friend. She supported me while I qualified for the bar." O'Neill waved her arm around the book-lined room. "She helped me find a position with this firm. She was so kind to me—I don't know what I would have made of my life without her."

"That was very sweet of her," replied Kenyon. "She must have been a very generous person."

"She was an angel," replied O'Neill. "I still can't believe she's, she's . . ."

She began to cry again; this time, Kenyon waited patiently until her sobs subsided into sniffles.

"You must think I'm an awful solicitor," she said.

"No, not at all. I wish more lawyers had a heart like you."

O'Neill smiled. "That's kind of you to say." She looked carefully at Kenyon's face. "You know, you remind me of her."

"Thanks. I should tell you, though, we weren't really related. I was adopted by her folks when I was a baby."

"She spoke of you often. She was very proud of you."

"She did?" said Kenyon, surprised. "I mean, she was? How come? I never even met her."

O'Neill shrugged. "I don't know. She said you were with the FBI, and she was very happy for you."

Kenyon returned to his chair and sat down. "You know, it's sad. Lydia and her dad never got along. Here she is, leaving me all this stuff, and I never even so much as saw a picture of her."

O'Neill came from behind the desk and stood beside him, pointing over his shoulder. "That's a picture of her, there."

Kenyon turned and looked at the nude in the oil painting. "That's *her*?" His ears burned red as he thought of his feelings of attraction the first time he looked at the painting.

"It was done in her home," continued O'Neill, oblivious of his discomfort. "She insisted I have it just before, you know, before . . ."

This time, Kenyon stood up and placed an arm around her and held her close, the top of her head resting against his chest. Her shoulders shook for a moment as Kenyon stroked her hair. It was soft, he noted, and smelled of peaches.

When she finally stopped, Kenyon leaned over to catch her eye. "Listen, maybe I can take you out for a drink while I'm here; you can tell me all about Lydia. I'd love to hear more about her."

She smiled briefly. "I'd like that."

"Great. Let me find a place to stay, and I'll give you a call and leave you a message."

O'Neill shook her head firmly. "I wouldn't even think of letting you stay in a hotel."

Kenyon held up his hand. "Thanks for the invite, but I couldn't put you out by staying at your place. You've got a lot to do, and I'd just be a distraction."

"I wasn't thinking of my home, you silly. I meant Lydia's."

Kenyon glanced around at the painting of Lydia, then back at O'Neill. "I don't know . . ." he started. For some reason, he felt creepy about staying in a nude dead woman's home.

"Don't worry, you'll be fine. Lydia had a housekeeper; I'll give her a call and have her pick up some groceries for you."

"You sure it wouldn't be easier for me to get a room somewhere?"

"No. It will be good to have someone staying there. You never know when a thief might read the obituaries and try to break in."

Kenyon hadn't thought of that. "Yeah, they do that in San Fran a lot," he agreed. "I guess it won't hurt for a day or two."

O'Neill returned to her desk. "I have the keys here somewhere." She dug in the desk drawer and pulled out a large ring. "These ones marked in red are for the house in Kensington," she explained. "The ones in blue are for the art gallery, and the rest I haven't figured out yet." She handed Kenyon the keys. "The addresses to her home and gallery are on the top of the inventory."

"So, where do we go from here?" asked Kenyon. "I'd like to get this cleared up as soon as possible."

O'Neill tapped her chin with a manicured nail. "I've got the will in probate court, and I can hire a professional evaluator to start inventorying the property. There are some checks for utilities and staff that you'll need to sign, but I don't think you need to stay in London for more than a week."

Kenyon breathed a sigh of relief. "Good, I really appreciate your help," he said. He turned and stuck Lydia's will into an exterior pouch on his luggage. "I'd love to stay longer and all, but I really have to get back to San Francisco as quick as possible."

"I understand," replied O'Neill. "Oh! I almost forgot." She lifted the alabaster vase from her desk and handed it to Kenyon. "This is for you."

The vase was smooth, and cool to the touch. "Thanks, it's beautiful," said Kenyon. "What is it?"

"Lydia," replied O'Neill. "She requested that she be cremated, and her ashes scattered."

Kenyon held the urn gingerly in his hands. He couldn't help but glance again at the nude portrait. "Did she say where?" Kenyon asked.

"She said you would know."

Kenyon eyed the urn dubiously. It was the first time he had ever even been in the same room as Lydia, and she obviously wasn't in a talkative condition. He wondered what had ever possessed her to think he would know where she wanted her ashes scattered. He shrugged, and tucked the urn in the cradle of his left elbow. "Thanks for your help," he said, shaking O'Neill's hand.

"It was my pleasure," replied the solicitor. She looked at Kenyon, burdened by his luggage and Lydia's urn. "Can I call a cab for you?"

"No, I saw some sitting in the square when I got here. I don't think I'll have any trouble flagging one down."

"Good." O'Neill gave Kenyon's arm a warm squeeze. "Give me a ring when you get settled in."

Four

Kenyon wheeled his luggage out to the sidewalk, then shifted Lydia's ashes to his other arm. It had become quite a hot day, and his white cotton shirt clung to his back under his suit. He began to regret sending the limo away.

Looking around for a cab, he spotted a taxi painted in purple and pink polka dots sitting at the curb about half a block down the street. Kenyon waved his free arm, and the cab approached.

As it pulled up, the agent noticed the picture of a chocolate bar painted on the side of the taxi. "Eat Me!" it screamed. Kenyon smiled, imagining how popular the cabby would be in San Francisco.

The agent leaned over and spoke into the open window. "You free?"

The cabby, a young, muscular man with short blond hair and a crooked nose, broke into a wide grin. "No, it's gonna cost you, guv," he said, in a broad, working man's accent. "Hop in."

As Kenyon clambered into the back of the cab, the driver glanced over the front seat at his luggage. "You here for a visit?"

"No, business."

The cabby handed a card over the back seat. "Well, if you want to see the town, just look up 'Appy 'Arry."

Kenyon read the card. "Happy Harry," it said. Underneath was cell phone number, then "Chauffeur Services, Guided Tours. Don't start the party without me."

"Thanks, I'll keep it in mind." Kenyon tucked the card into his wallet. He wondered what "Don't start the party without me" included.

As Kenyon settled into the back of the cab, Harry glanced into the rearview mirror. "This your first time in London, guv?"

"Yep."

"You in a big rush to get to this here address?"

Kenyon shook his head. "Not really."

"Well, why don't I take you by some of the sights, like? Won't cost but a few quid more."

"Go for it," said Kenyon.

Harry turned a corner and headed south, bumping down a cobble stoned lane. The cabby pointed to a series of low, ivy-covered brownstone buildings. "This here's the Temple, where all the barristers have offices," he said. "Dates back almost eight hundred years, it does, to the time when the Knights Templar owned it."

The cabby drove past several historical ships docked by the bank of the Thames River, then turned down another side street. "Scotland Yard started out here in the 19th century," he explained, pointing to a large, nondescript building. "They moved to new quarters a few years back."

The mention of Scotland Yard reminded Kenyon that he should call the office in San Francisco. He glanced at his watch. It was almost four local time, which meant it was about eight in the morning on the west coast.

Harry entered a wide boulevard that was jammed with tour buses. Hordes of tourists crowded the sidewalks, taking pictures, and gawking at the buildings. "Look up to your left, way up," said the cabby.

Kenyon strained his neck to look out the window. High above him stood the famous face of Big Ben, the clock that marked time over the Houses of Parliament.

The cab circled a large square. "That's Westminster Abbey on the right, where they had Diana's funeral."

Kenyon peered at the ancient cathedral, finely decorated with statues and stained-glass windows. "It's beautiful," he exclaimed.

"You think that's something—let me show you where Her Majesty lives."

Harry angled his car through several side streets, before emerging beside a large park. Buckingham Palace was an immense building bordered by a high, wrought-iron gate. In front of the palace was a memorial to Queen Victoria; the gold-covered statue of the monarch sat regally on a throne, surrounded by marble acolytes.

"That's about it, guv," said Harry. "We should be gettin' along, before the traffic builds too much."

"Fine by me," replied Kenyon. It was time to call San Francisco, anyway. He reached into his jacket and took out his cell phone. Within a few seconds, he was talking to the FBI's main switchboard. "Hey, Sally? It's Jack."

"How's England?" asked the receptionist.

"Jolly and old. Can I speak to Marge?"

There was a pause before Sally came back on the line. "No, she's not in yet. Do you want to talk to Jasmine?"

"Yeah, put me through."

His partner answered after two rings. "Leroi here."

"Hey, Jazz; it's Jack."

"Jack! How's everything going in London?"

Kenyon shifted Lydia's ashes in his arm. "Well, there's been a few surprises, but otherwise, pretty good. How's the Cyberworm investigation going?"

Leroi lowered her voice. "Not good."

"What do you mean?"

"We couldn't hold Dahg. He walked yesterday morning."

"Shit, what happened?"

"His lawyer gave the bail judge a blow-job. He showed that his client never received any stolen goods."

Kenyon cursed under his breath. He'd been afraid this would happen. Deaver had forced them to go off half-cocked before they could gather sufficient evidence, and now Dahg's lawyer was sinking their case. "What about the fact his pals murdered Simon? Didn't the judge think that was important enough to keep him locked up?"

"Nothing to tie him to the murder, except for a conspiracy that was based on an anonymous tip," said Leroi. "And it gets worse."

"Don't tell me."

"Dahg's lawyer found out about the e-mail you got. He says he's going to sue the state for infringement of rights."

Kenyon sighed. "Well, one good thing," he said.

"What's that?"

"Dahg's gonna be gunning for the guys who set him up. We got a bead on him?"

"Yeah, we got a twenty-four-hour tail. Judge won't give us a wire, though. Says we have to work up a better case."

"We'll get it." Jack pulled out the address Tanya O'Neill had given him and read off Lydia's phone number. "When Marge gets in, can you have her give me a call?"

"Will do. Hey, before I forget, I know there's something Marge'd love for you to bring back: a box of Cuban cigars. It's legal to buy them over there."

"Yeah, but not to bring 'em back."

"What are you, a boy scout?"

"Yeah, as a matter of fact. Anything for you?"

"A pair of sexy French shoes. Size eight."

Kenyon laughed. "Will do. Over and out."

The cab had stopped at a light, and Harry glanced in the rear-view at Kenyon. "Say, you with the CIA, or something?"

"No, FBI."

The light turned green, and Harry shifted the car into gear. "That explains it, then."

"What?"

"The guy what's been following us." Harry pulled his sun visor down, then tilted the mirror attached underneath until Kenyon could see out the back. "You see that Range Rover, about three cars back, next lane over? Friend a' yours?"

Kenyon leaned forward and peered at the mirror. He could see the large, black 4X4 amid the traffic. The side was dented, and mud had sprayed up from the wheel wells, covering the fenders. The driver was the lone occupant and appeared to be a man, but it was too far back for Kenyon to make out any more details. "How long's he been tailing us?"

"He was parked near me in New Square," replied the cabbie. "He's been followin' us since I picked you up."

"You sure it's not a coincidence?"

"Only one way to find out." Harry turned sharply to the right, cutting across traffic and racing up a side lane. Behind them, they could hear the honking of horns as someone tried to follow across the crowded road.

They reached the far end of the lane, and waited. A few seconds later, the Rover entered the side lane.

"What do you think?" asked Harry.

"We got a tail, all right," agreed Kenyon. "Can you shake him?"

"Course I can, guv." Harry accelerated the cab. "Don't you want to know who it is, though?"

"Yeah, but how are we going to find out?"

"Well, there's two of us lads and, as far as I can see, only one of him."

"So?"

"So, we find a nice, quiet spot, and ask him real polite like, why he's tailin' your arse." Harry grinned widely. Kenyon noticed several of his front teeth had been replaced with gold crowns.

"What's your plan?" asked Kenyon.

Harry reached under the seat and pulled out a cap. "Put this on and sit low in the seat, so only the cap shows in the back window."

As the cab rolled through Knightsbridge, the Range Rover caught up and resumed its tailing position three cars back. Harry made sure it got close enough for the driver to see Kenyon's cap poking above the seat, then sped up, putting more distance between the two cars as he entered Kensington.

"There's a row of shops along Gloucester Road," he explained. "As soon as we turn the corner, I'll slow down. You tuck the cap onto the back window ledge and dodge into a shop."

"What are you going to do?" asked Kenyon.

"There's an alley back behind the shops. I'll go down to the corner and turn. You wait until the Rover goes past, then follow us."

"What then?

"I'll park halfways up the alley. Unless I miss my guess, he'll stop and wait to see what we do."

Kenyon kept low in the seat until Harry warned him that Gloucester Road was coming up. The agent propped the urn on the seat beside him and pushed the cap back onto the rear window. "Take care of Lydia while I'm gone," he said.

Harry looked in the rearview. "Get ready."

Kenyon braced himself against the rear door and popped the latch. As they swung around the corner, Harry slowed, and Kenyon hopped out and slammed the door. The cabby roared off.

Wincing from the stitches, Kenyon limped as fast as he could through the front door of a wine store.

The counter clerk, a young woman, glanced briefly up, then went back to reading her *Hello!* magazine.

Kenyon stood behind a free-standing display of South African wine, staring out the window. A few seconds later, the black Range Rover rolled into sight. The side windows were tinted; Kenyon couldn't get a clear view of the driver. The 4X4 rolled past, and Kenyon eased out of the shop and followed the car down the road.

Traffic was slow on Gloucester Road, and Kenyon managed to keep up to the two cars with a brisk walk. He watched Harry's cab turn the corner at the end of the block, followed a few seconds later by the Rover. He slowed his pace in order to give them time to park.

By the time Kenyon reached the entrance to the alleyway, both cars had stopped. Harry's brightly colored cab was about two hundred feet up the alley; the Ranger was positioned behind a dumpster, about halfway back.

Perfect, thought Kenyon. Using a stack of old cardboard boxes as cover, he snuck forward. There was no way of avoiding the rearview. Hopefully, his pursuer was too intent on watching the cab to check it. Fortunately, Kenyon reached the back of the 4X4 undetected, and dropped out of sight below the back door.

Time for a distraction. A box of blackened potatoes had been discarded beside the rear door of a grocery shop. Kenyon dug through until he found a spud that was still fairly firm. Careful not to burn his fingers, he jammed the potato up the car's muddy exhaust pipe.

It took about thirty seconds for enough pressure to build up. Then, with a loud bang, the potato shot out of the exhaust pipe. Kenyon could hear the occupant moving around in the car, wondering what happened. A few seconds later, he heard the driver's door open.

Kenyon rose to a crouch and, when the driver came around the back, reached up and grabbed him by the lapels and spun him up against the wall. The man struggled weakly, but Kenyon twisted his right arm behind his back and shouted in his ear. "Freeze! FBI!"

"Please, Monsieur Jack," said the man in a French accent. "I mean no harm."

Harry came running up, brandishing a tire iron. "I got you covered, guv," he shouted, taking up a position to Kenyon's right.

Keeping the man's face pressed against the wall, Kenyon frisked him for a gun. Finding no weapon, Kenyon spun him around.

His pursuer was a man of around sixty with black hair streaked with grey. He wore a dark blue, pinstripe suit and a stained silk tie. He was slim and held himself erect, like a former military man.

"How do you know my name?" asked Kenyon.

"I am Raymond Legrand. I am—was—a friend of Lydia's." He reached one hand inside his suit jacket.

Kenyon slapped the hand away. "Keep your hands up!"

The man obeyed. Kenyon reached inside Legrand's jacket and withdrew the wallet, opening it up to inspect the contents. The wallet held about twenty pounds in bills. Kenyon found the driver's license, and pulled it out. "Legrand, Raymond Jacques," it said. Although the hair in the photo was darker, it still matched.

Kenyon handed Legrand the wallet and stepped back. The man

lowered his arms and began to move forward, but Kenyon held up a warning hand. "You're not going anywhere until you do some explaining, partner."

Legrand eyed Harry, who still stood brandishing the tire iron. "As you wish."

"Why were you following me?" Kenyon asked.

Legrand stared deeply into his eyes. "I wanted to meet you."

Kenyon found Legrand's scrutiny disturbing. "Why didn't you come to the reading of the will?" he demanded.

Legrand dropped his piercing stare to the ground. "It is a bit embarrassing. I do not wish to say."

"Know what's even more embarrassing, guv?" said Harry, smiling to show off his dental work. "No front teeth."

Legrand got the message. "I did not go because I expected my wife Ilsa to be there. We are recently separated, and I did not wish there to be a disturbance."

Kenyon pondered this for a moment. "So why were you following us?"

Legrand coughed. "I believe there was a behest in the will for me?"

Kenyon thought back. "Yeah. A Louis Vuitton briefcase."

Legrand raised his eyebrows in supplication. "I was hoping to retrieve it from Lydia's home."

Kenyon eyed Legrand closely. "No. I'll send it through the office of the lawyer who's handling the estate. You can pick it up there."

Legrand's eyebrows fell. The Frenchman reached into his jacket pocket and pulled out a card. "Please, if you should reconsider, I would be most grateful if you were to drop it off at my office."

Kenyon read the card. *R.L. Investigations, Raymond Legrand, President.* "What's R.L. Investigations?"

"We handle mostly international clients," he explained. "We investigate counterfeiting, industrial espionage, that sort of thing."

"You're a PI?" asked Harry.

"Oui," said Legrand.

"I'd brush up on my tailing, if I was you," said Harry, lowering his tire iron. "You stink at it."

Legrand gave Harry a withering glance, then, brushing at a shred of cabbage that clung to his suit, he walked back to his car. He gave Kenyon one more penetrating stare, then got into the battered Rover and drove off without another word.

"What do you think of that?" asked Harry, as the two men got back into the taxi.

Kenyon shook off a sudden feeling of unease. "I think he's so full of shit, his eyes are brown." Harry laughed long and hard as they returned to the car.

It was only a few blocks further to Lydia's home, and Kenyon added a generous tip when they reached 61 Herringbone Gardens. "Thanks for your help," said Kenyon.

"No problems, guv," said the cabby, pocketing the money. "You just remember what it says on my card, 'Don't start the party without me.'"

Five

Herringbone Gardens was a quiet side street just off Cromwell Road. Kenyon stood on the curb for a moment and looked around; Lydia's place was situated in a long row of Georgian townhouses. Each white-washed, three-story townhouse was fronted by black, wrought-iron fencing and a twin set of pillars. Across the street, large sycamore trees loomed over a well-manicured park.

With Lydia's ashes in one hand and his luggage in the other, Kenyon made his way up the steps to the front door. It was a massive oak affair with cut-glass panels and a large, round brass doorknob.

He put his luggage down and unlocked the door. "Hello?" he called, as he entered the foyer. "Anyone home?"

No one answered. Kenyon glanced around at the foyer. It had a warm, Mediterranean feel to it. The walls were painted in deep sienna and the floor was covered in black marble tiles streaked with creamy calcite veins. A spray of white calla lilies in a glass vase stood in memorium on a sidetable at the base of a grand, spiraling staircase. He put Lydia's remains down beside the flowers, then fetched his bag into the house and closed the front door.

When Kenyon entered the living room, he whistled out loud in amazement. The walls were covered in modern art and rose at least sixteen feet to the ceiling. The room was furnished with a suite of white, plush furniture. The drapes that covered the large bay window alone were more expensive than every stick of furniture in his apartment back home.

Kenyon's gaze focused on a suit of armor that stood near the fireplace. The suit, complete with helmet and a pole axe resting in a gauntlet, had been polished to a high gleam. Kenyon approached for a closer look. Fine filigree had been worked into the metal, and the pole axe had been sharpened to a razor edge. He resisted the urge to lift the helmet visor and peek inside.

Kenyon dropped his suit jacket onto the couch, then wandered into the adjacent dining room where eight upholstered chairs stood around an immense granite table.

Marveling at the taste and expense, Kenyon continued on to the kitchen. The countertops were a buttery marble. One corner of the kitchen, adjacent to a breakfast nook, had been closed off by a sealed-glass door to create a wine closet.

Thirsty, Kenyon poked around in the fridge and found several cans of beer in the back. He snapped the top of one marked "Caffrey's." He took a long gulp; the ale tasted smooth and creamy.

Carrying his beer, Kenyon wandered back down the hallway to the foyer. As he ascended the curving staircase, he absently ran his hand along the smooth wooden handrail. It felt cool under his fingers. At the top of the stairs he turned left and headed for the room overlooking the street.

It was the master bedroom. The curtains were semi-translucent, filling the room with a warm, soft light. A king-sized bed with an upholstered headboard rested against one wall, adjacent to a rosewood chest of drawers fronted by spiral columns. A flatscreen TV and DVD player were fitted into a cherry wood cabinet across from the foot of the bed.

Kenyon sat on a loveseat that rested in the big bay window; a pair of fluffy pink slippers poked out from underneath. He bent over and picked one up, turning it in his hand. He imagined Lydia sitting on this chair with a book, her bare feet curled beneath her, a cup of steaming coffee on the mahogany table. He softly placed the slipper back.

Just off the master bedroom was a long, narrow room that had been outfitted as a walk-in closet. A row of sliding doors flanked one wall, and a small vanity mirror and chair occupied the opposite side.

Kenyon opened a door at random, and the smell of expensive perfume greeted him; the closet was full of Lydia's blouses, all arranged by color. He checked several other closets. Most were filled with tailored jackets, leather shoes, and formal dresses.

The last closet on the right contained purses and suitcases. Most were ordered by color on shelves, but there was a big pile on the floor. Kenyon remembered the briefcase left to Legrand in Lydia's will. He scanned through the shelves, then got down on his knees and rummaged through the jumble.

Kenyon's initial search came up empty. He poked through the closet a second time, but nothing fit the description. He checked all the other closets, peering into the recesses in case he had missed it, but his careful scrutiny failed to turn up a briefcase.

He pulled out the vanity chair and sat down, puzzled. Where did Lydia put the briefcase? Kenyon could just imagine Legrand's reaction when he told him it couldn't be located; he thought back to the way the man had stared at him, and shuddered.

Just then, the doorbell rang. Kenyon made his way down to the foyer and opened the door.

A tall man of about thirty, with dark, short-cropped hair and large brown eyes stood outside. "Herr Kenyon?" he asked. "My name is Hadrian deWolfe." He spoke with a distinct German accent, and wore an expensive dark grey suit and shiny black Italian shoes. "I am sorry to intrude in your time of sorrow, but I was an acquaintance of Lydia's," he explained. He held out his right hand. "I came by to introduce myself, and offer my condolences."

"Thanks," said Kenyon. "Please, come in." He escorted his visitor into the living room, pointing toward an ornate chair.

Rather than sit down, however, deWolfe advanced to the suit of armor. He took out a magnifying glass and examined the suit closely, tracing his right index finger along the filigree. "A marvelous example of 15th-century Milanese ceremonial armor," he announced. "I have seen one just like it in the Duke of Kent's mansion."

"Are you some kind of expert?"

"Sorry," said deWolfe. "Where are my manners?" He pulled out a silver container, withdrew a business card, and handed it to Kenyon. It said, "Hadrian deWolfe, Art and Antiques Evaluator." There were addresses for Zurich and London.

"You're an antiques dealer?" he asked.

DeWolfe nodded. "I handle all aspects, from verifying authenticity to bidding at auction. Mostly, I work from my home in Switzerland, but I also have many clients in Britain."

"So, why are you here?"

"Lydia was always very kind and generous to me," said deWolfe. "I know it is not much, but I came here today to offer you my services, should you ever decide to liquidate her estate."

Kenyon slapped his forehead. "Oh, I get it; you're the guy Tanya promised to send on by to look at Lydia's stuff."

"*Ja,*" replied deWolfe.

"Would you like something to drink? A glass of white wine?"

DeWolfe glanced around the room, Kenyon already half forgotten. "That would be splendid."

The agent went to the kitchen and rooted around in the wine closet. He opened a bottle of Pouilly Fumé and poured a glass.

When Kenyon returned to the living room, deWolfe was examining the marble-topped sideboard. "Lydia had excellent taste," he commented, running a long finger across the smooth top.

"You could have fooled me," Kenyon replied, handing him the glass. "I don't know a thing about this stuff."

"No one could ever fool Lydia," he responded. "She could spot a counterfeit almost immediately. She had a very shrewd eye." DeWolfe sniffed the wine's bouquet then, satisfied, took a sip.

"You worked a lot with Lydia?" asked Kenyon.

"I came for her advice on several occasions regarding market prices." DeWolfe put his wine glass on a table, then got down on his hands and knees and peered under the couch. "I was, in turn, most helpful to her regarding the—how do you say it?—provenance of certain *objets*."

Kenyon eyed the crouching man. He wasn't quite sure what to make of him.

His inspection of the underside of the couch finished, deWolfe stood up and carefully dusted off the knees of his trousers. "Now, if you will pardon me for being so abrupt—what do you intend to do with Lydia's belongings?"

"Good question," said Kenyon. "I don't have room for all this in my apartment in San Francisco. I guess I'm going to have to sell some of it, but I don't know what."

"I understand; it's important to look carefully," agreed deWolfe. "One never knows what one might find." He pulled out a gold pen and leather-bound notepad. "Perhaps it would help if I walked around and made a note or two?

"Yeah, go right ahead." Kenyon glanced at his watch, remembering he hadn't heard from Marge in San Francisco. He also wanted to collect his e-mail. "Do you mind if I go? I've got some stuff I have to do."

DeWolfe waved absently over his shoulder as Kenyon departed.

Kenyon went upstairs and dug a netbook out of his luggage. He glanced around the room; there was nowhere to plug it in. The bedside table holding the phone was too tiny, and the coffee table in the bay window was too low.

He wandered down the hall; there were three closed doors. The first door let to an oversized linen closet filled with towels, sheets, toilet paper, and a vacuum cleaner. The second concealed a steep stairwell that climbed to the attic floor above. Curious, he put down his computer, then, advancing with his left leg to avoid straining his injury, he made his way up.

The third floor had been set up as a studio. A large wooden easel, now empty, dominated the center of the room. An old wooden chest covered with tubes of oil paint sat off to one side. A white lab coat hung from a peg. A second room, adjacent to the studio, had been fitted out as a workshop for framing paintings. The air in the studio was stale and dusty; it had the melancholy air of disuse.

Returning to the second floor, Kenyon walked to the end of the hall; a loose floorboard let out a loud squeak as he opened the third door. This time he was lucky; it led to what was obviously Lydia's home office. It was a small room with wooden wainscoting and a Persian rug, dominated by a large oak desk and a pigeonhole shelf. A large window looked out onto the back alley.

Kenyon carried his netbook over to the desk. He noticed immediately that the office contained no home computer; it didn't even have a printer or a cable jack. Lydia's Filofax, a diary bound in black leather, was the only item resting upon the desk surface. He sat down in the desk chair and idly opened the daybook. The back flap was stuffed with business cards, phone numbers, and credit card receipts. He placed the diary into an empty slot in the pigeonhole shelf.

Kenyon spotted Lydia's American passport tucked into an adjacent pigeonhole. He flipped it open to study her photo. The color picture had been taken two years before, when Lydia had last renewed her passport. Her blond hair was longer, but her picture bore little resemblance to the oil portrait Kenyon had seen in O'Neill's office. Her expression was almost defiant; Kenyon wondered what she had been thinking that moment.

Just then, the phone rang. Startled, Kenyon picked it up. "What?"

"How-are-ya?" said Gonelli, in her thick New York accent.

"Great, Marge. I'm the proud owner of this big house in London. Man, the drapes alone are worth more than my car."

"Sounds hoity-toity."

"You bet. I hired this guy just to count the ashtrays."

"Listen to the big-shot," said Gonelli. "You'll never want to come home."

"Are you kidding me? I miss you guys already." It was true. Kenyon hadn't even spent a night here, and already he was homesick.

"We'll see," said Gonelli. "You'll meet some rich cutie with a snooty accent and forget the bunch of us."

"Don't count on it. Hey, I hear Dahg got sprung."

"Yeah, but he ain't going far."

"What about Deaver? How'd he take it?"

Kenyon could hear Marge spit a piece of cigar tobacco out of her mouth. "He's running around trying to make a case from the other end."

"You mean, with Simon's killer?"

"Yeah. He's got the boys over at State Department trolling their files."

"Find anything?"

"If he did, he ain't sharing it with me."

Kenyon didn't like the sound of that. Deaver off on his own could cause a lot more trouble than he was worth. "Give my best to the gang, and tell them I'll be home soon."

"Will do. And Jack? If you get the time, there's a little something I wouldn't mind you picking up."

"A box of Cubana Havanas?"

"I luv ya, kiddo."

"Talk to you later."

Someone knocked on the door. "Mr. Kenyon, are you in there?"

"Yeah, come on in."

DeWolfe stepped into the room and flipped open his notepad. "I have some good news and some bad news. The good news is that Lydia had an extensive and, I might say, desirable collection of art and antiques."

"And the bad news?" asked Kenyon.

"Her taste was very eclectic. In order to properly liquidate her estate, it will require time and effort to identify all the best bidders."

"That's a problem," said Kenyon. "I don't have much time to fuss with all that stuff. I have to get back to San Francisco real quick."

"With your permission, then, shall I begin to make some inquiries?"

"Good idea," said Kenyon. "Let's grease this pig."

DeWolfe's left eyebrow arched up in a bemused expression. "An excellent idea. Perhaps we could meet for dinner in a day or so?"

"Great," said Kenyon. He stood up and escorted deWolfe down the staircase to the front door. "I'd love to hear more about Lydia, as well."

"I would be delighted," said deWolfe. "There are many amusing tales to tell. *Auf Wiedersehen.*"

Kenyon walked back into the living room. Through the bay window, he could hear the distant sound of traffic, but he felt no urge to go out and explore. He felt tired and jet-lagged, at loose ends.

He picked his jacket up off the couch and absently noted that it felt heavy. He suddenly remembered the DVD Tanya O'Neill had given him. He pulled the disc out of the jacket pocket and read the label; *Sisters of Mercy Charity Auction.*

Kenyon went to the kitchen and poured a glass of wine, then went upstairs and plugged the disc into the player. Settling onto the bed, he pressed play on the remote.

A stately country mansion appeared on the screen. It was daylight, and expensive cars were pulling up to the front entrance. Several people dressed in formal evening gowns and tuxedos got out of a stretch limo, and the camera followed them up a set of wide marble steps into the house.

"Welcome to the ninth annual Sisters of Mercy Charity Auction," announced the voice-over in a plummy BBC accent. "On behalf of our host, we are happy to invite you all to Ingoldsby Manor."

The picture cut to a tall, striking woman. The title beneath her picture told the viewer that this was Mrs. Ilsa Ingoldsby-Legrand. The host was beautifully attired in a black velvet evening gown that clung to her slim hips. Her hair flowed down her back like a waterfall of gold. Kenyon guessed she was in her mid-fifties, but her skin was so white and smooth, it was almost alabaster. "We're so delighted with the turn-out tonight," she said, in a low, husky voice. "We have a lovely selection of people from a wide variety of society, as well as from the performing arts."

The camera cut to an enormous grand piano. A large, well-known tenor was singing an aria from *The Marriage of Figaro*. Curiously, no one was accompanying him on the piano.

As the announcer blathered on, the camera panned around the

room, lingering on several of the items up for auction. Kenyon shook his head in wonder as he gazed at a small sheep floating in a tub of formaldehyde and a pair of mannequins with genitals molded to their foreheads.

The camera continued and the agent caught a glimpse of Tanya O'Neill. She was dressed in an emerald green ball gown that complemented her dark red hair. Beautiful, thought Kenyon.

Legrand passed through, dressed in a black tuxedo and carrying a brandy snifter. He glanced irritably at the camera before moving out of view.

Suddenly, Kenyon sat up in bed. He pressed the reverse button, and the picture swam backwards. There. Standing against a pillar, staring out into the distance, was Lydia. He pushed the frame-by-frame button, and the picture began to move slowly forward.

Lydia turned her gaze toward the camera. She wore a stunning red silk evening gown and a string of pearls, but the expression on her face was dark and full of foreboding.

Six

Saturday, July 9

The next day Kenyon woke at mid-morning. He hadn't slept long—rolling over on his stitches had taken care of that—but the bed was firm and comfortable, and he felt refreshed. He arose and pulled back the curtains, letting light stream into the room. It was going to be a hot Saturday.

Kenyon went to the adjoining bathroom. The soap in the shower stall smelled of lavender. He had a quick shower and a shave, then dug a golf shirt and a pair of jeans from his luggage and got dressed.

The smell of frying sausage hit his nostrils as he walked downstairs. He paused on the stairwell for a moment, listening. He could hear the rattle of pots and pans in the kitchen. Cautiously, he inched down the stairs and advanced quietly to the entrance of the kitchen.

A woman was standing at the stove, her back to Kenyon, singing in Spanish. She was about forty, short and stout, with her hair dyed a brilliant red. She threw a dollop of butter into a frying pan, then cracked several eggs.

Kenyon advanced into the kitchen. "Hello?" he said.

The woman jumped in fright, then spun around, clutching a spatula to her ample bosom. "You scare me!"

"Sorry. What are you doing in my kitchen?"

The woman peered closely at him. "You Mister Yack Kenyon?"

"Yeah."

"Oh, Mister Yack." She came over and gave him a big hug, her short arms barely reaching around Kenyon's chest. She started to cry.

Kenyon patted her on the back as she sniffled into his shirt. "Uh, it's okay," he said. He reached across and pulled a section off a roll of paper towels and offered it to her. "I didn't mean to scare you."

The woman blew her nose in the towel. "No, no. I cry for Miss Lydia."

Kenyon suddenly understood. "You're the housekeeper?"

The woman beamed. "Ya. I am Señora Santucci." Kenyon held out his hand, but the woman hugged him again. "I am so sorry for your auntie."

"Thank you." Kenyon glanced at the stove, which was beginning to smoke. "Is something burning?"

Señora Santucci quickly turned and removed the frying pan. "You hungry? See—I make you breakfast."

Kenyon's stomach growled in appreciation. "Thanks, I'd love some." He glanced around the room. "You brew any coffee, Señora Santucci?"

She removed a carafe from an automatic brewer and poured him a cup. "Si. Cream?"

Kenyon held up a hand. "Black is fine."

"Good. You sit, and I make big meal."

Kenyon sat down in the nook and watched the housekeeper bustle around the kitchen. Within minutes, she had a steaming plate of sausage and eggs on toast set before him. Kenyon avidly dug in with his knife and fork. "This is great."

"You like? Good. Then you keep Rosita as housekeeper, no?"

"I'd be happy to, until I leave, anyway."

Santucci's smile faded. "You no stay?

"I've got a job in San Francisco. I have to go back."

"I see." The woman wiped her hands in her apron and turned back to the stove.

Kenyon stopped eating. He suddenly realized that, in effect, he was now Señora Santucci's employer, and it was up to him to decide her future. He didn't know what to say. "How long did you work for Lydia?" he finally asked.

"Four years."

"Where did you work before that?"

"Ingoldsby Manor."

"You worked for Ilsa?"

Santucci sat down at the nook table, across from Kenyon. "I no want to, but I have a bad husband. He has the hot Italian blood. He get drunk and beat me, so I go away and work in the country."

"What was Ilsa like?"

"She very bad. She say, 'You do what I want, or I send you back to your husband.' I am so worried, my hair fall out."

Kenyon shook his head in sympathy. "That's awful."

Santucci nodded. "One day, your auntie, she come to the Manor, she see me sad. She say, 'Why you cry?' I tell her, my mistress is bad."

Kenyon was intrigued. "What did she do?"

"Miss Lydia give me a job and a place to stay that very day. She very sweet, like an auntie to me."

Kenyon stared down at his unfinished eggs. "You don't have to go back to your husband, if you don't want to."

Santucci crossed herself. "He is dead."

"Well, I guess that's good," said Kenyon. "Listen, I'll talk to Tanya. I'm sure there's someone who needs an excellent housekeeper like you."

The woman stood up and began to clear up the pots and pans. "You are very kind, Mister Yack, but don't you worry about me," she replied. "I be okay."

Kenyon picked up his coffee and left Santucci to the dishes. He wandered down the hall and stood in the living room, staring out the large bay window. He had only been thinking of the physical assets; he hadn't considered the people in Lydia's life. How the hell was he supposed to deal with all of that?

His thoughts were broken by a phone ringing. He looked around the room; a cream-colored desk set sat atop a sideboard. He put down his coffee cup and picked it up. "Hello?"

"Hullo. This is Charles Strand from the Morgan dealership calling about your motor car."

"What car?"

"The Plus 8. Have you decided what you want to do with it?"

It took a few minutes, but Kenyon finally got the story from the car dealer. Lydia had owned a Morgan sports car, the one she had been killed in. The wreck had been towed back to the dealership and they needed a decision about whether to repair or scrap it.

"How far are you from Herringbone Gardens?" Kenyon asked.

"About four streets south," replied Strand.

Kenyon got directions from the manager. "I'll be along in a few minutes."

The agent walked south until he came to Old Brompton Road. The road was lined with shops; customers bustled in and out of the florists, wine merchants, and bakeries as they did their Saturday morning shopping.

The Morgan dealership was located on a cobbled alleyway off the main road in what would have been a row of stables a century before. The barn doors had been replaced by modern glass windows, and the interior remodeled into a showroom.

Kenyon glanced through the windows. Six Morgans sat in the showroom, their paint gleaming in the morning light. They were all convertibles with a design from the 1940s, with long hoods, flaring wheel wells and large, bulging headlamps. Kenyon pictured Lydia in her fluffy pink slippers, puttering around the countryside at thirty miles per hour.

As Kenyon entered, a short, fat man with a monk's fringe of hair stepped from behind a desk. "Can I help you?"

"I'm Jack Kenyon. I just had a call from Charles Strand."

The man stuck out his hand. "Strand, here. I'll show you Lydia's car." He escorted the agent around to the garage beside the showroom.

Inside the garage, the whine of pneumatic tools filled the air as several mechanics in overalls bent over partially dismantled cars. Spare tires, car fenders, and tailpipes littered the floor. An automobile rested to one side of the workshop under a canvas tarpaulin. Strand walked over and pulled off the cover.

Once upon a time, Kenyon imagined, it had been a beautiful car. The body was indigo, and the interior was upholstered in red leather. Now, however, the front wheel wells and hood were bent and scraped. The windshield had been crushed flat, and the interior was spattered with leaves, dried dirt and gravel. Kenyon noted, almost clinically, that there was no evidence of blood or other human remains.

"If you want me to repair it, I can do the job for five thousand pounds." said Strand.

Kenyon was amazed. "Is that all? It looks like a total write-off."

"We build the Morgans tough, and we build them smart," replied Strand. "The engine and chassis are still intact. Most of the damage is cosmetic. We just need to replace the body parts, and she'll be good as new."

Kenyon rubbed his chin. He pictured himself flying up the Pacific Coast Highway, the winding, two-lane blacktop that bordered the Pacific Ocean. "Is it a good car to drive?"

Strand smiled. "That it is. It's very quick, going from 0 to 60 in under six seconds. It has excellent handling abilities on curves, and a top speed of one hundred and thirty miles per hour. We rent them by the day, if you'd care to try one out."

"Maybe I will," said Kenyon. "You know, it sounds like a lot of car for Lydia to handle."

"She'd have boxed your ears for that, lad," replied Strand. "Miss Kenyon qualified for her competitive driving license ten years ago. She placed fifth at the time trials at Silverstone racecourse just last summer."

Kenyon whistled. "I didn't realize she was such a good driver."

"That's the odd part," said Strand, his glance returning to the car. "She's the last person I imagine would lose control and kill herself."

Kenyon stared silently at the wreck. Every time he thought he had a handle on Lydia, someone turned it upside down. He glanced over at one of the gleaming models, and made up his mind. "I'd love to fix it," he said. "Is any of the cost covered by insurance?"

Strand frowned. "I thought that was already settled." He pointed at the car. "Didn't *you* send it here?"

"No. I just got to London yesterday."

"That's odd," replied the manager. "We had an assessor from the insurance company in last week after it arrived from the police compound."

Kenyon scratched his head. "Lydia's lawyer must have had it released. Listen, I'd like to get the ball rolling. Mind if I use your phone?"

"Certainly. Let me take you to my office."

Strand's office was a little cubbyhole just big enough for a desk and chair. Kenyon pulled out Tanya O'Neill's business card and dialed her number.

The solicitor was glad to hear his voice. "How was your first night at Lydia's?"

"You want to know the truth? It was spooky. I kind of expected her ghost to come up the stairwell at midnight."

O'Neill was sympathetic. "It can be unsettling sleeping all alone in a big house like that," she replied.

Kenyon liked the direction their conversation was taking. Before he got sidetracked, however, he wanted to get the information he needed to start the garage working on the car. "What's the name of Lydia's car insurance company?" he asked.

"I have no idea," replied O'Neill. "Why do you need to know?"

She listened while Kenyon explained the situation.

"I didn't release the car," the solicitor replied. "I have no idea how it got there."

Well, if you didn't do it, and I didn't do it, then who did? wondered Kenyon. "Let me check it out, and I'll get back to you."

Kenyon returned to the garage. He found Strand filling out a work order form on a clipboard.

"How did the car get here?" he asked the manager.

Strand thought for a moment. "It probably got towed here."

Kenyon pointed to the clipboard. "Is there a release form?"

Strand shook his head. "Not at this end. The tow-truck operator might need something at the police compound, though."

"Let's have another look at the car," Kenyon suggested.

The door handle was a simple latch. Kenyon opened the driver's side door and squeezed inside. The dash had four small analog dials for gasoline, temperature, oil, and voltage. There were two larger dials behind the wood-grain steering wheel, a speedometer and tachometer. Kenyon leaned across and checked the small glove compartment on the passenger side. It was empty.

He got out of the car and had a closer look at the exterior. From what he could tell, the front right side seemed to have taken the worst damage. "Do you know how the accident occurred?" I asked.

"The article in the *Times* said she rolled it late at night," replied Strand. "I don't know much else."

Kenyon walked around to the back of the car, which was relatively intact, except for a broken rear taillight and a black smudge, like that from a bumper. It looked like it had been rear-ended by another car. He pointed out the damage to Strand. "Is this old, or new?" he asked.

Strand bent over and looked closely. "I certainly don't recall it being there when she brought it in for tuning the week before," said Strand. "Maybe it happened during the crash."

"Did the insurance assessor leave a number to call?" Kenyon asked.

"No, but they rarely do."

"Do you remember what he looked like?"

Strand shrugged his shoulders. "We get so many assessors through here, Mr. Kenyon . . ."

"He was a tall man, older."

The agent turned. A mechanic with Rasta-curls was sitting nearby on a pair of tires, drinking his tea and eating an apple. The name "Cecil" was stenciled on his blue coveralls.

"Do you remember anything else?" Kenyon asked.

Cecil shrugged. "Didn't seem like much of an assessor, you know?

He just looked in the secret compartment. Wasn't interested in the damage, man."

Kenyon glanced at Strand. "Morgans have a secret compartment?"

"Not all," replied the manager, "just Lydia's." He pointed to the unlatched windows. "As you can see, it's child's play to get inside." Strand walked to the back, and flipped open the trunk. "Lydia wanted a place to store oddments securely, so we custom-built her one." He pulled on the rear cover of the trunk to reveal a compartment big enough to hold a case of wine.

Kenyon leaned into the trunk and peered into the compartment. There was nothing inside. He backed out of the trunk and closed the lid. Something wasn't right; an unauthorized assessor pulls the car out of the police compound, then all he does is search a secret compartment? "Do you remember which pound it got shipped from?" he asked.

Cecil took a sip of his tea. "Somewhere from the south of London. The lad with the tow truck, he bitched about the traffic around Richmond."

Kenyon turned to Strand. "Do you mind if I hold off on a decision about the car for a day or so? There's a few things I want to check first."

Strand shrugged. "We're not too busy at the moment, we can keep it here while you make up your mind."

"Good. Don't touch it until I give you the say-so."

Kenyon left the dealership and returned to Lydia's home, pondering the strange events as he walked along. When he reached 61 Herringbone Gardens, he went up to the office and phoned O'Neill. "The insurance assessor sounds like a phony," he explained. "Lydia had a secret compartment in the Morgan. My guess is, he wanted to get it out of police custody so he could search the car."

"It doesn't make any sense," replied O'Neill. "Unless, of course, he was a thief, and he thought there might be something valuable left in the car."

Kenyon pondered that for a moment. "If a thief was looking for something to steal, he would have broken into her empty house. I haven't seen any evidence of a forced entry here."

As they talked, Kenyon idly pulled Lydia's Filofax out of the pigeon-hole and flipped to the calendar section. There was a page for each day. Lydia's notations were entered in clear, legible fashion, not at all like Kenyon's own chicken-scratch writing. Most of the entries were for picking up dry-cleaning, meeting clients for lunch, and various appointments.

Curious, Kenyon turned to the day she died, Saturday, July 2. There was a notation for "Auction, 8:00 PM." "The video of the auction you gave me; was that the night Lydia died?" Kenyon asked.

"Yes. Lydia was coming home when she ran her car off the road."

Kenyon thought for a moment. "There's some damage on the back of the Morgan that the dealership can't account for. It almost looks as though someone rear-ended her car."

"You think it wasn't an accident?" asked O'Neill.

"I want to talk to the police investigator," replied Kenyon. "Do you have a contact name?"

O'Neill put down her receiver. She was back on the phone quickly. "Here's a name; Sergeant Barker. He's listed on the accident report as the collision investigation officer at Scotland Yard."

"Scotland Yard?" Kenyon thought back to his brief meeting with Stan Fairmont at Heathrow airport; what was the FBI's contact name at Scotland Yard? He fumbled out his wallet and found the card; Detective Inspector Humphrey Arundel. "I'll call and see if they'll speak to me," said Kenyon.

"Ring me later," O'Neill replied. "I'd love to hear what you discover."

Seven

Kenyon had been amazed how quickly Scotland Yard responded to his request. He had spoken to Arundel, and the detective inspector had given him directions to a park near the south edge of London. They were to meet that afternoon at the parking lot, and proceed from there.

Kenyon returned to the Morgan dealership and rented a car. Strand was right, thought Kenyon, as he drove the Morgan through the streets of London; this car was a hell of a lot of fun to drive. There wasn't much to it but a big engine, a tough suspension, and a tight steering arc. Except for some discomfort from the bullet wound as he worked the clutch, it was a joy.

Driving on the left wasn't as difficult as Kenyon thought it would be, except for the roundabouts. The first time the agent headed into one of the circular intersections traveling left, he went completely around the circle, twice. He quickly got the hang of judging when to enter and exit, however, and was soon making good time as he drove south.

Traffic was heavy, but no worse than San Francisco on a Saturday afternoon. The sun was hot and bright, and he was glad that he had packed his shades.

The diesel fumes from an ancient Mercedes sedan ahead of Kenyon poured into the cockpit of the car. A break appeared in the oncoming traffic, and he hit the accelerator. The sports car whipped effortlessly ahead of the lumbering sedan.

Kenyon crossed the Thames and drove past Kew Gardens and Richmond Park. The suburbs, packed with row after row of brown-brick houses, gradually gave way to fields and stretches of forest preserve.

Kenyon soon spotted the North Downs Park sign; the entrance was just ahead. He geared the Morgan down and it responded with a throaty growl. He turned right, across the road, pulling into a graveled car park.

A large man dressed in the dark blue uniform of the Metropolitan Police was standing beside an ancient limousine. It was a 1936 Bentley Sedan in mint condition. The officer was busy polishing the dark blue paint until it gleamed.

Kenyon parked the Morgan beside the Bentley and climbed out of his car. "Excuse me, I'm looking for DI Humphrey Arundel."

When the officer turned, Kenyon saw he was a large and beefy man. He had small brown eyes and the dark shadow of a beard on his jowls. He glanced Kenyon up and down, then, without a word, turned to the back door of the limousine and opened it.

Intrigued, Kenyon stepped through the wide door. In spite of the heat of the day, the rear passenger compartment of the limousine was cool and dry. The seats were upholstered in burgundy leather, with brass fittings on the door. A sliding glass panel separated the driver's section from the rear compartment.

The man sitting inside was slight of build and dressed in an expensive, single-breasted suit. He extended a carefully manicured hand. "Detective Inspector Humphrey Arundel, Special Branch," he said in a languorous accent.

"Special Agent Jack Kenyon, FBI."

"Simply charming to meet you," said Arundel. "Please, have a seat."

A crystal set of brandy snifters tinkled as Kenyon eased himself onto the burgundy upholstery. "Some squad car you have here."

Arundel pulled out a silver cigarette case and lit up. "We're not allowed to smoke in police vehicles, so I bring the family car when expeditions arise." He pointed to the officer standing outside. "In case he didn't introduce himself, that is Collision Investigation Officer Barker. He was in charge of investigating Lydia's accident."

"I'm glad you could meet me on such short notice," said Kenyon.

"I know what a collision officer does, but I'm not familiar with Special Branch."

Arundel pushed back a patch of lanky blond hair that hung over his forehead. "Oh, you *know* . . . we handle *special* situations."

Arundel's intonation was very precise, and he had a way of emphasizing every third word that reminded Kenyon of a florist who had a shop near his apartment in San Francisco.

"What do you mean, *special* situations?" asked Kenyon.

"It's quite simple: Lydia knew everyone, and everyone knew her," Arundel explained. "She was very special to us all."

Kenyon was trying to puzzle that one out, when Arundel continued. "Oh, by the way, Mater sends her condolences."

"Mater?"

Arundel lit the cigarette with a malachite-inlaid lighter. "Lady Beatrice, my mother. Lydia helped her acquire an absolutely delightful Renoir statuette last Christmas. She was appalled to hear about her death. So senseless."

"Did you ever meet Lydia?"

Arundel rolled down his window and blew the cigarette smoke to one side. "Once, at Ascot. She was sitting in our box. Charming woman. Full of life. Just a bit of sadness there, behind the eyes, to make her mysterious. Do you know what I mean?"

"Yeah, she was big on mysterious." Kenyon glanced up as Barker, his polishing task finished, eased his large bulk into the driver's seat. "I don't want to take up too much of your time, but it's very important to me to see where Lydia's accident took place."

"We understand perfectly, and it's no problem at all," replied Arundel. He leaned forward and pulled down the partition. "Always ready to help our cousins across the pond, right, Barker?"

The large man nodded solemnly. "Right, sir." His voice was flat and emotionless.

Arundel finished his cigarette and crushed it into an onyx ashtray mounted on the door. "You don't mind if we proceed in my sedan, do you?" he offered. "Your car should be safe here until we return."

Kenyon had no objections, and Barker meshed the car into gear. They rolled out of the parking lot and turned onto the main road.

They drove for several miles past pastureland bordered by hedgerows and wooden fencing. The smell of freshly cut hay reminded Kenyon of his childhood ranch in Montana. "I had no idea London still had farms in it," said Kenyon.

"We're actually in Surrey county right now, out of Scotland Yard's jurisdiction," replied Arundel. "But there is a sliver of London that extends south, and Lydia happened to cross into it before her accident. We shall arrive there, presently."

Barker came to a signpost that said "Abbey Lane," and the stately Bentley turned off the main road. The heavy car began to climb a steep hill, and the pastures gave way to deciduous trees along the slope. Even though he had only driven the Morgan for a short time, Kenyon couldn't help thinking this would be an excellent test road for the small, powerful sports car.

As they ascended, the asphalt lane narrowed between a steep wall of chalky dirt to the left and a dry ravine bed on the right. About halfway up the hill, they came to a spot shaded by a canopy of oak and yew trees. Barker pulled off the road and parked, and the men got out of the car.

"It happened here," said the sergeant, as they walked up the road. "A local woman reported an accident around midnight." He pointed down into the ravine. "This is where we found the car."

To the right, the road dropped steeply for about fifteen feet. Kenyon could still clearly see where the brush had been crushed. A large tree bore a white scar on its trunk where the bark had been violently peeled off.

"Was the woman a witness?" asked Kenyon.

"No," said Barker. "She lives just over the rise. She heard the car coming up the hill fast, then heard a crash. She drove down the road, but couldn't find anyone near the wreck, so she went back and called us."

"The police arrived about fifteen minutes after the call," continued Arundel. "They combed the underbrush and found Lydia's body near the car. She was pronounced dead at the scene and taken to the mortuary."

"I got here shortly after they discovered Miss Kenyon," said Barker. "I was assigned to examine the scene and determine the cause of the collision."

Barker turned and walked down the road, back toward the Bentley. They stopped in front of some gouges in the dirt on the uphill side of road. Rain had fallen since the accident, and the markings were already guttered and worn, but Kenyon could still see that they had been made with some force.

"From what I saw," Barker said, pointing to the ruts, "I concluded that the driver was traveling up the hill at a high rate of speed when she lost control and swerved to the left, gouging the dirt with her front wheels." Using his hands and shoulders to mimic the motion of the accident, Barker continued, "her car rose up on a sharp angle, flipped over and slid across the road and dropped into ravine."

All three men stood silently for a moment, fixing the tragedy in their minds. Kenyon wondered if her life had flashed before her eyes. Did she have time for a short prayer, or had it happened too fast? "What killed her?" he finally asked.

"She wasn't wearing her seatbelt," replied Barker. "The pathologist determined that she was flung from the car, then crushed by it. My understanding is that she died quickly."

Kenyon nodded. "Was she drunk?"

"She had a low level of blood alcohol, consistent with one or two glasses of wine. Drug tests were negative."

Kenyon took a small comfort in the fact that she hadn't been impaired. "So, what caused the accident? A mechanical problem?"

Baker shook his head. "We towed the car to the police compound, where I examined it. There was no sign of brake wear, tire problems, or loose steering linkage. The car was in excellent mechanical condition.

Most of the damage was consistent with sliding along the roadway, then dropping into the ravine and hitting the trees and bushes."

"Except for the damage on the back," said Kenyon.

"Ah, you noticed," said Barker, becoming animated for the first time. "A car that simply leaves the road suffers patches of damage from trees, rocks, and bushes. On the other hand, a car that is rear-ended off the road will show damage to the bodywork in a straight line, with paint, plastic, or chrome chips embedded in the damage. Just like the crease in the back of Miss Kenyon's car."

"I take it you spotted that right away."

Barker nodded. "It looked like someone had collided with her from behind, which could have caused her to lose control."

Kenyon was irritated. "So, why did you ignore it?"

If he heard Kenyon's tone, Barker ignored it. He walked down the road about twenty feet and squatted on his haunches. "First of all, if there had been a collision, there would have been taillight glass or similar debris on the road. We didn't find anything, not even skid marks. We concluded that this particular damage occurred earlier."

Kenyon shook his head. "You're wrong. The mechanic at Lydia's Morgan dealership told me he serviced the car a week before her death, and he didn't notice any damage."

This time, Barker did seem irked by Kenyon's tone. He stood and advanced, his eyes fixed on the agent.

Arundel stepped between the two men, smiling. "Let me assure you, Mr. Kenyon, that Scotland Yard did a full and thorough investigation." He pointed vaguely south. "I personally went to Ingoldsby Estate. Witnesses at the auction the night of your aunt's death confirm that she damaged her car while pulling out of the parking area. There was no mysterious collision."

Kenyon still wasn't convinced. "If it wasn't drinking, and it wasn't mechanical, and it wasn't a collision, what *was* it?"

"Loss of attention, most likely," said Arundel.

"What?"

"You know, fussing with a cigarette, tuning the radio. It just takes a split second of inattention."

"Bullshit," replied Kenyon. "She didn't smoke, there's no radio in the car, and she was an excellent driver."

"Not according to the District Licence Centre," countered Barker. "She had several speeding tickets and a seatbelt violation."

"Something stinks," said Kenyon. "I just can't *believe* she was killed by a split second of inattention."

Barker crossed his arms. "I've been investigating collisions for seventeen years. If you think I've missed something, you tell me what it is."

Kenyon stared straight at the big man. "How do you sign a wrecked car out of the police compound?"

Barker looked puzzled. "You don't, strictly speaking. The compound is actually a local garage contracted to remove cars from the scene of an accident and store them until the investigation is finished. After we've examined the car, we call the next of kin, and if they still want it, they have a tow truck pick it up."

"Why do you ask?" queried Arundel.

"Somebody signed Lydia's car out on the sly." Kenyon explained how the Morgan mysteriously arrived at the dealership. "They must have walked into a tow-truck office, paid cash, and told them where to pick up the car."

"Why would anyone bother with a wreck?" asked Arundel.

"Maybe they were looking for something," said Kenyon.

"What, pray tell?"

Kenyon stared up the road, at the place where Lydia had died. "I don't know."

Arundel sighed. "You make it sound like some nefarious conspiracy. It could simply have been a bureaucratic foul-up at the insurance company."

Kenyon stared silently down at the crumpled brush littering the site where Lydia died, saying nothing.

Arundel continued. "I understand this is important to you, but you're not the first person to feel that there is more to someone's death than senseless tragedy. We do understand, and we sympathize."

Kenyon looked up at Arundel, then at Barker. "I'm sorry. I didn't mean to suggest you didn't do a good job."

Barker nodded, satisfied, and began to walk back to the sedan. Arundel took Kenyon by the arm and escorted him back. "Why don't you relax and enjoy your stay in London. There are some excellent mysteries playing in the West End right now. Just your cup of tea, I should think."

Kenyon stopped in the middle of the road. "There is something I'd like to do. Do you know how to get to Ingoldsby Estate from here?"

Just then, two women on horses emerged from the forest. They glanced at the men, then crossed the road and continued up a dirt path.

"Well, if you had a horse, you could ride down this bridle path a quarter mile or so," said Arundel. "Otherwise, it's about five miles by road." The DI held his chin in one hand. "But why would you wish to go there?"

"I want to meet the family."

Arundel rolled his eyes. "Well, don't we have strange tastes."

"What do you mean?" asked Kenyon.

"They're terribly *gothic*, if you know what I mean."

"I don't. Tell me."

Arundel lowered his voice. "You must understand, I'm not one to gossip, but they are quite a colorful tribe, especially the old man."

"Who?"

"Sir Rupert, Ilsa's father. Nasty old tiger, he is. Always on the prowl."

"What's his game?"

"Military contracts. Secret Service during the war, you know. Very hush-hush. Knows all the high and mighty."

"Quite a player behind the scenes, is he?"

Arundel nodded. "He certainly was."

"*Was*? What happened to him?"

"Had a stroke last winter. Drools out of the side of his mouth now."

"He's retired?"

"Pretty much. His daughter Ilsa handles the business end of the family."

"What's she like?" asked Kenyon.

Arundel lit a cigarette. "Mater tells me she's the Francis Drake of the charity scene. The Ladies who Lunch flee in terror when she appears on the horizon, ready to pillage and plunder their trust accounts in the name of a good cause."

"How about her husband, Legrand?" asked Kenyon. "Is he involved in the business?"

"As little as possible, from what I've heard. He's in what you Yanks call 'the doghouse' with his wife."

Kenyon narrowed his eyes. "Over what?"

"Can't you guess? He *is* a Frenchman, after all."

Kenyon stared blankly at the DI. "I haven't a clue."

Arundel blew a smoke ring. "Word has it, she caught him with another woman, old boy."

Eight

After Arundel dropped him off at his car, Kenyon drove the Morgan to the T-junction at the bottom of Abbey Road. He turned west and continued for several miles, until he came to a long, thick hedgerow on the right. It was broken by two large stone pillars holding up a set of black, wrought-iron gates. A brass plate with the inscription "Ingoldsby Manor" was attached to one of the pillars.

The gate was open, and Kenyon entered. The lane passed by several tall cedars, then ran along the edge of an equestrian circuit. Nobody was training, but Kenyon reckoned the white wooden jumps, straw bales, and water hazards were frequently used, judging by the gouges in the turf.

Kenyon rounded a corner and spotted a large, square red-brick mansion with white arched windows. Ingoldsby manor stood three stories tall, with a mansard roof covered in slate tiles. He pulled around to the front of the mansion; a semi-circular expanse of stairs led up to the main, colonnaded entrance.

A gardener was pruning wilted flowers from a rose bed at the base of the stairs. He stood up as Kenyon got out of the car. "Nice Morgan," he commented, as he wiped his brow. "Saw one just like it 'ere a few weeks ago."

Kenyon stuck out his hand. "I'm Jack Kenyon. The car probably belonged to my aunt, Lydia Kenyon. Did you know her?"

"I certainly did." He took off his glove and shook Kenyon's hand. "Name's Bernie. Miss Lydia always complimented me on 'ow lovely me flowers looked."

Bernie was about sixty, with round, sunburnt cheeks. He took a checkered hankie out of his denim coveralls and wiped his bald pate.

"It's a shame, the accident. I must have been one of the last people to ever see the dear alive."

"You were gardening at *night*?"

"No, no—I was serving as a valet, parking the cars." He nodded toward the house. "The old squire's been letting go of most of the staff, you see. Miss Ilsa needed an extra hand sorely, and I didn't mind, keeps 'em from parking on me gladiolas, it does."

Kenyon nodded. "Did you talk to Lydia that night?"

"Only when she banged her car."

Kenyon was all ears. "What happened?"

Bernie turned and pointed to a spot on the edge of the cindered parking area. "Lydia was here first that night, so I put her Morgan on the edge."

"Did somebody crack her taillight when they parked?"

"No, that happened while I was trying to clear her a ways out," said Bernie. "It was takin' me a few minutes to move the other cars, see, and she got all lathered, and started her car up before I could finish."

"You mean, she lost her temper?"

Bernie nodded. "She popped the clutch, like, and smashed it into the bumper of the car parked behind 'er."

"What did she say?"

Bernie gave a short, barking laugh. "'Bloody Hell!' is what she said."

"I guess she was upset at the accident," replied Kenyon.

"If you ask me, she was upset before she smacked her car."

"What do you mean?"

Bernie plucked at his ear. "She just stuck it in gear and drove off, without so much as a by-your-leave to me. Not like her at all. Mad as a wasp in marmalade, she was."

Mad enough to lose her concentration and crash her car? "Tell me, where can I find Mrs. Ilsa Ingoldsby-Legrand?"

Bernie pointed to the front door. "Go on up to the house, and Gladys will suss 'er out." He returned to his pruning.

Kenyon headed up to the steps to the main entrance. There was a large brass knocker shaped like the head of a lion on the door, and he banged it, twice. He waited for a few moments, wondering if he should try a side entrance, when the door was opened by a woman dressed as a maid.

"Can I help you?" she asked.

"Are you Gladys? Bernie sent me up here to ask you where I might find Mrs. Ingoldsby-Legrand."

Gladys was a small woman of about fifty with her hair pulled into a bun. "Miss Ilsa is with her father, out on the grounds," she explained. "If you come through the house, I can show you where to find her." She opened the door fully, and beckoned Kenyon inside.

The foyer to the mansion was devoid of furniture. The floor was covered in cream limestone, and the walls were paneled in brown-stained wood. It gave the entrance a chilly, dark atmosphere.

Gladys led the way down a wide hallway, to the right. They passed a set of doors opening into the ballroom that he recognized from the charity auction DVD. Kenyon paused to glance inside. The room was large; he estimated that one hundred guests could fit comfortably inside. A series of six paneled floor-to-ceiling windows overlooked the lawn. Except for the large grand piano sitting in the corner, the room was also bare of furnishings.

"Nice piano," said Kenyon. "It must sound great in this room."

"I wouldn't know," said Gladys. "It hasn't been played since 1939."

"Is it broken?" asked Kenyon.

Gladys raised one eyebrow. "Sergey Rachmaninov played his Third Piano Concerto for the last time in public on this piano. Sir Rupert had the keyboard sealed the day after."

Well, la-de-da, thought Kenyon. That explained the solo singer on the DVD.

They continued down the main hallway and into the kitchen. An ancient, blue-enameled cast-iron stove was flanked by two natural gas ranges and a rotisserie large enough to hold a dozen roasts.

They came to the rear entrance, and Gladys opened the door. "Follow that path through the stables," she explained, pointing to a red gravel walkway. "There's a field behind the far trees. You'll find Miss Ilsa there."

Kenyon thanked her and walked across the lawn. The stable was a long, low structure of red brick trimmed in white and roofed in slate, like the main house. The smell of horse manure hung strongly in his nostrils. It reminded him of Cyrus's ranch in Montana. On a whim, he detoured into the building.

It took a moment for Kenyon's eyes to adjust to the darkness of the interior, but he soon distinguished a series of enclosures laid out along one wall. There was room for almost two dozen horses, but most of the stalls were empty.

As Kenyon walked by a stall labeled "Evening Star," a chestnut mare stuck her nose out, nuzzling for a treat. Evening Star was sleek and strong. Kenyon petted her snout, and the mare whickered. "You remind me of Lady," he told the horse. "Been a while since I rode her, though."

Kenyon continued down the stable to the tackroom at the far end. The door stood open, and he glanced inside. The room was deserted, but the rich smell of leather oil permeated the air, and several saddles hung on pegs on the wall. Kenyon entered.

One wall of the tack room was covered with framed photos of various riding competitions. He stopped in front of a picture showing a woman making a leap over a white barrier. A logo for an event held in Belgium was superimposed on the corner. Kenyon peered closely at the caption. It read, "Ilsa Ingoldsby-Legrand, Silver Medal."

A row of upright clothes lockers had been bolted to the back wall. Feeling slightly guilty, Kenyon opened one and peeked inside. A woman's riding kit hung neatly on a peg, along with a pair of pantyhose. He closed the locker door and retraced his steps.

Kenyon returned to the bright afternoon sunshine and continued down the path toward a stand of walnut and birch. The shade of the trees was deep and cool; a flock of small birds flashed between shadow and light as they flew among the moss-covered trees. It was so peaceful and quiet and ancient that, for a moment, Kenyon felt as though he was walking through Sherwood forest. Any moment now, he expected Robin Hood to hop out from behind a tree and demand his gold.

His mood was interrupted by the sound of a shotgun blast, quickly followed by a second report. He crouched and cocked his head to the right, trying to judge the direction of the shots. As far as he could see, the trees ended at the edge of a field. Kenyon approached slowly, wary of making himself a target.

He didn't see his assailant until the end of the shotgun barrel was almost in his face. Kenyon staggered back in surprise, tripping over a root and landing on his back. Helpless, he stared up at the attacker, an ancient man with a ruddy complexion and large ears.

"Caught you trespassing!" the man shouted, pointing an ornate, double-barreled twelve-gauge at Kenyon's gut.

Kenyon noticed that the man's left arm hung limp at his side, but his right arm was still strong enough to hold the gun.

"I'm not trespassing, I'm here to see Ilsa," said Kenyon, as calmly as possible. "Put the gun down."

The old man ignored the order and stared malevolently at the agent. "Who are you?" he demanded.

"My name's Jack Kenyon."

"Kenyon?" whispered the man, almost to himself. He stared at the agent, a mad hatred in his eyes. "You little bastard!" He cocked the hammers of the deadly gun. Kenyon cringed, awaiting the blast.

"Father!" a woman admonished. "Stop it this instant!"

Ilsa Ingoldsby-Legrand stepped up to the old man and grabbed the gun from his hands. She snapped the breech and emptied the shells from the barrels, then turned around and shouted to the bushes. "Harold! I told you to keep an eye on Father!"

A short, heavyset man in a camouflage hunting jacket came out from behind a hunting blind. "Sorry, Miss Ilsa," he replied, doing up his fly. "I just stepped away for a moment."

Ilsa shoved the empty shotgun into his hands. "Take Sir Rupert back to the house. And have the firing pins removed from this gun. Is that understood?"

"Yes, Miss Ilsa," he replied. "At once, ma'am." Harold took his charge by the arm and began to lead him back toward the house. As they walked away, the old man dragged his left foot slightly in the dust.

"You must forgive Father," Ilsa said to Kenyon. "There have been so many burglaries around here."

Kenyon turned his attention to the woman. Her long, slim legs were covered in black leggings, and she wore a navy sweater with a marksman's leather shoulder padding. Her long blond hair was tied up in a bun, but her skin was as pale and translucent as it had appeared in the video. One detail that Kenyon hadn't noticed in the DVD; her eyes were the color of lake ice.

She reached down and clasped Kenyon's hand, pulling him to his feet with surprising strength. "Might I ask who you are?"

The agent dusted himself off. "My name's Jack Kenyon. I'm Lydia's . . ."

Her smile immediately disappeared. "What do you want?" she coldly asked.

Kenyon was surprised by her abruptness. "Lydia left a bequest in her will. To one of your charities."

Ilsa turned her back on Kenyon and walked toward the blind. "Oh, she did, did she?

"Yes. The Daughters of Mercy."

Ilsa snorted, a short, sharp laugh. "How ironic."

Kenyon felt vaguely irritated. "What's so funny?"

Ilsa didn't reply immediately. Instead, she paused before a rack of shotguns. There were six weapons, all silver-filigreed 20-gauge Perazzis with walnut stocks. Kenyon had once guided a party of European hunters for a two-week horse trek across the Rockies. One of them, an Italian count, was very proud of his .410 Perazzi; it had, he noted, cost him forty thousand American dollars.

Ilsa stroked the barrel of one of the guns, a smile playing across her lips. "Are you familiar with the Daughters of Mercy?"

Kenyon shook his head. "No, I'm not."

"They help single mothers care for their children," replied Ilsa.

Kenyon shrugged. "It sounds like a worthy charity."

"It is." Ilsa lifted a shotgun and placed two shells into the over/under barrels. She took her stance, then shouted out to the field, "Ready!"

In the distance, Kenyon could see some movement as beaters worked the long grass at the far edge of the field. "Does any of the money from your annual art auction go to the Daughters of Mercy?" he asked.

Ilsa turned one eye back to Kenyon. "Some. Are you interested in art, Mr. Kenyon?"

"I'm more interested in auctions."

"How so?"

"I'm interested in knowing what happened the night of yours."

Ilsa squinted down the gunsights, into the field. "Many things happened."

"I want to know what happened to Lydia."

"In what way?"

"When she left here, she was very angry."

"And you naturally assume I was responsible?"

"I didn't say that . . ." replied Kenyon.

Ilsa turned to him. "You came here hoping that I would tell you we had an argument and that Lydia was so angry that she crashed her car and killed herself. Well, Mr. Kenyon, it simply didn't happen that way."

"What did happen?"

"I don't know." She nodded down the lane, toward the house. "Father was not feeling well, and I spent the latter part of the evening in his chambers, overseeing his care. I wasn't downstairs when Lydia left."

"Look, I know you and Lydia didn't get along," Kenyon pressed on, "but it's important to me to find out what happened."

Ilsa returned her gaze to the field. "Then I suggest you ask my husband, Raymond Legrand."

"Why?"

There was a sudden flurry, and a pair of ground birds burst from cover and hurtled toward the blind.

"Because he was the one fucking her, not me."

The gun went off, twice, and the two birds dropped to the ground.

Nine
Sunday, July 10

The phone rang, and Kenyon stirred. It was late morning; Lydia's bedside clock said it was just after eleven. He lifted the receiver. "Hello?"

"Hello, Jack. It's Tanya. How did everything go yesterday?"

Kenyon sat up and rubbed his face. After driving back from Ingoldsby Manor and returning the Morgan to the dealership, he had sat for several hours in the park across the street, nursing a bottle of Jack Daniels. "Not so good."

"Why don't you come over for breakfast and tell me about it? We could kill two birds with one stone; I've got some papers for you to sign."

Kenyon smacked his dry lips together; the inside of his mouth definitely tasted like the bottom of a birdcage. "You got any coffee?"

O'Neill did, and, after writing down directions to her flat, Kenyon promised to meet her within the hour. He shaved and brushed his teeth, then hustled outside to Cromwell Road and grabbed a cab.

O'Neill's apartment was located in Holland Park about one mile north of Lydia's home. The neighborhood was just west of Kensington Palace and consisted of old mansions that had been divided into flats. Kenyon buzzed O'Neill's apartment, then trudged up four flights to the top floor.

She was waiting for him at her door, barefoot. She was wearing a short skirt and a light cotton blouse. Without the formal legal attire, she looked younger, more appealing, thought Kenyon. "Come on in," she invited.

The flat was bright and airy. One side was a combined living room, dining room and kitchen; the back half held a bedroom and ensuite bath. Kenyon glanced into the bedroom. Women's clothing was strewn about on the floor and the bed was un-made. There was no sign of a man's clothing.

Kenyon went into the living room. The hardwood floor was partially concealed by a large Persian rug, the furniture dotted with bright silk pillows. Lydia's nude portrait hung over an ornate marble fireplace.

O'Neill caught him staring at the painting. "What do you think?" she asked.

"Lydia looks almost at home here," he said.

She handed Kenyon a large mug of black coffee and pointed to a set of French doors. "Why don't you sit down outside while I finish breakfast?"

The doors opened onto a small patio on the roof of the building. Coffee in hand, Jack went outside and sat down at a wrought-iron table. In the distance, he could see the forest of trees marking Hyde Park. Fat white clouds scudded quickly across the sky from south to north. Kenyon wondered if that meant good weather, or bad.

O'Neill came out with a tray filled with smoked salmon, cream cheese, and bagels and a bowl of cut mangos.

Kenyon dug in, his appetite whetted. "How did you know this was my favorite breakfast?" He asked between mouthfuls.

"I didn't," replied O'Neill. "It just happens to be Lydia's. Is this what you ate in Montana?"

"Nope. I don't think I even saw a bagel until I was eighteen, let alone lox."

After they finished their food, O'Neill fetched the carafe from the kitchen and refilled their coffee mugs. "So, tell me what happened yesterday."

Kenyon leaned back and stared out over the rooftops. He had been wondering whether to say anything. Finally, he decided honesty was the best policy. "Lydia was having an affair with Legrand." He turned back to O'Neill. "Did you know?"

Her expression was hidden behind a large pair of sunglasses. "Yes."

Kenyon turned his gaze back to the rooftops. "Why would she do that? Why would she chase around with another woman's husband when she could have anyone?"

"Does it really matter, now?"

"It matters to me," said Kenyon.

"Why?"

"Well, because . . . shit, I don't know." Kenyon rubbed his face in his hands. "I guess because I wanted her to be someone nice."

"She was one of the loveliest people I ever knew," replied O'Neill.

"I wanted to be proud of her."

"You can be proud of her," said the lawyer. "She did many wonderful things in her life."

"Yeah? Like screwing somebody else's hubby?"

O'Neill stood up and headed into the apartment. "Don't talk of her like that."

Kenyon followed her inside. "Why not? It's the truth, isn't it?"

O'Neill stopped in front of Lydia's portrait. "Sometimes the truth is the smallest part of reality."

"Okay, then maybe you can explain it to me."

O'Neill turned to face Kenyon. "Explain what?"

Kenyon sat down on the couch. "What was going *on* between the three of them? I mean, if Lydia was running around with Legrand, then what was Ilsa doing letting her organize this big art auction she holds every year?"

O'Neill sat down beside Kenyon. "It's a little complicated."

"I like complicated."

O'Neill thought for a moment. "Charity work is very important to Ilsa. Her family, the Ingoldsbys, have been trading on public service for centuries. The problem is, all of her friends are the horsey crowd. Unless you have Prince Charles out to your auction, nobody covers it. Ilsa needed Lydia to pull in the media."

"How did she do that?"

"Lydia knew the A-list: the rock stars, the movie actors, the ones who guaranteed newspaper coverage. She was their trusted art adviser. One phone call to Bono or Naomi from Lydia, and the society columnists poured out in droves."

Kenyon sat back. "This is too weird. You're telling me Ilsa tolerated Lydia and Legrand fooling around because it meant her charity event was a success?"

O'Neill hung her head. "I don't know, Jack. I don't want to talk about this just now."

Kenyon looked at her. "I'm sorry." He looked out the window at the beautiful day. "You want to do something? Maybe show me the neighborhood?"

She lifted her head. "Do you like ice cream?"

"I love it."

O'Neill took him by the hand. "Come on, then."

They left the apartment and walked several blocks east, until they came to a wide street lined with immense homes on one side and a large mansion on the other. "That's Kensington Palace, where Diana lived," explained O'Neill.

They entered Kensington Park, a large, open area dotted with ponds, ancient oaks and bandstands. Children sailed boats in the water, and nannies walked by wheeling their prams.

"This is great," said Kenyon, as they stood and waited in line at an ice cream stand. "It reminds me of Mary Poppins."

"Come on," said O'Neill. "I'll show you something special."

They wandered down a lane of rose bushes until they came to a huge monument. Marble statues stood at four corners, and a cupola supported by granite columns stood over an immense, gold-leaf statue.

"What is it?" asked Kenyon.

"It's the Albert Memorial," said O'Neill. "Queen Victoria had it built for her husband, Prince Albert, just after he died."

Kenyon stared at the one hundred and fifty-foot tall monument. "She must have really been nuts about the guy."

"It's amazing what people will do in the name of love."

They wandered along a path until they came to a cafe by the Serpentine, a long, sinuous lake in the middle of the park. They bought two glasses of white wine and sat by the water. Some teenagers on in-line skates came by, laughing and shouting.

"That looks brilliant," said O'Neill. "You ever try it?"

"Nope."

"What did you do for fun when you were a kid?" she asked.

"We'd pack our horses and go camping in the mountains," he said. "Find a glacier lake and set up our tent and do a little fishing and hiking. How about you? What did you do for kicks?"

O'Neill took a sip of her wine. "I grew up in Ireland, near the sea. I'd ride my bike across the green hills to the ocean and spend my evenings with friends by a fire on the shore, dancing under the stars."

"It sounds beautiful."

"It was."

"Why did you leave?" asked Kenyon.

"Why did *you* leave?"

Kenyon leaned over and pulled a stalk of grass from the turf. He chewed on it absently. "You talked to Cyrus?"

"Your foster father? Yes."

"How was he?" asked Kenyon.

O'Neill thought for a moment. "He was greatly saddened by the news of the death of Lydia."

"Really? He said that?"

"No. He cried, though."

"Well, you got one up on me," said Kenyon. "I lived with Cyrus for eighteen years and I never heard him cry once, not even when my stepmom, Daisy, died of cancer."

O'Neill reached over and ran her warm hand along Kenyon's arm. "Was it hard, living with Cyrus?"

Kenyon snorted. "Not if you did exactly what he said. Man, he was always on my case about something. If he caught me so much as standing still, he'd shout at me, 'Quit wasting your time daydreaming, boy!'"

O'Neill leaned forward and stared at his eyes. "You were a day-dreamer? What did you dream about?"

"You really want to know?"

"Yes, I do."

Kenyon stared at the grass. "I never told anyone this before."

O'Neill gave Kenyon such a nice smile, he couldn't resist.

"Okay." He took a breath. "When I was around seven or eight, I used to dream about my parents."

"Sorry?"

"My real parents. You know, the ones who gave me up for adoption."

O'Neill nodded. "Tell me about your dreams."

"I pictured myself sitting on the porch of our ranch house. This big car would pull up, and out would get my mom and dad. He'd be wearing this nice suit and smoking a pipe, and she'd be all gussied up in this pretty dress. They'd give me a hug, then say, 'Oh, Jack, we finally came for you,' then they'd take me back to this nice, suburban home with a yard and big dog. And everything would be perfect."

Kenyon stared out over the lake. "Well, they never did show up. By the time I finished high school, I knew it was up to me to get out. Cyrus said I was welcome to stick around and work the ranch, but I won an athletic scholarship at Stanford, and I lit out for the big lights of San Francisco when I was seventeen."

"By the time I was seventeen, I wasn't welcome in my home," said O'Neill. "I was too outrageous for my folks to handle."

Kenyon turned his head to one side. "Except for that axe in your purse, you don't look too dangerous to me."

O'Neill sipped her wine. "Axe murderers are fine. I was something worse."

"What?"

"I developed a crush on my teacher."

Kenyon nodded. "I can see how people would be outraged."

"I was attending The Bleeding Sacred Heart of Jesus. My teacher was Sister Mary Ignatius."

"Ooh," said Kenyon. "And that was uncool?"

"Are you kidding me? Falling in love with a nun, in Ireland? My father thought I was deranged; he wanted to send me off to a sanitarium." Rain began to fall from a cloud drifting overhead. O'Neill brushed a drop from her face. "I told the lot of them to get stuffed, and I came to London."

They finished their wine and began walking back across the park. "Did you meet Lydia in London?"

O'Neill nodded. "I was painting portraits on Portobello Road. Lydia liked my drawings and offered to help me out. She spoke to some people and got me an art scholarship."

"Were you a good artist?"

"Fair," replied Tanya. "That portrait of Lydia? I painted it."

"No way!" said Kenyon. "That's a great portrait. How come you're not hanging in the Tate Gallery by now?"

O'Neill smiled. "My art professors were very kind, but London is a difficult city to make a living in as an artist. I switched to law." It began to rain a little harder, and they began to walk faster. "Tell me about being an FBI agent," said O'Neill. "Do you arrest spies?"

"Sometimes. We also chase mad bombers, extortionists, and the Mafia."

"How about aliens?"

"Just the ones from Earth."

The wind picked up, and the rain came down harder. They laughed as they ran, splashing in puddles and slipping on the wet pavement. By the time they reached O'Neill's apartment building, they were both drenched.

"Take off your clothes," demanded O'Neill, as soon as they were in her flat.

Kenyon looked up in surprise. "What, all of them?"

O'Neill laughed. "Come on, don't be so shy. I've got three brothers."

Kenyon went into the bathroom and stripped down to his boxer shorts. When he came out, O'Neill was in the bedroom, changing out of her wet clothes. Kenyon hung his jeans and shirt over a chair by the French doors.

"There's some port in the kitchen," shouted O'Neill. "Pour us a drink."

Kenyon found a bottle of Ware's Special Reserve and fished some glasses out of a cupboard. He went back to the living room and sat down on the couch below the portrait of Lydia. He tilted his glass at the picture.

O'Neill came out of the bedroom dressed in an emerald green silk bathrobe, her hair brushed back.

"You look lovely in that color," said Kenyon.

"You're such a charmer," said O'Neill. "Let me get you something with that port." She went to the kitchen and dug around for a few minutes, then came back holding a platter. "You have a choice; chocolate-dipped almonds or parmesan cheese. What's your preference?"

"I think I'll try the parmesan." Kenyon took a slice of cheese and put it on a cracker. When he bit in, however, the cracker split, showering him with crumbs.

"Oops, a bit messy," said O'Neill. She ran her hand across Kenyon's bare chest, brushing away the crumbs. "You should stick to the almonds." She picked one up and placed it in her lips, sucking on the chocolate.

O'Neill looked up and caught him watching her. "Tell me something, Jack, do you find me attractive?"

Kenyon smiled. "Yes, I do."

"Why?"

"I like the smell of your hair, and your soft skin, and your pretty smile."

O'Neill sat down and kissed him on his shoulder.

"Do you like me?" asked Kenyon.

"Yes."

"Why?"

O'Neill ran a fingernail down his chin and gazed into his dark brown eyes. "Because you care about people."

"I do?"

O'Neill kissed him on the neck. "Uh-huh. I knew that from the moment I met you."

Kenyon tilted her head up and softly kissed her warm, full mouth. O'Neill responded, thrusting her tongue between his lips. He tasted almonds and chocolate.

Kenyon kissed her neck, then worked his way down across the soft skin of her shoulder. She had a small butterfly tattooed on her right shoulder blade. He licked it playfully.

O'Neill untied her robe and her breasts fell free of the silk. A silver ring ran through her nipple.

Kenyon cupped her breast gently in his lips and kissed it until it stood erect.

O'Neill stood up and ran to the bathroom, returning with a condom. She stood by the couch and let her robe drop to the floor. Underneath she wore a pair of black, silky briefs. She leaned forward and pulled off Kenyon's boxer shorts, then clasped his penis in one hand, unfurling the condom over his erection.

Kenyon, filled with desire, pulled her back onto the couch and ran his tongue along her earlobe. Goose bumps rose on her skin.

O'Neill pushed him onto his back and climbed astride his flat stomach. She pulled the gusset of her panties to one side and slid Kenyon inside her. Arching her back, she thrust her hips against his loins, first pushing, then grinding. Rivulets of sweat ran down between her breasts to join the moisture on his belly and thighs.

Panting, O'Neill leaned forward, and their bodies slid against one another, seeking out every sliver of skin.

Kenyon gripped her tightly as she began to convulse, her muscles flexing in joyous spasm. She cried in his ear, an animal wail of pleasure, and Kenyon answered with a guttural moan of joy as he came.

She gradually subsided onto him, her soft breasts pressing onto his chest. "Hold me, Jack," she whispered. "Just hold me."

Later that night, Kenyon sat on the balcony of Lydia's home, staring out into the street below. He was alone. The dusty aroma of ozone hung in the air. When he tilted his glass up to take a sip of wine, he could still smell O'Neill's perfume on his skin.

The phone rang. Kenyon stood and entered through the doors leading into Lydia's bedroom and picked up the phone. "Hello?"

"Hey, cookie."

"Hey, Marge." Kenyon could hear a baseball announcer in the background; Gonelli must be watching the Giants game. "Are the good guys winning?"

"Those bums? Don't get me started. What are you up to?"

The cord on the phone was long enough for Kenyon to walk back to the balcony chair. "I'm just sitting here watching the world go by."

"You should get out and have some fun. Meet some nice girls."

"Oh, I've been doing that," said Kenyon. "Anything new on the case?"

"Yah. Dahg flew the coop."

Jack sat up. "What?"

"He blew our tail. Vamoosed."

"What did Deaver do?"

"Shit a brick."

"Is that all?" asked Kenyon.

"What do you think? He's bitchin' to Washington. I should have shot the little turd when I had the chance."

"Don't worry about him, Marge. I've just got a few loose ends to tie up, then I'll be home and we'll get these guys nailed."

"That's my boy. Meantime, you watch your back for Dahg. This guy is ex-CIA. He could turn up anywhere."

"Will do, Marge."

Kenyon hung up and stared out into the sky. There were several flashes of lightning high in the night clouds, but no peal of thunder. Kenyon craned his neck, but try as he might, the buildings blocked his view of the approaching storm.

Ten
Monday July 11

Kenyon woke up at six the next morning. His wound felt much better, and he decided it was time to test it out with a run. He got into his jogging shorts and shoes and headed to Hyde Park.

The morning sun cut through the tall trees of the park, dappling the statues and lawns with light. There were only a few pedestrians out that early in the morning, and he felt like he had the whole place to himself. He ran slowly along the cycle path that circled the perimeter.

By the time Kenyon got back to Lydia's, he felt much better. The house was empty; he was used to starting the day alone, and had asked Senora Santucci to begin work later in the day. He had a quick shower and shave, then dressed in a pair of black Levi's and a white T-shirt. He walked around the corner and picked up a *Times* newspaper and a coffee at the local deli, then returned and sat on the balcony overlooking the park.

He had just finished his coffee when the phone rang in the bedroom.

"Hello, you," said O'Neill.

Kenyon smiled. "Hello, to you, too."

"What are you up to, today?"

"I'm going to Lydia's art gallery to check things out," said Kenyon. "How about I meet you for lunch after?"

"I would love it."

"Good. Your office, around one?"

"Perfect," said O'Neill. "Oh, and don't forget to take the cheques I gave you. Zoë's the assistant manager at the gallery. She's positively desperate for them."

"Thanks for reminding me."

Kenyon hung up the phone and went back to Lydia's office. He found a black leather portfolio and stuffed the folder of papers O'Neill had given him into it, along with Lydia's Filofax and gallery keys.

He was halfway down Herringbone Gardens heading toward Cromwell Road when someone shouted, "Oi, Jack!"

Kenyon turned. Happy Harry's taxi was parked across the street, the cabby waving out his window. "Need a lift?"

Kenyon walked over to the taxi. "Have you moved in, or what?"

"It's a great spot to take a tea break," said Harry, drinking from a thermos.

Kenyon climbed in, and they were soon rolling down Cromwell Road.

Sitting in the back of the taxi, Kenyon pondered what to do with the art gallery. His first instinct was to sell it, but on the other hand, there were employees that would lose their jobs. He tapped the cabby on the shoulder. "Harry, if you inherited an art gallery, what would you do?"

"Keep it," said Harry. "You should see the lovely birds what show up at an opening. It's like honey to bees, it is."

Kenyon laughed. "I hadn't thought of that."

Traffic was light, and they made good time. Harry followed Piccadilly until he reached New Bond Street, then turned up the road lined with jewelers, fashion shops, and art auctioneers.

Kenyon watched the sidewalk. Most of the women were dressed in fine clothing. There were one or two fat Asian men escorting tall, leggy blondes in short skirts and black high heels.

Kenyon Fine Arts was located on a side road just off New Bond Street. "I'm going to lunch with a friend," said Kenyon, as Harry pulled up. "Can you come by and pick me up at half past noon?"

"No probs, guv," said Harry. "See you then."

The facade of the art gallery was mostly glass, trimmed with marble. An abstract oil painting sat on an easel in the large front window.

Kenyon tried the front door, but it was locked. He started to fish out the set of keys, but was interrupted by a female voice over the intercom.

"May I help you?" she asked.

"My name's Jack Kenyon. Can I come in?"

"Just a minute!"

Within a few seconds, a young woman opened the door. She held out her hand. "I'm Zoë Tigger," she said. "It's such a *pleasure* to meet you." Tigger was in her early twenties, with long brunette hair, a peaches and cream complexion, and a private school accent that Kenyon suspected cost her daddy a bundle.

"Tanya tells me you're the real boss down here," said Kenyon.

Tigger laughed, a high, giggle. "She's so *sweet*. More like the official dogsbody, I am."

Tigger relocked the door and led Kenyon into the reception area. The gallery was a modern, multi-level space with white walls, soft leather chairs, and a huge skylight. Paintings, statues, and other works of art were distributed throughout the space in an uncluttered, informal manner. The only incongruous touch was a security camera and several motion detectors installed on the walls.

"I brought some cheques down," said Kenyon, taking a folder out of the leather portfolio. "Tanya says you needed them."

"Thank you," Tigger replied, taking the folder. "It's been an absolute fiasco around here." She started through the folder, but suddenly stopped. "Listen to me, what an ass." She stepped toward Kenyon and gave him a hug. "I'm terribly sorry about Lydia. I was deeply shocked."

"Thanks," Kenyon replied. "I'm learning just how much she meant to so many people."

Kenyon was distracted by an American woman's voice further in the gallery. "Bruno, *stop*! You're simply outrageous!"

Kenyon glanced up as a young man appeared from a back room. He was dressed in a black T-shirt and grey silk jacket that looked as though it had been professionally wrinkled. He had two-day's growth of beard on his face, and his dark, curly hair spilled over his forehead.

The man was walking arm in arm with a middle-aged woman. Her cheeks were flushed, and her bottle-blond hair was slightly askew. "These Italians are such flirts!" the woman said to Tigger, adjusting the jacket on her Dior suit. Her voice was clearly American. "Don't you just die?"

The receptionist smiled. "Mrs. van Pectin, I'd like you to meet the gallery owner, Mr. Jack Kenyon."

"Pleasure's all mine," she replied, extending an expensively manicured hand. "I gotta run, though, I'm meeting a viscount or something at eleven. Bruno, could you walk me out to the car?" The man escorted her out to the waiting limo, kissing her hand as she alighted.

He quickly returned to the gallery and extended his hand to Kenyon. "How do you do?" he said in an Italian accent. "I am Bruno Ricci, the gallery manager."

Kenyon shook his hand. "Nice to meet you. I guess we should talk."

Ricci turned to the receptionist. "Zoë, take some cash from the float and go buy biscotti at Luigi's."

Tigger turned and pointed toward the back. "But I picked up some delightful scones this morning . . ."

Ricci tapped his finger once on the reception desk, hard. "Biscotti. Now."

Tigger jumped up and almost scurried out the door.

Ricci turned to Kenyon, a languid smile on his lips. "A good girl, but one must be firm," he said.

Kenyon's lips smiled back, but his eyes didn't. "What is it exactly you do around here, Ricci?"

The Italian turned on one heel, waving his hand. "Everything," he replied. "Without me, this is nothing."

"You're too modest."

Ricci pointed out to the street. "You saw that woman? She knows nothing of art. But when she comes to me, I tell her, Madam, you are exquisite, you are divine." Ricci walked over to an abstract watercolor landscape on the wall, a rich pattern of greens, blues, and reds flowing like clouds across the canvas. "I tell her, when you stand beside this masterpiece, it is like the moon to the sun."

Kenyon walked over and read the sticker beneath the artwork. The painting was a work by a German artist, Emil Nolde, and priced at two hundred and fifty thousand pounds. "She bought this?"

"She will." Ricci motioned toward the interior of the shop. "Come with me."

Kenyon followed the manager through the gallery. There were perhaps a dozen works on display, ranging from late 19th century to contemporary abstracts. Kenyon recognized several of the artist's names, including Renoir, Cezanne, and Warhol. Even to his untrained eye, it was obviously a very tasteful and sophisticated selection.

They entered a glass-fronted office in the rear of the gallery. Ricci sat down behind a modern, bare desk and propped his feet up on the surface. He pulled a pack of cigarettes out of his jacket pocket and lit one with a silver lighter, motioning Kenyon to take a seat in a comfortable leather chair.

Ricci squinted at Kenyon through the curl of smoke. "You know, this industry is full of predators, my friend."

"Oh?" replied Kenyon. "How so?"

Ricci tapped beside his eye. "You sit in America, you cannot see the sharks. They will eat you alive."

"What do you suggest I do?"

Ricci put his feet down and leaned over the desk. "You sell the gallery to me. I make you a good offer."

Kenyon shrugged, unimpressed. "I'll consider it."

Ricci waved his hand. "You have one week."

Kenyon was about to reply when he heard the front door slam. "Biscotti's here!" Tigger called.

Both men rose and walked down toward the gallery. "By the way," said Ricci. "Lydia changed the locks last week, but she forgot to order keys for me. Can you do it?"

"Yeah, sure," said Kenyon. "Just get me the name of the locksmith."

They reached the front reception desk, where Tigger had placed their lattes and biscotti. Kenyon picked up one of the long biscuits and dunked it in his coffee, softening the hard biscuit.

Ricci was about to do the same, when he glanced at the desk. "When did this come?" he asked, picking up an envelope addressed to him.

Tigger cringed. "Mr. Kenyon brought it just now, Bruno."

Ricci ripped the envelope open. "And you did not tell me?"

"I was going to, but you told me to get . . ."

"Silly cow." Ricci held the check up. "I will deal with you later." He turned and headed to the door. Before leaving, he glanced up and down the street, then hurried across the sidewalk to a Porsche Boxster and roared off down the street.

Hell would get a hockey team before he sold this gallery to Ricci, Kenyon thought to himself. He turned to the receptionist, who was sitting behind her desk staring down at the biscotti. "Hey," he said. "How about a fifty-cent tour of this place?"

Tigger lifted her chin and smiled. "I'd be delighted."

She arose from her desk and gestured around the gallery. "This used to be a dingy old store, but Lydia had it redone. Isn't it brilliant?"

Kenyon agreed, and they moved back through the gallery toward a side hallway. "You can make a cup of tea in the copy room here," said Tigger. "That big steel door leads down to the storage basement."

"Where's Lydia's office?"

"In there." The receptionist pointed to a locked wooden door. Kenyon dug out his set of keys and fumbled around until Tigger reached over and found the right one. He thanked her and opened the door.

Lydia's office had a large skylight, but no other windows. Her desk was a modern, sculpted wood affair that had been stained green. Kenyon glanced at the shelf on the wall; it was crammed with reference books on contemporary and Impressionist art.

The agent sat down behind the desk. Except for a telephone console and a large ceramic ashtray with a fish painted on it, the top was clear.

"That's the ugliest thing I've ever seen," he said, picking up the ashtray and dropping it into the waste basket.

"It's a Picasso," said Tigger, delicately retrieving it and placing it back on the desk. "Bruno would give me what-for if it disappeared!"

"Don't you worry about Ricci," said Kenyon. "I've got a feeling he isn't going to be here much longer." He leaned back in the chair and folded his arms across his chest. "So, what do we have to do while I'm here? Tanya tells me there's some bills, and stuff."

Tigger nodded. "I think I've got most of it, but I'd feel better if you had a look. I'll go get the mail file." The receptionist stood up and left the office.

As Kenyon waited, he swiveled from side to side, examining the rest of the office. A closed circuit TV console and digital recorder sat on a low, steel filing cabinet beside the desk. The split screen showed four views, including the gallery, front door, storage room and Lydia's office. Kenyon glanced up at the tiny camera behind the door, then back to his grainy, reversed image.

Tigger returned with the mail file and plopped it on the desk. It contained a thick stack of opened envelopes.

"Anything I should watch for?" asked Kenyon.

"I tagged most of the bills and client checks," said Tigger. "I think the rest is tosh. Have a look, though." The reception phone rang, and Tigger rushed out.

Kenyon pulled his chair closer to the desk and began to work through the pile. He placed the top portion of bills and checks to one side; the rest consisted of solicitations for donations, invitations to exhibition openings and wholesale catalogues for art gallery supplies.

Tigger was still on the phone, so Kenyon re-sorted through the mail to make sure he didn't toss anything important out by mistake.

One envelope was from the Organ Donor Foundation. Kenyon had passed over it the first time, thinking it might be a solicitation, but when he glanced at it the second time, he noticed it was addressed to "The Estate of Lydia Kenyon."

Kenyon opened it up; it was a thank-you letter.

> On behalf of the Organ Donor Foundation, we wish to thank the family of Lydia Kenyon for her generous contribution to our program. We are happy to say that her specific donor card request to harvest her skin was fulfilled, and we used grafts to treat victims of a serious house fire. As well, her corneas helped to repair the sight of two glaucoma sufferers. Unfortunately, we could not, as per her wishes, donate her retinas to research, as the tissue had been damaged beyond the realm of use.
> Sincerely yours, Dr. Clive Merton.

Kenyon stared at the letter for several moments; it simply didn't make sense. He finally dialed the number listed for the Organ Donor Foundation. It took several minutes for the agent to get through to Dr. Merton. "It says in your letter that the Organ Donor Foundation couldn't use her retinas because they were damaged beyond the realm of use," he said. "I don't understand."

"She suffered from photo retinopathy," the physician explained.

"What's that in layman's terms?" Kenyon asked.

"Sun blindness. It often occurs when people stare at the sun too long during solar eclipses."

"How bad did she have it?"

Merton flipped through the file, reading. "Her case was severe. Her retinas were too damaged to function."

"You mean, she was blind?" asked Kenyon.

"Totally," replied Dr. Merton.

Kenyon laughed out loud. "I hate to tell you this, but she drove at least five miles on the night of her death."

"That's impossible," replied Merton.

"I can round up a room full of witnesses, if you want," Kenyon replied.

"I simply don't understand," said Merton. "One of my colleagues had a soccer-playing patient who suffered only a fraction of the damage in Lydia Kenyon's eyes, and he was blind for a week."

"How long did he stare at the sun?" Kenyon asked.

"He didn't. Hooligans shone a laser pen in his eyes during a match."

"A laser pen?"

"Yes. They're intended to be used as pointers in lectures, but some of them are so powerful they can severely blind a person."

Kenyon felt his head swim. "Could the damage in Lydia's eyes have come from a laser pen?"

Dr. Merton paused for several seconds. "Yes," he finally replied.

Eleven

Detective Inspector Arundel sat in Lydia's office at the gallery, listening intently on the phone. He held the Organ Donor Foundation letter by one corner, pinched between the thumb and index fingers of his right hand.

"Yes, Dr. Merton," he said, staring at the letter. "I understand."

Kenyon watched from the other side of Lydia's desk. When the FBI agent had called Arundel with his revelation, the Scotland Yard detective had been skeptical at first, but had finally agreed to come down and examine the evidence at the gallery.

"Thank you, Dr. Merton," Arundel concluded. "We shall be in touch." He hung up the phone and laid the letter from the Organ Donor Foundation down on the desk. "This is most peculiar."

"It's not peculiar," said Kenyon. "It's murder."

Arundel stood up and walked over to a shelf in Lydia's office. He stared blankly at the books for a second, lost in thought. "As I said, it *is* most peculiar."

Kenyon squinted his eyes warily at Arundel, sniffing trouble. "What's your problem with this?"

"You are basing your claim on one piece of evidence," Arundel replied. "What if the Organ Donor Foundation made a mistake at the lab and mixed up Lydia's retinal tissue with someone else's?"

"We can double-check."

"Dr. Merton just told me her retinal tissue was destroyed," Arundel said, pointing to the phone.

"That doesn't matter," Kenyon said, slapping his hand on the desk. "I *know* what happened."

Arundel leaned against the wall and crossed his arms over his chest. "Then, do tell."

Kenyon had spent the last half hour trying to piece it together. "You saw where Lydia was killed," he began. "The murderer stood behind a tree in ambush and waited for her car to come up the hill. Once it came around the bend, he shone the laser pen into her eyes and blinded her. She lost control and flipped the car. Pow. She's dead."

"Allow me to play the Doubting Thomas," said Arundel. "Under your scenario, the killer needed to know in advance where she would be that night."

"Easy," Kenyon said, flipping a sales pamphlet to the desk. "The auction was sponsored by Lydia's gallery. It was widely promoted. You didn't have to be a genius to think she would be there that night."

"Agreed. But, secondly, and more significantly, the killer needed to know when she was leaving."

"Not that important," said Kenyon. "It's a lonely country lane. The killer simply had to keep out of sight until she came up the hill. You can hear a Morgan coming from quite a distance, and those headlamps would be easy to spot."

Arundel nodded. "Finally, and this is important, the killer needed to know which route she would take back from the auction into town."

Kenyon fell silent for a moment. "Maybe she made a habit of going that way."

"Perhaps," Arundel said, pulling out his cigarette case and lighting one. "Assuming, for the moment, that all that is true, then why would someone go to the trouble of using a laser pen? Why not simply use a gun?"

"Because they wanted it to look like an accident," said Kenyon.

"But a laser pen? I've never heard of such a thing."

"Exactly," said Kenyon. "It was brilliant—there was no way any coroner would pick it up. Why check a driver for blindness? The killer only got caught out because Lydia donated her eyes."

"I agree, it is rather ingenious, but it still leaves one question: why kill her in the first place?

Kenyon stared at the surface of the desk. "I don't know."

"I'm afraid that's not good enough."

"What do you mean?"

Arundel waved his hand vaguely in the air, swirling the smoke from his cigarette. "What you've told me, without a motive, dear chap, it doesn't make a case."

Kenyon stared at the detective. "You're telling me you're *not* going to launch an investigation?"

"I simply cannot go to the chief inspector and ask him to commit valuable resources based on suppositions and evidence that no longer exists."

Kenyon punched the surface of the desk with his fist. "What more do you want? You think she blinded *herself*?"

"Be reasonable, Kenyon. What would your superiors say if you showed up with such a nebulous postulation?"

Kenyon pointed to the door. "Get out of my office, you stuffed-up piece of shit."

Arundel's eyebrows rose. "I shall pretend I never heard that." The detective crushed his cigarette in the Picasso ceramic and straightened his jacket, then brusquely left the office.

Kenyon sat at Lydia's desk, staring at the still-smoldering butt in the ceramic. He felt like hurling the ashtray against the wall and smashing it into a million pieces, but he resisted the urge. It took several minutes to calm down, but he finally regained his temper enough to dial the phone.

The telephone rang three times before it was picked up on the other end.

"Gonelli here," croaked the familiar voice.

"Marge, it's Kenyon calling from London."

There was a second's pause. "It's three o'goddamned clock in the morning. What the hell is going on?"

"I'm sorry, but I have to talk to you. They murdered Lydia."

That snapped her awake. "What? *Who* murdered her?"

"I don't know," Kenyon said, taking a deep breath. "I just know she was."

"Okay," she said, half talking to herself. "I'm gonna put on some coffee. Then you're going to tell me everything what happened."

While Gonelli filled the percolator in her kitchen, Kenyon related finding the letter from the Organ Donor Foundation and his thoughts on how Lydia was killed with a laser pen.

"The first thing you do, you call Stan Fairmont, the legal attaché in London," said Gonelli. "He's a good man."

"I can't, he's in Belfast," said Kenyon.

"Oh, yeah, I forgot," replied Gonelli. "You try the contact at Scotland Yard?"

Kenyon snorted. "Yeah; he didn't believe any of it."

"You're shittin' me?"

Kenyon mimicked Arundel's voice; "I simply *cannot* go to the Chief Inspector and ask him to *commit* valuable resources based on *suppositions.*"

"The bureaucratic butt-wipe," said Gonelli.

"Somebody killed her, Marge. And nobody cares."

"Jack, it's time for you to come home."

"I'm not coming back until I catch the murderer," Kenyon said, sitting straighter at the desk.

"Whoa! You start mucking around, you're going to end up screwing up the case."

"What case?" retorted Kenyon. "There is no fucking case."

Gonelli's voice firmed. "You come home on the next available plane."

"No."

"That's an order!"

"I'll quit."

Gonelli sighed, then fell silent for a moment. "As your commanding agent, I must inform you that any exploitation of your position as an agent of the FBI in this situation is unauthorized. You are strictly a private citizen with no official status."

"Fair enough," said Kenyon. "Now, are you going to help me find Lydia's killer, or not?"

"What, you gotta ask?" replied Gonelli.

"Thanks, Marge," replied Kenyon. "Where do we start?"

"The murderer seemed to know a lot about her habits," said Gonelli. "Let's start with her pals."

Kenyon thought of the people he had met so far. "Well, there's Tanya O'Neill, her lawyer, and Bruno Ricci, the gallery manager, and Ilsa and Raymond Legrand. Oh, and there's this art evaluator named Hadrian deWolfe."

"Okay," said Gonelli. "Who had the means, motive, and opportunity?"

"Well, I know the means; somebody blinded her with a laser pen."

"These laser pens; can you get 'em in England?" asked Gonelli.

Kenyon scratched his head. "I don't think they're illegal—you can probably order one on the Internet and have it mailed in."

"Okay, so that ain't gonna help much. What about motive? You know; jealousy, hate, greed."

Kenyon sat up. "Yeah—Lydia was having an affair with Raymond Legrand. His wife Ilsa knew about it."

"Hoo-hoo," said Gonelli. "Did she have an opportunity for revenge?"

"Ilsa was hosting the auction the night Lydia was killed," said Kenyon. "If she did it, she had to sneak out of the auction and cut across country in an evening dress and high heels."

"What about Lydia's loverboy, Legrand?"

"Same problem, only no high heels."

Kenyon could hear a rustling coming from the other end of the phone. He imagined Gonelli unwrapping the foil from a cigar. "What about dough? Who stood to gain financially from her death?"

Kenyon thought about Bruno Ricci. "The gallery manager's a real slimeball. I don't know how he'd profit, though."

"Okay. Here's what you do next. You got access to all her banking records and stuff?"

Kenyon glanced around the office. The low, steel filing cabinet looked like a good place to start, and he remembered tucking Lydia's Filofax into the leather portfolio. "Yeah, there's plenty of stuff."

"Good. I want you to go through it all and establish a pattern, you know, how she lived normal."

"Okay, then what?"

"Then you look for something that don't fit." Gonelli took a slurp of coffee. "Did she drop a lot of dough somewheres? Take a quick trip to Rio? When you find it, check it out."

"Thanks for the help, Marge. Sorry I had to wake you up."

"Don't worry about it, sweets. Give me a call when you got something."

Kenyon hung up the phone and turned to the steel filing cabinet. It was locked, but he soon found the key and opened it.

The top drawer was for the gallery business, the hanging folders carefully labeled with utilities, tax statements, and client files. He closed the drawer and tried the bottom one.

The second drawer held personal files. Kenyon glanced through the papers. There were telephone bills, credit card charges, and other documents, all arranged by date. Kenyon was thankful that Lydia had a neat streak. He lifted out the files and placed them on the desk.

The agent examined the phone bills first. British Telecom listed each call made, including date, time, and duration. The most recent month wasn't in the file; he had to dig through the pile of new mail on Lydia's desk until he found it. Kenyon scanned the list until he came to the day of her death. There were half a dozen phone calls spread throughout the day; he would have to cross-reference them to numbers listed in her address book.

He put the phone bill down and looked at her credit card bills. The most expensive item on the card Lydia used most often was lunch at the Ritz Hotel. There were also some purchases at Harrod's department store and other shops around town. Nothing unusual stood out.

He put the credit card statements aside and continued. The rest of the papers in the file were for property taxes, health insurance, and various other official documents, each in chronological order going back several years. Kenyon thought about his own filing system, a cardboard box that he kept under the bed. He couldn't imagine anyone ever making sense of that mess.

Kenyon dug Lydia's Filofax out from the leather portfolio and opened it up. He hadn't examined it that closely the day before. This time, he flipped to the night of her death: Saturday, July 2. "Auction 8:00 PM," was written neatly in ink.

Out of curiosity, Kenyon flipped through the days after she was murdered. On Wednesday, July sixth, his own thirty-third birthday, she had written, "Call Jack."

Kenyon put down the diary and stared up at the skylight, wondering. Why had Lydia planned on calling him on his birthday? He opened her address book and looked through it. His phone number wasn't listed. He concluded it must be some other Jack.

He flipped back to the days before her death. Lydia's appointment with Tanya to sign her will was marked in on Thursday, June 30. There was very little else, except for an afternoon appointment at "TEQ" on Wednesday, June 29; a cryptic "Techno 69" written in on Tuesday, June 28; and "Archie Lump, 100k," on Monday, June 27.

Kenyon wondered what the large sum was for; perhaps a payment? He suddenly realized that he hadn't seen any banking statements. He went back to the steel filing cabinet, but there were no other files in the personal drawer. He opened the business drawer, but the bank statements were all for the gallery.

He went back to the desk and sat down in the chair. The desk contained three drawers; a narrow one under the desk surface for holding pens and paper-clips, and two side drawers large enough to hold folders.

Kenyon tried the side drawers; they were locked. He examined his set of gallery keys, but none of them fit the desk. He finally pulled out a pointy steel letter opener and, with a silent apology to Lydia, jimmied the drawers open.

The top drawer was empty, but Kenyon hit pay dirt on the second.

He drew out a file marked "Personal Chequing," and flipped it open. The latest bank statement was also for the month of May. The canceled cheques showed various payments to creditors and utilities. Kenyon glanced down at the bottom and whistled; Lydia had over three hundred thousand pounds in cash in the account.

Where was the next statement? Kenyon dug through the pile until he found an envelope from Lloyd's Bank, then ripped it open. It was the record for the month of June. Kenyon scanned down the page until he came to June 27; Lydia had withdrawn one hundred thousand pounds in cash that day. It had to have been for "Archie Lump." He returned to the address book, but there was no one by the name of Lump listed in it.

Kenyon searched through the older statements from March and April. The most cash Lydia had drawn out of her account at any one time over the previous year was five thousand pounds. The one hundred thousand pounds was definitely unusual. Who was Archie Lump?

"'Allo, 'allo!"

Kenyon started in surprise. Happy Harry was standing in the doorway. The cabby flexed a thumb over his shoulder. "Taxi's out front. You ready to go?"

Kenyon suddenly remembered his lunch with O'Neill. He glanced at his watch; it was almost 12:30 PM. "I'll be right out," he said.

Harry stared at Kenyon closely. "You all right, then?"

"Yeah, I'm fine. I just need a minute to clear my head."

Harry left, and Kenyon took a moment to gather up the Filofax and bank statements. He locked Lydia's office door and headed toward the front of the gallery. He doubted Tanya would be much interested in getting something to eat after he told her his news.

Twelve

Kenyon sat quietly in the back of Harry's taxi as the cabby wheeled through central London. He stared out at the busy boulevards, oblivious to the double-decker buses, street buskers, and crowds of tourists. His mind was still numb from the discovery of Lydia's murder. He shook his head angrily, trying to draw himself out of the shock-induced lethargy.

Gonelli was right; most murderers knew the victim. Certainly, Ilsa had a motive: Lydia was fooling around with her husband. And Legrand's sneaky trick of tailing Kenyon back from Tanya's was suspicious as hell. And as far as Bruno Ricci was concerned, Kenyon trusted the gallery manager about as far as he could throw him.

But none of that added up to murder in Kenyon's book; especially when you considered the trouble the killer had gone to in order to cover up his crime. It was too well planned, too methodical.

Too professional?

Kenyon sat up straight in his seat. Was this the work of a hired assassin? The more he thought about it, the more sense it made. A late-night attack on a lonely country road meant there would be no witnesses, the use of the laser pen all but guaranteed nobody would spot the murder. But that kind of planning went far beyond a Mafia hit-man; you would almost expect someone with CIA training to come up with the plan.

Someone like Charlie Dahg?

It was just possible, thought Kenyon. He worked it through in his mind. Lydia was killed around midnight on Saturday, July 2. Because of the eight-hour time difference, Dahg could have caught an early morning flight from Heathrow on Sunday, and still been in San Francisco that afternoon in time to meet Simon at the hotel.

But why would he kill Lydia in the first place? What possible connection did she have with the stolen software, other than the fact she was Kenyon's aunt? No, it just didn't make sense. He warned himself not to get lost down some dead-end conspiracy nightmare. He needed to look for the facts.

Traffic was slow, and it took the cabby almost forty minutes to reach Tanya's office. Harry shook his head. In all that time, Kenyon hadn't uttered a word.

"You sure you're all right, guv?" Harry asked as Kenyon got out of the cab.

"I'll be fine," Kenyon said. "Wait for me."

O'Neill was waiting in the reception area when Kenyon entered. The pretty lawyer had taken off her solicitor's robe to reveal a light, raspberry-colored cotton dress. "You're late," she said, kissing him on the cheek.

"Sorry, we got held up in traffic."

"Not to worry." O'Neill began moving toward the front door. "I'm sure they'll still have two pints left when we get there."

Kenyon reached out and took her by the arm. "Tanya, there's something we have to talk about, first."

His tone was enough to make the solicitor stop dead in her tracks. "What is it, Jack?"

Kenyon glanced over his shoulder at the clerk, who was suddenly very interested in their conversation. "Not here. Let's go back to your office."

Puzzled, O'Neill led Kenyon down through the maze of corridors to her office. When they entered, she closed the door, then crossed the room and sat behind her desk.

Kenyon leaned against the closed door. He stared at O'Neill, suddenly unsure what to say. He wondered how close had Tanya been to Lydia. She had wept at the recollection of her funeral; how distraught would the lawyer be to learn her friend had been murdered? He stood for several seconds, mute.

O'Neill's look of concern slowly became mixed with impatience. "Well, what is it, Jack?" she asked.

He licked his lips, then rushed it out; "I'm sorry to have to tell you this, but Lydia was murdered."

O'Neill tilted her head to one side, as if she hadn't heard quite right. "Murdered?" she repeated. "I don't understand. She died in a car crash. It was an accident."

"No," said Kenyon. "That's what they wanted everyone to believe. Someone forced her off the road and killed her intentionally."

"Did the police tell you this?" O'Neill said, her eyes wide.

Kenyon shook his head. "I discovered it when I was opening up some mail in Lydia's office." He explained the letter from the Organ Donor Foundation, and his talk with Dr. Merton.

O'Neill struggled hard to retain her composure. "Did you contact Scotland Yard?"

Kenyon nodded. "Yeah, I told them."

"What did they say?"

"They said there wasn't enough evidence to warrant an investigation."

O'Neill shook her head. "I don't understand."

"It's not so difficult. Scotland Yard doesn't like somebody coming into their turf and telling them how to do their business."

"What do you mean?"

"They'd rather ignore a murder than admit they fucked up."

O'Neill stared at Kenyon, incredulous. "I can hardly believe *that*."

"Oh, you can believe it, all right. I've seen it happen a dozen times when the FBI comes into a case. Some cops would just as soon let the bad guys walk than let the Feds in."

O'Neill picked at a pen on her desk. "What are we going to do?"

Kenyon stared into O'Neill's eyes. "If Scotland Yard won't help, then I'm going to find the killer myself."

"How are you going to do that?"

"I'm going to need as much information as I can get about the last week of her life."

"What kind of information?" asked O'Neill.

Kenyon sat down. "I've got some of the stuff: bank statements, credit card and telephone bills, but I need more. I need to build up a profile of her last days."

O'Neill squared her shoulders. "How can I help?"

"How about the auction she organized at Ilsa's home the night she was killed?" asked Kenyon. "Do you have any information about that?"

O'Neill thought for a moment. "Would an invitation list help?"

"That's a good start. I'll also need anything else you can find."

O'Neill picked up a cardboard file box from the floor and pulled out a booklet. She handed it to Kenyon. "This is the auction brochure. It shows all the items up for bid that night, and who donated them."

Kenyon opened the brochure at a random page and glanced inside. It showed the color photograph of a small bronze statue of a nude dancer. The text below the photo explained that the figure had been carved in wax by the French artist Degas, and cast after his death. At the bottom of the text was written, "Suggested opening bid: £100,000."

Kenyon suddenly remembered the notation in the Lydia's Filofax. "Lydia took one hundred thousand pounds cash out of her banking account just a few days before she was killed," he said. "Do you have any idea why?"

O'Neill looked up from digging around in the cardboard file box. "No, I don't."

Kenyon continued. "There was also a name, Archie Lump."

O'Neill opened her mouth several times to speak, but nothing came out.

"Are you all right?" asked Kenyon, alarmed.

O'Neill groped for a second before replying. "I'm sorry, I just can't think. This is all so much . . ."

Kenyon came around the desk and took her in his arms. "What's wrong?"

"I don't know." She pointed at the box. "What's the point of all this?"

"What do you mean?"

"Why are you doing this?"

Kenyon stared at O'Neill intently. "To find her killer."

"Finding Lydia's killer won't bring her back," she said, struggling against him.

Kenyon let go and stood back a pace. "Don't you want to see her murderer caught?"

O'Neill folded her arms, rubbing them as though against the sudden cold. "I'm frightened."

"Don't worry," he said, stepping closer, "everything will be all right."

O'Neill looked up into his eyes. "Jack, leave this to the police."

"I can't. They won't do anything."

"Please. Just leave it alone." O'Neill placed a hand on his arm.

Kenyon backed away, confused. He'd thought Tanya was Lydia's friend. "What are you *really* frightened of?"

"A week ago, *you* didn't even care if Lydia existed." O'Neill pointed a finger in Kenyon's face. "Now you just come in here, a complete stranger, and you want to crawl inside her skin and rip her apart."

"That's not true."

"Isn't her money enough for you?" asked O'Neill. She began to cry. "Must you destroy her, as well?"

Kenyon was filled with a flood of anger and frustration. He gripped the top of a chair, then turned and rushed from the office and down the hallway, out into the clear sunlight.

Destroy her? he thought. How does wanting to find out who her killer is *destroy* her?

Harry was sitting in his cab, the driver's door open to the curb, talking on his cell phone. He looked up as Kenyon bolted outside, and quickly shut the phone. "Oi, what's this?" he called out, as Kenyon climbed into the back seat.

"Go!" shouted Kenyon.

Harry glanced at the solicitor's office, but no one was pursuing. "Right you are, then," he said, turning on the diesel. "Where to?"

"Just get me out of here."

Harry turned the cab into the road and motored off. "Bad news?" he asked.

Kenyon looked up at the rearview mirror, meeting the cabby's eyes. "The worst."

Harry glanced at the traffic, then back at Kenyon. "Sometimes it helps to talk, mate. Why don't we find a nice spot an' go for a lager. The round's on me."

When Kenyon didn't reply, Harry took it as a yes. He wheeled around a corner and parked adjacent to a pub called the Final Drop. Its sign featured a hangman's noose.

The Final Drop was located within the shadows of the tall spires of the Royal Courts of Justice, and most of the pedestrians were either solicitors attired in black robe and wig, or defendants dressed in business suits.

There were several wooden picnic tables outside in the sun. Harry went inside to order, while Kenyon sat and stared at the street.

The cabby returned with two pints of lager and sat down opposite Kenyon. "Cheers," he said, tilting his glass. "Now, what's eatin' you?"

Kenyon shook his head and mutely stared into his beer.

"Don't you worry about me repeating anything," Harry admonished. "We cabbies have an unwritten rule; never blab wot's done in the cab."

Kenyon still remained silent. He felt reluctant to talk, not because he didn't trust Harry, but because he didn't want the humiliation of not being believed.

Harry nodded over his shoulder toward the cab. "I seen a few things in this taxi, my son, you just wouldn't believe. Things made of rubber."

Kenyon couldn't help but look at Harry.

The cabby, noticing Kenyon's interest, continued. "I once got it in the back of me neck with a leather whip, I did. Nearly drove into the Thames."

Kenyon smiled, in spite of his mood. "What I have to say isn't pretty."

"Neither is me mom when she takes her teeth out, but I still love her."

Kenyon sighed. "My aunt, Lydia, was murdered, and nobody in London believes me."

"That's 'cause you ain't told me, yet," replied Harry.

Kenyon explained how everyone thought Lydia had been killed in a car accident, but his subsequent discovery of the letter from the Organ Donor Foundation proved it was murder. "I mean, it's bad enough that the cops didn't believe me, but Tanya, Lydia's friend, thought I was nuts. She said I was trying to destroy Lydia. How can I destroy her?"

The cabby shook his head, equally perplexed. "Maybe it was just too much of a shock to her," he said. "Did you think of that?"

"No, I didn't." In his mind, Kenyon ran through the encounter again, and realized how insensitive he had been to her feelings. "I feel like a brass-plated asshole."

Harry waved his hand. "She'll be all right. Give her a bit. She'll see it your way."

Kenyon took a long drink. "I hope so. I'm going to need her."

"If it means anything, I believe you."

Kenyon smiled. "Thanks. It does."

"Listen, I'll help." The cabby tapped his thumb against his breast. "Old 'Arry, here, he knows this town, like. You just ask me anythink."

"I don't know." Kenyon stared at his beer for a moment. "You ever hear of a guy named Archie Lump?"

"Sure have," said Harry.

Kenyon was delighted. "Who is he?"

"Just the biggest bookie in town, is all."

Thirteen

Harry drove the taxi west for several miles, finally pulling off the main road onto a quiet side street. "This here's Belgravia," said the cabby.

Kenyon surveyed the neighborhood. Belgravia had the look of old money, and lots of it. The streets had long, ornately planted parks running down the middle of the boulevards, and Rolls Royces and Ferraris were parked by the curbs. Large baskets of geraniums and petunias hung from wrought-iron light standards. Except for a Royal Mail postie pushing a three-wheeled cart, there were no pedestrians on the sidewalks.

Harry pulled the cab over to the curb in front of a large, well-kept home. The residence appeared identical to the rest of the mansions along the street; white, four stories high, with grey-and-rose granite pillars flanking a large black door.

On closer inspection, however, Kenyon noticed the CCTV cameras mounted in the vestibule and under the eaves of the house.

"Archie Lump's one heavy bookie," said Harry. "Whatever you want to bet on, he'll take it."

"I thought gambling was legal in the UK," said Kenyon. "Can't you just go down to a betting shop on the corner?"

"Yeah, but then it's all recorded," said Harry. "This here's for folks who don't want no tax man looking too closely at what they got, if you get my drift."

Kenyon understood. A drug baron who wanted to throw a few million away at craps had to choose his venue carefully if he didn't want the Feds on his tail. "What's Lump like?"

Harry chewed on a toothpick. "Smooth, but don't let that fool you, mate. He's got a mean streak, he does."

"How mean?"

"A few years back, some stockbroker in the city run up a couple hundred grand on credit with Archie, then tried to welch when he lost his dosh in the market crash. They found him swinging on a rope under Waterloo bridge."

"I take it the cops didn't think it was suicide."

Harry snorted. "Tough to hang yourself with your eyeballs in your back pocket."

Kenyon couldn't help but think of Lydia's blinded eyes. Had she been killed over unpaid gambling debts? It didn't make sense: she had paid out one hundred thousand pounds. Did she owe Lump more? Kenyon opened the door. "If I'm not out in an hour, send in the Marines."

Harry laughed. "Don't you worry none; I'll keep an eye out for you."

Kenyon groaned at the bad pun as he got out of the cab. He walked up the tiled stairs to the front mansion and pressed the doorbell.

A few seconds later, a female voice came out of an intercom box. "Who's calling, please?"

The agent stared into the camera lens in the box. "Jack Kenyon. I'm here to see Archie Lump."

"One moment, please."

Kenyon stood at the doorway staring back at Harry's cab for almost a minute before he heard the electric buzz of the lock being released.

"Please step inside, Mr. Kenyon."

The agent advanced into the vestibule. A large, burly man dressed in a three-piece suit was sitting at a desk behind the door. He stood up and, without formality, frisked Kenyon for weapons. He then picked up a small bug detector and ran it over Kenyon's clothing. Satisfied, the man returned to his chair and pressed a button under his desk. "The reception room is first door on your left," he said, pointing down the hall.

Kenyon's footsteps echoed down the hall as he advanced into the building. From somewhere deep inside the house he could hear phones ringing and people talking. The first door on the left was inlaid with intricately cut glass. He opened it and stepped into a large reception room that had been decorated in shades of blue, with elegant curtains gathered back in gold tassels to let in the light. It was well furnished, with Regency chairs and side tables gracing the walls. An informal setting of stuffed chairs sat in the bay window.

It seemed as though the room had been purposely laid out to exhibit an impressive display of artwork, ranging from early impressionist to post-abstract modern. Kenyon strolled around, idly examining the pieces, until he came to a still life. He stood before the oil painting, fascinated. It depicted a bowl of fruit, a vase, several flowers, and a small statuette, all done in a primitive brush-stroke, but with a complexity and understanding of color that transfixed the observer.

"Matisse," said someone behind him. "Cost me a packet, that did."

Kenyon turned to face Archie Lump. The bookie's fat, round face poked out of the top of a finely cut silk suit. The few strands of hair that still clung to his head had been neatly trimmed. Almost incongruously, he clutched an ancient, white toy poodle in his left hand, the animal almost hidden by immense, thick fingers. "Name's Archie Lump," he announced, in a broad, East London accent. "And this 'ere's Cuddles."

Kenyon shook the bookie's hand. "Jack Kenyon."

Lump motioned toward the set of stuffed chairs. "You any relation to Lydia?" he asked, as he lowered himself into his chair.

"Yes, she was my aunt."

"Sorry to hear about your auntie," he replied. "Always sad when someone in the family dies."

Kenyon wondered if the bookie felt that much sympathy for the dead stockbroker's next-of-kin.

The guard at the door appeared carrying a silver tea set.

"Cup o' tea?" asked Lump, as the man placed it on the coffee table. "Try these bickies, they're lovely." He fed one to Cuddles, who gummed at it gingerly.

Kenyon sipped his tea and ate a biscuit. "You have a wonderful collection of art," he said.

"Thank you. I do love it, I do. Some of it came from your auntie's shop. I've got a Degas statue at home, and a Maggote here in my office."

"Did you say *maggot*?"

"Yep, only the French, with an *e* on the end."

"Is that the artist's real name?"

"No, he changed it. Thought of himself a bit of a shit-disturber, he did."

Kenyon put down his teacup. "I came here to ask you about a recent dealing you might have had with Lydia's gallery."

Lump cocked one eyebrow. "What is it, lad?"

"Why did Lydia give you one hundred thousand pounds cash?"

Lump shrugged. "That's a private affair, lad."

"Private or illegal?"

"None of your business."

Kenyon drew out his FBI badge and flashed it at Lump. "I can make it my business."

Lump sat back in surprise. "You got no jurisdiction here."

"We can extend enforcement on money laundering worldwide, Lump."

The bookie absently petted Cuddles, his beady eyes fixed on Kenyon. "I'm clean."

"Maybe you are, but what about your clients? How would they feel if we started asking them questions about their dealings with you?"

Abruptly, Lump's demeanor changed. "In that case, I shall be delighted to explain."

Lump rose from his seat. Placing Cuddles gently on the chair, he walked over to a piece of art on the wall, the one he had purchased from Lydia's gallery. "You see this here?"

Kenyon approached warily. The abstract painting was about one foot wide and eighteen inches tall. It consisted of electronic bits and pieces—transistors, chips, and wiring boards—attached to a panel in a geometric form, then splattered over with bright blobs of red, yellow, and blue paint. It looked like R2D2 barfed, thought Kenyon. "What is it?" he asked Lump.

"This here was painted by Marcel Maggote. I knew him when he was alive. Screwy French bastard, he was, but he had talent."

Kenyon looked from the painting to the bookie. "What happened to him?"

"He got a taste for heroin. Bought a bad batch two summers ago and went into convulsions." Lump smiled a feral grin. "Choked on his own vomit, he did."

Kenyon stared at the bookie silently, waiting for him to continue.

Lump tapped the painting. "Before he died, I got old Maggote drunk one night, and he showed me this." With a delicacy that belied his thick fingers, Lump pried away a flat microchip from the surface of the painting. He turned it over. There, hidden from view, was a small portrait of the Fred Flintstone cartoon character.

Kenyon examined the tiny likeness. "Why did he do that?"

"It was like his little joke, see? Nobody knew he did it, but him."

As Lump carefully replaced the chip, Kenyon stared at the Maggote, puzzled. "What does this have to do with you and Lydia?"

Lump finished his task and turned to Kenyon. "A couple a months back, when I was in Monaco, one of me lads got a call from Lydia's gallery. The gallery told him they had one of Maggote's works up for private sale, and was I interested?"

"What did you do?"

"I jumped at the chance. They wanted fifty grand, and that seemed reasonable. Old Maggote was dead by then, and his stuff was worth a lot more. I had my boys pick it up."

Kenyon felt the bookie was getting off topic. "Where does Lydia's payment come into all this?"

Lump pointed to the agent's chair. "I was sitting right there last week, admiring my new Maggote, when I thought, 'ere, Archie, let's

113

have a look an' see what the lad's got painted under this new one. But, you know what? I couldn't find nuthink."

"Nothing?"

"No. And you know why? Cause it was a fake, it was."

"I don't understand."

Lump leaned forward and tapped Kenyon on the chest with a meaty finger. "Your Auntie sold me a forgery, she did."

Kenyon was stunned. "A forgery?"

Lump, enjoying his discomfort, continued. "I called her up, real polite-like, and told her I wanted me money back. She came right over that afternoon with one hundred grand cash and took it off me hands. No questions asked."

Kenyon's face reddened. "I had no idea . . ."

Lump smiled cruelly. "Well, now you do." He picked up a silver bell from the tea set and shook it. It tinkled. The guard appeared immediately at the french doors. "Now, get the fuck out o' me house, FBI man."

Kenyon turned and quickly retreated. The sound of the toy poodle's bark, and Lump's laughter, followed him down hallway.

Kenyon sat in Lydia's kitchen, drinking a beer. It was late at night, and the room was dark. Sitting on the table in front of Kenyon was Lydia's set of keys. They glowed dully in the faint moonlight that streamed through the kitchen window. He picked them up and weighed them in his hand. He shook them, and they jingled softly, whispering their secrets.

The phone rang. Kenyon stared at it for a moment, wondering who would be calling this late. He finally put down the keys and picked up the handset.

"Yeah?"

"Did I wake you up, kiddo?" asked Gonelli.

Kenyon could hear the sounds of the FBI's San Francisco office in the background. It must be late afternoon there right now. "No, I was just sitting here."

"You sound like crap."

"I feel like crap."

"What's up?"

Kenyon took a pull on his beer. "Oh, nothing much. Lydia was a forger."

"What?"

"She was selling fake paintings."

"How do you know?"

"One of her customers complained."

Kenyon could hear Marge chewing on her cigar. "Who was the customer?"

"Archie Lump."

"The bookie?"

Everybody seems to know this guy but me, thought Kenyon. "Yeah. He was pretty pissed off, too."

"Hey, maybe Lydia didn't know it was a fake."

"Yeah? Then why did she gave him back twice what he paid for it? Lydia bought him off."

There was a long pause from Gonelli. Finally, she continued. "What are you going to do now?"

Kenyon sighed. "I don't know. I just want to come home."

"What happened to finding Lydia's killer?"

Kenyon thought of O'Neill's reaction when he had asked her about Lump. Had she known about the forgery? Was she covering for Lydia? "If I continue, I'm going to open a can of worms."

"Yeah, but if you stop now, you know what will happen?"

"What?"

"You'll regret it for the rest of your life."

Kenyon leaned forward, silent, his head down. Finally, he spoke. "You're right, Marge."

"Of course I'm right. So here's what we're gonna do. First off, who knows Lydia was murdered, besides you and the cops?"

"I told Tanya O'Neill, Lydia's solicitor."

"Who else?"

"Um, Happy Harry."

"Who?"

"He's a cabby. He's been helping out."

"From now on, don't go blabbin' about this murder stuff. Until you got motive and opportunity, everyone's a suspect, right?"

"Right."

"Okay. Now we nail down the motive."

"I haven't come across a good one, yet," said Kenyon.

"What about this fake painting stuff? Don't that sound like good motive to you?"

"You mean Lump?" said Kenyon. "Lydia paid up. He's got no beef with her."

"You know the old saying, kiddo: where there's smoke, there's fire. Who *else* might be mad enough over a bum painting to kill her?"

Kenyon sat up straight. "I didn't think of that. You ever cover any forgery cases, Marge?"

"There was one out in Hawaii a few years back. Some clown sold a ton of fake Dali prints to tourists off a cruise ship. Made over two million before he got nailed."

"How'd he get caught?"

Gonelli sipped her coffee. "Spelled Dali's name wrong."

"And he still sold a *ton*? How could you ever get so many stupid people in one place?"

"I take it you never been on a cruise ship."

Kenyon smiled in spite of his mood. "Okay. So you figure there could be more of these Maggote forgeries out there?"

"Yeah," said Gonelli. "But this don't sound like no simple fake prints scam like the Dali thing. What you need to do is talk to someone who knows the local scene."

Kenyon immediately sat up. "I know just who to call."

Fourteen

Tuesday, July 12

The next morning, Kenyon arose bright and early from a restful sleep and went down to Lydia's kitchen. He plugged in the kettle and made a cup of instant coffee, then sat down at the kitchen nook.

Normally, having to drink a cup of instant coffee would have put Kenyon in a foul mood, but he felt happy, almost buoyant: he had a plan of action.

Taking a business card out of his wallet, he picked up the phone and dialed a local number. After three rings, voice mail kicked in. "This is Hadrian deWolfe," a male voice said. "Please leave a number and I will ring back presently."

"This is Jack Kenyon calling on Tuesday morning around ten. Please give me a call when you get in." Kenyon hung up.

The agent was just finishing his coffee when the doorbell rang. He went to the foyer and found Raymond Legrand standing on the front step.

"What do you want?" asked Kenyon.

Legrand looked down at his shoes. "I came to apologize."

"For what?" replied Kenyon. "Tailing me, or screwing around with my aunt?" The agent stared hard at the man, waiting for an argument, but Legrand hung his head contritely and said nothing.

In fact, the man had such a whipped dog look that Kenyon couldn't hold his anger long. He sighed, and stood back from the door. "You want a coffee?" he asked.

The Frenchman looked up. "Yes, please."

They walked down the hall to the kitchen. The water in the electric kettle was still warm. "All I have is instant black," he said.

"That will do fine," said Legrand.

Kenyon poured the coffee and handed it to the Frenchman. Legrand took one sip, and his eyes went wide. "Perhaps I shall forego the coffee," he said. He went to the sink and poured it down the drain, careful to lift a large bar of soap out of the way first.

Legrand then joined Kenyon at the breakfast nook. "My gardener Bernard told me you came out to Ingoldsby Manor," he said.

"Yeah. I spoke to your wife."

Legrand looked Kenyon in the eye as he spoke. "It was wrong for me not to come to the reading of the will the other morning. But now that you have met Ilsa, I think you can understand my reluctance to face her."

Kenyon didn't disagree; he remembered the way she had plugged those grouse with her shotgun. "That doesn't excuse you from following me."

Legrand stared at his black coffee. "I was not completely truthful with you about the briefcase." His gaze returned to Kenyon. "If it were to go through Lydia's solicitor, then Ilsa's lawyers might learn about it."

"So?"

Legrand coughed. "In the event of a divorce, I would prefer if the contents remained confidential."

"Well, it's a moot point right now," Kenyon replied. "I can't find it."

Legrand idly fingered Lydia's keys on the breakfast table. "That does not surprise me. Lydia had a special hiding spot."

"Where?" asked Kenyon.

Legrand pointed over the agent's shoulder. "There is a false ceiling in the wine refrigerator."

Kenyon opened the glass door. The ceiling *did* appear to be about two feet lower than the rest of the room. "How do you open it?" he asked.

Legrand fetched a stepping stool from under the kitchen counter. "There is a latch on the side."

Kenyon stood on the stool and felt along the edge where the wine shelf met the ceiling; he quickly found the latch that held a hinged panel shut. The agent eased the panel down, exposing a dark cavity above. He could discern a bulky mass looming in the shadows.

Standing on his tiptoes, he was just tall enough to ease his head through the opening. It took a second for his eyes to adjust, but the bulky object turned out to be the compressor for the wine cooler. "I don't see any briefcase," he said.

"Have a careful look," replied Legrand, from below.

Kenyon turned, scanning the dark recess. The light didn't penetrate far; he had to stretch one arm and search blindly through the space. He checked a second time, but all he found was thick dust. He eased out of the recess and closed the latch. "Nothing up there," he said.

Legrand shrugged. "Well, it was worth a try. Lydia liked to hide things—I fear she may have hidden this one too well." He turned to leave.

The agent followed him down the hall. "Don't worry, I'll keep looking," he said. "I'll give you call when I find it."

Legrand turned and clasped his hand warmly. "Thank you. You're a good boy." He opened the front door and quickly left.

Kenyon watched the Frenchman climb into his beat-up Range Rover and drive off, then returned to the kitchen. His hands were filthy with dust. He went over to the sink and ran some water over his hands, but to his chagrin, he couldn't find the bar of soap.

Just then, the phone rang. Wiping his wet, dirty hands on the tea towel, he grabbed the kitchen unit.

"Hello, it's deWolfe calling," said the evaluator. "You left a message?"

"Yes. I'd like to get together with you. Is lunch okay?"

"Lunch would be splendid."

"Great," said Kenyon. "My treat. Where would you like to meet?"

"Have you ever been to the Ritz?" asked deWolfe.

Kenyon recalled the name on Lydia's credit card bill. "No, but I'd like to go. Where is it?"

"It is near Lydia's gallery," said the evaluator. "You can simply hail a cab and tell them the Ritz, and they will know."

"Fine," said Kenyon, glancing at his watch. It was almost eleven. "I'll meet you there at noon."

"Splendid. Oh, and wear a suit jacket. It's rather tony," said deWolfe.

When Happy Harry picked Kenyon up at half past eleven, the street was busy with traffic. Kenyon was getting used to the route now, and recognized the Wellington Arch as they passed Hyde Park Corner.

The taxi pulled up in front of the Ritz Hotel. It was a large, impressive stone structure on the south side of Piccadilly. Kenyon glanced at his watch as he paid the cabby his fare. "Come back for me in an hour, okay?"

"Right, guv." The cabby beeped the horn as he drove off into traffic.

DeWolfe was standing in the lobby when Kenyon entered. "I was very pleased when you called," he said as he shook Kenyon's hand. "What do you think of the Ritz?"

Kenyon stared at his surroundings. "It's wild," he admitted. The foyer opened onto a long indoor promenade decorated in gold leaf and marble. Halfway down the promenade was a piano bar with large palm trees reaching toward a thirty-foot ceiling.

The dining room was located at the end of the promenade. A maitre d' in a tuxedo stood guard. A silver pin on his lapel announced that this was Artur.

"Table for two," said deWolfe.

The maitre d' glanced down his nose at Kenyon's jacket and Levi jeans. "Have you a reservation?" he asked in a French accent.

Kenyon shook his head. "No."

Artur checked his book and shook his head. "I am sorry, but we are full for lunch."

Kenyon looked over the maitre d's shoulder into the empty restaurant. "Are you kidding me? You could hold bazooka practice in there."

Artur's lip curled slightly. "I repeat, there is no room."

Kenyon was ready to walk away when deWolfe intervened. "Artur, this is Mr. Jack Kenyon, the nephew of Lydia Kenyon."

The expression on Artur's face suddenly transformed. "I am so sorry to hear about your aunt's demise," he said. "She was an absolutely lovely woman." He extended his hand and shook Kenyon's warmly. "Please accept my condolences on behalf of all the staff."

"Thank you," Kenyon replied, astonished at the sudden reversal.

"Do you have anything in the garden?" asked deWolfe.

"But of course, Monsieur," he replied. Artur turned on his heel and led them through the restaurant.

The restaurant's decor matched the opulence of the rest of the hotel. The floor was covered in a carpet of burgundy and robin's egg blue, and marble columns capped in gold leaf rose to a ceiling covered in a trompe l'oeil fresco of fluffy clouds.

They passed through glass doors onto a patio overlooking Green Park, and Artur sat Kenyon and deWolfe down at an ornate, wrought-iron table.

A waiter soon appeared. He wore a gold cluster of grapes on his lapel, and reverently carried a bottle of Bordeaux wine in the crook of his arm. "On behalf of the Ritz, we would like to offer you a complimentary bottle of wine in the memory of Miss Lydia Kenyon."

DeWolfe leaned forward to read the label. It was an Haut Medoc Superior, vintage 1966. "An excellent selection, Sommelier," replied deWolfe. "We shall be more than delighted to accept."

Kenyon watched the waiter depart to open the bottle. "They sure seem to have thought a lot of Lydia around here."

"This was Lydia's favorite entertaining spot. Whenever one of her celebrity clients came to town, she always brought them to dine at the Ritz."

"And that's why they're springing a nice bottle of wine on us?"

"They hope Lydia's nephew will carry on the tradition."

Another waiter brought menus, and the two men perused the contents. Kenyon stared at the entrees; half of them were listed in French. He noted, with alarm, that there were no prices listed.

The wine steward returned and poured a glass for sampling. Kenyon swirled a sip in his mouth. The wine was strong yet smooth, and tasted of wild berries. He nodded; the sommelier filled the glasses, then departed.

DeWolfe placed his glass back on the table. "I am flattered, of course, that you have asked me to dine, but might I inquire the reason for the invite?"

"I had hoped to learn a little about the art business from you," Kenyon replied.

"Are you thinking about running the gallery yourself?"

"I'd like to explore my options. I was hoping you could fill me in on how things work in this town when it comes to art."

"Why don't we order first?" said deWolfe. "Shall I pick something for both of us?"

Kenyon nodded gratefully. "Go right ahead."

DeWolfe called the waiter over and ordered several courses, then sat back in his chair and pondered where to start. "Art in Britain is big business," he began. "Several billions' worth of paintings and other artwork are sold annually, and London is the center for most of the action."

"Several billion?" Kenyon whistled. "I had no idea it was that large."

DeWolfe nodded. "The recent recession took a big bite, but Christie's and Sotheby's auction houses alone still have annual worldwide sales in excess of a billion. And there are a handful of UK-based houses that turn over 100 to 250 million pounds annually."

"And the Kenyon Art Gallery?"

"There are about one hundred galleries in London that do ten to one hundred million pounds. Lydia's gallery would fall into that range."

The waiter returned with an oval baking dish. "What's this?" Kenyon asked.

"Terrine of foie gras," replied deWolfe. "It is made from the liver of a goose. Try some with the fig chutney."

Kenyon spread some paté onto a cracker and topped it with the chutney. The meat was spicy and sweet, with a rich, gamey flavor. Kenyon chased it with a sip of the Bordeaux.

"Tell me," Kenyon asked. "Is art profitable?"

"It is one of the most profitable businesses around," said deWolfe. "If Lydia was grossing 21 million pounds a year, she would have a pre-tax profit of around 33 per cent, or 7 million pounds, and a post tax profit of 3.5 million pounds."

"Whoa. That's like winning the lottery every year."

"That it is, only a lot easier."

"Tell me, who can afford to buy this art?" asked Kenyon. "I mean, there's stuff hanging in Lydia's gallery worth over a million bucks."

DeWolfe spread some paté onto a cracker. "There are several thousand people worldwide who can pay 100 million pounds for a painting by Van Gogh or Monet without a moment's hesitation."

The two men finished the appetizer, and a busboy whisked it away. The waiter then returned with their soup, a rich, rose-colored lobster bisque. Kenyon spooned up some; it was filled with succulent meat. "I know I'm going to sound like a hick, but why do they pay that much for a scrap of canvas with paint on it?"

DeWolfe savored his soup for a few moments before replying. "That is actually a very good question, one that the art industry devotes a lot of time and energy pondering."

He put down his spoon. "There are three main categories of buyer. The first is the aesthete, who buys art for the pleasure. Art for him is a hobby, a passion."

"What's the second category?"

"The investor, who buys for value. The art market has outperformed all stock exchanges in the last twenty years."

"And the third?"

"The nouveau riche."

"Who?"

"The new money; the recent arrivals who wish to buy credibility by owning something famous and valuable."

"How does a gallery connect up with all these people?" Kenyon asked.

"Through a mix of socializing and networking. Ascot and opera for old money, night clubs, film openings, and rock concerts for new."

"What did Lydia do?"

"Lydia cultivated the new crowd: software billionaires, rock musicians, and movie stars. They all trusted her."

The waiter returned, wheeling a silver carving trolley. With a flourish, he opened the lid to reveal a roast rack of lamb. He carved the roast into separate chops, serving them with rosemary potatoes and buttered carrots.

Kenyon ate hungrily; deWolfe with more restraint. After the main course, they paused for a few moments, in silence.

"Is trust important?" Kenyon finally asked.

"Extremely important. Most people don't know how to recognize whether a painting is genuine or not. That's why they go to a gallery, because they are paying for the expertise and reputation."

"Did Lydia have a good reputation?"

"*Ja*. All of her catalogue is first-rate quality."

Kenyon felt relieved to hear it. He hadn't wanted to believe that Lydia would knowingly sell a forgery.

The waiter returned to remove the plates. They both declined dessert, and ordered coffees.

"Have there been many scandals recently?" Kenyon asked.

DeWolfe thought for a moment. "A forgery ring infiltrated the Tate gallery's files a few years ago and authenticated false paintings."

"Did they catch the guys?"

"No, it was only discovered accidentally, several months later. They were long gone by then."

"Have there been any scandals involving modern stuff?"

"Oh, yes. A gallery in Hawaii was caught selling counterfeit Dali prints."

"I heard about that. What about modern originals?"

"That is very uncommon."

"Why?"

"Modern originals are very difficult to pass off. Any potential buyer with suspicions can simply contact the artist to authenticate it." DeWolfe eyed Kenyon. "What are you getting at?"

Kenyon tried to look innocent. "What do you mean?"

"There is something you are not telling me. I insist that you explain."

"I can't right now."

DeWolfe gazed shrewdly at Kenyon. "Then, let me guess; Lydia's gallery has a forgery."

The agent couldn't conceal his surprise. "How did you know?"

DeWolfe lowered his voice. "Lydia called me last year. It was all very hush-hush. She was concerned about the provenance of a modern painting."

"What did you find?"

"It was a fake."

"Did you catch the crook?"

DeWolfe shook his head. "It had passed through too many owners to know who had made the switch. We couldn't prove who was the culprit."

"Well," replied Kenyon, "whoever it is, I think they're back. A fake showed up at Lydia's gallery, and I need to know if there's any more. I need your help."

DeWolfe nodded solemnly. "I will do anything for Lydia. And you can count on my utmost discretion."

"What should we do?" asked Kenyon.

"We should go to Lydia's gallery and look at the rest of the paintings, immediately."

Fifteen

Happy Harry's taxi was waiting out on Piccadilly when Kenyon and deWolfe emerged from the Ritz hotel.

The cabby took them north for several blocks on Bond Street, then turned onto the side road housing Lydia's gallery.

Tigger buzzed the two men through the front door. The receptionist looked carefully at Kenyon as he entered, clearly concerned about his abrupt departure the day before. "Is everything all right, Mr. Kenyon?"

"Yeah, I'm okay, Zoë," he said. He turned to his companion. "This is Hadrian deWolfe. He's going to help me evaluate some art. We'll be down in the storage room."

Hearing Kenyon's voice, Bruno Ricci emerged from his back office and approached the reception area. "Oh, there you are, Kenyon," he called, languidly pushing back the locks of curly black hair that had fallen over his forehead. "My banker is a pig. There is an overdrawn account, you can help, no?"

Suddenly, Ricci noticed deWolfe. Without another word, he exited the gallery and strode swiftly down the street.

Kenyon scratched his head. "What the hell got into him?

DeWolfe's eyes grew wide in perplexity. "Perhaps, I look like his banker, *ja?*" He shrugged, then turned and headed toward the back of the gallery.

Kenyon glanced briefly out the window at the rapidly retreating form of Ricci, then followed deWolfe. He would ask the gallery manager about his rude behavior later; right now, he had more important concerns.

The storage room was located in the basement of the gallery. Kenyon pulled out Lydia's ring of keys and unlatched the two deadbolts that firmly fixed the door to the frame. He flicked on the light switch and the two men descended the heavy wooden stairs.

The basement walls of the gallery were bare concrete. A workshop was situated on the near side of the cellar, with a long, flat table and a toolkit holding a saw, hammer, and various other implements.

DeWolfe ignored the workshop and headed directly for the far wall, which was covered by a long storage cabinet. Constructed of steel, the cabinet held twenty vertically mounted drawers. He strolled slowly up and down the length of the cabinet, carefully reading the contents list on each drawer. He finally turned and came back to the center of the cabinet. "Please, unlock this one," he said, pointing to a drawer. DeWolfe then went to the workbench and fished through the toolkit. He returned with a portable fluorescent light in one hand, a blacklight in the other, and a jeweler's loupe on a chain around his neck.

Finding the correct key, Kenyon unlocked the first vertical drawer and slowly drew it out. Four paintings hung on a steel-mesh frame. They depicted various English outdoor scenes, including a fox hunt and a young, cherub-cheeked boy eviscerating a grouse for his master.

Kenyon glanced dubiously at the dark, lacquer-encrusted paintings. "Why are you looking at these?"

"These landscapes are 19th-century oils after the school of Constable." DeWolfe tapped a stag hunting scene with a long finger. "Remember, I mentioned a forgery that we uncovered in Lydia's gallery last year? It was by this artist, Johnson. It had already passed through several hands before we caught it."

"How did you spot the fake?"

DeWolfe turned on the fluorescent light. "Fortunately, it is easy with 19th-century works. The lacquer used to preserve the surface remains clear under daylight, but glows yellow when exposed to fluorescence."

He held the light close to the painting, and the surface glowed a distinct amber.

"Well, it appears that this one is authentic—hardly surprising, considering Lydia's experience in the past."

Kenyon closed the first drawer and pulled open the second. It held four paintings depicting cattle skulls resting in various desert landscapes. "I recognize these from art class in high school," he said. "They're by an American artist."

"Georgia O'Keeffe," agreed deWolfe. "Early and mid-20th century. A very prolific painter, and quite desired by you Americans, hence the popularity among forgers."

DeWolfe peered closely at the horn on one painting. "O'Keeffe used a white pigment with a high calcium content that glows purple under ultraviolet light. They don't concoct it anymore, and only the most dedicated forgers go to the bother of mixing authentic pigment." He sniffed. "Lazy lot."

The evaluator turned on the black light and held it up to the paintings; on every work, the white pigment glowed a healthy violet hue. He looked at Kenyon and shook his head; the paintings were genuine.

"You sure?" said Kenyon. "Every single one of these works is okay?"

DeWolfe glanced down the long row of drawers. "I could go through the rest, but I would need more sophisticated equipment, and a lot more time."

Kenyon leaned against the workbench, dejected. "Well, thanks for trying."

DeWolfe walked over and joined Kenyon beside the workbench. "Of course, if you were to be more explicit, it might help me narrow the search considerably."

Kenyon stared hard at the evaluator. How much could he really trust deWolfe? If word got out that Lydia's gallery had a plague of fakes, it would ruin the reputation of the business. On the other hand, he felt he had to trust somebody. What good was the gallery if Lydia's killer went free?

Kenyon made up his mind. "Lydia got a call the week before she died. A client claimed she sold him a fake. She bought it back."

DeWolfe leaned toward Kenyon. "Who was the artist?"

"Some Frenchman named Maggote."

"Ah," replied deWolfe, straightening. "It is beginning to make sense."

"What is?"

"Lydia rang me a few weeks ago in Zurich. I cannot remember when, exactly. She asked me to come in and have a look at one of Maggote's works, when I had the time."

"Did she say why?" asked Kenyon.

"No, but that is not unusual. You do not want the evaluator to come in with any preconceived notions."

"What did you find?"

"I never made it here," replied deWolfe. "I was just leaving to examine a collection of 19th-century lithographs in Hungary when she called. By the time I returned, Lydia was dead."

Kenyon walked over to the cabinet and examined the content lists. "There's a couple of drawers with Maggote's stuff in it. Do you want to have a look now?"

The evaluator looked dubious. "Well, post-modern is not exactly my cup of tea . . ."

"I think I can help. Maggote had a secret way of identifying his works. I know what it is."

"Indeed?" said deWolfe. "I am already intrigued."

Kenyon unlocked the first of the drawers containing Maggote's work and drew it out. There were four paintings, all done in the same style that Kenyon had seen in Lump's collection: bits of electronic hardware affixed to a plywood surface and splashed with paint.

Kenyon bent over the first painting. "Maggote would paint a cartoon character behind a microchip and hide it on each work." The agent pried off a memory chip from the upper left corner. A profile of the French cartoon character, Tintin, had been neatly painted on the rear. "See?"

DeWolfe placed the loupe back in his right eye and examined the character. "How did you discover this?"

"I have my sources," said Kenyon.

DeWolfe turned to Kenyon. "There is more to you than meets the eye, Herr Kenyon." He tested the three other paintings. All of the works in the drawer had a hidden character. "It appears as though all these ones are authentic," said deWolfe. "Let's look at the rest."

There were a total of fifteen Maggote works in the storage room. They worked their way down through the drawers, but each painting contained a hidden cartoon character.

Kenyon pushed the last drawer shut, strangely disappointed that they were all real. "I guess that shoots that lead down."

"Not necessarily," said deWolfe. "Sometimes, what's not there is just as important as what is."

"What do you mean?"

The evaluator tapped a list on one of the drawers. "This inventory says that there should have been four paintings in this drawer, but there are only three."

Kenyon glanced at the list. "That's right." They pulled open the drawer again, and deWolfe checked the numbers on the back of each work against the list.

"*Techno 69* seems to be the one missing," said deWolfe. "Odd name; it sounds familiar."

Kenyon stared at the list. "Yeah, it rings a bell." Where had he seen that name?

"Well, it's the only one that appears to be missing," said deWolfe. "Perhaps it was the one that Lydia wanted me to look at."

Suddenly it struck Kenyon; Lydia had written *Techno 69* in her Filofax a few days before she was murdered. Careful to conceal his excitement, he turned to deWolfe. "Where do you think she might have put it?" he asked.

DeWolfe shrugged. "Perhaps it was sold. We can check the files."

Kenyon nodded in agreement. "Sounds like a plan."

The agent closed the drawers, and the two men went up to the main floor. After locking the storage door, Kenyon led deWolfe down the hall to Lydia's office.

The agent pulled open the client drawer on the filing cabinet and went through the contents. Each artist had their own file, arranged alphabetically. He flipped through the folders until he found Maggote's, then returned to the desk.

The folder was quite thick; each work had an authentication certificate, color photo, and provenance listing the ownership trail. The works in the basement storage room were filed up front; they showed Maggote's estate as the owner. Kenyon flipped to the back; there were about a dozen paintings marked sold. He worked through the pile until he found *Techno 69*.

The color photograph showed a painting similar to the rest of Maggote's work; electronic components had been affixed to a plywood board and splashed with blobs of red, yellow, and orange paint. As far as Kenyon could see, the only item differentiating *Techno 69* from the rest of the works was a square, glistening solar panel in the lower left corner. Kenyon handed the photograph to deWolfe, then read through the paperwork. "*Techno 69* was sold last year," he said. "Some outfit called TEQ Plc bought it."

"Oh, dear," replied deWolfe, waving the photograph in the air. "Now I know why the name is familiar." He stood up and ran through a pile of magazines on a shelf until he found a slim catalogue. He flipped through the slim volume until he found what he was looking for. "It's in here," he said, handing the catalogue to Kenyon. "It was donated to the auction."

Kenyon glanced at the cover. "Charity Auction, Ingoldsby Estate, Surrey," was written in large script across the top. "Saturday, July 5," the day of Lydia's death, appeared beneath.

"I wonder who bought it?" said Kenyon.

"I believe Regency House handled the actual auction," said deWolfe. He pointed to a pile of mail. "They may have sent a list of the sales."

Kenyon found a large manila envelope from the auctioneer. He ripped it open, pulled out the list, and scanned the contents until he found what he was looking for. "Someone named Garbajian bought it for ninety thousand pounds."

DeWolfe leaned back in his chair. "Abdul Garbajian—I know the man. A very important patron of modern art. Also very guarded of his privacy."

Kenyon handed deWolfe the rest of the *Techno 69* papers. "You think it might be a fake?"

DeWolfe scanned the papers. "Everything seems to be in order. Certainly, there is no way that Lydia would knowingly sell TEQ a forgery."

"Yeah, but anything might happen once it's out of her hands," said Kenyon. "I think we should see this painting for ourselves."

"I agree," replied deWolfe. "I do have a concern with Herr Garbajian, however."

"What's that?"

"He has a bad temper. He might not react well to being told he spent ninety thousand pounds on a forgery."

"Yeah, well, that's understandable," agreed Kenyon. "I don't see any way around not telling him, though."

DeWolfe lowered his voice conspiratorially. "Perhaps there is a way we can check its authenticity without unduly alarming our dear friend."

"What do you propose?"

The evaluator rubbed his hands together. "Just a harmless ruse. Do you have a white smock?"

"Say what?"

"Oh, what do you Americans call them? A lab coat."

Kenyon thought he'd seen one in Lydia's studio. "Yeah, I think there's one at home."

"Excellent. You go fetch it, and in the meantime, I shall arrange everything with Garbajian."

Kenyon escorted deWolfe out the gallery door and onto the sidewalk and waved down a passing taxi. "Give me a call when you have something set up."

"Will do," replied deWolfe, nodding as the cab drove off.

If Kenyon hadn't followed the cab with his eye as it departed down the street, he never would have noticed the man crossing the road at the corner. As it was, deWolfe's taxi passed the pedestrian when he was almost in the taxi's lane, forcing him to abruptly turn back. He was wearing a cap over his short hair and a large pair of sunglasses, but there was no concealing the distinctive limp.

"Dahg," said Kenyon aloud.

A bus driver honked his horn in anger as Kenyon crossed the busy thoroughfare. He tried to close the gap between himself and his prey, but the sidewalk was clogged with people. He jumped high several times to try and keep Dahg man in sight, but the man suddenly disappeared from view.

It took Kenyon fifteen seconds to reach the point where he had last seen the fugitive. He stopped in front of the entrance to a long, narrow arcade filled with jewelry shops. The walkway was crowned with an arched glass ceiling and crowded with shoppers eyeing the diamonds and pearls. There was no sign of Dahg.

Kenyon approached an ancient Warder standing guard at the entrance to the arcade. "Did you just see a man about six feet tall, with short blond hair and a limp go by?"

The Warder removed his thick glasses and rubbed them on his bright red tunic. "No, sir. Ain't seen no gentleman like that."

Dahg had disappeared so quickly, for a moment Kenyon doubted his eyes. But in his heart, he knew what he'd seen.

Sixteen

As Kenyon walked back toward the gallery, his mind raced. What was Dahg doing in London? He was disturbed but also excited by the sudden appearance of the ex-CIA man. In his preoccupation with tracking down Lydia's killer, he had almost forgotten about Cyberworm: now, the theft of the software program, and the murder of Simon, was back, front and center.

When he reached the gallery, he stopped by the front desk and questioned the receptionist. "Zoë, did you see a man out front, about my height, short blond hair, walks with a limp?"

Tigger shook her head. "Doesn't sound familiar."

"If he happens to show up and I'm not here, whatever you do, don't let him in."

A look of concern crossed Tigger's face. "Why?"

"Mr. deWolfe tells me there's been a suspicious character in the area casing out galleries."

"Ah!" Tigger nodded her head. "Don't want them reconnoitering our place, do we?"

"Exactly. I've got to go out for a few hours. You hold down the fort."

Tigger gave him a brilliant smile. "Roger, boss." She saluted as Kenyon exited.

Out on the street, Kenyon glanced up and down the road, but there was no sign of Dahg. He turned and headed up the street.

By now, he was starting to get his general bearings. To the south was the Thames. To the north was Oxford Street, part of London's busy shopping district. To the west was Hyde Park, a wide expanse of greenery separating the gallery from Lydia's home.

Kenyon reached the eastern edge of the park and turned south along Park Lane, a wide avenue lined with fancy hotels. The stroll helped him calm down and collect his thoughts. Dahg in London just didn't make sense. The guy was on the lam; why come here? Maybe he had been mistaken; maybe it hadn't been Dahg at all.

A long black Mercedes limousine crossed the sidewalk in front of Kenyon. When he glanced up he found himself right in front of the Dorchester Hotel. There was a stand of taxis waiting by the door. Kenyon decided to grab one.

The cab paralleled the park for half a mile, then headed west for another two. Kenyon was glad he had taken a taxi: Hyde Park was a lot larger than he had suspected.

As the cabby drove past the expanse of green, Kenyon mulled over what he had learned about the forgeries. Someone had planted a fake Maggote that Lydia had sold to the bookie Lump. Lydia had made good, but now it seemed there was another fake out there, one that might have been sold to Abdul Garbajian. What had deWolfe said about this cat? He had a bad temper. Bad enough to murder Lydia over a forgery?

No, that didn't fit: Lydia died the night of the auction, just after it was sold. It was unlikely that Garbajian would figure out immediately that it was a phony and set up a murder in the middle of the night. On the other hand, if it *was* a fake, then there had to be some connection to Lydia's death. All in all, Kenyon liked deWolfe's idea of using a ruse to check the painting.

The taxi stopped in front of Lydia's home. Lydia's housekeeper was sweeping the steps as he came up the walk.

"Hello, Señora Santucci," said Kenyon.

The housekeeper sniffed and turned her back.

"What's wrong?" asked the agent.

Señora Santucci turned to face Kenyon. "Poor Miss Lydia, if she knew her nephew so greedy! You cannot wait to grab her money and go."

"I am not."

"You are, too. You try to sell this house, I know it."

"Whoa, wait a minute." Kenyon scratched his head. "I haven't talked to anybody about selling Lydia's house, honest."

"Then why a man come around this morning and ask to see? He say you want to sell."

Kenyon felt a stir in the pit of his stomach. "What did this man look like?"

"He big and tall, and Yankee, like you."

"Short, yellow hair?"

"I think, maybe. He wear a hat."

"Limp?"

"Yah. He walk funny."

Kenyon's eyes grew wide in alarm. "You didn't let him in, did you?"

Señora Santucci placed her hands on her hips. "No! I tell him, go away."

Kenyon gave her a hug. "Good for you. If he ever comes back and I'm not around, you call me right away, okay?"

The housekeeper beamed. "I chase him away with broom."

Kenyon went into the house and hurried upstairs to the office. He glanced at his watch; it was close to four, making it almost eight in the morning in San Francisco. He closed the door and dialed the FBI headquarters. The receptionist quickly put him through to Gonelli's office.

"Marge, it's Jack," he said when he got her. "Dahg's in London."

"Hey, it's a little early in the morning to be pulling my chain, kiddo."

"I'm not kidding, Marge. He's here."

"You sure?"

"Yeah. He tried to sneak past the housekeeper into my place this morning. I saw him myself this afternoon, sniffing around Lydia's gallery."

"So, Dahg's in London, is he?" said Gonelli, almost to herself.

"What I can't figure out: what would he want with Lydia?" said Kenyon.

"You mean, what would he want with you?"

"Me?"

"Yeah, *you*," said Gonelli. "Remember the e-mail that set Dahg up? It came to you."

"So?"

"So, whoever did it, did it through you."

"Yeah, but *I* don't know who sent it."

"I know that, you know that, but Dahg don't. You didn't bring any Cyberworm files to London, did you?"

"No, I left everything with Jasmine."

"Good. 'Cause he'll be back."

Suddenly, Kenyon wished he had his sidearm. "Can we put out an international warrant on him through Interpol?"

"Will do. Listen, you want protection? I can call the embassy and have them put a detail on ya."

Kenyon pictured two burly Marines with carbines following him around everywhere. "No. I can take care of myself." The agent made a mental note to check out the house for security as soon as possible. "What else is going on in the Cyberworm case? Anything new?"

"Nebula Labs ain't talkin' to us," said Gonelli. "Deaver slapped a clamp on 'em, and they're hiding behind it. I can't even find out what the damn software does."

"Jesus," replied Kenyon. "What a lot of horseshit."

"Hey, at least we found a pony. I got a source in Deaver's office."

"Yeah?"

"Yeah. Word is, the US attorney's office thinks it was all set up off-shore. They're chasing down some leads in Europe. Now, Dahg shows up in London. I'm gonna have Leroi go through the files and pin down any UK connections."

"Could be IRA."

"They steal guns, not secrets," said Gonelli. "I'm thinking maybe Iran or one of their pals are behind this."

Kenyon felt better. "At least that gives us somewhere to start," he said.

"What about Lydia's murder?" asked Gonelli. "You find out anything on the forgery angle?"

"I think there was another fake that might have been bought through Lydia's gallery," said Kenyon. "A painting called *Techno 69*."

"*Techno 69*, huh? Who bought it?"

"An English company called TEQ. Then it was donated to a charity auction, and some dude named Abdul Garbajian bought it."

Gonelli pulled out a pen. "Gimme those names again, and I'll check 'em from this end."

Kenyon spelled out the names of TEQ and Garbajian while Gonelli wrote them down.

"How are you going to check if Garbajian's painting is a fake?" asked Gonelli.

"I mentioned to you an art evaluator named Hadrian deWolfe," said Kenyon. "He knows the buyer, and he's going to arrange a meet with this guy so we can secretly examine the painting."

"You trust this deWolfe?" asked Gonelli.

"Don't worry about this guy, he's an old pal of Lydia's."

"Well, *that's* a good recommendation," said Gonelli.

Kenyon ignored the jibe. "I'll give you a call when I find out more."

"You take care, cookie. Watch your back."

"Will do, Marge. Thanks."

Kenyon hung up the phone; time to do a security check. Rule number one: examine all windows and external doors. The office window faced out to the alleyway, secured by a heavy brass lock. He glanced out. It was at least twenty feet to the ground, but workers on the adjacent home had set up scaffolding not six feet away. A cat burglar could make the leap to the outside window ledge, if he were agile enough. Not good.

Kenyon then went back downstairs. At the main door he examined the locking mechanism. It was a good-quality deadbolt, extending two inches into a heavy wood frame. However, someone could smash the lead paneling in the side window and reach right in.

In the living room Kenyon examined the bay windows that faced the street. Heavy brass locks secured the glass on the inside, and access to the windows from the outside was limited by the iron fence and the stairwell that descended to the basement level. But a determined thief could lay a plank across to the outside window ledge and pry a window up with a crowbar; not any easy thing to do undetected, but still possible.

Next, Kenyon headed for the basement. Passing through the kitchen, he noted with satisfaction that the window facing the alleyway had been filled in with glass brick. It would take a sledgehammer to force a way through there.

In the basement, the bottom floor had been divided into a wine cellar on one side and servant's quarter's on the other. The door leading to Señora Santucci's apartment was sturdy. Kenyon would have to check with her later on the quality of the basement doors.

Back upstairs, the windows in the third floor studio didn't have sturdy locks, but a burglar would have to scramble up the drain pipe for three floors just to reach them. One slip, and he would drop onto the pointed iron fence below.

All in all, Kenyon was pleased with the security of the house. A locksmith could easily install a double-keyed mechanism on the front door, but the scaffolding at the back was a problem. Maybe the locksmith would have to think of something to secure the office window.

The white lab coat was hanging where he had last seen it. Kenyon lifted it off the peg and turned to leave, when he stopped. The hairs on his neck tingled; something was wrong.

Kenyon cast his eyes around the room, slowly surveying the furniture. Years of experience had sharpened his senses to the point where, like a cat, he could instantly tell if the tiniest detail of a room had been altered.

Everything appeared to be in the same spot, except for a brush; the tip now faced the easel. He walked over and examined it closely, careful not to touch it.

Maybe Señora Santucci was here and cleaned up, he mused. If that was the case, why be so fussy about returning everything to its exact spot?

Kenyon turned and walked to the second room. He bent down and stared at the floor. There, in the sawdust, were the unmistakable footprints of a man. They led straight to a garbage bin in the corner. When he opened it, Kenyon could see it held a short piece of wood. He lifted the scrap of frame wood, painted burgundy, then dropped it back into the bin.

A phone rang. Kenyon returned to the main studio room but, for a second, he couldn't locate the source of the sound. The agent finally found the receiver under a pile of newspapers and picked it up.

"DeWolfe here," said the evaluator. "I have arranged to meet Herr Garbajian this evening at ten at his residence. Do you have the white smock?"

"Yeah, I got it."

"Excellent. I will meet you out front of Lydia's at nine-thirty."

Kenyon hung up the phone and returned to the framing room. Who had been up here, and why? he wondered. Suddenly, it hit him: deWolfe. The evaluator must have come up during his cataloguing of Lydia's possessions; it was only natural that he check the studio.

Kenyon tucked the lab coat under his arm and made his way down the stairs, chuckling. You're getting jumpy, he thought. Soon, you'll think everyone's out to get you.

Seventeen

DeWolfe arrived promptly at nine-thirty, driving a boxy, blue Volvo sedan.

Clutching the lab coat under one arm, Kenyon climbed into the front passenger seat. "So, what's the plan?" he asked.

DeWolfe put the car into gear and headed south. "Word has leaked out that a quantity of depleted cesium accidentally got mixed in with cadmium yellow paint at the chemical plant," he explained.

Kenyon's eyes went wide. "Really?"

"No, of course not," replied deWolfe. "That is the ruse. Garbajian has an obsessive fear for his own safety, *ja*? When I called and told him the deception this afternoon, he begged for my help to ensure his collection was harmless."

DeWolfe reached King's Road and turned right, driving down through Chelsea. Chic fashion boutiques and trendy restaurants lined the high street; a group of rowdy men in soccer jerseys spilled out onto the street from a pub.

"Where do I fit in?" asked Kenyon.

"You are an atomic energy official from the United States over here to talk with high-level scientists," explained deWolfe. "I convinced you to come over and have a look at Garbajian's collection."

"Now I see why you wanted the lab coat."

"Yes; a nice touch to go with your Geiger counter." DeWolfe withdrew a small, black device from his jacket and handed it over.

Kenyon was impressed. "You seem to have thought of everything."

"I *do* try to be prepared," agreed deWolfe, solemnly. "You will check all his collection, *ja*? When you get to *Techno 69*, I will distract him long enough for you to examine it for the hidden cartoon character."

DeWolfe turned off the busy King's Road and headed south. They drove toward several modern highrises situated on the north shore of the Thames. As they approached, Kenyon could see that the highrises were encircled by a tall brick wall. A guard at the entrance to the compound confirmed their license plate on a guest check list before allowing them to pass through the road barrier.

Inside the compound, the towers were clustered around a marina filled with large yachts and powerful speed boats. Kenyon could see the Thames through the gate that closed off the canal leading to the river. It was high tide, and tour boats, their cabins empty of sightseers, chugged upstream.

DeWolfe parked in a section marked "Visitors." Kenyon donned his coat and tucked the Geiger counter in one pocket, then the two men approached the front entrance of the largest tower.

The foyer of the tower was protected by a private security guard seated behind a barrier of steel and bulletproof glass. The evaluator spoke into a microphone by the door. "DeWolfe and Professor Kenyon here to see Herr Garbajian," he announced.

The guard dialed a number, then spoke briefly on the phone. Satisfied, he pushed a button, and the door on the security barrier swung open. "Please come in. Someone will be right down to escort you up."

A few minutes later the doors to the elevator opened, and a small, wiry Middle Eastern man in a double-breasted suit stepped out. His left eye was sewn shut; he squinted at them briefly with his good right eye, then beckoned them forward. "I am Hazzim," he said. "My master awaits."

The three men stepped into the mirrored elevator, and the doors closed behind them. Kenyon noted that there were no floor buttons in the device; the elevator began to rise on its own. Judging by the time and speed of the ascent, Kenyon guessed that they were somewhere near the top of the twenty story building by the time it stopped.

"Does your master own the top floor?" asked the agent.

"My master owns the entire building," replied Hazzim.

The elevator doors opened up into a marble-tiled foyer. Standing there awaiting them was the largest Arab that Kenyon had ever seen. The man stood over seven feet tall, and his wide girth was covered in a flowing white robe. His black hair glistened with styling gel.

The guard held up a hand to stop deWolfe and Kenyon from advancing any further. He beckoned them to hold up their arms for a weapons search.

The giant quickly and expertly frisked both men. He pulled out the Geiger counter, examined it briefly, then returned it to the agent. He then silently motioned deWolfe and Kenyon to follow. Hazzim remained in the foyer.

Both men glanced curiously around as they advanced through the apartment. Garbajian's home consisted of several large rooms furnished with an impressive mix of Western and Oriental furniture, including a carpet collection that Kenyon figured would do a museum proud.

Most striking, however, was the art collection. In addition to the Warhols and Picassos, Kenyon recognized an impressionist oil painting depicting water lilies; Monet.

The Arab turned down a hallway and stood to one side of a door-way. He beckoned deWolfe and Kenyon to enter.

The room was a large semi-circle of about twenty-five feet in diameter. The outer wall was a phalanx of floor-to-ceiling glass; Kenyon could make out the cruise boats on the Thames, far below. The three inner walls were decorated with an eclectic display of modern art. One oil painting looked like cans of white, yellow, and red paint had been poured onto a block of rapidly spinning plywood; another display consisted of a large, sealed aquarium in which a pickled lamb floated in formaldehyde. Kenyon idly wondered what you were supposed to do if it if ever sprung a leak.

DeWolfe nudged Kenyon. "There it is," he whispered.

Techno 69 was tucked into one corner, almost out of sight. It measured only one foot by eighteen inches and, like Maggote's other works, was a mix of electronic components fixed to a flat surface and daubed with bright paint. It struck Kenyon as almost ludicrous to think that someone might have been killed over it.

"Gentlemen, it is a pleasure."

Kenyon and deWolfe turned to face a small, rotund man. Abdul Garbajian was in his mid-forties, but his smooth, round features and large brown eyes gave him the appearance of a much younger man. He was dressed in a dark grey business suit, blue shirt, and red silk tie. He turned and pointed to the large bodyguard. "Please forgive Ali for having to search you for weapons. He is very thorough when it comes to my safety."

DeWolfe waved a hand dismissively. "Think nothing of it, Herr Garbajian." He turned toward Kenyon. "May I introduce Professor Kenyon, of the Atomic Energy Commission."

The two men shook hands. "It is an honor to meet such an esteemed scientist," said Garbajian.

"You have a lovely home," replied Kenyon. "I can't help but admire your collection."

Garbajian smiled shyly. "It is a trifle," he said. "But it is something that I hold very dear."

"*Ja,*" interrupted deWolfe. "And we would not want anything untoward to happen to it, now would we?"

Garbajian's tentative smile disappeared. "This issue that we spoke about, it is dangerous?"

DeWolfe turned to Kenyon, raising one eyebrow.

"Probably no worse than minor genetic mutation," said Kenyon. "You weren't planning to have children, were you?"

Garbajian turned white and placed his hands over his groin.

DeWolfe placed a protective arm around Garbajian's shoulders. "Why don't we leave Professor Kenyon to his work? I would love to examine that charming Matisse hanging over the bar."

Garbajian slapped his head. "Where are my manners? Perhaps you would like a schnapps, yes?" The two men departed for the main living room.

Unfortunately, to Kenyon's dismay, Ali remained behind, his arms crossed, staring at him intently. When Kenyon pulled the Geiger counter from his lab coat pocket and turned it on it emitted a low clicking. He slowly and methodically ran the sensor over the pickled lamb, hoping that the guard might lose interest.

No luck. Ali kept his gaze focused closely on Kenyon. The agent crossed the room, nearer to the Maggote, and pointed the Geiger counter at an oil painting that depicted a group of nuns despoiling a Hun. He flicked the volume control on the device and the clicking rose to a cacophonous shriek.

Still, Ali held his place. Probably doesn't have any family jewels to worry about, thought Kenyon to himself. The Maggote was only a few feet to his right, but he couldn't think of a way to distract the guard.

Suddenly, Garbajian let out a piercing shriek. It was followed by a second wail. In a flash, Ali was out the door, racing for the front of the apartment.

Kenyon wanted to follow, but he quickly turned and stepped toward the Maggote. Dropping the Geiger counter, he ran his fingers over the artwork, searching for a loose component. There. He tugged at a two-inch microchip, and it immediately came loose from the surface. Turning it over, he held it up toward the light.

A tiny figure of Mickey Mouse waved brightly back. The painting was real.

Kenyon had no time to think; a third scream, this time from deWolfe, jerked his attention back to the living room. Jamming the microchip into his pocket, he raced out of the den and down the hall.

The scene in the living room pulled him up short. Garbajian was writhing on the floor, pulling on the back of his shirt in an effort to drag the tails out of his trousers. Ali stood across the room, pinning deWolfe by his neck against the wall. The art evaluator, his feet at least a foot off the ground, struggled vainly to breathe.

"Drop him!" shouted Kenyon.

Ali simply looked back and forth between Garbajian and deWolfe, torn between helping his master and throttling his attacker.

Kenyon needed to act quickly. He stepped forward and grabbed the prone Garbajian by the shoulders. "Tell him to drop deWolfe!"

In a flash, Ali dropped the art evaluator. He also pulled out a knife from his waistband and advanced on Kenyon.

The agent stood up and stepped back. "Whoa! I'm not going to hurt anyone!"

Ali lunged forward, his knife held high.

The agent spun to his left and kicked Ali hard in the knee. The big man screamed and bent forward in pain. Kenyon cracked him on the chin with his elbow. Ali went down in a heap. He kicked the knife from Ali's hand, then went to deWolfe's aid.

The art evaluator was crumpled against the base of the wall, grasping his throat.

"Can you breath?" asked Kenyon.

"Barely," deWolfe gurgled, as he pushed himself into a sitting position.

By this time Garbajian, the back of his shirt fully out of his trousers, was on his feet. "Hazzim!" he shouted. "Come here!"

Hazzim appeared at the door carrying a Czech-made submachine gun. He flipped the safety and pointed it directly at Kenyon, then looked at his master.

"Get out of my house, at once!" demanded Garbajian.

Kenyon gripped deWolfe by the shoulder and turned him toward the foyer. "Come on, Hadrian, we got what we wanted." The men retreated to the elevator, the snout of Hazzim's weapon following them until the door closed.

As soon as they were descending, Kenyon turned to deWolfe. "What happened?" asked the agent.

DeWolfe coughed, clearing his throat. "The guard was not about to leave you alone, so I had to improvise."

"What did you do?"

DeWolfe smiled slyly. "I dropped an ice cube down Garbajian's back."

Kenyon grinned. "I guess that would make me scream, too."

Both men laughed until they reached the bottom.

Eighteen

The Anne Boleyn pub was located on King's Road, about half a mile north of Garbajian's apartment. Outside the pub, a small, deserted patio opened onto a side street that ran off the busy main street.

DeWolfe and Kenyon sat at a table on the patio, quietly nursing their drinks. The agent pulled out the microchip and showed the cartoon figure of Mickey Mouse to the evaluator. "It's definitely a genuine Maggote," said Kenyon.

"*Ach*," replied deWolfe, shaking his head. "I was certain that it would be a forgery."

Kenyon sipped at his pint of beer. It was warmer than he usually liked, but it had a full, nutty flavor he enjoyed. He looked at deWolfe. "So, what to do now?"

DeWolfe stared at Kenyon closely, his snifter of cognac forgotten. "This escapade is not really about forgery, is it?"

Kenyon glanced away from deWolfe. "No, it's not."

DeWolfe kept his gaze focused on the agent. "I am waiting for an explanation."

"I'm sorry," said Kenyon. "I can't tell you everything."

DeWolfe turned his attention to the street. "I have gone along willingly and have not asked too many questions because I trust you." He placed his snifter down on the table and crossed his arms. "Now it is time to trust me. Otherwise, I must leave."

Kenyon thought about Gonelli's advice to keep his mouth shut, but he needed deWolfe's help. He took a deep breath. "I know you may not believe this, but Lydia was murdered."

DeWolfe stared openmouthed at Kenyon. "She died in a car accident," he finally blurted out. "The police said so."

"Yeah, well, I know different."

DeWolfe picked his glass up and took a gulp of his cognac. That seemed to help his nerves. "How do you know differently?"

"Somebody blinded her and forced her car off the road. The police didn't spot it at first, but I have proof."

"Why on *earth* would anyone want to kill Lydia?"

"I don't know." Kenyon twirled the beer in his glass. "All I can think of is it has something to do with these forgeries."

DeWolfe leaned back in his chair. "*Mein Gott*, I had no idea." He took another drink of his cognac. "I have not been completely truthful with you."

"What?" asked Kenyon.

DeWolfe stared down at the patio tiles beneath his feet. "When Lydia called me in about the forgery last year, she had her suspicions about someone. We just couldn't prove it."

"Who was it?" asked Kenyon.

"That young man who works for her: Bruno Ricci."

It was almost midnight by the time they arrived at the Kenyon Gallery in Mayfair, and the evening sky hung black and cloudless. The streets were deserted and deWolfe had no problem parking his Volvo sedan directly in front of the gallery.

Kenyon pulled out his keys and unlocked the front door. He punched the code into the keypad that deactivated the alarm, and the two men entered the gallery.

Light from the street filtered into the main display room. The shadow cast by a small Degas bronze extended its way across the floor like a long crooked finger. Kenyon fumbled against the left wall until he found a dimmer switch, then turned up a series of halogen display lamps just enough for them to see their way around. The agent didn't want to attract the attention of a roving bobby; no point in having to explain what they were doing there at this late hour.

"Ricci's office is over here," said Kenyon. The two men moved to the back of the display room and stepped behind a jutting wall that hid them from view from the street. Ricci's office door was open and they went inside and turned on the light.

The gallery manager's office was about the same size as Lydia's, but without the skylight. The room was decorated in modern Scandinavian chrome and leather chairs, and the desk was made of frosted glass and rough-cast aluminum. A still life of animal intestines on a hubcap hung from one wall.

The wall shelf was crammed with art books and catalogues. DeWolfe began to examine the books, lifting each one out and fluttering the pages to see if anything had been tucked inside.

Kenyon sat in the chair behind Ricci's desk. The side drawer was empty except for a carved wooden box about the size of a hardcover book. Kenyon lifted the box out and placed it on the top of the desk.

The carving featured a naked Asian man and woman entwined in a convoluted sex position, an illustration from the Kama Sutra. Kenyon lifted the lid and peered inside; it contained nothing but a small mirror, a safety razor blade, and a rolled up bank note.

Kenyon removed the mirror and held it to the light. He could see traces of white powder on the surface. He licked the end of the bill; the acrid taste of cocaine emanated from the end of his tongue.

DeWolfe turned from the bookshelf. "Nothing here," he announced.

Kenyon held up the mirror and rolled note. "It seems Ricci has a taste for coke."

"Vile habit," deWolfe said, wrinkling his nose.

"Yeah, and expensive, too." Kenyon continued his search, checking for a false bottom in the desk, poking around in the chairs, but finding nothing. He finally nodded to deWolfe, and the two men retreated to Lydia's office.

Kenyon sat down in Lydia's chair, facing deWolfe across her desk.

He rubbed his forehead. "You were telling me how tough it is to fake a modern artist, right?

"*Ja.*"

"So how come Ricci chose Maggote?"

"I was referring to a live artist," said deWolfe. "If the artist is recently deceased, you can arrange a scam that is known as the 'Greedy Buyer.'"

"How does the scam work?"

"When an artist dies, he normally leaves behind a large supply of unsold pictures," began deWolfe.

Kenyon interrupted. "Like that stuff of Maggote's in storage?"

DeWolfe nodded. "Exactly. It isn't in the interest of the estate to flood the market all at once, because that will lower the value of all the rest. On the other hand, if you do not release any at all, people lose interest, and the market value also drops."

DeWolfe leaned back in his seat, pursing his fingers together. "Generally, an astute executor announces that they are only going to sell half a dozen or so a year, in order to keep the price increasing."

Kenyon began to catch on. "I take it some collectors start to get too eager?"

"Indeed, they do," replied deWolfe. "Hence the name, the Greedy Buyer."

"Let me guess the rest," Kenyon offered. "A forger with an inside to the dead artist's gallery approaches a collector and says, 'I'll give you a break and sell you one outside of this year's quota, but you have to keep it quiet.'"

DeWolfe nodded. "Essentially, yes. The forger uses the cover of the gallery to fake the authenticity, and the buyer hides it so that no one will know he got the inside break."

"It sounds almost foolproof."

"It is. The forger generally has a much greater knowledge of the techniques used by the artist, and can fool any amateur investigation of authenticity that a buyer might muster."

"Unless, of course, the buyer knows more than the forger." Kenyon flipped open one of the buyer's files. There was a personal number listed in the address. He picked up the phone.

"Who are you calling at this late hour?" asked deWolfe.

Kenyon looked up as he dialed. "An unsatisfied customer."

The phone rang once. "Yeah?"

Kenyon recognized the bookie's voice. "Mr. Lump, it's Jack Kenyon."

"Well, well, if it ain't my favorite little Fed in the whole wide world. I got to tell you, lad, I ain't larfed so hard since me dear, fat ol' mum got stuck in the loo." Lump's voice lost its levity. "What do you want?"

"I want to apologize," said Kenyon. "I was wrong to threaten your clients. It was an abuse of my official powers."

There was a brief silence on the other end. Kenyon had no doubt it was the first time anyone in law enforcement had ever said he was sorry to Lump.

"Apologies accepted," said the bookie. "Now, why did you really call?"

"I have some unfinished business I want to attend to at this end."

"What's that?" asked the bookie.

"Did Lydia personally handle this transaction?"

Lump covered the phone; Kenyon could hear a muffled conversation with someone else in the room before the bookie came back on. "No. It was some bloke at the gallery. The little pimp, Ricci."

"That's what I thought. Thanks."

Kenyon hung up the phone and went to the steel filing cabinet. He unlocked the top drawer and lifted out several files. "Give me a hand with this stuff," he asked.

DeWolfe spread several of the files out on the surface of the desk, including the one for Maggote. "What are we looking for?"

"Lump says Ricci sold him the fake Maggote, but I doubt if the word of a bookie is going to stand up in court. We need some solid evidence. There has to be a paper trail."

DeWolfe thought for a moment. "The only way that Ricci could have pulled this off was by operating under the legitimate guise of the gallery. Let's start with the sales receipts."

Kenyon dug through the file cabinet until he found the sales ledger. It was a small, hardcover book bound in black leather. "I would have thought she'd need something bigger," Kenyon mused aloud.

"Not when you're only doing sixty sales a year," said deWolfe.

Kenyon opened the book up. Each sales slip was divided into three parts; blue, yellow, and pink. The front half was filled with pink slips, all filled out.

Kenyon examined the pink slips. The first was for the beginning of January of that year; the final one was filled out just one week before her death. The smallest purchase was for fifty thousand pounds, the largest for two million pounds. "I see what you mean," he said. "She must have made ten million pounds in three dozen sales."

DeWolfe took the book from Kenyon's hands and placed it under the desk lamp. He quickly examined each of the slips, then flipped through the rest of the book, examining each of the unused receipts. Finally, he straightened up and beckoned Kenyon over. "I suspected this."

"What?"

"There is no slip for the painting sold to Lump."

"Then how could he scam Lump? Did he use a fake receipt as well?"

"Not necessary." DeWolfe flipped to another pink slip. "See this one?"

Kenyon bent over and looked. "It just says, 'voided.'"

"Exactly." DeWolfe cocked an eyebrow, waiting for Kenyon to get it.

It didn't take long. "Oh, right. Ricci pulled the blue and yellow parts off, then wrote 'void' on the pink. He gives the blue one to Lump, throws away the yellow, and leaves the third so that Lydia won't notice one is missing." Kenyon flipped through the book. "He must have done the same with the sale of *Techno 69*."

Kenyon reached the end of the book; the sale to TEQ was marked in on the final receipt. He stared at it for a moment, then leaned back in the chair, puzzled.

"What is wrong?" asked deWolfe.

The agent turned the book around, so that the evaluator could see. "It's filled out by Lydia. It's got her signature on it."

DeWolfe stared at the receipt. "How can this be?"

Kenyon rubbed his face in his hands. "I don't know."

"Perhaps Ricci forged her signature?"

Kenyon shook his head. "Why bother? The voided receipt scam was working. No, that's Lydia's signature, all right." The awful feeling that Lydia was involved in the forgery scheme began to fill his heart.

DeWolfe stared at the wall, thinking. "I wonder if the receptionist knows anything?"

"You mean, Zoë?"

"*Ja*. Perhaps she saw or heard something. Perhaps we should meet back here tomorrow and ask her?"

Kenyon was about to reply, when the phone rang. He snatched it from the cradle. "Yes?"

"Mister Yack?"

The voice was almost whispering, but Kenyon immediately recognized his housekeeper. "Señora Santucci? Are you all right? What is it?"

"There's somebody upstairs, in your home."

Nineteen
Wednesday, July 13

Kenyon slammed the phone down and thrust his hand out to deWolfe. "Give me your keys!"

Startled, the appraiser dug in his pocket. "What is going on?" he asked.

"Somebody's in my house." Kenyon had no doubt who the prowler was: Charlie Dahg.

The front door locked itself as they sprinted from the gallery. Kenyon leapt into the driver's seat and started the Volvo.

"Er, have you ever driven on the left before?" asked deWolfe.

"Yeah. Piece of cake."

DeWolfe put on his seatbelt and cinched it tight.

Except for a few late night buses, traffic was light. Kenyon gunned the car up to one hundred miles per hour and roared through a round-about.

Two bobbies walking the pavement stared in amazement as Kenyon did a controlled, four-wheel drift around a corner onto Cromwell Road. Seeing them, the agent hammered on the brakes and screeched to a halt beside the startled pair.

"61 Herringbone Gardens!" he yelled out the window, before roaring off again. Glancing in the rearview, he could see the policemen radioing in for back-up.

As they approached the corner to Lydia's house, Kenyon eased up on the gas and turned off the headlights. He wheeled onto Herringbone Gardens in neutral, slowing to a stop about one hundred feet from Lydia's home.

There was just one light burning, over the front porch. Kenyon couldn't see any movement or wayward flashlight beams inside. He turned to deWolfe. "I'm going to look for Mrs. Santucci. Wait here for the cops." Kenyon got out of the car and quietly closed the door. He moved slowly toward the house, keeping as close as possible to the iron fencing that paralleled the sidewalk.

As he neared the house, he spotted a shadow moving in the front stairwell that led to the basement of Lydia's home. Crouching, he slowly advanced, wishing that he had his Sig Sauer.

Suddenly, the shadow turned and flew from the stairwell directly at him. Kenyon braced himself as Señora Santucci leapt into his arms.

"Mr. Yack!"

"Shh!" said Kenyon. "Is he still inside?"

"Yah!"

"Did you see him?

"No, I just hear some glass shatter, and then I hear noise upstairs. I remember what you say, and call you at work."

"You got anything I can use as a weapon?"

"Just this," said Santucci. She pulled something from the front pocket in her apron.

Even in the dim light of the street lamps, the large cleaver glistened. "That'll do," said Kenyon. "Come with me."

The pair slipped down the stairs and into Santucci's basement apartment. "Where's the back door?" whispered Kenyon.

Señora Santucci motioned to follow. They tiptoed through the maid's flat until they came to the door that led to Lydia's basement. Kenyon mimed to Señora Santucci to wait there, then, as quietly as he could, he eased back the bolt and advanced into the wine cellar.

The basement was deserted. He cautiously advanced up the stairs into the kitchen.

The darkened room was quiet and devoid of occupants. Kenyon stood for a moment, wondering if the woman was imagining things.

Then he heard it: the sound of scraping somewhere in the house.

Kenyon cautiously advanced. He glanced into the dining room; the silver drawer had been opened, and a trail of spoons led into the living room. Clutching the cleaver tightly, he crept into the front living room, ready to strike, but it, too, was deserted. Placing the cleaver on the couch, he advanced to the suit of armor. The pole axe came away from the gauntlet easily. He hefted the weapon. It was well balanced and intimidating, but the shaft would make it difficult to maneuver in the narrow hallway upstairs. He returned it to the suit of armor and retrieved the cleaver.

As he reached the hall, Kenyon heard the scraping sound again. He moved to the bottom of the circular stairs and glanced up. As close as he could tell, Dahg was pushing furniture around on the floor above. The agent hoped that nobody was acting as lookout. Gripping his weapon in his right hand, he advanced up the stairs.

The second floor hallway was deserted. A sudden flash of light caught his attention; Dahg was in Lydia's office. Keeping low and to the wall, Kenyon advanced down the hallway toward the partially opened door. He leaned forward, his face inches from the crack, trying to peer inside. Without thinking, he placed his foot upon the loose board, and it squeaked.

Oh, shit, was all he had time to think before the heavy door slammed violently shut, knocking him across the hall.

When Kenyon came to, he was laying on Lydia's bed. An ambulance man was pressing an icebag against the top of his head.

Detective Inspector Arundel was sitting on a vanity chair. "Ah, Sleeping Beauty awakens."

Kenyon tried to focus his blurred eyes on the detective. "What happened?"

"Your house guest seems to have made a hasty exit," said Arundel. "By the time we arrived, he was long gone. Did you get a look-see at the culprit?"

Kenyon sat up in bed and took the ice bag from the attendant. "No."

"Any suspicions who it might be?"

"No."

"Does the name Charles Dahg, late of the CIA, ring a bell?"

A bolt of pain shot through Kenyon's head, and he winced as he lay back into the pillows. "How do you know about Dahg?"

"I received a call from a Mr. William Deaver. I believe he is the assistant attorney for the federal district of San Francisco. Are you acquainted?"

"I've heard of him."

Arundel leaned back in his chair. "He is well acquainted with you. And not fondly, I might add. He tells me that Mr. Dahg has jumped bail and headed for these parts. He wanted to know . . ."

They were interrupted by a constable entering the room. "He broke a window and came in through the back, sir. There's scaffolding in the mews; he probably used that to reach the window."

A second constable entered. "Some silverware missing from the dining room, sir."

"It would appear we interrupted his search," said Arundel. "Any ideas what this nefarious cur wanted in your home?"

"I have no idea," replied Kenyon.

Arundel looked at him dubiously. "You seem to be making a career out of that."

Kenyon wanted to kick Arundel in his well-pressed trousers, but his head still swam. "Speaking of ignorance, what's happening with your investigation into Lydia's murder?"

"We have some surprising new leads."

Kenyon sat up, his headache forgotten. "What are they?" he demanded.

Arundel stood, carefully adjusting the crease on his trousers. "Haven't you ever heard? Information is a two-way street." He nodded to the two constables, and they followed the DI out.

After the police left, Jack called the FBI office in San Francisco. It was late afternoon on the west coast, and Gonelli was still at the office.

"Marge, Dahg busted into my house."

"Are you all right, sweetie?"

"Yeah. I got a bump on my head, but I'll live. He wasn't after me, he was after something in the house."

Gonelli thought for a moment. "You sure you didn't bring none of your Cyberworm notes along?"

Kenyon shook his head. "No. Like I told you, I left it all with Jasmine."

"Then it must have been something of Lydia's."

"Yeah, but what? He isn't the kind of guy to steal a painting, Marge."

"Did the London cops have anything to say?"

"Plenty," said Kenyon, bitterly. "Deaver's been spilling his guts to Scotland Yard."

"*What*?"

"He's been telling them about Dahg and the Cyberworm investigation."

"So that's it," said Gonelli. "Ya know, that little runt is starting to piss me off big-time. He's been stonewalling us from the git-go, and here he's yapping to Scotland Yard. He'll make dead meat look good when I'm finished with 'im."

"Good for you, Marge. Anything else on Cyberworm?"

Kenyon could hear someone come into Gonelli's office. She covered the phone for a moment, then came back on. "I gotta go, cookie. You get some rest, I'll give you a shout later."

"I just thought . . ."

But before he could finish, Gonelli had hung up.

Kenyon put the phone down, then lay back in bed. *Why do I feel like such a mushroom?* he wondered. He found the ice pack, and placed it on his head.

When Kenyon awoke in the morning, his mouth felt like an ashtray, and his head pounded. He got up and closed the front window, shutting out the noise of traffic.

Wearing nothing but his boxer shorts, Kenyon headed downstairs and put the kettle on to boil, wondering as he did so why Dahg would want to get into Lydia's house. Kenyon had told Gonelli the truth: all of his notes were back in San Francisco. Even if Dahg had simply been waiting in ambush to revenge his arrest, he'd certainly had the opportunity to kill the unconscious Kenyon before the police arrived.

Kenyon poured the boiling water into a mug and stirred in a spoon of instant coffee. No, there was something here that Dahg was after, he thought. Taking the mug with him, he wandered into the dining room.

The spoons on the floor had been gathered up and taken away for fingerprinting. Scotland Yard might make a match against Dahg's CIA set. Kenyon closely examined the silverware drawer. There were no false compartments that he could detect, nor any cryptic markings. He turned the drawer over and felt the unfinished wood. There were no sticky spots where an envelope might have been taped.

Kenyon walked through the living room, which appeared untouched, and headed back up the stairs. As far as he knew, Dahg had confined his search to the dining room and the office.

In the office Kenyon made note of the broken window pane. The window was still unlocked; he pulled it open and peered down into the alleyway. Shards of glass glinted in the well surrounding a basement window. That must have been the noise that Señora Santucci heard, thought Kenyon.

The agent almost had his head back into the room before he realized that something was wrong. Why were the shards of glass on the *outside* of the house, if Dahg was trying to break *inside*?

He got down on his hands and knees and carefully examined the floor beneath the window. There were no shards of glass, not even a speck. He looked out the window again. As far as he could tell, it was all down in the alleyway.

Kenyon went over and sat down at Lydia's desk. His head still hurt, and it distracted his concentration. Why would Dahg smash a window and steal some spoons? Suddenly, the agent recalled the scraping sound he had heard: Dahg had been shifting furniture around. Kenyon arose from the chair and stared at the desk. It had been slightly shifted. When he looked behind the desk, at first, there appeared to be nothing to see but the telephone line and wainscoting. On closer inspection, though, he realized that part of the telephone line seemed to disappear into the wall. He shifted the desk aside to get a closer look. Sure enough, the telephone line had been pinched under the wainscoting for several feet before it emerged near the wall plug. He tugged on the telephone line, but it was firmly wedged under the wainscoting. He gave a harder pull and a portion of the wainscoting popped away from the wall.

Puzzled, Kenyon peered closely at the top of the wainscoting, noticing a small slot, about a half inch wide. Digging in the drawer of the desk, he found a slim letter-opener. He eased the metal blade into the slot and heard a latch click; a three-foot section of the wainscoting, mounted on embedded hinges, swung free to reveal the door of a grey steel safe.

So, *that's* what Dahg was looking for, Kenyon thought. The safe stood about two feet wide and three feet high. It was an older model, protected by a skeleton key and a combination dial. Kenyon pulled on the handle embedded in the steel door, but it was locked. He remembered the key ring Tanya had given him and wondered if one of those keys would fit the safe. He arose and went to the bedroom and fetched the key ring from his jacket.

Getting back down on his knees in front of the safe, Kenyon tried an old-fashioned skeleton key. Sure enough, the key fit. He could feel the latch inside give way. The door resisted his attempts to open it, however. He still needed the combination.

Disappointed, Kenyon sat down at the desk and pondered his next move. When it came to PIN numbers or combinations, most people either used easy-to-remember ones like their birth date, or wrote it down in their daybook or wallet.

Lydia's Filofax was still at the gallery, so he couldn't check to see if she had written the combination down. As far as he could recall, however, none of the pages contained a heading saying "Secret Combinations."

What was her birth date? he wondered. All he knew was that she was born in the late 1950s. Cyrus rarely talked about Lydia, and they never celebrated her birthday.

Kenyon remembered Lydia's American passport, tucked into a pigeonhole. He flipped it open. The passport listed her birth date as February 28, 1958. He knelt in front of the safe and blew on his fingers like they did in the movies. He spun the tumbler twice clockwise, stopping at 2, then one full rotation back to the 28, then finally, clockwise to 58. Inside the safe door, Kenyon could hear the tumblers drop into place. He turned the handle, and it rotated.

Just then, the phone rang. Kenyon wanted to ignore it, but it might be Gonelli calling back. He reluctantly arose and picked up the phone.

"DeWolfe here," said the evaluator. "Are you all right?"

"Yeah, I'm okay," replied the agent. "What happened to you last night?"

DeWolfe cleared his throat, nervously. "I did not want to get under foot. I kept well clear."

Kenyon rubbed the bump on his head. "I wish I'd done the same."

"I understand you are not well. We had intended to talk to the receptionist Zoë today. Do you wish to postpone it?"

"No," replied Kenyon. "Meet me at the gallery in one hour."

"Very good."

Kenyon hung up the phone, then knelt back onto his knees and gripped the handle firmly. He took a deep breath, then pulled the steel door open.

Except for a small rectangle of paper, the safe was empty. Disappointed, Kenyon leaned in and picked up the paper; it was one of Raymond Legrand's business cards.

He turned it over; on the back was a handwritten message.

"Please forgive me" was all it said.

Twenty

Harry was in his usual spot outside Lydia's home when Kenyon came out of the house. "I hear you had a little fun last night," said the cabby as the agent climbed in.

"Who told you that?" asked Kenyon.

"Mrs. Santucci," said Harry, winking. "She's a bit of a peach, that one."

"It wasn't fun, and I don't want to talk about it," said the agent. "Just drive me to the gallery."

Harry shrugged, putting the car into gear.

As they drove, Kenyon tried to piece together the significance of the business card. "Please forgive me," it said. Was it addressed to him, or Lydia? He had no way of knowing how long it had been there, but it made no sense for Legrand to break into his house and rob him.

Or did it?

What had Legrand said the day he came looking for the suitcase left to him by Lydia? That Lydia had a hiding spot. Maybe that nonsense about searching in the wine cooler had been a distraction so that Legrand could run up and check the safe, thought Kenyon.

No, that didn't work; he had only been in the cooler a few seconds. Kenyon tried to picture the kitchen scene again: him in the cooler, Legrand sitting at the kitchen nook table playing with Lydia's set of keys.

The keys.

Kenyon dug the set out of his pocket and sure enough, there, tucked under the tooth of the safe's skeleton key, was a tiny fleck of soap. All of the other keys appeared clean, but when he held the front door key up to his nose, he could smell the faint aroma of lilac.

So, the Frenchman had distracted Kenyon long enough to make a soap impression of the front door and safe keys and one of Legrand's assistants at his private investigation firm could make copies. The broken window and stolen spoons had been a misdirection. Legrand wanted it to look like a simple burglary.

Kenyon shook his head. Why go to all that trouble to steal something that was already yours, and then leave a calling card?

The cab entered the short side street to Lydia's gallery, and Kenyon reluctantly pushed the puzzle out of his head for a more immediate concern—what to do about his gallery manager, Bruno Ricci. He hoped that the receptionist knew something that might be relevant.

By the time he reached the gallery, Kenyon's head had cleared enough to put together a plan of attack. He paid the cabby, but before he got out of the car, he leaned forward. "Sorry about snapping at you, Harry. The last few days have been hard."

"That's all right," Harry replied affably. "I know what it's like to get a bump on the old noggin'."

Kenyon held out a fifty-pound note. "I'm worried about Señora Santucci. Do me a favor and keep an eye on the house for a few hours?"

Harry pushed away the bill. "Consider it done, mate."

Kenyon smiled. "You see Raymond Legrand snooping around, you give me a call, okay? But if you see a guy around six feet tall, short blond hair, walks with a limp, you give the police a call."

Harry held a thumb up. "You got it. You an' me, we'll give 'em what-for, right?"

Kenyon held his thumb up. "Right."

As Kenyon approached the front door, deWolfe got out of his parked car and approached the agent. "How shall we do this?" asked deWolfe, nodding toward the gallery.

"If Bruno is in, you put the whammy on him so we can talk to Zoë alone," said Kenyon.

The receptionist buzzed the two men through the doorway. Kenyon had a quick look around; the gallery appeared deserted.

"Is Bruno in?" asked Kenyon.

"Not today," replied Zoë. "Would you like me to make you a cup of tea?"

"Yeah, that would be great," said Kenyon. "Meet us in my office when it's ready. I'd like to have a talk."

The two men went to Lydia's office. A few minutes later, Tigger appeared with a tray containing three cups and a porcelain teapot shaped like a cabbage. She set the tray on Lydia's desk and sat down beside deWolfe, opposite Kenyon.

"When does Bruno usually get here?" he asked.

The receptionist shrugged. "It's hard to say. He sort of comes and goes as he feels."

Tigger poured the tea and handed a cup to deWolfe and Kenyon. The agent blew on the hot surface for a moment, then sipped the beverage; it was tart and bitter, with a hint of lemon. "You don't like Bruno, do you?" asked Kenyon.

Tigger sipped her tea for a moment. "No," she finally replied.

"Well, can I let you in on a little secret?" said Kenyon. "I don't like him much either."

Tigger smiled into her teacup, but said nothing.

"In fact, I like you a lot more," continued Kenyon. "My guess is, you do most of the real work around here, don't you?"

A blush spread across Tigger's cheeks. "I try my best."

"I'll bet Lydia trusted you a lot."

"I'm the first one here, opening up the shop," said Tigger.

Something twigged; Kenyon suddenly remembered that Ricci had asked for a new set of keys. "So, when Lydia got the locks changed just before she died, she gave you a set, but not Bruno?" he asked. "Why is that? Isn't Bruno the manager?"

The receptionist's shoulders sagged. "I'm not supposed to say anything."

"Who told you not to?"

"Bruno."

Kenyon's face darkened. "He threatened you?"

Tigger nodded, silently.

"It's okay," said the agent. "I'm here. Nobody's going to hurt you. Please, tell me what happened."

Tigger took a long breath. She glanced once at deWolfe, then returned her attention to Kenyon. "It was just a few days before Lydia died. Bruno and Lydia had a big fight. I was on front desk, but I could hear the shouting."

"What were they arguing about?"

"I don't know. They were down in the storage room. It was too far away to hear clearly."

Kenyon glanced at deWolfe, then continued. "What happened then?"

"Bruno stormed out," said Tigger. "Lydia asked me to call for someone to change the locks and codes."

"Did Bruno ever come back to the gallery while Lydia was alive?" asked deWolfe.

"No," said Tigger.

"Did you ask Lydia what happened?" continued Kenyon.

"She didn't want to talk about it," said Tigger. "We were too busy arranging the auction. It was only two days away, and I had to take over all of Bruno's work."

"I take it Bruno wasn't at the auction that night," said Kenyon.

"I think Lydia would have strangled him if he did show up," said Tigger.

I wish he had, thought Kenyon.

"Who collected the donated pieces for the auction?" DeWolfe asked. "Was it Ricci, before he left?"

"No," said Tigger. "Most were gathered by the auctioneers, except for one that Lydia insisted on picking up herself."

"Which one was that?" asked Kenyon.

Tigger pondered for a moment. "A piece by Maggote. A company called TEQ donated it. I can't remember the exact name."

"A picture called *Techno 69*?" asked Kenyon.

Tigger brightened. "That's the one."

"Did you ever notice a copy of *Techno 69* in the gallery?" asked Kenyon.

Tigger looked puzzled. "Why would anyone make a copy?"

Kenyon changed the subject. "Before Lydia changed the locks, did Bruno have a key to the downstairs storage?"

"Of course," said Tigger. "He was in charge of storage. Lydia never went down there."

Bingo, thought Kenyon. "Thank you, Zoë, you've been a big help. Do you mind returning to the reception desk? Mr. deWolfe and I have something to discuss."

Tigger stood, taking her tea. She smiled at the two men and left.

Kenyon closed the door, then returned to his seat. "I think I know how Garbajian ended up with the real *Techno 69*," he said.

"How?" asked deWolfe.

"Bruno had a forgery made that was an exact duplicate of *Techno 69*, and swapped it with the real one down in the storeroom," began Kenyon.

"*Ach!*" replied deWolfe. "That is very good. That way, when Lydia sells the fake, his tracks are covered. Bruno can market the real one to a buyer on a different continent at his leisure, with little fear of being caught."

"But Bruno outsmarted himself," continued Kenyon. "After Lydia sold the fake to TEQ, he hid the real one in storage, where only he ever went."

"Until Lump's fake turned up," said deWolfe. "Then, Lydia went to check the rest of the Maggotes herself."

"And what did she find?" continued Kenyon. "A painting she had already sold months before!"

"She must have been furious," said deWolfe.

"She blew her top," agreed Kenyon. "Lydia raked Bruno over the coals, then threw him out the door and changed the locks."

"That *would* explain why Garbajian has the original," agreed deWolfe.

"Yeah, Lydia must have swapped back the real *Techno 69* for the fake when she picked it up for the auction," Kenyon's face became grim. "And it also explains why Ricci killed Lydia."

"So it would seem," said deWolfe. "Should we go to Scotland Yard?"

Kenyon shook his head. "Arundel would laugh me out of the building. I need solid proof."

DeWolfe tapped a finger against the side of his jaw. "If Bruno has the fake, then we *will* have solid proof, *ja*?"

"He'd be nuts to hang onto it," said Kenyon.

"Perhaps not," replied deWolfe. "If he is in such dire need of cash, he may think he can alter it enough to create a whole new Maggote. That is why he is still hanging around: he is waiting for the moment to sneak into the gallery records and create a new authentication."

"Which he hasn't been able to do, because he doesn't have keys," agreed Kenyon.

"The trick is, how do we get him to cough it up?"

"I suggest that another ruse is precisely what is in order," replied deWolfe. "But what?"

"I got it," said Kenyon. "I'll offer him a deal: either he gives up the fake *Techno 69*, or I spill the beans." He opened up Lydia's daybook and began to search for Ricci's home number.

"Do you really think he will turn over the painting if you threaten to expose him to the police?" asked deWolfe.

Kenyon found the number, and began to dial. "Who said anything about the police?"

The appraiser's eyes went wide in sudden realization. "Ah, brilliant." He leaned forward and pushed the speaker button. "Do you mind? I want to hear the scoundrel's reaction."

"Okay," said Kenyon. The phone in Ricci's apartment began to ring. "Just keep quiet and let me do the talking."

Someone answered the phone. "*Ciao.*"

"Ricci? It's Kenyon calling. I've got a deal for you."

"Ah, you have accepted my offer for the gallery, no?"

"No," said Kenyon. "This is another deal, one you're going to be a lot more interested in."

"I am all ears."

"I know about your forgeries, Ricci."

There was a brief silence on the other end of the phone. "What do you mean?"

Kenyon continued. "You had quite an operation going with the Maggotes."

"I deny everything."

"I found the proof in Lydia's files," countered Kenyon. "You've committed a very serious crime."

"You cannot prove anything in a court of law."

"I'm not thinking of telling the police, Ricci. I'm thinking of telling Archie Lump."

An audible gasp emanated from the speaker phone. "You cannot . . ."

"Oh, I can, and I will, Ricci, unless . . ."

"Unless, what?"

"Unless you hand over something I want."

"Anything. Please, what is it?"

"The fake *Techno 69*, Ricci. I want it. Now."

"I cannot."

"Oh, yes, you can, Ricci. You know how angry Mr. Lump can get. It's either your eyes, or the fake."

"I cannot give it to you, because I do not have it!"

"You're lying, Ricci."

"No! It is the truth!"

Kenyon glanced at deWolfe, but the appraiser sat transfixed, staring at the speaker. What to do now?

Suddenly, Ricci broke the silence. "I cannot give you the painting, but I have something better."

"What?" asked Kenyon.

"I know what happened to Lydia."

DeWolfe was so startled that he fell forward, his arm outstretched toward the phone. Kenyon reached over a grabbed him by the wrist at the last moment, before he hit the console. He eased deWolfe back into his chair.

"What happened to Lydia?" Kenyon asked.

"Not over the phone," said Ricci. "Meet me at my house. Tonight, at midnight. I will tell you what I know, in exchange for your silence."

"Tonight, at midnight," repeated Kenyon. He pressed the speaker button, and the phone disconnected.

"You can't possibly trust him," said deWolfe.

"I don't."

"He's setting up a trap."

"Don't you worry. I'm going in with back-up," said Kenyon.

Twenty-one

After arranging the rendezvous with Ricci, Kenyon left the gallery and returned home by taxi. It had been a tiring day, and though his wound was healing well, his head still hurt from being bumped by the door. He wanted to lay down and rest before evening.

He was almost through Lydia's front door when he suddenly realized that Harry wasn't around. He glanced up and down the street, but the cabby's distinctive taxi was nowhere to be seen. He went inside and called Harry's cell number, but only got his voice mail. Kenyon left a message, then ascended the steps, worried. *If Harry doesn't get back to me in time, I'm screwed*, he thought. *There's no way I'm going to see Ricci without someone at my back.*

Kenyon laid down on the bed, exhausted. Fatigue overtook his worries, and he immediately passed into a sleep that was heavy, but not dreamless. The agent found himself sitting in the passenger seat of Lydia's Morgan sports car. It was a beautiful, sunny day, and the top was down. Alpine mountains towered above, and the air was full of the smell of summer forests.

As the Morgan roared through a steep canyon pass, Kenyon slowly turned toward the driver. It was Ilsa Ingoldsby-Legrand. She was driving with one hand on the wheel, the other holding a sharpshooter's pistol. The wind was blowing her hair around, and she carelessly brushed it back into place with the barrel of the gun.

Suddenly, Ilsa took her eyes off the road and turned to stare at Kenyon. It wasn't mere hatred in her ice blue eyes, it was something deeper, darker. She lifted the gun and pointed it at him.

Kenyon tried to leap from the car, but his legs were frozen. He scrabbled at the door, but he couldn't find the latch. He turned back toward Ilsa, but she had disappeared; the car was careening down the road without a driver. It slowly turned toward the chasm to the right.

Kenyon awoke with a start; he was covered in sweat, and his hands trembled. It was sometime in the evening. The sound of the phone had broken the nightmare's evil spell. The agent picked up the receiver, with relief.

"Jack, it's 'Arry calling back."

Kenyon glanced at the bedside clock; it showed just after 9:00 PM. "Where you been all day?" he asked.

"Sorry, 'ad to take a day-fare out-of-town," said Harry. "Any problems?"

"No," said Kenyon. "I was calling about something else. You available for some back-up tonight?"

"You got it, mate. What's the plan?"

Kenyon outlined what he wanted, and Harry agreed to pick him up at 11:20 PM.

Later that evening, Kenyon was still turning the nightmare over in his mind when Harry rang the buzzer. He grabbed his coat and headed to the front door. Once again, he wished he had his sidearm. In his gut, he felt Ricci was too much of a coward to threaten him to his face, but he also knew the Italian was perfectly capable of any sort of skullduggery.

Kenyon joined the cabby in his taxi. "You get the stuff?" he asked.

"Right here." Harry took out a wafer-thin cell phone and a thin, black cord. "It's all charged and ready to go."

Kenyon took the black cord and pinned the end to the inside of his coat. He plugged the other end of the cord into the hands-free extension on the tiny cell phone, dialed a number, then tucked the phone into the breast pocket of his jacket.

Harry's cell phone rang. The cabby closed the partition and answered.

"Can you hear me?" asked Kenyon, holding his head erect.

"Clear as a bell," said Harry. He re-opened the partition.

Kenyon turned off the cell phone. "I'll keep my unit on when I'm upstairs in Ricci's apartment," he said. "If I yell for help, you call in the cavalry, okay?"

"Got it, mate."

Ricci's address was in Knightsbridge, about a mile from Lydia's home. The taxi drove east on Cromwell Road, past the immense, ornate Natural History Museum and the equally lavish Victoria and Albert Museum, until they came to a busy commercial sector lining Brompton Road. The street was crowded with interior decorator outlets, travel agencies, and fashion boutiques.

Just ahead of them, a young woman with short auburn hair pulled up in a silver Porsche and dashed into an all-night pastry shop. Something about the pretty woman reminded Kenyon of Tanya. He thought about her smile, her green eyes, and her smooth white skin pressing against his. Since their argument over Lydia, they hadn't spoken. Kenyon thought about calling her, but what would he say? I'm sorry I bugged you by trying to find Lydia's killer? The thought depressed him.

Harry slowed the cab as they approached the address. Ricci's apartment was located in a large, modern brick building on the south side of Brompton Road. The front of the building was lined with antique stores, draperies, and a chic cafe. Harry turned at the corner and drove down the side street paralleling the building, and parked.

Kenyon glanced at his watch. They were about twenty minutes early. "Wait here, I'll be right back," he told the cabby as he got out of the cab and entered Ricci's building.

The entrance to the apartment portion of the building was reached by walking down an aisle between the cafe and an antique shop specializing in clocks. The glass door leading to the apartment's tiny foyer and elevator was locked. A row of buzzers by the door indicated about twenty apartments in the building, and Kenyon spotted Ricci's immediately. The penthouse, naturally.

A little old lady with a ginger-colored Pekingese came out of the elevator. Kenyon helped hold the door open for her as she exited. "Thank you, young man," she said. Kenyon noticed that the collar on her jacket was made of fox. The head of the animal, still on one end, made it look like roadkill.

Kenyon returned to the street and walked up to Brompton Road. The sidewalk was still crowded with tourists in garishly colored running shoes, most of them gawking at the floodlit facade of the nearby Harrod's department store. The tiny patio of the corner cafe was full of customers enjoying cappuccinos and French pastries.

Kenyon sauntered past the cafe to a newsstand. He bought a *USA Today*, noting that, even though it was two days old, he was still charged the full price. He stood beneath a street lamp and flipped through the pages. The Giants had lost their last game to the Angels, eight to seven. Damn, they gotta get a bullpen, he thought.

His reading was interrupted by squealing tires. Kenyon glanced up to see a scuffed-looking Range Rover come around the corner and tear off down Brompton Road at a fast rate. He had only a second to peer at the driver, but even a quick glance was enough to confirm that it was Raymond Legrand.

Kenyon walked back to the road where Harry was parked. "That Range Rover that just drove by—you see where it came from?" he asked.

"Yeah, it must have been parked behind the building," said Harry.

"It was Legrand," said Kenyon. "Think he was following us?"

"Not a chance," said Harry, puzzled. "I'd a spotted him in a second."

Kenyon glanced at his watch; it was almost midnight. "We'll worry about it later," he said. The agent took out his cell phone and dialed Harry's number. "We got work to do."

With phone contact established, Kenyon headed for the front door. He pushed the button for Ricci's apartment, then waited. There was no answer. He pushed again and waited for another minute, but still no response. Kenyon turned and glanced out toward the street, wondering if Ricci hadn't come home yet.

Their nightly promenade done, the old lady with the dog came walking up to the entrance. She unlocked the door, and Kenyon held it for her again.

"Who are you here to see?" the old woman asked.

"Mr. Bruno Ricci," Kenyon replied.

"Oh, such a delightful young man," responded the woman. "He is so fond of my little Pierre." She held up the Pekingese, who tried to nip Kenyon's hand when he gave it a pat on the head. Since Ricci hadn't answered the buzzer yet, Kenyon simply entered behind the pair.

The foyer was done in a reddish marble, with large, stuffed chairs that looked too uncomfortable to sit in. The little old lady headed down the hallway of the first floor; Kenyon got onto the mirror-lined elevator and rode up to the fifth.

Kenyon found Ricci's apartment door at the end of the hall and rapped twice on the brass knocker. He stood quietly and listened, but couldn't hear anyone moving around inside. He waited for a few moments, then knocked again. Frustrated, he leaned forward and glanced through the peephole, though he couldn't see anything. He rapped on the door once more, this time, harder. Still no answer. Kenyon reached forward and tried the doorknob. To his surprise, it was unlocked. He swung the door open and leaned in. "Ricci? It's Jack Kenyon."

The apartment faced east, toward Harrod's. Advancing slowly into the foyer, Kenyon could see the upper-most part of the department store's façade: a thousand tiny lights twinkling in the darkness.

Off to his right, Kenyon could hear Latin music playing on a stereo. It sounded like the Gypsy Kings. He cautiously moved in that direction.

A wide arch marked the entrance to the living room. The carpet was a pale lilac, and the furniture was finished in a rich green fabric. Several modern abstracts hanging on the wall added bright splashes of red and blue. Kenyon didn't recognize the artists. The overall impression was expensive and outlandish.

A pale oak dining table rested in a large bay window facing north over Brompton Road. A cup of tea and a plate with bread crumbs sat beside a copy of the *Times*. Kenyon walked over to examine the paper; this morning's edition. He continued through the kitchen. There was a pot of tea brewing on the counter; it was still warm to his touch.

Kenyon came to the main hall and headed toward the bedroom door, which was ajar. The deserted room was dominated by a queen-sized bed on a modern sculpted steel frame. A large duvet was jammed to one side, and several pillows spilled to the floor. Articles of men's clothing were tossed haphazardly about the room. A wallet and keys sat atop a bleached wood bureau. The agent could hear water running in the bathroom adjacent to the bedroom. Kenyon thought Ricci was in the shower and hadn't heard him at the door.

"Ricci?" he called out again, louder, but there was still no reply. Kenyon moved cautiously forward. The agent came to the closed door of the bathroom; he noticed a dark puddle running from under the door. He pushed the door open; a thin veneer of pink water was lapping the black and white tile floor.

Ricci rested in the bathtub, nude, his head rolled back, his eyes closed, his lips pursed in silent thought. It looked as though he were asleep, except for the slashed wrists and the bloody knife on the floor.

Kenyon moved forward. Ricci's wrists were a mass of blood. He checked for a pulse on the gallery manager's neck, just below the left jaw. The skin was warm to the touch, but there was no pulse. Carefully, Kenyon lifted one eyelid. Ricci's sockets had rolled up, lifeless.

Kenyon stepped back into the bedroom and lifted the cell phone out of his pocket. "Harry? You there?"

"Yeah," replied the cabby. "What's up?"

Kenyon took a deep breath. "You better call the cops. Ricci killed himself."

Twenty-two
Thursday, July 14

The police arrived fifteen minutes later. The man in charge, a heavyset detective sergeant named Ruffy, asked Kenyon to wait in the living room while his men dealt with Ricci.

Kenyon sat at the dining room table, staring absently at the unfinished toast on the plate. Before the police arrived, Kenyon had done a quick search through the apartment. He had hoped that Ricci might have written something down detailing Lydia's death, but he hadn't found a scrap. Whatever Ricci had known about Lydia's death, he had taken it to his grave.

An assistant forensic practitioner was just carrying his photographic equipment out the front door when Detective Inspector Humphrey Arundel arrived. Arundel didn't even glance in Kenyon's direction, but immediately went with Ruffy down the hall. They inspected the scene for several minutes, before Arundel returned and entered the living room.

The detective sat in the chair opposite Kenyon. He turned the *Times*, glanced at it, then returned it to its original position. "What, may I ask, is your relationship with Mr. Ricci?"

"He's the manager of Lydia's—my—gallery."

"When did you last speak to him?" he asked.

"This afternoon."

"Did he seem despondent? Depressed?"

"No."

Arundel nodded, almost to himself. "When did you arrive?"

"Shortly before midnight," said Kenyon. "I buzzed, but Ricci didn't answer. One of the residents let me into the building. When I got to his door, I knocked, but nobody opened the door."

Arundel stood and walked over to the teapot and placed his palm against the side. "What did you do then?"

"The door was unlocked, so I opened it and called out. I could hear music playing, so I came inside."

Arundel lifted the pot and glanced idly in. "What did you see?"

Kenyon pointed to the table. "Pretty much what you see here."

Arundel sniffed at the contents of the teapot, then dipped a finger in and tasted the contents. "Did you touch anything in here?"

Kenyon thought for a moment. "The front door, then that teapot, to see if it was warm."

Arundel returned to his place across from Kenyon. "How did you discover the body?"

"I spotted water coming under the door, and pushed it open."

"Did you touch or disturb anything in the bathroom?"

"I touched his neck." Kenyon indicated a spot below his own jaw. "He was still warm, but there was no pulse."

"And then?"

"I had Harry call you."

"Ah, yes. Mr. Happy Harry. How does he fit into this scenario, exactly?"

"He's my cabby."

"Ah," said Arundel, flatly. "Your cabby."

"Yeah, my cabby."

"And was he acting in any other capacity for you this evening?"

Kenyon immediately recognized the warning in the question. He glanced at his watch. It was almost one, plenty of time for Arundel to interview Harry. Arundel was telling him it would be dangerous to lie. The agent took a deep breath, and let it out. "Yeah. He was my back-up."

"Why would you need a back-up to visit your gallery manager?"

"Because I discovered Ricci was forging paintings and selling them through the gallery."

Arundel raised one eyebrow. "You suspected a felony, and you didn't report it to the police?"

Kenyon stared down at the newspaper. "I didn't know for certain. I came here tonight to find out."

Arundel stood and walked over to the counter. He idly opened a drawer. "It might make for a good mystery novel, but it is my general experience that organized criminals do not spill the beans as soon as someone confronts them with the evidence."

Kenyon winced. "I was hoping to talk some sense into him."

"At the very best, you were hoping to intimidate him." He lifted a bread knife out of the cutlery drawer and examined the grip. "You don't strike me as a brutish man, so I will eliminate violence. What was it, Kenyon? A threat to go to the police?"

"No."

Arundel turned his head to one side as he peered at Kenyon. "Something more subtle, then."

Kenyon stirred in alarm. *Harry knows about Lump, but he wouldn't say anything about that,* thought Kenyon. Kenyon decided to keep his mouth shut.

Arundel continued. "Yes, I think it must have been something so devious, so diabolical, that Mr. Ricci had no alternative but to take his own life." He replaced the bread knife and closed the cutlery drawer. "Now, would you be so kind as to submit to a voluntary search?"

Kenyon stood up. "I'm assuming I either comply or face the consequences."

"An excellent assumption," said Arundel. "Now, place both of your hands here on the counter, palms down, and spread your legs."

Kenyon did as he was told, smiling grimly.

Arundel turned and signaled to a burly constable standing nearby. "If you would be so kind as to do the honors?"

The constable stepped forward and began to frisk Kenyon, removing each item from his pockets.

"What do you expect to find?" asked Kenyon. "A matching carving fork?"

"I was thinking more of a suicide note," said Arundel.

The constable placed several items on the counter, including Kenyon's keys, his wallet, and the cell phone and extension mike cord.

Arundel flipped through the wallet as the constable continued his search, removing the wad of pound notes and riffling through them. He briefly examined the keychain, making particular note of the skeleton key to the safe. He picked up the cell phone, pressing the function key several times to check the stored data.

The constable finally finished his search and nodded to Arundel. The DI dismissed the man, then nodded to Kenyon to sit back at the table. "I am relieved to see, Mr. Kenyon, that among your many faults, concealing material evidence is not among them."

Just then, an investigator came in holding a small wooden box. Kenyon immediately recognized it from his search of Ricci's office at the gallery.

"Found this in his sock drawer, sir," the constable said to Arundel.

The DI admired the carving on the lid for a moment, then opened the box and lifted out a small bag of white powder. "Ah, it would seem that Mr. Ricci had nasal indisposition."

Arundel placed the cocaine back into the box and handed it to the constable, then turned back to Kenyon. "Let's assume, for the moment, that Ricci was motivated to suicide by a fear of prosecution over the forgeries. Not a normal fear, but, when you take into account the tendency of cocaine addiction to induce paranoia, not an unlikely one. All it took was your threat of exposure to push him over the edge, and he took the coward's way out."

Kenyon sat with his head bowed, saying nothing.

Arundel continued. "Odd that Ricci didn't write one, don't you think?"

Kenyon glanced up. "What?"

"A suicide note." He nodded toward the table. "He makes a last supper, laces his tea with some form of barbiturate, then retires to the bathtub for a nice, soothing soak before slitting his wrists. All very clean, proper and tidy. Except for the suicide note. Most unusual."

Arundel was interrupted by the return of the investigator. "Found this concealed in the closet, sir." In his gloved hand, he held a small metal tube about the size of a fountain pen.

Arundel snapped out a red silk handkerchief and took the object in his hand. He pointed the device out an open window and rotated its head a quarter turn. A powerful red beam of light instantly shot across the road. Arundel traced the thin, brilliant red dot along the side of the Harrod's store for a moment.

Kenyon sat motionless, staring out the window at the side of the store.

Arundel turned the laser pen off and placed it on the table. "Well, now we know what frightened him so, don't we?"

Kenyon turned to the DI. "I . . . I didn't know."

"No?"

Kenyon stared down. "No. I accused him of the forgeries and threatened to expose him if he didn't confess in full."

"And?"

"He offered information to keep me quiet."

"What kind of information?"

"He said he would tell me who killed Lydia."

Arundel's eyebrows rose. "He offered to confess to her murder?"

"No. He never said anything about confessing. His words were, 'I know what happened to Lydia.'"

Arundel nodded toward the laser pen. "I suspect he did. In fact, I don't doubt that forensics will turn up his prints, and only his prints, on this device."

The DI turned to Kenyon. "Now, since our prime suspect can no longer confess, you must tell me precisely what happened. And I warn you, leave nothing out."

Kenyon took a deep breath. "Ricci was forging works of an artist named Maggote."

"The Frenchman who overdosed on drugs?"

"Yeah. Lydia represented his estate. It was easy for Ricci to whip up new works, authenticate them through the gallery, and sell them to clients under the table."

"How did Lydia uncover his scheme?"

"By chance. One of the clients discovered he had a fake, and called her up. She paid to keep his mouth shut."

"But her suspicions regarding Mr. Ricci were aroused."

Kenyon nodded. "She dug around and discovered Ricci had made a copy of a painting, *Techno 69*, and swapped it for the real goods. Lydia unknowingly sold the fake to a corporate client."

"How did Lydia react to this discovery?"

"Zoë, her receptionist, told me she had a big fight with Ricci, then threw him out and changed the locks."

"When was this?"

"Two days before her death."

Arundel nodded. "So, Mr. Ricci had time to set up an 'accident.' Very clever, really. If it hadn't been for the entirely fortuitous donation of her retinas, we would never had discovered it."

"It still doesn't make sense," said Kenyon.

"How so?" asked Arundel.

"I never said anything about Lydia's murder. Why would he confess?"

Just then, the coroner wheeled the remains out of the bathroom. Both men watched silently as the dolly containing a black plastic bag passed by.

"Well," said Arundel. "It would appear that we shall never know." He sighed, and nodded toward the laser pen. "Normally, I would thank you for uncovering the means and motive for a murder. But this is not a normal situation. You have behaved in a manner that casts disrepute upon the FBI. Not only have you hopelessly tainted any opportunity for the Crown to prove a case of murder against Ricci, but you have precipitated a suicide. I hold you personally responsible for the death of this man." Arundel motioned for Kenyon to pick up his wallet, keys, and phone. "Get out of my sight."

Kenyon rode down in the elevator, silently steaming. Arundel was right, he had acted like a fool. He had rushed in blindly, not knowing how close he was, and now he would never know the whole truth of his aunt's death. "I'm sorry, Lydia," he said, aloud. "I'm sorry."

———

By the time Kenyon left Ricci's apartment building, it was very early in the morning. It was raining hard, and the streets were deserted of traffic and people. Kenyon turned up his collar and began to walk home.

He passed the V&A Museum, its immense, illuminated facade glistening in the rain. A street sweeper rumbled past, the driver glancing briefly at the lone pedestrian. A taxi slowed as it passed, but Kenyon waved it on; he wanted to be alone and let the rain wash away his misery.

By the time he reached Herringbone Gardens, he was soaked through to the skin. As he walked up the steps, he heard a car door slam behind. He turned around to see deWolfe crossing the street.

"Jack! I've been waiting for hours," he said. "Thank goodness you're all right. Did you locate the forgery?"

"No."

"What happened?"

"Ricci killed himself."

"Good Lord." DeWolfe reached out and steadied himself against the iron railing. "Why on earth would he kill himself over a forgery? It defies all common sense."

"He didn't kill himself over that."

"No?"

Kenyon stared down the quiet street. "The police found evidence he killed Lydia."

"What, the laser pen?"

Kenyon nodded silently.

"But what about the forgery?" continued deWolfe. "Did they find that?"

"No."

"We must continue looking. It has to be somewhere."

"I don't give a shit about the forgery, anymore," said Kenyon. "It's over, Hadrian. Go home." Kenyon turned toward the door.

"But . . ."

Kenyon went inside and left the other man standing on the steps.

The interior of Lydia's home was in darkness, except for a faint yellow light from the streetlamp pouring into the living room. Kenyon grabbed a tea towel from the kitchen to dry his face and hair, then went to the sideboard in the dining room and poured himself a good, stiff scotch. He returned to the living room and sat on the couch, facing the bay windows.

God, how I hate this town, he thought. *Everything about it stinks: the people, the cops, the weather. I'm going to sell this house and everything in it. With any luck, I'll never have to come back here again.*

The phone rang. Kenyon glanced at his watch; it was after three in the morning. He reached over and picked up the receiver.

It was Gonelli, in San Francisco. "Hey, watcha up to, kiddo?"

"Not much, Marge. Just driving people to suicide." Kenyon quickly explained what happened.

"Hey, it ain't your fault," said Gonelli. "The guy was a slime. He robbed Lydia, then killed her. Why are you feeling so guilty?"

"I feel bad for Lydia," said Kenyon. "I feel like I let her down, somehow."

"You caught her killer. You done great."

Kenyon rubbed his face. "Thanks, Marge. You know, I really miss you guys. I'm coming home on the next flight."

"No, you ain't," said Marge. "That's what I'm calling about. Remember I promised to run traces on Abdul Garbajian and TEQ?"

"Yeah, what about them?"

"Well, Garbajian's also known as Abdul Al Zabol, among a few other aliases. He's got a few sidelines going, like embargo-running of chemical weapons for Iran."

Kenyon sat up in his chair. "What about TEQ?"

"Some high-tech outfit involved in military research. Ain't much on it in the public records. It's controlled by a numbered company."

"Any connection to Garbajian?"

"Not to him, but you're gonna like what we did find. Before Deaver clamped down on the Cyberworm investigation completely, we managed to subpoena Simon's long-distance phone bills. Our boy made some calls from San Francisco to England several months ago. Guess who?"

"TEQ?"

"Yup. My gut feeling is this is what Deaver's after. I want you to check these TEQ guys out. Pronto."

Twenty-three

Happy Harry was busy Thursday morning, and it wasn't until noon that the taxi driver finally picked Kenyon up at Lydia's home.

"Where to, guv?" asked the cabby.

"You know a town called Reading?" asked Kenyon.

"Yeah. Just west of London."

"That's the one. Let's go."

The cabby drove along Cromwell Road until it connected to the M4 motorway running west of London. Kenyon was amazed how quickly the city disappeared. As soon as they had passed Heathrow, the rows of brick houses gave way to rolling pastureland.

Traffic was light heading out of town, and the taxi made good time. Shortly after one, they reached Reading. Kenyon had expected a quaint village, but the city was a sprawling industrial center with endless row houses, low squat warehouses, and narrow streets crowded with trucks and buses.

Harry drove through town and descended down into the Thames River Valley where the crowded city gave way to modern buildings surrounded by landscaped parks. The taxi pulled up in front of a modern, four-story building. Three large, stainless-steel letters were affixed over the front entranceway; TEQ. The cabby parked the taxi near the entrance, and Kenyon disembarked.

The agent noticed that the landscaping around the building looked in rough shape. Several shrubs had spilled over their borders, and the flower beds were littered with old Styrofoam coffee cups and candy wrappers.

A large, black Mercedes sedan was parked near the front door. As Kenyon passed, he glanced down at the tires; they were a puncture-resistant style favored by security firms. He wondered who at TEQ needed a bulletproof car.

The front door was locked. Kenyon peered through the doorway, but he couldn't see anyone in the interior. He pushed the buzzer at the side of the door.

"Go away!" said a man's voice over the intercom.

"What?" asked Kenyon, surprised.

"Go away with you, and quit bothering me. If you have any credit enquiries, you can direct them to our solicitors."

"I'm not a creditor. I'm from the FBI."

"Oh! I do apologize," said the voice. "Be there in a flash."

About a minute later, a man in a lab coat opened the door and invited Kenyon in. He was short, with a fringe of reddish hair circling the top of his head. "I'm Dr. Hamish MacQuaig, president of TEQ," he said, shaking the agent's hand. "And you are?"

"Jack Kenyon, special agent for the Federal Bureau of Investigation."

"Splendid!" replied MacQuaig. "Agent Gonelli contacted me from San Francisco. Please allow me to inspect your identification papers."

Kenyon reached into his jacket and pulled out his ID. MacQuaig glanced at it briefly, then took it over to a device adjacent to the reception desk. He cleared a pile of bills off a computer keyboard and turned on a monitor. "Won't take a sec," he explained, as he placed the ID on a scanner.

MacQuaig punched several keys, then waited as the machine did its work. In less than thirty seconds, a bell rang the all-clear. "International verification scanner checks out," he explained, handing the ID back to Kenyon. "Can't be too careful, can we?"

"No, I guess not," said Kenyon. "Dr. MacQuaig, I have no official police standing in the UK, but do you mind if I ask you a few questions?"

"Ask me all the questions you like," replied MacQuaig. "Shall we retire to the boardroom?"

MacQuaig led the agent down a deserted hallway. Kenyon noted that most of the offices were empty, stripped bare of all furniture.

The boardroom, however, was still furnished with a large oak table and upholstered swivel chairs. Several flatscreen monitors were mounted against one wall. Picture hooks marked the former locations of artwork on the walls. Only one remained, a portrait of an older man posing in hunting gear, deerstalker cap, and shotgun. He looked vaguely familiar, but Kenyon couldn't place the face.

"I'm sorry I can't offer you a coffee or tea, but as you can see, we're rather short-staffed at present," said MacQuaig.

MacQuaig closed the door, then sat down at the boardroom table beside an electronic panel and pushed several buttons. "Just activating the cone-of-silence," he explained with a grin.

Kenyon wondered if he hadn't come out all this way on a wild goose chase. He took out a notebook and pen and placed them on the table. "Dr. MacQuaig, I specialize in counter industrial espionage at the FBI."

The scientist held up a hand. "We comply with all American security regulations regarding encryption. As you can see, we maintain a top level of security. Our lab uses the latest generation of security passes, computer firewalls, and eavesdropping inhibitors."

Kenyon made a note in his book. "That's very impressive, doctor. Have you ever been in contact with a software engineer named Simon?"

MacQuaig's bushy eyebrows bobbed up and down in annoyance. "Yes, yes. I've already told all this to your colleague, someone named Beaver, or something."

"Assistant US attorney Will Deaver?"

"Yes, that's it." MacQuaig pulled a pair of glasses from his lab coat and rubbed the lens in agitation. "He was here yesterday. Rather rude, I must say. All these questions about Simon, and not a word of explanation. All I know is that Simon is no longer at Nebula Labs. Would you mind terribly telling one what's going on?"

Kenyon leaned back in his chair and studied MacQuaig. His gut instinct told him he could build the scientist's trust with information. "He was caught trying to sell some of Nebula's software to spies."

MacQuaig's face went white. "Not Cyberworm?"

Pay dirt, thought Kenyon. He leaned forward, an earnest expression on his face. "Yes, doctor, it was Cyberworm. I take it you're familiar with the software?"

"I know it."

"Doctor, I'm not an expert like yourself; could you please explain what it is?"

MacQuaig took out a handkerchief and wiped his face. "Damned computer virus, that's what it is. Didn't like it from the time we were first approached." He nodded toward the portrait on the wall. "But the old boy took it on, said we'd make millions controlling the code."

"Doctor, what kind of computer virus are we talking about?"

"The Pentagon commissioned Nebula Labs to design a cyberattack virus."

"You mean, this virus can be used in the event of war to destroy an enemy's computers?" asked Kenyon.

"There's no point in taking out an enemy's computer; they can back it up with another cheap PC," said MacQuaig. "Cyberworm is far worse; it eats up the communications links."

"You mean the telephone and satellite connections?"

"Yes. It attacks the switchers and devices that relay the data. It effectively shuts down telephones, electrical grids, air lines, everything down to the level of an outhouse."

Kenyon whistled aloud. "Man, that's one nasty virus."

"Too nasty, I'm afraid," said MacQuaig.

"How so?"

"There's no way to stop it. Once you activate the virus, it can spread completely around the world, paralyzing the global economy." MacQuaig tapped the boardroom table. "Thank God the code is safe here."

"The code?" asked Kenyon.

"Yes. Cyberworm can't be activated unless you have the encryption code. It's part of a two-step security program. That's what our company supplied to Nebula Labs on a blind basis for security reasons."

Kenyon began to nod in understanding. "Did Simon come here from Nebula to try and get the encryption code?"

"Yes. But we refused to give it to him."

"Why?" asked Kenyon. "Didn't he have proper clearance?"

"Oh, he had that all right," replied MacQuaig. "What he didn't have was the cheque."

"What?"

"Once they learned it was too uncontrollable, the Pentagon pulled the plug on the funding," said MacQuaig. "Nebula wouldn't pay us for the work on the code." The scientist vaguely waved his hand in the direction of the office. "In case you hadn't noticed, we're in a bit of a financial bind as a result."

"Is there any way of anyone getting hold of the encryption code?" asked the agent.

"No," replied MacQuaig. "The lab's strictly off limits to non-technicians. Not even the president of TEQ had access."

"Was the code ever taken outside of the labs?" asked Kenyon.

"It was demonstrated on occasion in this boardroom, but the room is designed to be completely secure," said the scientist. "The walls, floors, and ceiling are lined with lead, and the room is periodically swept for bugging devices."

They were interrupted by a knock at the door. MacQuaig glanced at a monitor, then pushed a button. The door unlocked, and a woman dressed in a short-skirted business suit and black high heels entered.

"Hamish, I need you to sign some papers," she began, then stopped short when she saw Kenyon. "What are *you* doing here?" she demanded.

Kenyon stood up and faced Ilsa Ingoldsby-Legrand. "I was going to ask you the same question."

The woman turned back to the scientist. "What is he *doing* here?"

"He's with the FBI, ma'am," said MacQuaig, weakly. "He's part of an ongoing investigation."

"Throw him out," said Ilsa. "Immediately. "

MacQuaig looked helplessly at Kenyon, then back at Ingoldsby-Legrand. "But, ma'am . . ."

She stared at MacQuaig. "I see I am going to have to find someone with a spine do it for me." She spun around and stalked out the door.

Kenyon turned to MacQuaig. "What the hell is *she* doing here?"

MacQuaig nodded to the portrait. "She's the boss's daughter."

Kenyon turned and stared at the portrait. The last time he had seen the man, his face had been distorted by illness, but the shotgun looked pretty familiar. "Sir *Rupert* owns TEQ?"

"That he does. Or did. The old boy had a stroke last year, not been himself, daughter runs the show now."

Kenyon could hear Ilsa berating someone as she returned down the hall. She appeared shortly with a rosy-cheeked man dressed in a chauffeur's uniform. Kenyon recognized Bernie, the gardener he had met on his visit to Ingoldsby Estate.

Ilsa pointed a finger at Kenyon. "Get rid of this intruder right now, or heads will roll. Do I make myself clear?"

Bernie shrugged helplessly at the agent.

Kenyon held up a hand. "No need to worry, Bernie, I was on my way." He turned and shook MacQuaig's hand. "You've been a tremendous help, doctor. Thank you."

He walked to the entrance, Ilsa's glare following him the entire way.

Traffic was heavy as they headed back into town and finally ground to a halt as they passed Heathrow. Harry stared at the long line of motionless cars ahead, cursed, and put the car into neutral. "Bloody hell, I hope the trip out here was worth it," he said. "What is this TEQ, anyway?"

"It's a software firm," replied Kenyon. "They specialize in military applications."

"You mean, like encryption?"

Kenyon glanced up toward Harry. "How did you know that?"

Harry shrugged. "Oh, I must have 'eard it from one of my customers, like."

Kenyon caught Harry's eyes in the rearview. "I meant to ask you, did Arundel give you a hard time the other night?"

Harry turned his gaze away from Kenyon. "Who's that?" he asked.

"Nobody important." Kenyon stared out the window. *Why was Harry lying to him?*

By the time Harry dropped Kenyon off at 61 Herringbone Gardens, it was almost five. The agent sat on the living room couch and dialed FBI headquarters in San Francisco.

"Marge, I know what Cyberworm is," said Kenyon.

"Spill, kiddo," said Gonelli.

Kenyon explained the workings of the device, including the Pentagon's involvement.

"*That's* why Deaver put a clamp on it," said Gonelli. "They want to keep its existence from leaking out."

"Yeah, and in the meantime, they let it walk out the back door."

"What about this encryption code thing?" asked Marge.

"Simon came to England to get the code, but the Pentagon hadn't paid up, so TEQ stiffed him," said Kenyon.

"Lucky day," replied Gonelli. "Where's that leave us?"

Kenyon sat with his head bent, thinking. "Thanks to Simon, the spies have the cyberattack virus, but until they get the encryption code, the program is gibberish."

"Can they get it from TEQ?" asked Gonelli.

"I don't think so. MacQuaig's a queer duck, but he's got that place locked down tighter than a bull's ass in fly season."

"Hey, I'm from New York," said Gonelli. "Is that good or bad?"

"That's good," said Kenyon. "The spies still need the second half. If they can't get it from TEQ, they'll be desperate to get it somewhere else. Maybe we can flush them out using the code as bait."

"I'm coming to London," said Gonelli. "Don't do anything till I get there."

"Sure, Marge, but listen, I haven't told you the best part. Guess who owns TEQ?"

"Who?"

The front doorbell rang. From where he was sitting, Kenyon could see a police constable standing at the door.

"Shit, it's the cops. I'll call you right back."

Kenyon hung up and went to answer the front door.

Twenty-four

The constable was accompanied by Detective Sergeant Ruffy, the lead investigator at Ricci's suicide investigation.

"What can I do for you, detective?" asked Kenyon when he opened the door.

"If you don't mind, sir, we'd like you to return to Mr. Ricci's apartment."

"Why?"

Ruffy's face was fixed in the impassive expression that all cops wore. "We need your assistance in some further inquiries."

Sensing that it was pointless to ask further questions, Kenyon fetched his jacket from the hallway and joined the two men in an unmarked car parked outside. The driver placed a flashing light on the dash, and the heavy evening traffic parted as they moved down Cromwell Road.

The night was warm and clear, and the streets were full of pedestrians. Kenyon, sitting in the back seat, watched them staring as they passed. He recognized the smug, disapproving looks on their faces: angry that he had broken the law, happy that it wasn't them sitting in the back of the cop car.

Kenyon thought back to what Gonelli had told him about Deaver. He couldn't believe the moron was hiding such important evidence. If it hadn't been for the chance association of the *Techno 69* fake with Sir Rupert's company, it might have taken the FBI months to find the lead.

Kenyon thought about his encounter with Ilsa earlier in the day. It was funny how she kept cropping up. Not only did her father own the company that designed the encryption code for Cyberworm, but her husband had been fooling around with Kenyon's aunt. He wondered where else she would turn up: bad luck always came in threes.

They parked in front of Ricci's apartment, and the policemen took up flanking positions as they escorted Kenyon into the foyer. The agent had the distinct impression they were concerned he might make a run for it, and were covering his getaway. Whatever was waiting for him upstairs, Kenyon thought it must be a doozy. He wondered fleetingly if they had discovered the *Techno 69* fake, and wanted him to identify it.

Kenyon and the cops were met by another constable when they arrived at Ricci's floor. He escorted them into the apartment and gestured for Kenyon to continue on into the living room.

Detective Inspector Arundel was sitting at the kitchen table, a pair of black-rimmed spectacles propped on the end of his nose. He was reading a report. He glanced up as the agent entered. "Ah, there you are." He pointed to a chair on the opposite side of the table. "Do sit down."

Kenyon settled into the opposite seat. While Arundel read the report, Kenyon glanced around the room. The food, newspaper, and teapot had been cleaned up. Otherwise, everything else looked the same.

Arundel finished reading the report and placed it on the table. "Do you know what this is?" he asked, tapping the paper.

Kenyon read the heading upside down; "City of London Mortuary Office: #SD447." "The autopsy?"

"Indeed. Would you care to guess what it says?"

Kenyon shrugged. "You tell me."

Arundel took off his reading spectacles and tapped the report with one of the arms. "It says that Ricci was murdered."

Kenyon's mouth fell open. "Murdered!" The agent pointed toward the bathroom. "But I saw him! He slit his wrists!"

Arundel kept his gaze on Kenyon, studying his reaction. "At first glance, that is what it would appear. There were no signs of struggle to indicate an altercation. Even the barbiturate in the tea was prescribed

by his doctor. Except for the lack of a note, it looked like a straightfor-
ward suicide."

Kenyon stared intently at the detective. "So, why does the coroner
think he was murdered?"

"Because the assailant made one basic mistake." Arundel went
to the kitchen and pulled a bread knife out of the cutlery drawer.
Returning to his chair, the detective rolled up his sleeves to expose
his wrists. "When a suicide slits his wrists, he does it by starting near
the thumb and cutting down," he explained, miming the motion for
Kenyon's benefit. "He then swaps hands, and does the second wrist.
The coroner can easily determine the orientation of the knife and
the direction of the stroke by looking at the serrations in the wound
through a stereoscope."

Kenyon knew all this from his training at Quantico. "So?"

"When the coroner looked at Ricci's wrists, both the cuts were
running in the same direction," said Arundel. "Whoever killed Ricci
simply lined his arms up against the tub and slit them together, like he
was cutting a loaf of bread."

Kenyon sat, stunned by the news and trying to absorb the implica-
tions. The room was very quiet. He suddenly glanced up; all the men
in the room were staring at him. "Whoa, wait a minute," he exclaimed.
"You don't think *I* did it."

Arundel nodded. "As a matter of fact, yes, I do."

"Are you nuts? I was with Happy Harry! He saw me go up. There's
no way I could have faked his death in the few minutes before you
arrived."

"A curious point that," said Arundel. "According to the coroner,
the time of death is uncertain. It seems that the warm water in a bath
tends to keep the body temperature of the victim higher than normal,
making the time of death appear shorter."

"I don't follow you."

"No need to make yourself sound any less ignorant than necessary,"
said Arundel. "We have a detailed itinerary for your movements on

the day in question. It seems there were several hours of unaccounted activity. You could have murdered Ricci between 10:00 and 11:00 PM, walked home, then proceeded over here with Harry as your alibi. Any cursory examination by a pathologist on site would assume it had happened within the hour."

Kenyon fought to keep his anger under control. "Okay. Let me take a page from your book. When I told you that somebody had killed Lydia, you said, 'what's the motive?' Well, Arundel, what's my motive for killing this guy?"

The detective stood up and walked over to the kitchen. He leaned his elbows on the island counter and contemplated Kenyon. "I understand you are acquainted with a Mr. Archibald Lump, noted art collector and freelance bookmaker?"

Oh shit, thought Kenyon.

"As an investigator yourself, it will come as no surprise that the Metropolitan Police take an active interest in Lump," said Arundel. "Imagine our surprise when, within days of your arrival, you made an appearance at his home. Would you care to explain your presence there?"

Kenyon let out a long breath. "Lydia made a note in her daybook that she paid Lump a hundred grand. I went there to find out why. It turns out he was the guy Ricci sold a bum painting to. Lydia made good, and then some."

Arundel nodded. "Ah, so that is where you obtained evidence of Ricci's forging. I can imagine that it made you very angry."

"Not enough to kill him."

Arundel cocked his head to one side. "What *would* make you angry enough?"

"What do you mean?"

"What else did Mr. Ricci have over Lydia?"

Kenyon swallowed, hard. What did they know about *Techno 69*? "I don't know," he said.

"Oh, I think you do." Arundel arose. "Come with me."

The detective walked into the living room and sat down at the couch in front of the TV console. He motioned for Kenyon to sit down in the adjacent chair. Puzzled, the agent complied.

"After we received the coroner's report, we came back here for a more thorough look," said Arundel. "We found this DVD in the recorder."

Arundel picked up the remote and activated the recorder. The TV picture flickered for a second, then an image appeared on the screen.

"Do you know the location?" asked Arundel.

Kenyon stared at the TV. The tape was from a security system recorder, with the image split into four. The black and white image was grainy, and there was no sound, but he immediately recognized it as a tape from Kenyon Gallery. "Yeah. It's Lydia's place."

"Can you tell what's going on?"

The top left corner showed the front entrance to the gallery. Men and women in fancy clothes were entering into the foyer. The upper right corner showed a boisterous crowd jammed into the main gallery. "It looks like some kind of party," said Kenyon.

Arundel pointed to the date stamp in the corner that read 12/21. "It was a charity reception that Lydia held every year before Christmas. This is from last year."

The party was obviously in full swing, with people laughing and gesturing in drunken abandon. The agent recognized several movie actors and other celebrities dancing. A large-breasted woman was lifting her miniskirt and rubbing the face of a well-known rock star into her crotch.

"Quite a riotous event, by any standard," said Arundel. "Do you see Lydia anywhere?"

Kenyon peered closer at the image. There was Legrand, dressed in a tuxedo and clutching a cigar, and he saw Ricci darting in and out of the crowd. He even recognized Ilsa Ingoldsby-Legrand, her face sour, chatting with a man in the corner, but he couldn't see his aunt. "Maybe she went out for some fresh air," said Kenyon.

"No, she didn't," said Arundel. "Watch the lower half."

The bottom left image showed the storeroom, empty of any guests. The bottom right showed Lydia's office; Kenyon recognized her desk and filing cabinet. It was also empty.

Suddenly, the door to her office opened, and a woman entered. She turned toward the camera, and Kenyon recognized her as Lydia.

He leaned forward to study the image. She was dressed in a dark dress, something long and flowing. It covered one shoulder, leaving the other bare. She wore a diamond choker around her long and graceful neck. Even though the image was black and white, she looked radiant.

A second woman entered the room. Her back was to the camera. Her hair was dark, and cut to shoulder length. Lydia advanced to the woman and kissed her full on the mouth. The other woman responded, pushing Lydia back toward her desk. Lydia began to kiss the woman on the neck, working down her shoulders, pulling the back zipper down.

Kenyon began to feel his face flushing, but he couldn't take his eyes from the image.

Lydia, her eyes aflame, pulled the top of her lover's dress off and ran her hands up and down the woman's naked back.

Kenyon finally averted his eyes. "I've seen enough."

Arundel stopped the tape in mid-frame. "I believe that is Lydia, is it not?"

Kenyon stared at the floor. "Yes."

Arundel turned to the agent. "You come to me claiming that your aunt was murdered by a laser pen. Then, you just happen to discover the body of her gallery manager. You call the police, and, lo and behold, they discover the murder weapon, just as you had predicted."

Kenyon sat quietly, saying nothing.

Arundel continued. "The case is closed. Until, of course, we see through the deception. We return and investigate more thoroughly and, look what we discover; the murder victim just happens to have a very embarrassing DVD of Lydia in his recorder."

Kenyon's head began to swim. He almost felt as though he were going to pass out if he didn't get some fresh air.

"Was Bruno blackmailing Lydia?" asked Arundel, quietly.

"I don't know."

"Oh, I think you do. Ricci invited you here the other night to discuss a business deal, all right, but when you found out what the deal really was, you became angry."

"No."

"So angry, in fact, that you decided then and there to kill him."

"No."

Arundel stood and began to pace the living room. "Perhaps you went to the bathroom and found the barbiturates in his medicine cupboard. There was an empty vial there. A few tablets in his tea, and he was soon insensate and helpless. You carried him into the bathroom, removed his clothing, then staged the suicide."

"No," Kenyon said emphatically. "I didn't kill him. I swear."

"Then who did? Who had a better motive than you?"

"I don't *know*!"

Arundel sighed. "You're in over your head on this one, Jack. Until you tell me the truth, I cannot help you."

Kenyon stood up from the couch. "I don't need your help."

"As of this moment, you are to stay within the city limits," said Arundel. "Any attempt on your part to leave town will be construed as an act of flight, and I will have you detained. Do you understand?"

Kenyon nodded. He rose to go.

"One final question." said Arundel. "Do you have any idea who the other woman is?"

Jack glanced back at the image on the TV. "No," he replied.

Arundel nodded toward the door, and Kenyon silently left.

As soon as he was out on the street, Kenyon walked up to a garbage can and gave it a good solid kick. The stupid fuck, he thought. How dare he accuse me of killing Ricci. He kicked the garbage can again, this time putting a serious dent in the side and stubbing his toe.

Kenyon limped for a step or two, favoring his foot, but the brief outburst seemed to help. He leaned against a building and took a deep breath of air. What the hell was Arundel up to? Was he setting him up so that the real killer could go free?

No, that's paranoia, he thought to himself. Arundel was just doing his job. But, come to think of it, what kind of police branch handled everything from road accidents to murder, anyway? Arundel had been riding his shoulder right from the beginning.

"Think, damn it," he said aloud. "Think." He couldn't believe that the police suspected him of murdering Ricci. It just didn't make sense. If they really thought so, they would have arrested him.

He stopped. Unless they wanted him out and about on the streets, a sitting duck for the real killer. Kenyon squared his shoulders. If that was the case, then he'd have to redouble his efforts and find the real killer first. And the best place to start was with the other woman in the DVD.

Kenyon had lied to Arundel. He knew who Lydia's lover was, the woman with the tiny tattoo of the butterfly on her shoulder.

He turned and began walking toward the home of Tanya O'Neill.

Twenty-five

Kenyon headed west along Cromwell, then turned north on Gloucester Road, toward Kensington Gardens. The sun had long set, and the streets were dark. The windows of several pubs were open, and laughter spilled out onto the street.

Kenyon noticed none of it, the image of Lydia and Tanya burning in his mind. He was not a prude. Certainly, living in San Francisco had inured him to gay and lesbian couples. But this wasn't just any couple. This was his aunt and his lawyer. His aunt and his *lover*.

Kenyon thought about Lydia. Suddenly, he knew why Cyrus had driven his only daughter out of the house, never to return. Cyrus was a God-fearing man. To him, homosexuality was an abomination, something to cast from your midst. He thought about the heartbreak that Daisy, his foster mother, must have gone through. He felt sorry for Lydia. He felt sorry for them all.

He had no such sympathy for Tanya. No wonder she had reacted so badly to the news that Lydia had been murdered; she was probably worried that he would uncover their secret. He thought of the hot, passionate love-making between him and Tanya, and his face flushed.

Kenyon came to a small lane running off Gloucester Road. He turned and wandered down the quiet, deserted lane, past a row of tiny, brightly colored houses that must have been the servants' quarters a century ago.

The lane curved gently to the right. Kenyon walked about two hundred feet before he realized, to his annoyance, that it was sealed off at the end by an ancient churchyard.

Kenyon turned around, and immediately spotted someone entering the lane behind him. The man was wearing a black windbreaker and a Chicago Bulls cap pulled down over his face, but there was no doubt in Kenyon's mind who it was: Charlie Dahg.

Kenyon realized he was trapped. The wrought-iron fence surrounding the churchyard stood eight feet high. Grabbing hold of one of the iron bars, he boosted himself up, ripping his jacket as he clambered over the pointed tips.

Kenyon landed in some bushes on the other side. Pulling himself out of the shrubbery, he surprised an elderly woman tidying a grave. He smiled and waved to the startled woman as he scrambled over a marker stone and hurried out the main gate.

Kenyon found himself on a quiet residential street bordered by tall, red-brick townhouses on one side and the church on the other. He sprinted down the block as fast as his injury would allow.

He reached Church Street and turned north. Kenyon counted to thirty, then walked slowly back and peered around the corner. Sure enough, about two hundred feet back, he spotted Dahg moving cautiously along the street in pursuit.

Damn, he needed to alert the police, but he didn't want Arundel to know where he was going. The moment the Scotland Yard detective saw O'Neill, he would know that Kenyon had lied to him about her identity. He turned and ran the next two blocks, heading for the bright lights of a busy street ahead.

He came out onto Kensington High Street. Many of the shops lining the streets were closed, but the sidewalks were packed with people out for a breath of fresh air. The stitches in his butt were starting to ache and he knew he couldn't run much further. He needed to do something, and fast. Kenyon slowed down and looked around and spotted a tube station ahead. He entered, hoping to blend in with the crowd.

The underground station was part of a large shopping mall. A pharmacy was still open, and a uniformed security guard stood by the door. It was a large store, with security cameras in the ceiling and detectors at the exit. Perfect, thought Kenyon. It was time to snare Dahg.

Kenyon entered the mall adjacent to the drugstore. A decorative fountain stood in the middle of the main aisle of the mall. The agent paused on the far side and watched the entrance. As soon as his tail appeared, he stepped into plain sight and headed for the drugstore.

Entering the store, Kenyon walked up to the fragrance counter and picked up a boxed vial of perfume. As he examined the label, he carefully peeled the bar code off the slippery cellophane. It curled into a tiny cylinder in the palm of his hand. The agent put the perfume back on the shelf and started back toward the main exit.

Dahg had entered the store and was busy trying to blend in, his face buried in a copy of *Sports Illustrated* at the magazine rack. He was studiously facing away from the agent.

Kenyon strolled straight toward Dahg. As he passed, he softly placed the bar code sticker onto the back of his pursuer's windbreaker. The agent then kept on going right out the front door of the drugstore.

He was about fifty feet down the street when the siren at the exit went off. Kenyon turned to see Dahg being detained by the security guard. The ex-CIA man knocked him to the ground with a vicious punch, but a second guard came out and grabbed him by the torso.

Kenyon didn't stick around to watch the rest of the fight. He continued on his way, taking several doglegs and detours until he was fairly certain he wasn't being followed by any of Dahg's henchmen.

It was almost midnight by the time he reached O'Neill's building. The street was deserted, the only movement came from the wind swaying the sycamore trees that lined one sidewalk. Kenyon stood staring up at O'Neill's apartment. The windows were open to let in a late night breeze, and there was a light burning inside, but he couldn't see anyone on the patio. He climbed the steps to the front door and pushed the buzzer.

A few seconds later, O'Neill answered. "Yes?"

"It's Jack."

There was a brief pause, then the door unlocked.

O'Neill was waiting at the front door when Kenyon reached the top of the stairwell. She was wearing a short cotton nightdress that ended at mid-thigh. She stared at Kenyon for a moment, noting his haggard look. The chill of their last encounter hung in the air.

"It's late, Jack," she finally said.

"I know. I need to talk to you."

O'Neill hesitated a moment, then let him through the door.

Kenyon walked into the living room and glanced around. O'Neill appeared to be alone, preparing for bed. There was soft jazz on the stereo and a cup of tea sat on the coffee table. He stared at the couch and thought about her warm skin under his hands.

O'Neill approached Kenyon, her arms folded across her breasts. "What did you want to talk about?"

Kenyon turned to face the lawyer. "You haven't been telling me the truth."

O'Neill pushed her hair back over one ear. "What do you mean?"

"You know Ricci is dead." He stated it as a fact.

O'Neill nodded. "I read about it in the papers. He killed himself."

Kenyon shook his head. "He didn't commit suicide. He was murdered."

O'Neill's hand flew to her mouth. "How do you know?"

"The police told me. They think I did it."

O'Neill, unsteady, sat down on the couch. "But why? You had no reason to kill him."

"It seems I had several." He stared at the picture of Lydia over the fireplace, then turned to O'Neill. "I found out that Ricci was using Lydia's gallery to forge paintings."

Kenyon didn't have to ask if she knew; the solicitor blanched and turned her face away.

"I went to Ricci's apartment to confront him," Kenyon continued, "but he had already slit his wrists in the bathtub. I thought he killed himself because I had discovered his scheme. I told the police about it when they came to take the body away."

O'Neill said nothing; she continued to stare away from Kenyon.

"When they found out Ricci's murder had been faked to look like a suicide, they came back and did a more thorough search. Know what they found?"

O'Neill shook her head.

"They found a laser pen. Just like the one that must have been used to blind Lydia and force her to crash."

"It *couldn't* be Ricci," said O'Neill. "He's too much of a coward to kill anyone."

"But not coward enough to blackmail someone," countered Kenyon. "You know what else they found in Ricci's apartment? A DVD."

O'Neill turned toward the painting of Lydia.

"You know what was on it," said Kenyon. "You and Lydia. Making love."

O'Neill sat staring at Lydia's portrait, tears flowing down her cheeks.

"Bruno was blackmailing you and Lydia, wasn't he?" asked Kenyon.

"No."

Kenyon bent forward over the couch and gripped O'Neill by the arms, lifting her to her feet. "Godammit, you think this is some kind of game? Somebody killed Ricci in cold blood. Quit lying to me!"

"We didn't know *who* it was!" shouted O'Neill. "You have to believe me!" She began to cry in earnest.

Kenyon resisted the temptation to hold her close. He released her arms, and she sank back onto the couch, sniffing several times and wiping her nose on the sleeve of the nightdress. "A copy of the DVD came in the post several months ago," she began. "There was a note. They wanted one hundred thousand pounds."

"And Lydia *paid*?"

O'Neill nodded. "She put it in a plain brown bag under a bench in Kensington Park."

Kenyon cursed at their stupidity. "I take it the blackmailer wasn't through."

"That was the last I heard about it until you came and told me Lydia had taken out another one hundred thousand pounds for Archie Lump," said O'Neill. "I thought *he* must be the blackmailer."

"And that's why you tried to stop me from finding her killer? To hide your dirty little secret?"

Kenyon instantly regretted his choice of words.

"Is that how you see us?" asked O'Neill, suddenly defiant. "Two filthy dykes slutting in the closet?"

"No, I . . ."

O'Neill stood up and faced Kenyon. "She was the best thing that ever happened to me. She *believed* in me." O'Neill turned toward the portrait. "I loved her so much, I would have done anything for her."

"I'm sorry," said Kenyon. "I didn't know."

O'Neill turned back to the agent, her face knitted in anger. "That's bloody right, you didn't know. And it's something you'll never know." She turned back to stare at the painting. "Get out of my home."

Kenyon, his heart torn, turned to go. He was almost at the door, when he stopped. "I won't leave until you answer me one last question."

O'Neill didn't turn around. "What is it?" she asked.

"Did the blackmailer threaten to hand the DVD over to the media?"

"No."

"Did he threaten to show it to your boss at the law office?"

"No. I don't care about them."

"Then what *did* he threaten to do that was worth one hundred thousand pounds?"

O'Neill finally turned to face Kenyon. "To show it to Raymond Legrand."

Kenyon was thunderstruck. He suddenly recalled seeing Legrand outside Ricci's apartment the night he was killed. "Did the blackmailer carry through with his threat?" he asked.

O'Neill shrugged. "I don't think so. It wouldn't make sense—he'd never get another shilling out of her."

Kenyon nodded. "Did Lydia confess to Legrand?"

O'Neill cocked her head to one side. "Maybe. Lydia and Legrand had a big fight the night of the auction. When Lydia left, she was very angry."

Kenyon stared at O'Neill, her arms wrapped around her chest, tears streaming down her cheeks. He wanted badly to go over and hold her in his arms, to comfort her in her grief. Instead, he turned and walked out the door.

By the time Kenyon got back to Lydia's house, it was late. He poured himself a scotch on the rocks and sank into the living room couch. A few pale beams from the streetlights pierced the darkness.

Kenyon thought about Lydia. For some reason, her relationship with O'Neill made him strangely proud. It had been foolish of Lydia to have given in to the blackmailer, but he was glad that Tanya meant so much to her.

Kenyon also thought about Legrand. He never realized how deep Lydia's love for him must have run, to pay up that much money to keep her relationship with O'Neill a secret.

Kenyon glanced at his watch. It was nearing three in the morning, which meant it was almost seven at night in San Francisco. Thursday evening. He dialed Gonelli's home number, but her voice mail answered. "I ain't here," said the recorded voice. "Leave a message."

"Marge, it's Jack calling. Ricci didn't commit suicide; he was murdered. The cops think I did it, but I saw Legrand there that night. I think he was out to revenge a blackmail plot. I need to know how to handle this. Call me as soon as you can."

Kenyon hung up, then dialed the main switchboard at the office and got hold of Sue, the receptionist. "This is Jack, in London," he said. "Where's Marge tonight?"

"Marge is gone," said Sue.

"She's not at home yet," said Kenyon.

"No, I mean she's gone out of town," said Sue.

Kenyon cursed under his breath. "Okay. Put me through to Leroi."

Kenyon's partner was still at her desk. "Man, what you *doing* over there?"

"What do you mean, Jazz?" asked Kenyon.

"Shit, Marge was spittin' bullets all over the office this afternoon."

"Over what?" asked Kenyon, suddenly wary.

"Over you, cowboy. She got some message from Deaver, then she grabbed the first flight to London she could book."

Kenyon cringed at the mention of the assistant US attorney. "Give me a call as soon as you know what's up."

"Don't you worry," said his partner. "I got a hunch you are gonna find out soon enough."

Kenyon hung up the phone and trudged up to bed. God, he thought, what else can go wrong?

Twenty-six
Friday, July 15

Kenyon slept until eleven in the morning when he was awakened by the sound of Señora Santucci puttering around in the bathroom off the main bedroom.

"Don't you ever knock?" he asked, reaching for his shorts on the floor.

The housekeeper came in to admire Kenyon's butt as he pulled on his boxers. "Get up, lazy bone. I know you say not to come early in the morning, but today is big cleaning day. You go get some coffee in the kitchen."

"In a bit," Kenyon replied. "I'm going for a run first." He grabbed some sweat socks and a 49er's T-shirt, and headed out the door.

The morning was hot and hazy. Kenyon headed north on Gloucester Road to Kensington Park.

As he picked his way up the sidewalk past pedestrians and garbage cans, Kenyon's mind went over the past two weeks. First, Simon is killed, then Lydia, then Ricci. A computer virus that could destroy the world's economy was floating around in the hands of terrorists, and, to top it all off, the police thought he was a murderer. *The whole world is fucked*, Kenyon thought.

He considered Legrand. He had no doubt the Frenchman had murdered Ricci. He wondered how Legrand found out Ricci was blackmailing Lydia. He didn't think the gallery manager made good on his threat to tell Legrand; it made no sense for a blackmailer to lose the opportunity for further paydays.

No, Lydia must have revealed the blackmail to Legrand on the night of the auction. The private investigator had then found out who was doing it by his own means. He simply had to look at the tape to know it had to be someone inside the gallery. It wouldn't take long to zero in on Ricci.

Kenyon stopped on a corner to let a cab screech by. However Legrand had found out, he concluded, the result had been the same: he killed Ricci in revenge, then tried to make his death look like a suicide.

Kenyon thought about the one piece of the puzzle that didn't fit: the laser pen found in Ricci's apartment. If the gallery owner was successfully blackmailing Lydia, what sense did it make to kill her? Maybe Legrand knew. He'd call Arundel when he got back, and have the police pick up the Frenchman.

When he reached Kensington Park, Kenyon cut across the flower walk and joined the other joggers on the outer perimeter path. His wound had healed to the point where he was almost back to full gait. For the first time in two weeks, Kenyon pushed himself hard, running at full speed until the sweat rolled down his back and his lungs ached. It felt great.

After thirty minutes, Kenyon eased up to a slower pace, angling for a line of shady trees. An older Philippina maid was out walking a herd of long-haired dogs, and a young Swedish nanny pushed a blue stroller along the path. Both gave Kenyon the eye as he passed.

For the first time in days, Kenyon smiled. The hard run had helped clear his head and improve his mood. There were still quite a few unanswered questions regarding Lydia's murder and the Cyberworm case, but the agent had a feeling deep in his gut that something was about to break. He turned south and cruised home at a leisurely pace.

As Kenyon walked up to his house, he noticed a police van parked out front. The front door was wide open. A constable came out the front door carrying a box.

"Hey, what are you doing?" demanded Kenyon

"Talk to the guv inside," was all the constable said.

Kenyon stormed up the steps and into the foyer. "Can someone tell me what the hell is going on?"

"We're seizing evidence," said Will Deaver, standing in the living room with Detective Inspector Arundel. Both men looked grim.

"You'd better have a good explanation for this," said Kenyon, advancing into the room.

"No, it's you who better have the good explanation," Deaver replied. "Maybe I'll waive the death penalty."

Kenyon stopped short. "What are you talking about?"

"I've been conferring with Mr. Deaver for the last few days," said Arundel. "I'm afraid that he has a compelling case not only for murder, but for treason, as well." He pointed to a chair. "Sit down."

Kenyon complied, staring at them, wide-eyed. "You guys think I'm a spy?"

"Don't play stupid with me," Deaver snapped. "I've had my eye on you from the very first day."

"What do you mean?" asked Kenyon.

"That hot tip you got about the stolen software stank like shit," Deaver said. "You sent the e-mail to yourself."

"Why the hell would I do that?" asked Kenyon.

"Actually, it's not half clever," said Arundel. "It allows you to set up and control your own alibi. Right under the nose of the FBI, you kill Simon, steal the software, then run off in pursuit of some imaginary felon in order to hand it off to a confederate. And the best part of all, you leave a hapless former CIA agent to take the fall."

Kenyon pointed to his stitched rear-end. "Aren't you guys forgetting something? This imaginary felon shot me in the ass."

Arundel turned and raised an eyebrow to Deaver.

"It was a slug from his own gun," said Deaver. "The FBI was too stupid to check his hands for gunpowder."

Kenyon shook his head in disbelief. "Deaver, you are so full of shit. If I'm the guy who stole the Cyberworm software, then who got the code? My evil twin Skippy?"

"No, the rest of your slimy spy ring," said Deaver.

"Oh, now I've got a gang," said Kenyon. "Deaver, are you on drugs?"

The other man ignored the taunt. "We've been down to the gallery, Kenyon. We spoke to a Miss Zoë Tigger."

Arundel pulled out a notepad and consulted it. "Miss Tigger tells us you have been searching for a copy of a painting entitled *Techno 69*."

Kenyon shrugged. "So?"

"We went through the records in Lydia's office, Kenyon," said Deaver. "The original was purchased by TEQ, the company working on the encryption code."

"Lots of people bought paintings from Lydia."

"Yes, but this one was subsequently sold at auction to Abdul Garbajian, a man with connections to known terrorists," said Arundel. "And it appears that you have been spending an inordinate amount of energy pursuing the copy. That's what you were really doing at Ricci's flat, weren't you?"

Kenyon stared at the floor. "No."

Arundel closed the notebook and stared at Kenyon. "You went to his apartment and demanded the copy, and when he handed it over, you killed him and made it look like a suicide."

"We got you lock, stock, and smoking barrel, Kenyon," said Deaver.

Kenyon bent over and rested his forehead against his knees. This was all so crazy, he thought. It had to be some kind of bad dream.

"If you turn over the copy of *Techno 69* now, we may be able to arrange for leniency," offered Arundel.

"I don't *have* it!" said Kenyon.

"Who screwed up?" asked Deaver, leaning forward. "Was it Bruno Ricci? I'll bet he was holding out for more money. Is that why you murdered him?"

"I could never kill anyone in cold blood," said Kenyon.

Deaver stood up and hooked his thumbs in his belt. "A man who would kill his own mother is capable of anything," he said.

"I'm an orphan."

Deaver smiled. He was clearly enjoying himself. "You didn't think we'd find out?" He reached into his suit jacket and pulled out a yellow, aged document and handed it to Kenyon.

The document crinkled as Kenyon unfolded it. It was a Montana birth certificate for Jack Kenyon, dated July 5, 1978. He glanced to the bottom of the page. There was no name for the father. But in the line for the mother's name was typed Lydia Kenyon.

Tears welled in Kenyon's eyes.

Deaver leaned closer. "Who killed her Jack? Was it Bruno?"

Kenyon sat silently, the tears striking the birth certificate like drops of rain.

"Why did you have her killed, Jack?" Deaver pressed. "Because she screwed up? Or was it her taste in women?"

Deaver didn't even have time to scream. In one smooth motion, Kenyon came out of the chair and smacked the palm of his hand under Deaver's chin, hurling him backwards onto the couch.

Before Arundel could react, Kenyon grabbed the pole axe from the suit of armor and brandished it at him. "Don't make a sound," he ordered.

Arundel, eyes wide, mutely stuck his hands skywards.

Kenyon glanced toward the hallway. The constable was down in the basement, still rummaging around. Deaver was laying on the couch, moaning softly. Kenyon stepped toward the seated Arundel. "You carrying?"

Arundel, his hands held elegantly in the air, remained strangely calm. "No."

"Shh," warned Kenyon. He could hear the constable coming up the stairs.

Kenyon waved the battle axe as he passed the doorway. "You. Drop the boxes and come in here."

Perplexed, the cop did as he was told.

Kenyon pointed to Deaver. "Haul him downstairs."

Arundel nodded, indicating he should obey. The constable grabbed Deaver by the shoulders and headed for the basement steps. Kenyon ordered Arundel to follow.

"It's pointless to run; you can't get off the island," said Arundel.

"Just get moving," ordered Kenyon. "I don't have all day."

Arundel stopped in the kitchen and fished through a drawer.

"What the hell are you doing?" asked Kenyon.

Arundel pulled out a cork screw. "I noticed some excellent Montrachet down there," he replied. "Seeing as how we could be locked up for several hours . . ."

Kenyon shooed him down the stairs, then locked the door.

The agent leaned against the doorway. *This can't be happening to me*, he thought. The horror at being accused kept alternating with the shock of being Lydia's son. It was all too insane.

Kenyon placed the pole axe onto the kitchen counter. He leaned against the door for a second, wondering what to do next, willing himself to think clearly. He knew the cops would find the entrance to Señora Santucci's apartment any second. He had to get out of there.

All he was wearing was a pair of shorts and a sweaty T-shirt. Where was his wallet? He knew it was in his jacket, but where had he hung it the night before? He glanced down the hallway and saw it hanging on the deacon's bench by the front door. He hurried down the hall, grabbed the coat, remembering to leave his cell phone behind so they couldn't use it to trace him. He grabbed a ballcap and headed for the front porch.

"Stop right there."

Kenyon turned. Special Agent in Charge Marge Gonelli was standing at the turn of the stairs. Her shoulders visibly sagged from the long airplane journey from San Francisco.

"Marge," said Kenyon, taking a step toward her.

"Don't move," she ordered. "You're under arrest."

"Marge, I haven't done anything."

Gonelli stared grimly at the agent. "Not according to Deaver."

"None of what Deaver says is true," said Kenyon. "You have to believe me."

"What I believe is unimportant," replied Gonelli.

"Oh, yes it is," said Kenyon, squaring his shoulders. "Because if you honestly think I did any of this, Marge, then I have no one on Earth to prove my innocence except me."

Kenyon tucked the jacket under his arm and turned toward the open front door. He paused, but there was no response.

He walked slowly down the front steps to the sidewalk.

Still, nothing.

He reached the sidewalk and turned toward Cromwell Road.

Then Jack Kenyon, fugitive, ran as hard as he could.

Twenty-seven

Kenyon reached the end of the street and rounded the corner onto Cromwell Road. He figured he only had a few minutes before Gonelli let Arundel and his men out of the basement. They would immediately mount a pursuit.

He trotted west on Cromwell until he came to a busy intersection. He tried to flag down a cab, but they all drove by. Any second, a cop could appear around the corner.

Kenyon spotted an underground station. He sprinted across the street and into the dark entrance of the building.

He came to a stop inside and groaned aloud. The entrance to the trains was through a row of turnstiles, and two guards stood behind the barrier to ensure nobody hopped over.

A large crowd of students waited in line in front of the ticket office. Kenyon pulled out his wallet and walked up to the front of the line. "Kid, here's five pounds to let me butt in line."

"Que?"

Kenyon uttered a silent curse. The student was Spanish. He waved the note in the student's face. "Uh, esta cinco dinero para primero," he said, in his broken Spanish. "Hokay?"

The student smiled. "For ten, senor, si!"

Kenyon pulled out another bill and moved to the open ticket wicket. "That'll be five pound sixty for a day pass, love," said the clerk.

Kenyon paid and received a pink cardboard ticket. Glancing over his shoulder, he spotted the tall, rounded hat of a bobby entering the station. Bending over, he fumbled with the turnstile until it took his ticket. He rushed forward, but the turnstile refused to operate.

"Hoy, you," said the underground guard, pointing to Kenyon.

Kenyon froze.

"You got to take your ticket back out, mate."

Kenyon suddenly realized that his ticket was protruding from a different slot. He nodded to the guard and pulled it out. The turnstile clicked over, letting him through.

Without looking behind, he joined a large group of passengers getting onto an elevator. Just as he entered the enclosed space, he glanced up. A security camera stared balefully down at his face. He pulled down his ballcap, hustled inside the elevator and descended with the rest of the passengers.

The elevator stopped deep in the bowels of the earth and disgorged the passengers. Kenyon was carried along down a tunnel to the Piccadilly line platform where the crowd split into two: east and westbound. A train was standing at the eastbound platform. Kenyon rushed to an open door and pushed his way on board. He breathed a sigh of relief as the door closed behind him and the train accelerated into the dark tunnel.

Kenyon stood near the door, his tall frame nearly scraping the rounded roof of the car. He glanced around, careful to keep his cap pulled down. Most of the passengers were either tourists with daypacks or commuters reading their newspapers. They swayed on straps as the car bucked and squeaked down the ancient tracks.

The next station was South Kensington. Kenyon peered at the route map on the wall above the windows. He was heading toward the center of town. He tried to do some quick calculations. One of the first places the cops would look for him would be the underground. They would check the security tapes at the nearest station, but he estimated he had at least half an hour before the cops on patrol would have a picture or description. That gave him twenty minutes, or about five stops of the underground.

Kenyon was all too aware that he was still wearing his jogging shorts and 49er's T-shirt. The jacket in his hand was dark blue, but it had an

FBI insignia on the breast pocket. Might as well paint a bullseye, he thought to himself.

Three young men carrying bags from Harrod's got on at the next stop. One of them was wearing a Gap ballcap. He turned to his friend, who was wearing a Virginia Tech sweater, and poked him in the ribs. "Hey, Mel, tell Joe what the clerk said to you in the dressing room."

"I'd be *dee-lighted* to measure your inseam, *love*," Mel mimicked the clerk in a falsetto accent. "Man, I almost decked that fruit." They all laughed uproariously.

Kenyon looked at Mel. He was tall, with a crop of dark hair and a midwestern accent. He was ten years younger than the agent, but the resemblance was close enough.

"Excuse me," said Kenyon. "You boys go to Virginia Tech?"

"Yessir," said the one in the Gap cap. "We're criminology undergrads."

Kenyon pointed to Mel's sweater. "I'm going to meet my brother for his birthday, and he just loves the Hokies," he said.

The trio swelled with pride. "This year, we're going to win the Sugar Bowl," said Mel. All three whooped.

"I hope they do," said Kenyon, grinning. "Phil was going to go to Virginia Tech; that was, before the leukemia got him."

The three young men suddenly sobered. "Hey, I'm sorry to hear," said Mel.

"It's all right," said Kenyon. "The doctors here say he's going to be fine." Kenyon looked at Mel. "I didn't have time to buy Phil a birthday present, but you know, he'd love a Virginia Tech sweater. It would just make his day."

Mel didn't need a second hint. He put down his Harrod's bag and pulled his sweater over his head. "You give this to your brother, and you tell him Mel wishes he gets better soon," said the student.

"Hey, that's great," said Kenyon, taking the sweater. "Phil's gonna just love it. But let me give you something." Kenyon offered his FBI jacket. "Here, take this."

Mel's eyes went wide. "Is this for real?" he asked.

"One hundred percent," said Kenyon.

"Oh, man, the guys in criminology are gonna go nuts when they see this."

"Go ahead, try it on," said Kenyon.

Mel eagerly pulled the jacket on. "Fits perfect," he said, beaming.

The kid with the Gap hat glanced up as the train began to slow. "Hey, Leicester Square," he said. "This is our stop."

"You guys take care," said Kenyon, as they disembarked.

The agent waited until they had disappeared into the crowd, then slipped off the train and pulled on the Virginia Tech sweater. He tossed his ballcap onto a bench, and smoothed down his hair. He felt remorse at misleading Mel and his friends, but he was desperate.

A series of escalators carried the passengers up from the platform. Kenyon was careful to keep at least a hundred feet behind the students, wary of being spotted.

The station for Leicester Square was crowded with commuters and tourists trying to get in and out. Kenyon's heart plunged when he spotted two cops at each exit, carefully scanning the faces of people as they left.

Damn, thought Kenyon. Arundel had already got the word out. He stepped to one side to buy a cheap pair of sunglasses from a kiosk, hoping they wouldn't recognize him. It was a faint hope, but it was all that he could think of.

For the first time that day, Kenyon's luck took a turn for the better. As the three students reached the first exit, a bobby spotted the FBI jacket and grabbed his whistle. An ear-piercing shriek filled the air, and the other policemen came running. They pounced upon the unsuspecting student and wrestled him to the ground, along with his friends.

Kenyon felt terrible, but he knew it would make a hell of a story for their criminology classmates when they returned to the States. He said a silent thank you to the students, and fled up the unguarded exit.

As soon as he reached the sunshine at street level, Kenyon headed for Leicester Square. The pedestrian mall was crammed with tourists. The agent blended into the crowd, standing behind a fat man taking pictures of buskers with a video camera and an "I'm with Stupid" T-shirt.

Rather than watch the buskers, however, Kenyon scanned the crowd. He didn't spot any uniformed police, but he knew that Scotland Yard would have plainclothes in the crowd watching for pickpockets. He slowly made his way to the edge of the crowd, leaving Leicester Square and headed north, into Chinatown. Kenyon was surprised at the tiny size of the Asian neighborhood. Considering that London had almost ten million people, the oriental stalls and grocery stores only stretched for two blocks.

Kenyon continued north through Chinatown into Soho. The district was lined with theaters showing various plays. What had Arundel said? Why not take time out and go see a mystery. Kenyon laughed at the irony of that one. The theater district in Soho quickly gave way to the porno district, with Triple-X shops and nudie shows lining the streets.

As Kenyon walked past the Pussycat Exotic Show, a black man dressed in a gold vest stepped in his way. "We got gorgeous girls, we got well-hung lads," he said. "Come on sport, give it a go."

Kenyon was about to step around the tout and keep walking when he spotted a police car parked at the end of the street. He quickly ducked into the entrance. The foyer of the Pussycat was decorated in black velvet and a filthy red carpet. He paid his money to the bored ticket clerk and headed into the theater.

From what Kenyon could see in the gloom, the theater had once been an elegant music hall, but twenty years of skin shows had covered the walls in grime. As he sat down on a rickety bench, he noticed needles and condoms littered underneath. The only other people near him were a group of kids in raggedy clothes with spiked hair and they looked too stoned to even notice him.

The agent glanced at his watch. He had been on the lam for less than an hour. He figured he was safe for the next few minutes, but then what? Should he just turn himself in, he wondered? But he realized that if he was in jail, there'd be no way he would ever be able to figure out who was trying to frame him.

Kenyon thought back, trying to remember what Deaver and Arundel had said before he fled. Something about the e-mail he had received. It was too convenient. Kenyon had to agree. It was a great way to cover up the theft of the Cyberworm virus and build an alibi at the same time. The agent had to give his grudging admiration. Whoever had thought it up had done an excellent job of painting Kenyon into a corner.

What else had Deaver talked about? The stuff about the copy of *Techno 69*. They wanted it, and badly. What was so important about the forgery?

The question made his head ache. Kenyon was thirsty and tired. He had to find some cover to rest. He considered renting a hotel room, but he didn't have enough money for even one night. He couldn't go to the gallery; that would be the first place they'd stake out.

Kenyon thought for a fleeting moment about Tanya O'Neill, but he quickly dismissed the idea. Offering him sanctuary from the police was a felony, and she had a career in law at stake.

What about Happy Harry? No, Kenyon was certain that Arundel had the cabby under surveillance. One false move and he'd land in jail for aiding and abetting.

Who did that leave? Nobody.

No, wait. There *was* somebody. Kenyon pulled out his wallet and dug through it until he found the card he was looking for: *Hadrian de Wolfe*. The art appraiser had been a good friend of Lydia's. Would he help her son? The agent hated to ask such a risky favor of someone he hardly knew, but there was nowhere else to turn.

Kenyon returned to the foyer and found a phone booth. He went inside and closed the door, then dug out some change and dialed the number on the business card.

"DeWolfe here," said the art appraiser.

"Hadrian, it's me, Jack."

DeWolfe picked up the urgency in his voice. "What is it, Jack?"

"Listen, I'm in a lot of trouble. I hate to ask for your help, but there's no one else I can turn to."

The art appraiser didn't hesitate. "Whatever it is, you can count on me. Where are you?"

Kenyon breathed a sigh of relief. "I'm in central London, at the Pussycat Erotic Show," said the agent.

"I know where that is," said deWolfe. "It will take me fifteen minutes to get there—wait in the audience until I arrive."

"Will do," said Kenyon. "And one other thing."

"What?"

"Thanks."

"No need to thank me," said deWolfe, sounding pleased.

Thank God there's some people you can count on, thought Kenyon. He hung up the phone and headed back to his seat.

Twenty-eight

The show began just as Kenyon sat down. To the pounding of recorded rock music, a blond woman dressed in a schoolgirl's outfit wandered onto the stage, seemingly lost. The stage had been decorated in purple plush velvet curtains. A fireman's pole had been set up to one side, and a large, round bed dominated the center of the stage.

Kenyon leaned back in the bench and stared ahead, his eyes unfocused. He thought about the fact that Lydia was his mother. For the first time, his strange life started to make sense.

Kenyon knew that Lydia had come to London to study in the late 1970s. She would have been young, probably only twenty or so. For a small town girl from Montana, it must have been like another planet.

Suddenly, a large black man dressed in fireman's pants slid down the pole and landed at the blond girl's feet. He pulled down his pants to reveal a large, throbbing erection. The schoolgirl screamed in apparent fright.

Kenyon tried to picture a young woman with long, straight hair and chinos running into some British rock star in stovepipe jeans and a leather vest. Kenyon barked a short, loud laugh that made the stoned kids glance his way. For all he knew, his father could be Joe Cocker.

By now, the schoolgirl had gotten over her fright and was sucking the fireman's cock with great relish. He, in turn, pulled down her chemise to reveal an impressive set of breasts. He picked her up and flung her onto the bed.

It didn't matter a bit who the father was, thought Kenyon, Cyrus must have hit the roof when his daughter came home pregnant. An abortion would have been legal, but that wouldn't have mattered to Cyrus and Daisy: they were God-fearing fundamentalists. They would have ordered Lydia to have Jack, then arranged to formally adopt their daughter's bastard.

After that, guessed Kenyon, the old tyrant tossed his mother out on her ear, ordering Lydia never to darken his door again.

A second man, dressed in a Santa suit, came out and ripped off the schoolgirl's skirt. He and the fireman then took turns screwing her doggy-style.

How could Lydia abandon him just like that? Never a visit, never a card, never even a phone call. Maybe she just wanted to forget he ever existed. The thought filled his heart with sadness.

The agent glanced at his watch. What if deWolfe decided not to show? What if he called the police? The agent couldn't stand waiting any longer. He arose and went to the front door of the Pussycat, glancing out to see if the coast was clear.

Just then, deWolfe's car appeared, pulling up in front of the entrance. Abandoning caution, Kenyon sprinted over and hopped into the passenger side.

"Sorry about the delay, the traffic was dreadful," said deWolfe. He pulled away from the curb.

"Listen, I really want to thank you," said Kenyon, his heart pounding. "You don't even know what trouble I'm in."

"Tell me," said deWolfe.

"The police think I murdered Lydia and stole a military secret."

The driver glanced at his passenger askance. "Did you?"

"No. I'm being framed."

DeWolfe squared himself against the wheel. "Then I think you owe me an explanation," he said. "Now."

Kenyon didn't know where to start. "There's this computer virus called Cyberworm. Somebody tried to steal it in San Francisco. Only they set it up so it looked like I was the one stealing it."

"That's terrible," said deWolfe.

"It gets worse," said Kenyon. "The code to the computer virus was here in England. The police think I tried to steal it. Somehow, they think that fake *Techno 69* has something to do with it."

DeWolfe slammed on the brakes; a lorry behind almost rear-ended them. "Do the police have the fake?" he asked.

"No, they don't know where it is," said Kenyon.

The truck driver angrily beeped his horn. deWolfe pulled over for a moment and rubbed his face. "Dear God, what is the matter with this world?"

Kenyon patted him on the back. "It's all right. We'll catch them, don't you worry."

DeWolfe smiled grimly. "You are a very brave man, Jack Kenyon, to be thinking about catching the murderers when the whole world is pursuing you."

"Yeah, well, I got a personal stake here. Unless I figure out who did it, they're going to lock me up and throw away the key."

DeWolfe squared his shoulders. "Well, whatever you do, you will not do it alone. I will help you."

"Thank you, Hadrian. I'm going to need all the help I can get."

DeWolfe put the car in gear and pulled back into traffic. "Where do we start?"

Kenyon sighed. "I don't know. I just wish Ricci hadn't been killed. I think he was going to spill the beans."

DeWolfe turned his head to Kenyon. "What do you mean, killed? Did he not commit suicide?"

"No. The police called me back last night to his apartment. Someone drugged him and slit his wrists to make it look like a suicide."

"So, if we find out who killed Ricci, we have the mastermind."

"I think I know who did it," said Kenyon. "I saw Raymond Legrand outside Ricci's apartment the night he as killed."

"You mean, the husband of Ilsa?"

"Yeah. I think Legrand killed Ricci because he was blackmailing Lydia."

Suddenly, deWolfe stared ahead. Traffic had slowed to a crawl in front of the houses of Parliament. "Keep down," he warned. "There are always policemen on duty out front."

Kenyon kept low in the seat until deWolfe gave the all clear. By the time he arose from under the dash, they were near the Thames, heading west.

"Where are you taking me?" asked the agent.

"I have a friend with a small apartment in town," said deWolfe. "He is gone for the month. You will be safe there."

They drove in silence for a few minutes, until deWolfe spoke. "How do you know Ricci was blackmailing Lydia?" he asked.

Kenyon stared out the window. "The police found compromising footage in Ricci's recorder."

DeWolfe pondered this for a moment, then continued. "But if Legrand killed him and made it look like a suicide, why would he not take the film?"

"I don't know," said Kenyon.

"I do." DeWolfe slapped his hand on the steering wheel. "Because he planted it."

"What?" said Kenyon. "Why would he do that?"

"How much do you know about Sir Rupert Ingoldsby?" asked deWolfe.

Kenyon shrugged. "Not much. He owns TEQ, the company that made the encryption code for the stolen virus. Other than that, he's just an old, drooling fart."

DeWolfe shook his head. "There was a time he would have killed you for saying that. During the Second World War, he was a senior intelligence officer. He was well known for his angry temper and ruthlessness."

"He must have been hell on his family."

"Ilsa, worst of all."

"He beat her?"

"No, he adored her. But she could not wed. No man would risk her hand in marriage, they all feared Sir Rupert so much."

"Legrand did."

"Sir Rupert bribed Legrand with a senior position in his firm," said deWolfe. "He comes from a distinguished family, but they've been broke for years. For a penniless Frenchman, it was a dream come true: a beautiful wife and a secure job. All he had to do was wait until the old man died. Only, he could not wait."

"What do you mean?" asked Kenyon.

"Are you aware that Legrand and Lydia were having an affair?"

"Yeah, I knew that."

"So did Ilsa," said deWolfe. "She was going to divorce him."

"So?"

"Legrand was used to riches and high society. He needed a new source of wealth."

"Are you saying he's the one trying to steal Cyberworm?" said Kenyon, incredulous. "No way. The guy's a bumbling private investigator!"

"Do not let the exterior fool you," said deWolfe. "He is a former intelligence officer with the French military. He is quite capable of anything."

Kenyon sat back and pondered the concept of Legrand as mastermind. "You know, it almost fits," he said. "He'd know about the project through his wife. He could probably gain access to the encryption code somehow. All he'd have to do then is arrange for a mule to pick up Simon's end of the virus in San Francisco. He works it so that Lydia and I end up taking the fall."

"Ingenious," said deWolfe.

"Hang on, though. There's a problem."

"What is that?" asked deWolfe.

"They found fifty thousand dollars with Dahg in San Francisco," said the agent. "If Legrand was broke, where'd he get the money to pay the mule? He'd need at least one hundred thousand dollars to set this up."

DeWolfe thought for a moment. "How much money was blackmailed from Lydia?"

"I don't know exactly, at least one hundred thousand pounds."

"Ah. Who do you think was blackmailing Lydia, Jack?"

They drove on for a while in silence. Kenyon's head was reeling. It all tied together: the mysterious e-mail, the blackmail of Lydia. "He set it up all so perfectly," he said.

"Not quite," said deWolfe. "Legrand did not expect Lydia to stumble on the false *Techno 69*. He killed her before he realized she had hidden it."

"Oh, God," said Kenyon, aloud.

"What?" asked deWolfe.

"I know where Lydia hid it."

"Where?" asked deWolfe.

"She hid it in her last will and testament," replied Kenyon.

DeWolfe stared at the agent, puzzled. "I do not understand. How can you hide a painting in a document?"

"She bequeathed a suitcase to Legrand in her will," said Kenyon. "The fake *Techno 69* must be in the suitcase."

"Of course," said deWolfe, understanding. "All we have to do is find the suitcase."

"We're too late," said Kenyon, grimly. "Legrand has it."

"What do you mean?"

"He was the one who broke into Lydia's house the other night," said Kenyon. "He stole something out of a hidden safe. It must have been the painting."

"This is terrible," said deWolfe. "We must stop him."

"How?" asked Kenyon, bitterly. "He's got every cop in town after me."

"Open the glove compartment," said deWolfe.

Kenyon flipped it open to see a Luger 9mm pistol laying on top of some maps.

"We must find Legrand and take him at gunpoint to the police," said deWolfe. "They will drop the charges and you will be free."

The traffic began to slow. DeWolfe peered ahead. "Oh, dear," he said.

"What's wrong?"

"There appears to be some sort of police roadblock."

Kenyon could see the lights of a police cruiser reflecting off the buildings about a block ahead. He lifted the Luger out of the glove compartment and checked the clip; it was loaded. He tucked the gun into his pants and pulled the Virginia Tech sweater down over the butt.

"Time to bail," he said, opening the passenger door.

DeWolfe reached over to grab Kenyon by the shoulder, but he was already out the door. "Where are you going?" shouted the evaluator at the retreating agent.

"I'll call you when I get there," said Kenyon. He closed the car door and quickly disappeared into the stream of pedestrians on the sidewalk.

Twenty-nine

Kenyon sprinted down the street for a block. Conscious of people staring at him as he ran, he forced himself to slow down to a more leisurely pace.

He had to get out of his running shorts and sweater. By now, the police would have sorted out the arrest of the three students and realize he was wearing a Virginia Tech sweater.

Kenyon noticed a charity shop on Old Brompton Road and stepped inside. Nodding at the clerk, he dug through a large pile of used clothes until he found a pair of baggy jeans and a black cotton T-shirt. Inside the change room, he pulled off the Virginia Tech sweater and his shorts and tried on the clothes. The waist of the trousers was a little baggy, but the pockets were large enough to conceal the Luger. Leaving his old clothes in the changing room, he paid the clerk three pounds for his new attire.

His cheap sunglasses in place, Kenyon returned to Old Brompton Road and headed toward the South Kensington station. He knew that it would be too dangerous to use the underground, but he needed to find Legrand's office. And for that, he needed to buy a map.

The South Kensington station was packed with students heading for the nearby Victoria and Albert Museum, which suited Kenyon fine. He found a kiosk with maps for sale, and bought a fold-out that showed the streets and parks in the downtown core. He paid for the map out of his dwindling resources, and thanked the clerk.

Just as Kenyon was turning to leave the station, he spotted the police. There were two of them, a man and a woman, and they were ascending the stairs that led to the underground platforms.

Kenyon knew better than to run. Instinctively, he dropped to one knee and pulled his shoelace loose. With any luck, they'd walk right by.

The pair advanced over to the kiosk, stopping to talk to the vendor. "I'll take a *Daily Express*," said the male cop.

Kenyon glanced over at their well-polished boots. His hands began to shake as he tried to tie his shoe.

"Here, you all right?" asked the woman cop.

Kenyon turned his head slightly and spoke in a soft, Irish brogue. "Me, oh yes, ma'am, I just have a touch of MS."

"Here, let me help." She bent down and quickly tied his shoe.

"Thank you," he said. "You're very kind."

She smiled to him as she stood up. "Enjoy your day."

"I will."

The pair resumed their patrol. Kenyon, his back curled to hide his height, turned and slowly walked in the opposite direction.

Out on the street, Kenyon quickly straightened up and began to run. Just ahead, a double-decker bus was waiting at a stop. Kenyon entered onto the platform adjacent to the driver and pulled out his underground pass. "Is this good on the bus?"

The driver smiled. "Good for the whole day. Where you headed?"

"I thought I'd see some of the sights downtown," said Kenyon.

"This bus will take you right to Big Ben."

Kenyon made his way up the circular flight of steps to the top of the bus. There was an open seat near the front, and he made himself comfortable.

Sitting above the traffic was an unusual feeling. The agent could see far ahead down the road. It was around six in the evening and the streets were crowded with taxis. Everyone was making their way home for the weekend, he thought.

He longed to be home in San Francisco watching the Giants with Marge, or running on the pathways around the Bay, or just having a burger and a beer with the gang. With a start, he suddenly realized that he might never see his friends, or San Francisco, again. The thought depressed him. Somehow, he had to settle this mess and settle it fast.

Kenyon leaned back in his seat and turned his thoughts to Raymond Legrand. DeWolfe had said he was ruthless. He had a hard time imagining Legrand as a spy, but Kenyon had enough experience with counterespionage to know that the most innocuous people were often the most dangerous. He had already suffered a nasty bang on the head the night Legrand had broken into his home; he was lucky the man hadn't taken the time to finish him off for good.

The bus came to a stop. "End of the line," said the driver over the intercom.

Kenyon got off. The streets were crowded with tourists gawking at the Parliament building and nearby Westminster Abbey. Kenyon headed east, toward the Thames, and found a relatively quiet park. He sat down on a bench and pulled Legrand's business card out of his wallet, the one the private investigator had given him the day he and Happy Harry had waylaid him.

The address for R.L. Investigations was for Lincoln's Inn, near Tanya's office. Looking at the map he could see it was only about a mile from where he was sitting. He could walk there in half an hour.

Map in hand, he headed north. A little after seven the traffic in central London started to ebb. The narrow streets that ran between the long rows of office buildings in the downtown core fell silent. Kenyon could see the occasional cleaner moving through a building, emptying waste baskets. He picked up his pace, worried that everyone at R.L. Investigations would be gone by the time he got there.

Lincoln's Inn Road was a wide street that skirted a spacious park. Kenyon circled the open green space, glancing at the brass plates on the buildings as he walked, until he came to R.L. Investigations.

Legrand's building was four stories tall, with a facade of red brick. White limestone trimmed the arched windows. The entrance was guarded by a black, wrought-iron gate. Kenyon noted a security camera discreetly mounted on an arm to allow a full view of the entrance.

Legrand's car was parked out front. The battered Range Rover looked just as decrepit as the last time he had seen it.

A set of tennis courts were situated right across from R.L. Investigation's office. Several people were working up a sweat on the asphalt courts. Kenyon entered the park and found a bench that faced the building, then sat down to watch the play.

The agent wondered how far he would go to make Legrand talk. The weight of the Luger in his pocket was reassuring; he'd go as far as he had to.

Kenyon sat quietly at the bench, watching the front entrance, but no one came out. By ten, night had descended, and the tennis players were gone. It was time to make a move.

Crossing the park, Kenyon stopped at a garbage can. Someone had thrown away a small brown cardboard box with a courier sticker on the side. The agent picked up the box and crossed the street toward R.L. Investigations.

As Kenyon walked up the front steps, he scratched his forehead, obscuring his face from the security camera. He hoped that nobody was manning the monitor this late at night.

There was a buzzer to the left of the main door, on the opposite side of the camera. Kenyon gave a silent thanks to the incompetent technician who had set that up as he pushed the button.

"What is it?" came a man's voice.

"Delivery for R.L. Investigations," said Kenyon.

There was a pause. "We are closed."

"Says here, 'Attention Raymond Legrand. Special evening delivery.'"

There was a second pause. "Just a moment."

Kenyon stood by the door, careful to keep his face away from the camera and the package visible. *Come on, come on baby*, he said under his breath. *Show me how dumb you really are.*

There was the sound of a bolt being drawn, then the heavy door creaked open. The pale face of Raymond Legrand shone in the interior light. "Where do I sign?" he asked.

"Right here." Kenyon drew the Luger out from under the package and shoved it in his face. "Now step inside. Move."

Plainly shocked by the sudden appearance of the gun-wielding agent, Legrand did as he was told. Kenyon entered behind him and slammed the door shut.

The interior hallway led to a reception room decorated with dark wood wainscoting and cream walls. Kenyon glanced about, wary of taking his eyes off Legrand for long. The main floor appeared deserted.

"Anybody else here?" asked Kenyon.

"No," said Legrand. "I am alone."

Legrand was dressed in a dark blue, pinstripe suit and silk tie, only he had taken off the jacket. "Give me your tie," said Kenyon.

"What?"

"The tie. Take it off."

Legrand removed the tie from around his neck.

"Turn around and put your hands behind your back."

Legrand did as he was told, and Kenyon quickly knotted the tie around his wrists.

"Now we go upstairs," said Kenyon.

The two men ascended the stairs of the building, Kenyon close behind Legrand. At each landing, he paused and glanced quickly about, but the offices on each floor seemed to be empty.

The topmost floor had been fixed up as a living suite, with the floors covered in Persian rugs and the walls painted a pale cream. Glancing through the front window, Kenyon could see the distant spires of the Royal Courts of Justice. He took Legrand into the living room and pushed him down on a couch, glancing in at the single bedroom and bathroom. They were deserted. He came back into the living room and sat down across from his captive.

Resting on the coffee table between them was a Louis Vuitton briefcase. It was large enough to hold a small painting.

Legrand, his hands still tied behind his back, tried to shift around.

"Do you mind?" he asked. "This is very uncomfortable. My hands are beginning to go numb."

Confident that he could handle the older man, Kenyon came around and loosened his bonds. Legrand rubbed his wrists for a few moments until the circulation returned before he spoke. When he did, it was a question. "May I ask you something?"

"Go ahead," Kenyon said.

"Why are you doing this to me?"

"Because I know all about your scheme," said Kenyon.

Legrand stared at him, perplexed. "What scheme?"

"Your scheme to steal the Cyberworm virus."

"I don't know what you're talking about."

"I didn't expect you to admit anything," said Kenyon. "But we'll be able to prove it all in a court of law."

"Prove what?"

"For starters, you subverted Simon at Nebula Labs, then killed him when he delivered the goods."

"Ridiculous," said Legrand. "I don't even know anyone named Simon."

"Then, we'll prove you killed Lydia.

"You are truly delusional," said Legrand. "I *loved* Lydia."

"She was nothing to you," said Kenyon. "Just like Ricci."

"Ricci? Lydia's gallery manager?"

Kenyon leaned forward. "Yes, your accomplice. I *saw* you outside Bruno Ricci's apartment near Harrod's the night he was killed. You murdered him because he was going to squeal on you about *Techno 69*."

"This is complete madness," said Legrand.

"Is it?" Kenyon pointed to the briefcase. "Open it."

Legrand stared at the briefcase, his face suddenly pale. "No."

Kenyon stuck the barrel of the Luger in his face. "I said, open it."

Legrand reluctantly drew the briefcase to himself and unlocked the clasps. He began to lift the top open.

"Stop!" said Kenyon. "Hand it here."

Legrand pushed the partially open briefcase across the coffee table to Kenyon. Holding the Luger in his right hand, he cautiously opened the briefcase and peered inside.

The Louis Vuitton was filled with a large pile of papers and photographs. Most of the papers were newspaper clippings. All the photographs showed Kenyon.

The agent stared at the pile in disbelief. "What is *this*?"

"It is your life," replied Legrand.

Kenyon flipped through the pile. Some of the photographs were taken when he was a young boy. "Is this some kind of surveillance file you kept on me?"

"No," replied Legrand. "Lydia accumulated it, ever since you were a baby."

Kenyon read some of the newspaper clippings. One was an account from a Boseman, Montana, newspaper when he had won the state football championship with his high school team. Another was the notice of his acceptance into the FBI.

"This is what Lydia bequeathed to you in her will?"

"Yes," said Legrand.

"And this is what you broke into my house to steal?"

"Yes," replied Legrand. "I am sorry if I hurt you with the door. I did not mean to do it. I panicked."

"I just have one question," said Kenyon. "Why would my mother bequeath this to *you*?"

Legrand stared at his hands in his lap for a long moment.

"Because I am your father," he finally replied.

Thirty

Kenyon leveled the gun at Legrand's heart. "You're lying."

Legrand placed his hands on his knees and slowly eased himself erect. "May I pour a drink?"

Kenyon waved the barrel of the Luger in assent.

Legrand walked slowly over to a sideboard and opened a door to reveal a well-stocked liquor cabinet. He pulled out a dark bottle of liqueur and poured a thimble into a glass, then mixed it with soda water. The smell of black currant drifted across the room.

"Cassis," he explained, holding it up.

Legrand poured a second drink, this time a scotch. He returned to the couch and offered it to Kenyon. "I believe this is your favorite?"

"I'll pass," said the agent. "As I said, I think you're a liar and a fraud."

"You are perfectly correct," he agreed. "I am both. But even a scoundrel such as myself may have an interesting story to tell."

Legrand settled back into the couch and sipped his drink. "Let me take you back to the early 1970s," he said. "I was a young man, just out of military service for my native country of France, and I was living the high life in England."

Legrand tilted his head, recollecting. "You should have seen me then," he said. "I was young and brash, so full of myself. I could conquer the world." He nodded toward Kenyon. "When I look at you now, it is just like peering into a mirror into the past."

Kenyon scowled, not pleased with the comparison. "Does any of this have a point?"

"I bore you?" Legrand smiled. "The impetuousness of youth. Do not worry; there is, I assure you, a point to my story." Legrand took another sip of his drink. "As I was saying, it was the early 1970s. I began working for Sir Rupert Ingoldsby."

"I'd hardly call it a job," replied Kenyon. "You made a deal with him to marry Ilsa."

"Sir Rupert drove a hard bargain," said Legrand. "One of the conditions of my lucrative employment was the hand of his daughter in marriage."

"It must have been tough."

Legrand stood and went to refresh his drink. "I must confess, I found it easy, at first. Ilsa was not without her charms, and I looked forward to eventually inheriting the fruits of Sir Rupert's labors."

"But it went sour, didn't it?"

Legrand returned to the couch. "Ilsa wanted a family badly, but it was not to be. After several years of trying, the doctors finally told us Ilsa could not have children."

"That's not enough to ruin a marriage."

"You are correct. It is I who ruined the marriage. When Ilsa found out that she could not have a family, she threw herself with a passion into horse jumping. She was often gone for long periods of time to competitions."

"And you started tomcatting around."

Legrand waved his glass in the air. "I had affairs with a tennis instructor at Wimbledon and a young model at Ascot," he said. "They meant nothing to me. I was careful to keep my dalliances secret from Ilsa."

"Smart move," said Kenyon. "I've seen her shoot."

"She has her father's volcanic temper," agreed Legrand. "And it would have remained dormant, were it not for one mistake."

"What was that?" asked Kenyon.

"Lydia," replied Legrand. "It was the fall of 1977. By this time, Sir Rupert had set up this private investigation business to keep me busy."

"I'll bet you were snooping into his business partners," said Kenyon.

"What can I say?" replied Legrand. "The world is full of scoundrels."

It takes one to know one, thought Kenyon. He almost smiled.

"Ilsa was in Belgium at an equestrian event," continued Legrand. "The weather in London was very hot for that time of the year, and the streets were alive with young people. I went down to Soho one Saturday evening to a cafe. That is where I met your mother."

"What was she like?" asked Kenyon.

"She was very pretty," said Legrand. "Her hair was long and straight, like a golden waterfall, and she wore a tiny pair of blue granny glasses on the tip of her nose."

"Did you talk to her?"

"Oh, no. Not at first. I was too shy. I simply sat in a corner and listened to her play the guitar."

"She played the guitar?" asked Kenyon.

"And she sang," said Legrand. "She had a voice like an angel. I finally got up the courage to ask her to sing a song for me: 'Lili Marlene.'"

"Did she sing it?"

"No. She only knew Joan Baez. But she did laugh at my shirt and tie. She said I looked like a fuddy-duddy."

"What did you do?"

"I bought a pink silk shirt and came back the next night."

Kenyon couldn't help but smile at the thought of the hapless Frenchman in such a get-up. "What did she say when she saw you?"

"She said I looked like a circus clown," replied Legrand. "My ears burned in shame, and I turned away, but she grabbed my arm and hugged me. She said she was just *teasing* me. I did not like this teasing, but at the same time, she filled my soul with sunlight. I had never met an American girl before. She was so vibrant, so full of fun. For the first time in my life, I knew what it was like to lose my heart to another."

Kenyon picked up the scotch and took a sip. "Tell me more."

"I came to the cafe, night after night, and watched her perform," said Legrand. "Then, one evening, she disappeared."

"What happened?" asked Kenyon.

"The cafe owner told me she had gone to help some squatters take over a government warehouse by Waterloo Station. I rushed over, and there they were, hundreds of them, all trapped in the building by a ring of police."

"Where was Lydia?"

"On the rooftop, singing songs of protest," said Legrand. "I snuck inside through a back entrance and joined her, shouting defiance at the police"

"How long did you hold out?" asked Kenyon.

"Three glorious days," said Legrand. "Every day, we would hurl insults at the police, and every night we would sneak out to bring food back to our comrades. It finally ended when the building burst into flames."

"The cops set fire to it?" asked Kenyon.

"No. We were trying to roast a pig in an old steel drum and we set the floor ablaze," said Legrand. "We all had to flee."

Kenyon tucked the gun into his waistband. "What happened next?" he asked.

"We came back here." Legrand waved his hand around the flat. "It was late, and we were covered with soot. We lit some candles, and climbed into the old claw-foot tub in the *salle-de-bain*. I scrubbed upon her back with a bar of soap. She turned, and held me close, and kissed me. I knew that I would love her the rest of my life."

Both men sat quietly for a few moments. Finally, Kenyon broke the silence. "What happened?"

Legrand sighed. "Ilsa returned from her competition. I tried to keep my newly stirred passions hidden within my heart, but a woman can see right through a man. She knew that something was amiss. Then Lydia came to me with the news that she was pregnant."

"Me?" asked Kenyon.

Legrand nodded toward the bedroom. "You were conceived here, that night. When I learned, my soul was filled with joy, and I wanted to leave my wife and run away with Lydia."

"But you didn't?"

"No. Tragedy struck." .

"Ilsa found out?" asked Legrand.

"Worse. Sir Rupert discovered my transgression." Legrand smiled bitterly. "It seems that he kept an eye on all of his business partners, including me. He was terribly upset."

"What business was it of his?" said Kenyon. "This was between you and Lydia and Ilsa."

Legrand shook his head. "The old man was being considered for his knighthood, and he feared that the news would cause him to be taken off the Queen's Christmas list. He wanted to avoid a scandal, at any cost."

"What did he do?" asked Kenyon.

"He secretly went to Lydia," said Legrand. "He threatened to harm the child if she went through with the pregnancy. She packed her bags and fled."

"Why didn't you follow her?" asked Kenyon.

"I had no idea what happened," said Legrand. "The landlord of her flat said she left in a hurry, with no forwarding address."

"Didn't you wonder about your child?"

"Every day. The torment of not knowing what had happened almost drove me mad." Legrand gestured with his arm. "What had I said? What had I done? I thought she had left because of me."

Kenyon thought about the birth certificate that Deaver had shown him. "She went back to Montana, where I was born," he said. "Then she returned to London."

Legrand stared off into the distance, and sighed. "The day I saw her walking down the street, I almost fell to my knees," he said. "I hugged her and I wept for joy."

"And Lydia?"

Legrand arose, and went to stand by the window. "Something in her had changed. The spark of life still burned fiercely, but the joy was gone." He stared down into the empty street. "I asked her what had happened to our child, and she told me that she had terminated the pregnancy." Legrand turned to Kenyon. "For most of your life, I never even knew you existed."

Kenyon wanted to know more. "What happened between you and Lydia after she returned?"

Legrand shrugged. "We didn't speak of our passion for many years. Lydia opened a gallery and became very successful. She surrounded herself with the sparkling lights of society, including my wife. We all pretended to be happy."

"How long did that last?"

"Over thirty years," said Legrand. "And then, one night late last year, Lydia invited me to her home. She told me how Sir Rupert had threatened you with harm. She explained how she had hidden you at her parents' home, cutting off all contact."

"I can't believe he threatened her that badly," said Kenyon.

"I know Sir Rupert," said Legrand. "If he had known the truth, your life, and Lydia's, would have been in grave jeopardy."

"Why did she suddenly tell you, after so long?" asked Kenyon.

"Sir Rupert had a stroke," said Legrand. "It crippled him. Overnight, he went from being a dangerous enemy to a feeble old man. Lydia was no longer afraid of him. She could finally reveal the truth."

"And did the truth set *you* free?"

"No. I went to Ilsa and told her about Lydia and you, that it was all in the past. I had hoped she would understand in some way, but it was not to be." Legrand shuddered. "She was furious. She said she'd have her revenge on us all."

Kenyon thought about the time he had innocently wandered into her gunsights. He was glad she hadn't taken the opportunity to load him with buckshot right then and there. "What about me?" he asked. "When was I going to find out?"

"Lydia wrote you a letter," said Legrand. "She was killed before she had a chance to mail it."

Kenyon stood at the window overlooking the park for a long time, breathing the night air and thinking. Far off in the distance, the spires of the Royal Courts of Justice gleamed in their spotlights. *Where's the justice in any of this?* Kenyon thought. *Where's the justice for me?* Kenyon didn't even notice Legrand was gone until he returned with a humidor.

"Care for a cigar?" he asked.

Kenyon declined and Legrand lit one up, then sat down on the couch, where he silently puffed away.

There was something about the smell of the cigar that took Kenyon's memory back to the day in San Francisco. He thought about the stakeout, and how it had gone wrong. The pool of blood under Simon flashed before his eyes, then the chase through San Francisco. And finally, the abandoned warehouse, where he had stalked up to the office, following the suspect's scent.

The scent of a cigar.

Kenyon placed one hand on the butt of his Luger and turned to Legrand. "How do I know any of it is true? How do I know that it's not a complete pile of bullshit?"

Legrand put down his cigar and walked over to a small writing desk that served as a phone stand. "If there was someone you trust who could confirm my story, then would you believe me?" asked Legrand.

"Who?" replied Kenyon, laughing in derision. "Sir Rupert?"

"No. Someone you've known all your life." Legrand began to dial a number.

"Who are you calling?" asked Kenyon.

"Cyrus."

Kenyon held Legrand's phone, picturing the other end in his mind. Cyrus would be standing by the wood-burning stove, holding the ancient black hand-piece of the wall phone in his right hand.

"It's all my fault," Cyrus said, in a deep, cavernous voice. "I hated to live a lie, Jack. It hurt me deep."

"Why didn't you tell me?" asked Kenyon.

There was a pause. "I was ashamed. I couldn't stand folks around here thinkin' you was a bastard."

"Did you hate me for it?"

"No, I hated myself. But I took it out on you. I'm sorry, son."

Kenyon's throat constricted. It was the first time in his life Cyrus had ever apologized to him. For anything. "I forgive you," said Kenyon.

"Thank you, son. I love you."

That was the first time Cyrus had ever told him that, as well. "I love you too, dad."

There was a pause. For a moment, Kenyon thought the line had gone dead, but then he heard Cyrus' voice again.

"I ain't your dad anymore, Jack. I'm your grandfather. I don't know this Legrand feller, but he's your real father now. Don't let him slip away."

"I won't, Cyrus. I'll talk to you again, soon."

Kenyon hung up the phone and turned to Legrand. For several moments, the two men stood staring at one another.

Finally, Kenyon spoke. "You got a place I can stay for the night?"

Thirty-one

Friday, July 15

When Kenyon awoke on the couch the morning sun was coming through the window of Legrand's flat. The Frenchman was in the kitchen, cooking on the gas stove. The smell of coffee and bacon hung in the air, making Kenyon's stomach growl in appreciation.

Legrand noticed Kenyon was awake. "I hope you had a comfortable rest."

Kenyon pushed the blanket off his shoulders and sat up. "I slept like a log."

"Excellent. A good night's sleep always makes for a good morning's appetite, no?" Legrand carried the frying pan to a small dining table, where he loaded up a plate. With a flourish, he invited Kenyon to join him.

Kenyon sat down while Legrand poured the coffee. In addition to a large helping of bacon, the plate in front of him was heaped with toasted bread and an omelet. The agent realized that he hadn't eaten for over a day. He dug right in.

"This is great," said Kenyon, pointing to the omelet. "What's in it?"

"Some fresh mushrooms and onions." Legrand, coffee in hand, joined him at the table. "I fry them in butter and pepper, then fold the concoction into the omelet with a slice of brie."

"It's delicious," said Kenyon, his mouth full. "I could eat two."

Legrand laughed. "I am afraid this is all I have. I was not expecting company."

Suddenly, Kenyon realized the predicament his presence had put Legrand into. He put down his fork and stood to leave.

"Where are you going?" asked Legrand.

"Away," said Kenyon. "Just being here could get you into a lot of trouble."

"Do not leave," demanded Legrand. "It is extremely important that we talk, first."

Kenyon reluctantly sat down again. "About what?"

"Someone went to great lengths to set both of us up for some espionage plot. Whoever did that is far more dangerous than the police. Before you leave this house, I want to know who did it, and why."

Kenyon sipped his coffee. It was hot and strong, the way he liked it. "Before I say anything else, there's one thing I have to know," said Kenyon.

"What is that?"

"Did you kill Bruno Ricci?"

"No," replied Legrand, staring him straight in the eye. "I did not even know it was his apartment, until you told me."

"Then what were you doing there?" asked Kenyon.

"I was following a man. His name is Hadrian deWolfe."

"*Hadrian?*" Kenyon stared at Legrand.

"You know him?" asked Legrand.

"Yeah," replied Kenyon, suddenly on guard. "He's an art evaluator from Switzerland."

"That is his cover," said Legrand. "He was a paid informant for the SVR, the Soviet Foreign Intelligence service. For a while, he worked as a double agent for MI6. He was considered quite useful."

"What happened to him?" asked Kenyon.

"The SVR suspected his treachery, and he fled to Britain. There were rumors he was subsequently involved with arranging arms for terrorists in the Middle East. Nothing was ever proven, but he was too suspect for MI6 to keep on."

"Is that why you were following him?" asked Kenyon.

"No." Legrand stared at his hands in his lap. "I believe he was having an affair with my wife."

Kenyon's head started to spin. "*Ilsa?*"

"Yes. Once she learned of the ancient affair between Lydia and myself, she became very distant and cold. At first, I assumed it was because of me, but soon, I began to suspect there was someone else involved." Legrand stared off into the distance. "She would leave Ingoldsby Manor and come home at odd hours. There were phone calls. When I answered the other person would abruptly hang up." Legrand turned his gaze to Kenyon. "Eventually I had one of my staff follow her. He tailed her late one night to a small apartment in Kensington."

"Near Lydia's?" asked Kenyon.

"Yes," said Legrand. "My investigator observed deWolfe arrive shortly after. They stayed there until early in the morning."

"That doesn't prove they were having an affair."

"Of course not," agreed Legrand, ruefully. "Perhaps they were just playing bridge."

"Did you ever confront her?" asked Kenyon.

"I asked her face to face if she was involved with another man. She did not answer my accusation, she simply ordered me to leave Ingoldsby Manor." Legrand waved a hand around the apartment. "I have been here ever since."

Kenyon sipped his coffee for a moment, thinking about deWolfe. Why had he fingered Ricci as the man who might have the fake *Techno 69*? "Tell me about the night you followed deWolfe," he said. "The night Ricci was killed."

"I had been staked out for several hours in front of his apartment when I saw him leave at about 10:00 PM," said Legrand. "I thought he might be heading for an assignation with my wife. I followed him in my car."

Kenyon took another sip of his coffee. "What did he do?" he asked.

Legrand shrugged. "He parked behind Harrod's and went into the apartment. He stayed for about one hour, then came out. I followed him, but he simply returned to the flat."

"When did he leave Ricci's?" asked Kenyon.

"Shortly after 11:00 PM."

"Was deWolfe carrying anything when he left? Something fairly big, like a painting?"

"Not that I recall," replied Legrand.

Kenyon pondered for a moment. "You said deWolfe's apartment is in Kensington."

"Yes, it is near Lydia's—your—home," said Legrand.

Kenyon tucked the Luger into his pocket and headed for the stairs. "Let's go."

Legrand jumped up and followed him. "Where?"

"To pay a visit to Hadrian deWolfe."

The inside of Legrand's Range Rover was a lot cleaner than the exterior, which pleased Kenyon. He was also grateful for the tinted glass, He wouldn't have to crouch down to conceal himself from the police.

Traffic through downtown London was fairly light, and the two men made good time. After about twenty minutes, they reached Hyde Park, and headed west along Kensington High Street until they came to Gloucester Road. They turned left and headed south.

Legrand turned off Gloucester Road and meandered through a mews until he came to a spot just around the corner from Lydia's. He nodded to an empty parking stall marked "Private." "DeWolfe usually parks his car here," he said. "He must be out."

"Just as well," said Kenyon. "It gives us a chance to scout around."

A group of workmen were busy drilling a hole in the roadway near the front of deWolfe's apartment. Legrand pulled the Rover in behind their truck and parked. He then got out, flipped up the back hatch and began rummaging in the tailgate area, filling up a rucksack with various items.

Kenyon joined the PI at the back of the Rover. "What are you doing?"

"Since Monsieur deWolfe is not home, I suspect we will need a few things they did not hand out in Quantico." Legrand handed Kenyon a pair of latex gloves. "Put these on."

They walked toward the front door of deWolfe's apartment block. It was part of a row of townhouses similar in design to Lydia's, but divided into apartments. They reached the front door, which was locked. Legrand peered through the glass at the top of the door, then pulled a seagull's feather out of his jacket pocket. Inserting it through the crack at the top of the door, he began to wiggle it back and forth.

"What are you doing?" asked Kenyon.

"There is a motion detector that automatically unlocks the door as you leave," said Legrand. "The motion of the feather activates it."

"Where'd you learn that?" asked Kenyon.

"From a cat burglar in Marseille."

There was an audible click, and the PI pushed the door open. The foyer of the building led to a steep flight of stairs. They ascended for several floors, finally emerging at the topmost landing.

Legrand fished around in the duffel bag, pulling out a thin tube attached to a small LCD display panel. He pushed the tube under the door. An image of the flat appeared on the tiny monitor. Legrand gently twisted the tube, and the image did a pan of the interior. As far as he could see, the apartment was deserted. "No one is home," he announced.

"Great, but how do we get in?" said Kenyon. The door was solid wood, with a deadbolt locking it shut. "We'd need a forklift truck to bust down this door."

"We have something better," said Legrand. He fished around in his duffel bag again and drew out a small car jack and a telescoping steel pole. He attached the pole to the top of the jack, then expanded the pole until it was the width of the hallway. "Hold the end of the pole against the deadbolt," he commanded Kenyon, as he braced the base of the jack against the far wall.

The agent stared at the pole. "You know, I could get in a lot of trouble for this."

Legrand gave him a look. "Tell me, do they still hang spies in your country?"

"Good point." Kenyon lifted the pole and held it against the lock.

Legrand cranked the jack several times, until the pole was snug against the lock.

"This is going to make a hell of a bang when it goes," says Kenyon. "Won't somebody hear it?"

"Not if we time it correctly," said Legrand. Just then, the road crew outside began work and Legrand cranked the jack several times. The sharp crack of the splintering wood was drowned out by the din outside. The two men quickly entered the flat.

The tiny apartment consisted of a living room, kitchen, bathroom and bedroom. Legrand glanced through the kitchen cupboards. Most of the shelves were bare, with only a few condiments and scattered jars. The bathroom was equally Spartan, with a roll of toilet paper on the loo and a bar of hotel soap in the sink. There was no sign of a painting.

Kenyon entered the bedroom. A double bed occupied one wall; it had been slept in, but not made. A large bureau stood against another wall, closed. A gabled window looked north.

The agent walked over to the window and looked out. He was startled to see that the window overlooked the park that fronted Lydia's street. He could plainly see the front of her home.

A pair of powerful binoculars sat on a table beside the bed. Kenyon adjusted the lens for his eyes and peered out. The door of Lydia's home appeared so close it seemed he was standing on the front porch. He angled the sightlines higher and could see right into Lydia's bedroom.

Kenyon continued to scan the street. He suspected that the police would have set up a surveillance post in case he returned. The agent's practiced eye soon picked up the crew: an electrical contractor's truck was parked about one hundred feet up the road. Two men in coveralls were standing on the far side of the van, conferring. Kenyon glanced at his watch; it was eleven. Probably shift change, he thought. Curious to see if there was any other surveillance watching his house, the agent opened the window and leaned out.

The view down the street was blocked by a small saucer. At first, Kenyon thought it was a TV satellite dish, but he took a closer look and realized that it was the same type of dish used by the FBI when they mounted surveillance. A black electrical cord led out the back of the dish and into the room. Kenyon followed the line into the back of the large bureau. The agent opened the bureau. It was empty except for a large aluminum briefcase on the floor. Kenyon leaned forward and snapped the clasps on the case. Inside, couched in soft foam, were a sophisticated digital receiver, recorder, and cell phone.

"Raymond, get in here," said Kenyon.

Legrand entered and scanned the equipment. "It would appear deWolfe has a tap on someone's line." Legrand pressed rewind on the recorder and let it spin for several seconds, then stopped it and pressed play.

"Marge," Kenyon heard his own voice over the speaker. "It's Jack calling. Ricci didn't commit suicide; he was murdered. The cops think I did it, but I saw Legrand there that night. I think he was out to revenge a blackmail plot. I need to know how to handle this. Call me as soon as you can."

Kenyon sat down on the edge of the bed, stunned.

Legrand rewound some more tape, and the men heard Kenyon talking about his findings at TEQ. He rewound further and there was Kenyon's lament about Ricci's death.

"God, I yapped about the whole case!" said Kenyon. "No wonder deWolfe knew so much. The bastard's been stringing me along like a fool."

Legrand picked up the cell phone and turned it on. He activated the previous call's function and a number appeared on the screen. The investigator handed it to Kenyon. "Is that your number?"

Kenyon shook his head. "No, I don't know whose it is. Only one way to find out, though." He pressed the send button.

The phone rang for a moment, then was answered. "Hello?" said a woman's voice. "Hadrian?"

Neither man said anything. There was no need. It was Ilsa.

Kenyon disconnected the phone, and the two men left.

Thirty-two

Kenyon and Legrand sat on a park bench on the south shore of the Thames. A flock of pigeons mooched for crumbs at their feet. Legrand was staring out over the river.

"You okay?" asked Kenyon.

Legrand shrugged. He continued to stare silently into the flowing river.

The agent was glad that Legrand was quiet; he needed time to think. Ever since they had left the apartment, his mind had been racing to make sense of what was happening.

Obviously, deWolfe had used him to try and find the fake *Techno 69*. He had snuck in under the guise of Lydia's friendship and planted a bug, then strung him along. There was no doubt now in the agent's mind that deWolfe had murdered Ricci. But why? What made the forgery valuable enough to kill over?

It had to have something to do with the Cyberworm investigation. Deaver and Arundel had been willing to make a deal with Kenyon to turn over the painting. They already suspected he had the virus. Somehow it must have something to do with the encryption code.

Kenyon turned to Legrand. "You ever hear of a painting called *Techno 69*?"

Legrand stared at Kenyon for a moment, obviously caught up in his own thoughts. "Yes," he finally replied. "It is a Maggote."

"How do you know about it?"

"Ilsa bought it for the TEQ Corporation and hung it in the board-room. I hated it. Little blobs of paint on bits of transistors. That is not art, it is garbage."

Kenyon ignored the art criticism. "So, you worked at TEQ?"

"Yes. I consulted with Dr. MacQuaig over security."

"Then you know about Cyberworm," said Kenyon.

"Only in the vaguest terms. It is some sort of software, no?"

"Yeah, a real bad-ass virus. It was developed by Nebula Labs in San Francisco."

"Ah!" said Legrand, suddenly animated. "An American scientist showed up several months ago from Nebula. A very suspicious fellow. Dr. MacQuaig said he was trying to get the encryption code. He sent him on his way."

"What happened to the painting?" asked Kenyon.

Legrand thought for a moment. "Ilsa donated it to charity. Dr. MacQuaig told me Lydia came and picked it up two days before the auction."

So, Lydia had the painting for two days, more than enough to make the switch and conceal it, thought Kenyon. But it wasn't in her house; it wasn't in her gallery. Legrand didn't have it. Garbajian didn't have it. Where did she hide it?

Perhaps she had said something to Legrand. "When was the last time you talked to Lydia?" asked Kenyon.

The PI stood up and walked to the ledge overlooking the river. "On the night of the auction," he finally replied.

"I'm surprised you were invited."

Legrand turned and smiled ruefully at Kenyon. "Ilsa likes to keep up appearances. I was there as co-host."

"That must have been pretty uncomfortable," said Kenyon.

Legrand shrugged. "She was not there for much of the night, fortunately."

Kenyon was suddenly interested. "Why not?"

"Gladys, the maid, came down from the upstairs midway through the auction. It seems Sir Rupert had a setback, and was calling for her. I didn't see her again that evening."

"Tell me about the auction," said Kenyon.

"It was a large affair, with several hundred people" said Legrand. "Ilsa has been holding them for about ten years. We used to stage them in the main drawing room, but they had become so popular that we had to set up a reception tent on the lawn."

Kenyon thought back to the auction video. Lydia dressed in her long, red silk evening gown and string of pearls. "What was Lydia doing?"

"It would be easier to tell you what she was *not* doing," said Legrand. "Between greeting guests, attending the kitchen, and overseeing the preparations, she barely had a moment of rest."

"Did you speak to her before the auction?"

"I tried, but she only had her girl there, Zoë, and there was much to attend to. It wasn't until after the auction that we had a moment alone."

Kenyon thought for a moment. "What kind of a mood was she in?"

Legrand turned away from the river and came back to the bench. He sat down and faced Kenyon. "She was very agitated."

"Did you ask what was bugging her?"

Legrand nodded. "She brought out a letter from her purse."

"Who was it for?"

"It was addressed to you," said Legrand. "She said it revealed everything."

Kenyon wondered if Lydia had left a clue to the whereabouts of the fake painting. "Did you read it?"

"No," replied Legrand. "I did not want to read it. And I did not want her to send it."

"Why not?"

Legrand looked Kenyon in the eye. "I was afraid you would hate her, and that she would be crushed. I wanted her to leave well enough alone. When I told her that, she became very angry at me, and left." The PI turned and stared out over the river. "That is the last I ever saw of her alive."

Kenyon thought about what Bernie the gardener had told him; Lydia had stormed out of the house, smashed the rear of her car, then roared off down the road. To her doom.

"What became of the letter?" Kenyon finally asked.

"I called a friend in the coroner's office," said Legrand. "They did not recover the letter. I thought it might still be in her car."

Kenyon had a sudden flash. "So, *you* had it released from police custody, and searched it at the dealership," said Kenyon. "Did you find the letter?"

"No."

Another dead end, thought Kenyon. Lydia *had* to have left some sort of clue. "Did she ever say anything to you about the *Techno 69* painting?"

"No." Legrand held a finger up, as though remembering. "But, she did say one thing that puzzled me."

"What's that?"

"She said, 'If Jack should ever ask, tell him to look for the secret behind my smile.'"

Kenyon stood up from the bench and headed for the Rover. "Let's go," he called over his shoulder.

"Where are we going?" asked the PI.

"To check out a smile."

Legrand, bewildered, followed Kenyon.

They crossed the Thames and meandered their way north through side streets until they came to a quiet lane lined with tall, Georgian mansions. Kenyon directed Legrand to park at the side of the street under the shade of a plane tree.

"Who lives here?" asked Legrand.

"A mutual friend," replied Kenyon. "Come on, I want you to meet her."

The two men got out of the car and approached the building. Kenyon glanced up; the balcony doors to Tanya O'Neill's apartment were open. She was home. He pushed the buzzer at the front door. "Tanya, it's Jack," he said.

Kenyon glanced at Legrand. The older man's eyes had gone wide, and he looked a little pale. "You all right?" asked the agent.

Legrand nodded yes. The door lock clicked, and the two men advanced.

O'Neill was waiting for them at the top of the stairs. She wore a pair of cream-colored Capri pants and a sapphire blouse; Kenyon couldn't help but admire her beauty.

"What is *he* doing here?" she asked, when she saw Legrand.

"I asked him to come," said Kenyon. "We have something important to talk about. Together."

O'Neill looked skeptical, but she motioned the two men to enter her flat.

They all walked into the living room. Kenyon advanced to the painting of Lydia that hung over the mantelpiece; the burgundy frame was identical to the scraps of wood he had found in the garbage can in Lydia's studio.

O'Neill was studiously avoiding Legrand, turning her back to him. "Why are you here?" she asked Kenyon.

The agent pointed to the portrait of Lydia. "Why did you paint this?"

O'Neill turned to Legrand. "It was my present to her, to show my love."

Legrand remained silent.

Kenyon continued. "When we first met, you commented on how much alike Lydia and I looked. Do you remember?"

"Yes," said O'Neill. "I recall."

Legrand finally spoke. "There is a reason for that. Jack is Lydia's son."

At first, O'Neill stared speechlessly at Kenyon, then turned back to Legrand. "How do *you* know?"

Legrand squared his shoulders. "Because I am his father."

O'Neill sat down on the couch, clearly in a state of shock. Legrand went into the kitchen and fetched a glass of water.

Kenyon stared at O'Neill's pale face, wondering what might be going through her mind. He felt sorry for her, but he needed to continue.

When Legrand returned from the kitchen, Kenyon turned his attention to the private investigator. "What you don't know, Raymond, is that Lydia had another lover."

"Who was the scoundrel?" he demanded.

"Tanya," replied Kenyon.

Legrand also dropped to the couch, his knees suddenly giving way.

Kenyon, standing beside the portrait of Lydia, could see both of the people she loved looked miserable. He turned to O'Neill. "Tanya, I'm sorry I had to say that, but keeping it secret only allowed you to be blackmailed."

The agent turned to Legrand. "Raymond, I'm sorry I had to tell you, but the only reason Lydia paid the blackmail was because she thought she was protecting you. And that mistake may have cost her life."

"What do you mean?" asked O'Neill.

"Because it prevented her from going to the police when she discovered what she thought was a forgery ring," said Kenyon. "She decided, instead, to try and hide the evidence."

Jack turned and lifted the portrait of Lydia down from the mantelpiece. He flipped it over and pried out several of the pins holding the back-board to the frame. The backboard finally came loose, exposing a second, slightly smaller painting concealed within.

Kenyon lifted it out. It was a perfect copy of Maggote's *Techno 69*.

Thirty-three

A bank of fluorescent light bathed the electronics lab in the basement of R.L. Investigations in a cold, bright light.

Kenyon and Legrand stood to one side of a long, Formica lab table, watching as a man with receding blond hair and thick eyeglasses stood hunched over the fake *Techno 69*. "Ingenious," he muttered, as he examined the painting with a large, square magnifying glass.

"Tell us what you have discovered, Cruickshanks," ordered Legrand.

The technician straightened slightly, glancing at the men over his glasses. "This entire painting is designed to be a recording device." He removed a pen from his breast pocket and used it as a pointer. "Look here: this circuitry is a digital memory, and this," he pointed to a second patch of microchips, "appears to be the recording module."

Legrand tapped the picture. "But that is impossible. If this device were truly a bug, Dr. MacQuaig would have detected it when he swept the room. He had all the latest surveillance-detecting equipment."

"Not if it wasn't actively recording at the time," said Cruickshanks.

"But what good is a bug if it does not record?" asked Legrand.

"I didn't say it *didn't*," replied Cruickshanks impatiently. "I merely said it wasn't recording whenever they were checking for bugs."

"How is that possible without someone sneaking in and turning it on and off all the time?" asked Legrand.

"When it is activated by this," replied Cruickshanks. The technician tapped a glistening square of purplish, translucent material glued to the upper left corner.

Kenyon bent over the painting and examined the patch. "It's a solar-powered battery." He turned to Legrand. "It converts light into electricity."

"Yes, but this one is slightly different," said Cruickshanks. "This particular battery doesn't react to the visible light spectrum. It is designed to create a power source only when it is in the presence of electro-magnetic radiation released by a computer display."

Legrand looked perplexed, but Kenyon understood. "That's wild," said the agent.

Legrand crossed his arms in frustration. "I, for one, do not understand."

"Most bugs are detected when they're either transmitting or recording," said Kenyon. "That's when they're giving off an electro-magnetic field."

"That is easy to elude," said Legrand, unimpressed. "They turn the device on with a remote signal when they wish to record."

"Using a remote activator is very difficult to do when the recording device is inside a lead-lined room," said Cruickshanks. "Radio waves can't penetrate lead."

Kenyon continued. "So, what you do is design a bug that turns itself on only when the secret code is being broadcast."

"Will somebody please explain in plain language?" said an increasingly agitated Legrand.

"Computer screen monitors like the ones in the TEQ boardroom emit radiation," said Kenyon. He tapped the circuitry. "Whenever they ran a demonstration, this special panel powered up the bug."

Cruickshanks nodded. "The bug then recorded the encryption code and stored it in RAM."

Kenyon finished. "When the demo was over, the monitors would be turned off and the bug would go back to its dormant mode, where it was undetectable."

Legrand took Kenyon by the arm and led him off to one side, out of Cruickshank's hearing. "Ilsa bought *Techno 69* for the boardroom," he said. "Does this mean she is involved?"

Kenyon shook his head. "No. I think deWolfe learned from her that she intended to hang it in the boardroom, and had a copy made up with the bug. He knew Ricci was pulling a forgery scam, and twisted his arm into making the switch. All he had to do then was get it out."

Legrand pounded his fist against the lab desk. "He seduced my wife to convince her to donate it to the auction."

Kenyon nodded. "And it would have worked, if Lydia hadn't stumbled on the real one hidden in the gallery storage room. She switched them, and Garbajian bought the real one by accident."

"And before deWolfe and his gang realized what had happened, they killed Lydia," said Legrand. He sat down on a stool and buried his face in his hands. "The bastard," he muttered.

Kenyon placed a hand on Legrand's shoulder. "Don't worry, deWolfe's not going to get away with it."

Legrand glanced up. "What do we do now?"

Kenyon took the fake *Techno 69* and placed it back in the hiding place behind Lydia's portrait. "We jerk *his* chain around for a change."

Legrand drove through the streets of Kensington as dusk descended on the city. "What you propose is very dangerous," he said to Kenyon. "Why do we not simply turn the painting over to the police?"

Kenyon sat on the passenger side dressed in dark clothing and a baseball cap pulled down to conceal his face. "Because they think I killed Lydia in order to cover up the theft of the Cyberworm virus. If I show up with it, they're not going to believe deWolfe is responsible."

"So, what is the plan?"

Kenyon glanced into the back of the Range Rover at the portrait of Lydia. "We're going to give the painting to deWolfe."

Legrand turned his head toward Kenyon in surprise so quickly that he almost smashed into the bus ahead, barely hitting the brakes in time. "Are you absolutely insane?"

"We're just going to give it to him long enough to take it to his boss," Kenyon said, fishing around in his pocket and pulling out a metal disk about the size of a quarter. "See this? I got this from your boy Cruickshanks."

Legrand peered at the device in the gloom. "What is it?"

"A Global Positioning Satellite transmitter." Kenyon worked the disk underneath the frame of the painting.

"Ah, very imaginative," said Legrand.

Kenyon reached into his jacket pocket and pulled out a device that was the size of a pocket calculator. "This tells me the location." He turned the device on, and it beeped. "We can follow deWolfe wherever he takes it. Once he gets there, we call the cops."

Legrand nodded. "So, we simply give it to deWolfe and say, 'Here, take this to your master,' no?"

Kenyon laughed. "No. We have to fool him into thinking he's found it on his own."

They were nearing Lydia's home. Kenyon pointed to the alleyway that lead up to deWolfe's secret flat. "Pull in here, and stop."

Legrand wheeled the Rover to the side of the road. Night had descended, but Kenyon pulled the ballcap further down over his face. He got out of the car and slipped up the alleyway.

He found deWolfe's blue Volvo parked in the reserved spot. Glancing up, he saw a light burning at the top of the building. Good; Kenyon thought, deWolfe was in his lair.

Kenyon glanced back. He could see Legrand peering after him down the alley from the Rover, but the rest of the street was deserted. He bent down over the back of deWolfe's car and took the cap off the air valve on the rear tire. Using the tip of a pen, he pushed in the pin until the air began to rush out. After several minutes, the tire was flat. Kenyon put the cap back on the valve and returned to the Range Rover.

"Why did you do that?" asked Legrand as Kenyon climbed in.

"To give us some breathing time," said Kenyon. "Now we have to shake the surveillance team off Lydia's place." He took a bright yellow raincoat from the floor of the car and pulled it over his jacket, then handed a second one to Legrand. "You know what to do."

By now night had fully descended. Kenyon stood around the corner from Lydia's home beneath the towering limbs of a tree that stood in the fenced park. He was acutely aware of deWolfe's observation post directly above, and he had to will himself not to glance up.

Several pedestrians strolled past, obviously curious about the man standing out on a warm, cloudless evening wearing a raincoat. Kenyon ignored them, more concerned that he might be spotted by the surveillance team before the time was right.

He glanced at his watch. Legrand had been gone ten minutes; plenty of time to reach his appointed spot on Gloucester Road. It was time. Kenyon opened his raincoat and pushed the baseball cap back so that his face was clearly visible and began to stroll toward Lydia's home.

He spotted the surveillance van the moment he walked around the corner. It was the same one he had seen out of deWolfe's window the evening before; an electrical contractor's panel truck, parked adjacent to the park.

Kenyon slowed, then stopped beneath a street lamp. He waited for several seconds, then saw it; someone was moving in the van, causing it to sway. He could hear the side door being unlatched. He counted to three, then crouched and ran back.

As he rounded the corner, he peered over his shoulder. Sure enough, a man dressed in worker's coveralls was climbing out of the van and heading in his direction. He prayed that the second man would follow. Head down, Kenyon sprinted as fast as he could toward Gloucester Road. He rounded the corner, straight into Legrand.

"Go! Go!" he urged Legrand, who, dressed in a similar bright yellow garment, turned and ran for the Gloucester Road tube.

Kenyon stepped into the door of a betting shop and pulled off his raingear. Standing behind the door, he watched as first one cop, then the second, came sprinting around the corner and raced after Legrand.

Kenyon quickly left the betting shop and retraced his steps. The plan was for Legrand to ditch his bright raincoat in the station, then return out the door. With any luck, the agents would think Kenyon had disappeared into the underground and concentrate their search there.

Kenyon turned the corner back onto Lydia's street and approached her home cautiously. The van was empty. With the door thrown open he could see the radio equipment inside. The agent resisted the urge to pick up the handset and transmit a raspberry. Knowing that deWolfe was watching his every move, he pulled out a key and advanced up the steps. He quickly let himself in, then closed the door.

The interior of Lydia's home was dark. Kenyon stood for a moment at the door, sniffing the air, waiting for any sound or sign that someone was inside.

All was quiet. Kenyon advanced down the hall into the kitchen. Reaching into his pocket, he pulled out a portable bug detector and turned it on. A red diode light on the top flashed slowly as he turned it to the left and right, first around the stove and microwave, then around the wall phone. Nothing.

Kenyon continued into the dining room. He swept the detector under the large oak table and chairs, but the device remained silent.

Careful to keep from being silhouetted in the window, Kenyon moved around the living room in a crouch. He checked under the chairs, but there was nothing. He ran the detector along the mantelpiece; still no sign. Even the telephone on the coffee table showed no indication of being bugged.

Then, on a hunch, he followed the telephone line back toward the wall. At the window, mounted on a baseboard behind a curtain was a small white box. Kenyon pointed the detector and the red diode light began to flash faster and faster. He bent over for a closer look at the box. It resembled a voltage adapter, but it straddled the line between the phone and the wall socket. He recognized it as a dual bug. Not only could it record phone calls, but any conversation in the room, as well.

Kenyon returned to the telephone and picked it up. He dialed Legrand's cell number. The phone rang twice before Legrand came on the line.

"*Bonjour*," said Legrand.

Kenyon was relieved. "Bonjour" was the code word for free and clear. "I found the hiding spot," he said.

"Excellent," responded Legrand. "Where is it?"

"In the Rachmaninov," said Kenyon.

"Ah, ingenious," replied Legrand.

"We rendezvous there in two hours, at midnight." Kenyon then hung up.

He glanced out the bay window. The surveillance van was still empty, the door ajar. Kenyon quickly exited the front door and sprinted across the street to the fenced park. He grabbed the top of the wrought-iron gate and vaulted over the top and into the darkness beyond.

Thirty-four

Kenyon sat in the Range Rover for what seemed like an eternity, waiting for Legrand to return. Had the surveillance men from Scotland Yard managed to double back and capture him? He glanced nervously at the painting resting on the back seat. If he were caught now, he would spend the rest of his life behind bars. He leaned under the dashboard, wondering if he could hotwire the car.

A rap at the window made his heart leap into his mouth. Kenyon straightened up in the seat just as Legrand clambered into the driver's side, his face sweating. "I haven't had this much excitement since we torched Algiers," he said with a grin. He fired up the Rover engine, and the two men sped off into the night.

Traffic was light and they made good time heading south. They crossed the river and entered into the suburbs, following the path that Kenyon had taken a week earlier when he had driven out to see the spot where Lydia had died. It seemed like a million years before.

The bright lights of London dimmed as they left the city and entered the countryside. Legrand flicked on the high beams and roared down the back roads, picking the fastest way. Forty minutes after leaving Lydia's home, they turned onto Abbey Lane at the top of the hill.

Legrand slowed, easing the Range Rover down the steep, winding road and glancing around for a place to park. Kenyon pointed to a narrow, flat spot between two trees where the 4X4 could pull off. Legrand steered the Rover into the tight spot and quickly killed the headlights and turned off the engine.

They had no sooner stopped when they noticed the headlights of another car approaching down the road. They crouched down in the front seat, watching as a sedan appeared around the corner. It slowed slightly as it passed the parked Rover, then sped up and disappeared down the lane.

After the car passed, the two men sat in the Rover listening to the forest sounds coming through the car windows. All they could hear was the tick-tick of the engine cooling and the sound of the wind in the trees above. Somewhere in the night, an owl hooted.

Kenyon nodded to Legrand, and they got out and went around to the back of the car. The PI opened the rear door and fished around in the back for some dark clothing. Kenyon pulled deWolfe's 9 mm pistol from under a seat and tucked it into the back waistband of his jeans, then pulled his black sweater down over it. He then went to a side door and lifted the painting out from the back seat.

While Legrand changed clothes, Kenyon walked out to the road. He could still feel the heat of the day rising from the asphalt in the cool night air. He glanced both ways, but there were no telltale lights from oncoming traffic. They were alone.

Kenyon walked a few steps uphill. The light from a full moon peeked between the trees, illuminating the spot where Lydia's car had gone off the road. He could still see the scars on the trees where it had crashed to a halt. He paused and stared at the scene, so peaceful and quiet in the silvery illumination.

Legrand, dressed in black, joined him by the side of the road. "What is it?" he asked, peering down the embankment.

"Nothing," said Kenyon. He wanted Legrand to keep his mind on the task at hand. "I was just waiting for you." They continued up the hill.

About one hundred feet from the crash site, they came to the bridle path. "The Ingoldsby Estate is only half a mile away," said Legrand, pointing down the path. He glanced at the illuminated dial of his watch. "We will get there with an hour to spare."

Kenyon nodded. If he guessed correctly, deWolfe would try and get there before their rendezvous at midnight in order to steal the painting.

By letting the air out of his tire, he had given them at least a fifteen-minute head start. At best, they would only have a few minutes to plant the painting, then hide.

With Legrand leading the way, the two men headed down the path at a rapid walking pace. Even with the full moon, Kenyon could see little of the path, but he could smell the rich aroma of horse manure and feel the sandy earth beneath his shoes.

Legrand stopped. Something was moving on the path ahead. Deep in the shadows of the overlying trees, Kenyon could only make it a large, dark bulk. He pulled out the gun and flicked off the safety, taking aim.

Fortunately, he didn't fire. The metallic click of the safety startled the deer from its freeze, and it darted off the path, disappearing into the thick underbrush. Both men exhaled in relief.

They walked silently for about five minutes, then the path began to open up to one side. To his right, Kenyon could see a large field. High above, the dark sky was filled with a million stars. They followed a path along the edge of the field until they came to a shooting blind. Kenyon realized they were at the spot where Sir Rupert had tried to kill him with a shotgun. A shiver went down his spine.

Now that he had his bearings, Kenyon moved ahead of Legrand. The two men followed the pathway through the trees, finally coming out at the estate yard behind the numerous barns and outbuildings.

They paused. Except for a single electric bulb burning at the wide entrance door to the stable, the yard was dark. Legrand pointed, and they advanced to a smaller, unlit door.

Kenyon eased the door open and glanced inside. The stable was unlit. He could hear Ilsa's horse moving about, nervous at the sudden intrusion. He advanced along the aisle down the middle of the barn, stopping to stroke the horse's nose. "Shh, that's a good girl," he whispered. The horse nuzzled his empty palm. He wished he had an apple to give to her.

Legrand touched his arm and they continued toward the front of the stable. They opened the door cautiously and peered out toward the main house. The large mansion lay in darkness, except for a light burning over the back entrance to the kitchen. Kenyon couldn't see any cars in the yard, but from this vantage point, there was no way of telling if there were others parked out front.

Once again, Legrand pointed to the dark side of the mansion, and the two men advanced. Legrand led the way to a low set of steps that led to the basement of the house. At the bottom of the steps were a pair of massive, rough-hewn oak doors. Legrand took a skeleton key out of his pocket, then Kenyon saw the other man feeling around the door until he located the keyhole. Legrand turned the lock, then eased the squeaking doors open. Both men quickly darted inside. Kenyon left the door slightly ajar in case they needed to get out quickly.

Legrand removed a penlight and switched it on. The room was a series of brick arches supported by thick oaken posts and beams. A dozen large wooden barrels lined the walls. "We are in the wine cellars," he whispered. "There is a set of steps to the left."

Kenyon kept behind Legrand as closely as possible and followed the narrow, dancing beam of light as they advanced through the room. "Are you sure nobody's home?" he asked.

"It is the staff's night off," replied Legrand. "Just to be sure, I called on my cell phone. Nobody answered."

"Where is Ilsa tonight?"

"She normally takes Sir Rupert to the Governor's Club for dinner on Saturdays, then to the Royal Geographic Society talk. They are never back before midnight."

They reached the wide steps. Legrand went first, careful to keep the light from the tiny flashlight to a minimum. The steps ended at the main kitchen. The exterior light over the back door streamed through the large windows, illuminating empty countertops and large pots.

As they advanced toward the hallway, Kenyon glanced over his shoulder. He noticed a small portal leading to a flight of steep stairs. "Where does that go?" he quietly asked.

"That is the servants' stair to the bedrooms above," Legrand explained. "It is only used by Gladys."

Kenyon nodded, and the two men continued their journey.

The hallway was dark. Kenyon blessed Ilsa's penny-pinching ways, glad that she didn't leave all the lights in the house on.

The double doors to the reception hall stood wide open. Inside, moonlight flooded the polished wood floor, giving the room a cold, silver glow.

They crossed the floor to the Rachmaninov Steinway. The dark patina of the grand piano glistened in the moonlight. Legrand eased the lid up, and Kenyon placed the painting into the cavity. The piano strings cooed and sighed as Lydia's portrait nestled into its hiding spot. Legrand eased the lid down.

Kenyon pulled out the receiver for the GPS system and turned it on. The device emitted a soft ping to indicate that it was functioning. Nodding in satisfaction, the agent turned off the device and put it back into his pocket.

"What do we do now?" asked Legrand.

"We hide and wait for deWolfe to find it," said Kenyon. "Where's a good spot?"

"The drawing room next door."

Legrand was about to lead Kenyon to the drawing room when he stopped and nodded toward the windows. "Shh," he said. "I hear something."

The two men cautiously advanced to the patio doors and eased one open a crack. They could hear the distinct sound of several car engines in the distance, but there were no lights to tell how close they were. After a few moments, the sound died away. Legrand turned to Kenyon, and shrugged. He eased the patio door closed.

Once again, Legrand turned toward the drawing room, but Kenyon placed a hand on his shoulder and stopped him.

"What is it?" whispered Legrand.

From the moment they had started on their journey down the bridle path, something had been nagging at the back of Kenyon's mind. "That night of the auction, didn't you say Ilsa was away from the party?"

"Yes," replied Legrand. "She went upstairs to tend Sir Rupert. She was gone for over an hour."

Kenyon glanced out of the large reception room windows. From where he was standing, the horse barns weren't visible. He thought about the narrow back stairs leading from upstairs to the basement, then to the basement doors, then to the horse barn, and then to the bridle path. It had taken Kenyon and Legrand about fifteen minutes to traverse the path, but someone on a horse could reach the scene of Lydia's murder much faster.

"Oh, shit," said Kenyon. The agent turned and lifted the piano lid in an effort to grab the painting.

"What are you doing?" asked Legrand.

"We have to get out of here right now," whispered Kenyon.

They were interrupted by a noise in the house. Both men froze. From somewhere down the hall, they could hear the distinct *clump, clump, clump* of someone moving along in a walker.

"It is Sir Rupert," whispered Legrand. "What is he doing here alone?" He started toward the hallway.

Kenyon struggled to hold the heavy lid of the piano and lift the painting out. A corner caught on a string, and the plucked chord hung in the air, echoing around the room. Both men froze.

The sound of the walker stopped in front of the reception doors, and the room was flooded with light.

Charlie Dahg stood at the door, one hand resting on Sir Rupert's walker, the other pointing a gun at the two men.

Thirty-five

Kenyon and Legrand stood imprisoned in the wine cellar. Their arms had been looped around one of the stout wooden posts that supported the basement ceiling, their wrists bound by plastic handcuffs.

Dahg positioned himself beneath a light and closely examined the portrait of Lydia. Her skin glowed harshly beneath the glare of the bare light bulb. "Nice looking piece of ass," he muttered. "So, this is what everyone's been after."

"How did you find us?" asked Kenyon.

Dahg put down the painting and pulled a portable radio scanner out of his pocket. It was the kind used to monitor listening devices. "I overheard you were onto something. I tailed you out."

Kenyon winced at his own stupidity. Not once on their journey out from London had he bothered to look to see if they were being followed.

Dahg drew out a silencer and attached it to his gun. He stood at the base of the stairs and aimed it at the two men. "Nothing personal, but I don't want any witnesses."

Kenyon had to think fast. Dahg had forgotten to frisk the men, and the agent still had the Luger tucked in the back of his jeans. If only he could get his hands free.

"I assume you don't want fifty million, either," said Kenyon.

Dahg cocked his head to one side. "What?"

"That's what it's worth, in the right hands," said Kenyon. "I know the right hands."

Dahg shifted his weight to his good leg. "Tell me."

"I'll do better than that," said Kenyon. "I'll make you my partner."

A short, ugly bark of laughter escaped Dahg's lips. "I'd be a fool after you double-crossed me in San Francisco."

Kenyon shrugged. "That was a mistake. Nothing personal, but I didn't trust you. If I had realized how resourceful you were, I would have let you in on it in the beginning."

Dahg sat down on the steps and smiled. "Let's hear the story, *partner*."

Kenyon wet his lips. He had to play this very carefully. "The Cyberworm virus that Simon stole was only half the secret. The other half, the encryption code that unlocks the virus, is concealed in that painting."

"Where is it concealed in the painting?"

"Let me free and I'll show you."

Dahg, a rueful look on his face, shook his head no. "Who's the client?"

"I'm not going to give up my bargaining chip."

Dahg pointed his gun at Legrand. "Tell me, or I shoot your pal."

Kenyon glanced at Legrand. Sweat trickled down the older man's face.

The agent had to think fast. "Legrand's the technician—if you shoot him, we can't transfer the code to the virus."

Dahg paused for a moment, trying to make up his mind. "I don't believe you," he finally said. He pointed the gun at Legrand's crotch. "I'm going to count to three, then I'm going to shoot your friend in a very painful spot. One, two . . ."

Dahg never finished. Distracted by a noise, he turned and stared up the stairwell. "Who the fuck are you?"

A voice responded. "Your employer. Or, might I say, your former employer."

Dahg swung his gun away from Legrand and pointed it up the stairs. Before he could fire, there was a sharp crack of a gunshot, and his head exploded in a shower of blood and bone. He pitched forward off the steps, dead by the time he hit the cellar floor.

Kenyon and Legrand stared open-mouthed as Hadrian deWolfe came down the stairs, an ancient Colt .45 service revolver clutched in his hands. He nudged Dahg in the back with the smoking barrel. The victim didn't even twitch.

Satisfied, deWolfe stepped over the corpse and into the cellar. He stopped before the painting of Lydia. "Ah. What's this? Such a delightful portrait."

DeWolfe turned the picture over. "How ingenious!" He carefully withdrew *Techno 69* and held it up to the light. "At last, we meet again."

He turned and bowed to Kenyon, clearly jubilant. "Thank you, Herr Kenyon, I knew you had it in you."

"It was nothing."

"Don't be so modest," said deWolfe. "It was not in Lydia's house, or her gallery. And that cretin Ricci certainly did not have it. Without you, we might never have found it."

Kenyon nodded. "That was what the charade with Garbajian was all about. You wanted me to be your bloodhound."

DeWolfe smiled a toothy grin. "Our clients were becoming a trifle impatient, I must confess. Things were getting, shall we say, desperate."

"Desperate enough to kill your partner, Ricci?"

DeWolfe pursed his lips. "He was *hardly* a partner. If it wasn't for a little blackmail over his forgery scam, the sullen boy wouldn't have cooperated at all."

"Why did you set me up to call him?"

"Isn't it obvious? I wanted to find out if he was hiding the painting."

Kenyon nodded. "And when you learned he didn't have it, you killed him."

"He was going to confess my involvement," said deWolfe. "Really, you can't trust anybody these days."

"And what about Lydia?" asked Kenyon. "Couldn't you trust her?"

"Lydia never knew," said deWolfe.

"So, why did you kill her?" asked Kenyon.

"I didn't," said deWolfe.

"I don't believe you," said Kenyon.

"I have an unimpeachable alibi on the night of her murder," said deWolfe.

"Who?"

"You, of course." DeWolfe pulled out a cigar, then lit it. "By the way, how is the posterior? Any lingering soreness?"

"*You* tried to kill me?"

DeWolfe held up a protesting hand. "On strictest orders merely to wound."

"Orders from whom?"

"Why, Ilsa, of course. I must say, I found it sublimely clever." DeWolfe glanced at the painting. "She had a custom bug made in a replica of *Techno 69*, then suborned Ricci into swapping the real one for the fake in the boardroom of her own company."

Kenyon nodded at the dead CIA agent. "How did he fit in?"

"We hired Dahg to act as a mule and pick up the Cyberworm virus. He thought he was picking up control software for an air force attack drone."

"And you?"

DeWolfe grinned. "You mean, what benefits did I get above and beyond Ilsa's—how shall we say it—natural charms? A man of my tastes cannot satisfy them through a mere consultant's fees. Even the money we made blackmailing Lydia wasn't sufficient. When we finally turn the encryption code over to Herr Garbajian, we are to be paid one hundred million—more than enough to keep me in comfort for the rest of my life."

DeWolfe suddenly lost interest in the agent. Bending over *Techno 69*, he carefully began tucking it back into its hiding place behind Lydia's portrait.

Kenyon stared down at his bound hands. There was no way he could reach the Luger. He nudged Legrand in the foot, and the older man glanced up. Kenyon nodded imperceptibly toward his back.

Legrand nodded back. The PI shifted his weight, drawing his tied hands slowly around the post.

Kenyon arched his back, bringing his waistline closer. Legrand's fingers were only inches from the gun.

The butt of deWolfe's Colt suddenly cracked into the side of Legrand's head, knocking him to his knees. The spy reached around behind Kenyon's back, drawing the gun out. "Naughty, naughty." He glanced at the round in the chamber, then tucked the gun into the back of his own waistline. "Somebody could get hurt."

DeWolfe turned his head, sniffing the air. "What's that, a whiff of smoke? Dear me, I do believe something may be on fire."

Kenyon glanced up the stairs; the first traces of black smoke were curling down from the kitchen. "The police are already onto you," he said, in desperation. "You can't get away."

"That is a chance I intend to take." DeWolfe picked up Lydia's portrait and headed for the cellar door. "Thank you for finding the painting. *Auf Wiedersehen.*"

"Where do you think you're going?" a woman asked.

All three men craned their necks upward. Ilsa stood at the top of the cellar stairs, a silver filigreed Perazzi shotgun cradled in her arms.

DeWolfe placed the painting slowly to the ground. "Darling!"

Ilsa descended the steps, the shotgun pointed directly at deWolfe's chest. "Drop the gun."

DeWolfe threw the Colt down.

"Stand back."

DeWolfe took several steps back, toward the cellar doors. "I was just coming to look for you." He held his hands feebly in the air.

As Ilsa bent over the gun, deWolfe drew the Luger from his waistband.

He wasn't fast enough. The Perazzi flashed, and deWolfe hurled back into the cellar doors, his chest crushed by the force of the blast.

Ilsa stepped cautiously forward. DeWolfe, his breath wheezing out from his shirt in bright red bubbles, stared at the advancing woman. He struggled to raise his gun, but Ilsa fired a second round, this time at his head. His face dissolved in a pulp. She leaned over and pried the Luger from the dead man's hand, wiping the blood from the barrel.

Legrand roused himself. "Ilsa! Please, cut these bonds!"

"Shut up, worm." His wife then ignored him, her attention drawn to the painting.

Kenyon turned to the older man. "She's not going to set us free, Raymond. She's going to kill us."

Ilsa raised her eyes from Lydia's portrait. "I was, but now that my former partner has set fire to the family homestead, I think I shall let you burn, instead." The side of her mouth curled up in a crooked smile. "It seems that much more cruel."

"Why did you do it?" asked Kenyon. "For the money?"

Ilsa approached Kenyon. She stood very close, staring up into his eyes. She gently caressed his cheek with the tip of the Luger. "No, darling. I did it for revenge."

Kenyon stared back into her eyes, looking for some spark of humanity, but the cold blue orbs were devoid of life, like a deep pool of glacial water. "Revenge?"

"Yes." Ilsa stared down at the stream of blood running from a cut on Legrand's brow. "Revenge against my husband and his mistress." She returned her gaze to Kenyon. "But most of all, against the son I never had."

Ilsa kissed Kenyon softly on the lips, then placed a letter in his shirt pocket. "I believe this is addressed to you."

The smoke was beginning to pour down the cellar steps. Ilsa picked up the painting and headed toward the basement exit. She pushed deWolfe's corpse to one side, then opened the portal. She paused to look at Kenyon one last time, then closed and locked the double doors.

Thirty-six

Kenyon crouched low to the ground as the basement filled with black smoke. It was getting difficult to breath. He peered at the handcuffs in the dim light. The restraints were made of a thick band of nylon and held closed with a one-way, ratchet-and-lock. The system was impossible to pick, because it required no key. The only way you could remove the cuffs was by cutting them off.

"You have a pocket knife or anything sharp?" asked Kenyon.

"No," replied Legrand, coughing.

Kenyon rubbed the cuffs against the wood post. It chipped off a few slivers, but didn't even scratch the tough surface.

Legrand's coughs grew louder. Kenyon stared at Dahg and deWolfe, two dead sentinels in their prison. It was impossible to search their pockets as they were beyond reach.

Kenyon stood up and examined the post. The top was held in place by a large iron nail. Peering through the smoke, he could see that the wood around the nail had split.

Kenyon's heart rose in hope and he nudged the older man. "Raymond, stand up."

Legrand struggled to his feet. "What is it?"

"If we can push hard enough, maybe we can dislodge the top of the post."

The two men placed their shoulders against the post. "Heave!" shouted Kenyon.

The wood cracked and the post shifted a fraction of an inch.

"Again!" called Kenyon.

Legrand groaned as they pushed, but the post moved another half inch.

"Once more!"

The post screeched as the two men heaved one final time and, with a sudden crack of splitting wood, the post fell away. Almost simultaneously, the room was filled with a tremendous groan, and the wide ceiling beam came crashing to the ground. Kenyon was flung to one side, but the heavy beam landed squarely on Legrand.

The agent scrambled through the thickening smoke to the older man's side. "Are you all right?" he asked.

Legrand grimaced and pointed. "My leg . . ."

Kenyon followed his finger. Legrand's leg was pinned beneath the ceiling beam. He tried to lift it, but the large beam was too heavy. "Hold on," he said. "I'll get something to pry it up."

Kenyon scrambled around on his hands and knees, searching for a crowbar. He found an old axe handle discarded under a wine barrel. He returned and gently eased it under the beam, careful not to brush Legrand's leg. Then he heaved as hard as he could.

The beam rose an inch. Legrand tried to pull himself free, but the handle of the axe snapped, and the wooden beam fell back onto his leg.

The smoke swirled around the two men like a black, deadly fog. Legrand gripped Kenyon by the arm and tried to push him away. "Go, while you still can," he urged, between gritted teeth.

The overhead light flickered, then went out. Coughing, Jack reached through the darkness and took Legrand's hand. "It took me over thirty years to find you. I'm not going to leave without you."

Legrand grasped the Kenyon's hand and held it firmly for a second, but his grip began to weaken. Kenyon gasped as stars danced in his vision. It was only a matter of seconds.

As he stood on the threshold of unconsciousness, there was a brilliant flash of light, and the double doors exploded into shards. The agent lifted his head up in amazement as a figure clad in body armor and black helmet hurled through the door, an assault rifle cradled in one hand, a powerful strobe light in the other.

The apparition advanced on the two men, the assault rifle pointed directly at Kenyon's heart. Instead of shooting, however, the man flipped up the face mask and grinned at Kenyon.

"Wot a party!" shouted Happy Harry.

Harry slung one of Kenyon's arms over his shoulder and carried the agent out of the basement. As they came up the steps, the agent spotted Humphrey Arundel perched on a hunter's sitting-cane in the middle of the lawn. He was dressed in an SAS flak jacket and tweed pants, his face was lit by the brilliant fire that roared on the main floor of the mansion.

"Are you well?" asked Arundel.

Kenyon gulped at the fresh air and did his best to stand up. "Legrand is trapped under a pillar. I have to get him out."

Harry spoke into a radio receiver clipped to his body armor, and two similarly clad men came running up with what looked like a chainsaw. They dashed into the cellar, and Kenyon could hear the device cutting through wood, then a shout as they lifted the beam. Within thirty seconds, they emerged from the basement with Legrand and carried the limp man across the lawn. A field ambulance came from the other side of the mansion and met them.

Kenyon began to follow, but Arundel stood and blocked his way. "I do believe the medics can take care of Legrand," he said. "Right now, we have some equally important issues to attend to." He took the agent by the arm and began leading him toward the Bentley, parked at the edge of the lawn.

"Am I under arrest?" asked Kenyon.

"Technically, yes, but I think Lady Beatrice might allow you some liberty if you cooperate in our investigation."

"Your mom's got that much pull?" asked Kenyon.

"Well, she *is* the head of MI5," said Arundel. He opened the rear door, stepped inside, and signaled for Kenyon to follow.

Inside, a tall, elegant woman in her fifties was sipping tea. She placed her own cup down and reached for a thermos on a sideboard. "Young man, you look distinctly dreadful," she said. "May I pour you a cup of tea?"

Kenyon noted the same elongated nose and thin hands as her son. "Tea would be great, but we have to catch Ilsa. She's getting away with the painting."

Lady Beatrice turned an eye toward Arundel. "Humphrey, where is Ilsa now?"

The deputy inspector pressed a key on an electronic monitor embedded in a panel. "She appears to be moving northwards, toward London," he said.

Kenyon stared at the monitor, which displayed a roadmap of the region. "Hey, that's my GPS!"

"Thank you for your prescience," said Lady Beatrice. "I am afraid we are as surprised as you at her involvement."

Happy Harry appeared at the Bentley's open door and saluted.

"Harold, you smell abominably of smoke," said Lady Beatrice. "How is the operation proceeding?"

"Everything's secure and ready for inspection, ma'am."

Lady Beatrice got out of the car, followed by Kenyon and Arundel.

"Two men previously dead in the basement, ma'am, both hostiles," said Harry. "All our men accounted for and unharmed."

"What about Legrand?" asked Kenyon.

"He suffered a broken leg, but he's gonna be all right," replied the cabby.

"And what of Sir Rupert?" asked Lady Beatrice.

Suddenly, the air was rent by a horrible scream and they all turned toward the house. The noise hung in the air for several seconds, rising in pitch, until it was abruptly cut off as the roof collapsed in a brilliant shower of cinders and ash.

"That would be him, I reckon," said Harry.

They all watched silently for several seconds, until Lady Beatrice spoke. "Harold, if you would be so kind as to drive us into London?"

Harry snapped a salute. "Yes, ma'am!" He hopped into the front of the car.

Lady Beatrice beckoned to Kenyon to join her. "Perhaps we can compare notes?"

Kenyon followed Arundel and Lady Beatrice into the rear of the Bentley.

Sitting in a fold-down jump-seat, Kenyon faced Lady Beatrice and Arundel. "Thanks for pulling me out of that mess, but I have to get something straight: do you still think I'm the mastermind behind all this?"

"Oh, heavens, no," said Lady Beatrice. "We never did."

Kenyon pointed to Harry in front. "Then how come you've been following me from the moment I came to town?"

Arundel cleared his throat. "Perhaps we should backtrack a trifle. Several months ago, we received word through the chaps at MI6 that someone might make a play for the Cyberworm virus. It seems there was interest in it from certain well-funded terrorists in the Middle East."

"You mean, someone like Iran?"

"We weren't certain. All we really knew was the target. When we learned through our legal attaché in San Francisco that it had been stolen out from under the nose of the FBI, we focused our attention on TEQ labs and the encryption code, here in England."

"And me," said Kenyon.

"And you," agreed Lady Beatrice. "We were, of course, saddened when Lydia was killed." She reached forward and placed her hand on Kenyon's. "I offer you my condolences. Lydia was a wonderful woman."

"Thank you," said Kenyon.

Lady Beatrice sat back. "But we were also curious as to the coincidence of her association with TEQ and her nephew Jack Kenyon's involvement in the San Francisco theft. We assigned commander Harold Twiggley to place you under observation."

"Twiggley?" Kenyon turned toward Harry, who was grinning widely. He returned his attention to Lady Beatrice. "So, you didn't even know Lydia was murdered?"

"My apologies for downplaying the manner of her death," said Arundel. "We were, of course, grateful you had made the discovery, but we didn't wish to tip the cabal off."

"Because you didn't even know who they were," said Kenyon.

"Guilty as charged," replied Lady Beatrice. "We had our suspicions of the man whom you knew as Hadrian deWolfe, but we correctly assumed he wasn't acting alone. We needed to learn more, and quickly."

"So, you kept me in play as a stalking horse, just like deWolfe."

"Correct," said Arundel. "We wanted to round up the senior conspirators and regain control of the virus."

"Then why did you try to arrest me?" said Kenyon.

"You can thank assistant US attorney Deaver for that," said Lady Beatrice. "When he appeared in London with his accusations, we were compelled to go through the motions, as it were."

Kenyon turned to Arundel. "That's why you didn't put up a fight when I escaped."

"You were far more useful on-the-prowl, as it were," Arundel said, "than in jail."

Kenyon stared out the window. They were back in London, approaching the center of town. They passed Waterloo Station, then headed east along a major road. Kenyon caught sight of a road sign that read "Southwark Street."

Harry eased up on the accelerator and consulted a monitor in the front of the car. "She's slowed down, ma'am," he said. He tapped a hot key on the console, and the monitor flashed an enlarged map version of the neighborhood. There was a soft buzz as the console spit out a printed version of the map.

"Her destination appears to be in the warehouse district," said Arundel, studying the map

Lady Beatrice glanced at her son, nodding. "Prepare an assault."

Thirty-seven

The Bentley eased forward through the dark street. The neighborhood had an empty, hollow feel to it. Except for a few large trucks trundling past, the streets were deserted.

Southwark Street was flanked by long, low, two-story brick warehouses, many of them dirty and rundown. A brightly painted billboard advertising Woolwright's Guild, a condominium development, was nailed to an abandoned warehouse. Kenyon could smell a salty, tidal odor; they must be somewhere near the Thames, he concluded. Every minute or so, the air was filled with the roar of a large jet passing overhead, making Kenyon think that they were under the approach to Heathrow.

Harry dimmed the headlights and crept forward. Keeping a careful eye on the GPS console, he turned down a lane. Through the gap at the end of the street, the distinctive dome of St Paul's cathedral gleamed in the distance.

Harry finally came to a halt. He pointed to a warehouse directly ahead. "She's in there, ma'am."

The warehouse was two stories tall, made of cut stone and thick oak beams. It appeared to be abandoned. The front door was boarded-up and the windows on the second floor were broken. The interior was dark.

"Are you certain this is the one?" asked Arundel. "I don't see her car."

Harry pointed to several sets of double wooden doors covering archways at the front of the building. "You could fit a lorry through one of them," he said. "It must be inside."

"Right," said Arundel. "Where are the lads?"

Just as he spoke, three small buses with their lights out pulled up behind the Bentley. Each was painted flat black, had heavily tinted windows and the thick, knobby tires often seen on assault vehicles.

Kenyon, Arundel, and Harry got out of the Bentley and joined two dozen troops as they poured out of the vehicles. The men were all dressed in black and looked like they could snap a lumberjack like a twig. A Scotsman with strands of flaming red hair poking from under a dark cap stepped forward. "SAS Lieutenant Farnham here, sir. Fox, Viper, and Wolf units reporting for duty."

"Excellent," said Arundel. He spread the map out on the trunk of the Bentley. One of the men leaned forward with a flashlight, hooded so that it only cast a tiny light on the map. "Alert Thames patrol not to approach closer than Southwark bridge. Have them patch into communications band three. We'll call if we need them."

"Air support, sir?" asked Farnham.

"Bring in the helicopter, but keep it above three thousand metres," said Arundel.

"Right, sir."

As Farnham conveyed the commands through the radio, Arundel turned to the rest of the men. "Anybody familiar with the building?" he asked.

The men glanced at one another, then shook their heads no.

"I can have city planning check archives, sir," said Harry.

"I'm afraid we can't dally," replied Arundel. "Does anyone have a nightscope?"

One of the soldiers drew out a large pair of binoculars. Arundel lifted them to his face and peered at the building for several moments, before turning to Harry.

"Commander, what's your opinion on the second-story window to the right?"

Harry took the night scope and stared at the building intently. "Half-inch iron works held on by bolts, sir. Looks like the window's busted out behind it. Piece a cake."

"Right," said Arundel. "Wolf unit guards the rear and Viper stations out front, ready for assault. I shall lead Fox on the infiltration."

Kenyon took the nightscope from Harry's hands and peered at the building for a second. "Anybody know computers?" he asked aloud.

Several men turned back, blank looks on their faces.

Kenyon pointed to the roof. "See that dish? That's a satellite uplink."

"What of it?" asked Arundel.

"You don't put a fifteen-thousand-dollar dish on an abandoned building for nothing. They're going to launch Cyberworm from here. I'm going in with you."

Arundel glanced at the dish for a moment. "We'll secure the building, then we'll let you in."

"You want to take that chance?"

Arundel stared at Kenyon for a moment, then made up his mind. "You wear full body armor. No weapon. Keep to the rear. I don't want any heroics. Agreed?"

Kenyon smiled. "You got it."

The men quickly suited Kenyon up in body armor and a helmet. The helmet was made of light steel. The body armor was a long vest with a flap that extended over the crotch. It was much lighter than he expected. He pulled a plate out and hefted it. It appeared to be made of some resinous material.

"Graphite laminate," explained Harry as he walked past. "Stop a titanium-tipped bullet, it will."

Kenyon tucked the plate back into the flap and joined Fox unit as they crowded into the first bus. Arundel closed the door, then tapped the driver on the helmet. The bus moved slowly forward.

The driver eased the vehicle over the curb and pulled it up adjacent to the building. Arundel waved his hand once, and two men slipped out the rear door and took up positions clutching automatic pistols. The rest of the soldiers exited the front and waited beside the vehicle.

Farnham lifted a small, dual-tank torch mounted on a backpack and slipped the straps through his shoulders. He then grabbed the top of the rear door and vaulted onto the roof of the bus. Keeping against the wall, he lit the tip of the portable torch and quickly burned the heads of the main bolts holding the rusty grille over the window. He waited until a plane was passing directly overhead providing sound cover, then jerked the grille off its mounts.

The men below waited for a second, their guns ready, but no one appeared at the window.

"Right," said Arundel. "In we go."

The lead man quickly scaled the bus and clambered through the window, careful to avoid the red-hot bolts. He turned on a flashlight and examined the room. It was empty except for a moldering pile of carpet. He stuck his arm out the window and gave the all-clear. The rest of the soldiers entered the building, Kenyon following last.

The upstairs of the warehouse consisted of several large rooms connected by a wide hallway. Fox unit moved quickly down the hall, the large men astonishingly quiet on crepe-soled boots. When they got there, Kenyon was relieved to see that, except for some rubble and discarded machinery, the upper rooms were empty.

The hallway ended at a large steel staircase. Arundel crept to the top of the stairs with the nightscope and peered down. He returned a few seconds later. "No sign of anyone moving about," he said. "There's light coming from a room at the far end. I think they're inside."

"Should we call in Viper unit?" asked Farnham.

Arundel shook his head. "No, we'd just end up shooting each other in the arse." He glanced down the steps, then turned to his men. "Follow me."

One by one, the men advanced down the steps. Kenyon came last, careful not to make any noise.

The main floor was one large open space, supported by thick wooden beams. At the end of the main room was a smaller alcove. The alcove's door, a thick steel barrier that moved horizontally on rollers, had been drawn back, and they could faintly hear voices coming from within.

A shallow steel dyeing vat set into the floor about twenty feet from the alcove made a convenient point of concealment. Kenyon joined the rest of the men behind the vat and crouched down. The reek of ancient scum emanated from the empty container.

Arundel tapped Kenyon on the shoulder and motioned him forward. Bent low, the two men crept ahead until they had a better view of the lit room.

Inside, Kenyon could see a dark, swarthy man hunched over a computer terminal, busily typing on the keypad. Garbajian stood behind him, his eyes transfixed on the monitor.

"Does it work, Basid?" asked Garbajian.

Basid turned to Garbajian. "It is decrypting now. In a few moments, we shall have the virus."

A woman stepped into the light. "Excellent," said Ilsa. "You will transfer the funds, now."

Arundel stood up and trained his weapon at the trio. "You are all under arrest," he said, in a clear, loud voice.

The effect was like an electric shock. Garbajian, Basid, and Ilsa simultaneously spun towards the door, their mouths wide open in surprise.

Suddenly, Garbajian's guard Hazzim stepped into the doorway.

Arundel stopped in his tracks and pointed his gun at the one-eyed man. "Put your hands up," he ordered.

Hazzim's hands rose slowly from his side. Instead of raising them over his head, however, he turned the palm of his left hand forward, and a small, cylindrical object rolled out onto the floor of the main room.

Kenyon grabbed Arundel and pushed him backwards. They both tumbled into the large dye vat just as the grenade exploded.

Thirty-eight

His head ringing, Kenyon eased himself up onto his knees and peered cautiously over the lip of the vat, just in time to witness Hazzim swing the heavy door shut.

A barrage of gunfire erupted from Fox unit, ricocheting off the thick steel.

Almost simultaneously, a side door burst into splinters as Viper unit forced their way into the warehouse.

"Hold your fire!" shouted Arundel.

Fox unit instantly silenced their weapons.

"Viper! Take holding cover!" commanded Arundel.

The men from Viper unit joined Fox behind the vat, several men keeping their weapons trained on the door.

"What's the status, sir?" asked Farnham.

"We've got four suspects barricaded behind that door," said Arundel. "They've got hand grenades and God knows what else."

Farnham peered at the door. "Heavy gauge steel, by the looks of it. Probably cement core. Take a twenty-pound directional charge to budge it."

"Do it," said Arundel.

Farnham signaled to one of his men, who ran out the door under cover. He then turned to Arundel. "We'll have to evacuate this room."

Arundel nodded. "Right. Everyone out." The men quickly filed out the splintered entrance, until only Arundel, Farnham, Kenyon, and Happy Harry remained.

"Let's go, mate," said Harry. "Last one out buys the round."

"Wait," Kenyon said, turning to Farnham. "How long will it take to blow the door?"

"A few minutes," said Farnham. "Maybe three, at most."

"Shit," said Kenyon. "That's too long. They're almost ready to transmit. Once Cyberworm is out, it will destroy everything."

Arundel pointed at the imposing door. "There's no other way to reach the computers."

"What about the dish on the roof?" asked Kenyon. "We take that out, we stop the transmission."

"Good point," said Arundel. He turned toward the door. "We'll detail someone to take it out."

"No time." Kenyon grabbed Harry by the arm. "We'll go."

Two soldiers wearing thick gloves returned carrying a black metal box.

Arundel glanced at his watch. "We blow the door in three minutes. Stay off this end of the building in case the roof collapses."

"Piece a cake," said Harry. He synchronized the timer on his watch.

Harry and Kenyon sprinted back up the stairs, stopping at the top. They scanned the upper floor.

"You see any way out to the roof?" asked Kenyon.

"Gotta be a trapdoor somewheres," said Harry.

Using Harry's flashlight, the two men raced from room to room until they found a steel ladder bolted to the side of a wall.

They advanced cautiously until they were adjacent to the roof access. The small trapdoor was open, and they could see the landing lights of a jumbo jet blink as it passed above.

Kenyon studied the trapdoor for a moment. "Tight squeeze," he whispered.

Harry nodded in agreement. "What's the plan?"

"We just need to find the cable to the dish and cut it."

Harry pulled the bayonet off the end of his rifle "Give me thirty seconds." Gripping the bayonet in his teeth, he climbed the ladder. He cautiously peered over the lip of the trapdoor, then eased himself onto the roof. In a second, he was gone.

Kenyon reached thirty seconds, but there was no sign of Harry. He climbed the ladder.

Kenyon peered over the lip of the door. The roof of the warehouse was flat, with a two-foot wooden lip at the edge of the building. To his left, he could make out the silhouette of the large dish. A function light glowed bright red at the base: it was still in operation and Harry was nowhere to be seen.

"Harry!" hissed Kenyon. "Where are you?"

Kenyon could hear a mewling sound coming from the direction of the dish. Clambering out onto the roof, he advanced, wondering what a kitten was doing out there.

It wasn't a cat making the noise, it was Harry. Kenyon found the soldier sitting against the wooden lip of the roof. He was weakly clawing at something on his shoulder.

"Are you all right?" asked Kenyon. He crouched over to peer at whatever Harry was tugging at.

It was his bayonet. Someone had forced it through his arm, pinning him to the wood behind. Kenyon felt like retching.

Harry's eyes went wide as he focused on someone behind Kenyon.

Instinctively, Kenyon rolled to the left. A machete thudded into the lip, burying itself in the wood.

Kenyon spun to face his adversary. Ali stood behind him, tugging on the shaft of the machete in an effort to dislodge it. He launched himself against the man, tackling him in the midriff, but Ali flung Kenyon to one side, and resumed tugging at the machete.

Kenyon staggered to his feet. He was unarmed, but he couldn't leave Harry at the villain's mercy.

Suddenly, it struck him; Ali wasn't up there to attack the two men, he was there to protect the transmitter. Kenyon turned and rushed toward the dish, searching for the feeder cable. He found the line, wrapped several loops around his hand, and pulled it from the base of the dish.

With a bellow, Ali freed his machete and pursued Kenyon. The agent ducked behind the dish, trying to keep the end of the cable out of the giant's hand.

For a few frantic seconds, the duo lurched around the dish until Ali stomped down on the end of the cable, knocking Kenyon off balance. He stumbled against the lip of the roof and fell backwards over the edge. He would have plunged to his death, but the cable wrapped around his hand stopped him. He pounded against the side of the building, knocking the wind out of his lungs.

Swinging on the end of the cable, Kenyon glanced up. Through a haze of stars, he could see Ali standing above. The giant grinned wickedly, his machete held high.

Ali was interrupted by a beeping sound. He turned and glanced back toward Harry.

Kenyon grinned. "Time's up, big guy," he said.

There was a muffled clap of thunder, and the roof of the building rose. Ali and the dish hung weightless in the air for a moment, before plunging into the gaping hole in the roof.

Kenyon didn't have time to think. The cable, still entangled in the dish, whip-stocked him back onto the roof and across the tarry surface. Just as he was about to plunge after Ali, the dish came to rest, and Kenyon came to a halt at the lip of the hole. Directly below, amid the smoke from the explosion, Ali lay spreadeagled, unmoving.

The agent disentangled himself from the cable and ran over to Harry. A large pool of blood had formed beneath him, but he was still conscious.

"We'll have you out of here in a jiffy," said Kenyon.

Harry smiled weakly. "No worries."

"I'm going to get help." Kenyon squeezed through the trapdoor and descended the steel ladder. He found an SAS commando near the base of the ladder. "Harry's up top," said Kenyon. "He's injured. Call for an ambulance."

Kenyon headed back to the main room. Amid the swirling dust and smoke, he could see that the steel door to the alcove sat ajar, ripped from its mounts by the explosion. Inside the alcove, Garbajian and his henchmen lay face down on the floor, guarded by SAS commandos.

Kenyon scanned the computer monitor. A message flashed on the screen: "Transmission aborted." He breathed a sigh of relief, but the relief was short-lived. Arundel emerged from a passageway at the far end of the alcove. "Ilsa's escaped. She has the encryption code with her."

Kenyon ran back through the main room. He found a door leading into the lane adjacent to the warehouse. Pushing it open, he spotted Ilsa's car racing toward the end of the lane. A commando fired, bursting one of the taillights, but it didn't stop the car, which struck the wooden gate, smashing it off its hinges.

Kenyon ran down the lane and clambered over the remains of the wooden gate, staring at the retreating car. Lady Beatrice appeared at his side and grabbed him by the arm. "Come on, young man, she's escaping." She pushed Kenyon toward the Bentley. "I'll drive."

"No," replied Kenyon, climbing behind the wheel. "I'll drive. You have to let backup know where we're going."

Lady Beatrice switched the radio to multi-broadcast. "We have a suspect in flight heading east on Tooley Street in a black Mercedes. She is armed and dangerous. Use extreme caution."

With one of the rear taillights smashed, Kenyon soon made out its distinctive pattern. He floored the accelerator and the powerful car leapt ahead. A police van pulled from a side road, trying to block the Mercedes' path. Ilsa swerved sharply to the left, following an exit lane.

"She's heading north onto Tower Bridge Road," said Lady Beatrice into the radio. "Can someone block the north end?"

Kenyon turned onto Tower Bridge Road and peered ahead. "Doesn't look like we'll need anyone," he said. "They've closed the bridge."

A ship was approaching upstream, and the bridgemaster had initiated the raising of the leaves that allowed passage of large vessels under the structure. A pair of tall blue gates had been swung out onto the roadway to block traffic but the Mercedes didn't even slow down. Ilsa swung into the empty right lane and plowed through the barrier, accelerating toward the far end.

"The woman is completely insane," said Lady Beatrice. "What is she going to do, leap the gap?"

Kenyon sped in pursuit but by the time the Bentley reached the barrier, Ilsa's car was nearing the halfway point. The mechanical leaves had already started to inch slowly upwards, and a gap of several feet had opened. Kenyon could see the bridge master in his office frantically trying to reverse the widening gap.

It was too late. At the last moment, Ilsa tried to stop, but the Mercedes fishtailed out of control and plunged sideways into the gap.

Kenyon slammed on the brakes and brought the Bentley to a halt. He and Lady Beatrice ran to the edge and peered down.

The bridge had finally ground to a halt. There, stuck in the gap, was the Mercedes. Inside, they could see Ilsa struggling, trying to free herself.

The bridge began to lower. "Dear God, she'll be crushed," said Lady Beatrice. She turned and shouted at the bridgemaster. "Stop! Stop!"

The two mechanical leaves pressed upon the Mercedes like a nut cracker. The roof began to buckle, and the side windows exploded. Kenyon could see that the passenger window was a possible escape route. "Hang on," he called, clambering onto the side of the car.

Ilsa lay across the front seat of the Mercedes. "Can you move?" asked Kenyon.

Ilsa looked up. "My leg is stuck."

Kenyon glanced down toward the floor of the front seat. There, jammed between the dashboard and the gearshift, was the picture of Lydia. Ilsa's leg was pinned beneath the frame. "Give me your hand,"

Ilsa reached out, and their hands met. The agent pulled, but Ilsa's leg was stuck fast beneath the portrait's frame.

There was a loud clap as the Mercedes' windshield imploded, showering Kenyon with glass. The agent let go of Ilsa's hand and fell back as the immense weight of the bridge crushed the car. A scream arose from the mangled wreck, then silence, as the bridge finally came to a rest.

Far below, the river Thames flowed to the sea.

Epilogue
Friday, July 22. London

Jack Kenyon walked down the hospital hallway, the wheels of his carry-on luggage squeaking as they rolled over the spotless tiles. He stopped at the entrance to room 211. He could hear the sound of voices coming through the door. He rapped on the door, then walked in.

The room was painted in a faint peach, and the curtains had been drawn back to allow sunlight to spill through the large windows. Legrand was dressed in a standard issue hospital gown, his leg wrapped in a plaster cast and his arm covered in burn gauze. His mattress had been tilted up so that he could watch TV.

Tanya O'Neill sat in a visitor's chair beside Legrand's bed. Kenyon stopped short, surprised at her presence. "What is she doing here?" he asked Legrand.

Legrand smiled. "Seeing as how we both loved the same woman, I invited her here to compare notes, as it were."

"I was just going." O'Neill leaned forward and kissed Legrand's cheek. "I'll be back soon."

Legrand patted her arm. "Hurry back."

O'Neill walked toward the door and stopped in front of Kenyon. "There's something I'd like to say to you. Without your help, we never would have figured out who killed her. For that, I owe you my gratitude."

Kenyon stared into her eyes. "You loved Lydia with all your heart. For that, I owe *you* a debt of gratitude."

Tanya stood on her tiptoes and kissed Kenyon on the lips. She turned and waved to Legrand, then left.

Kenyon turned his attention to his father. "How are you feeling today?"

"Comme-ci, comme-ça," replied Legrand. He shrugged, pointing to the cast. "I do not like to sleep on my back, but what can I do?"

"I'm on my way to the airport, and I thought I'd stop by and give you these." He handed Legrand a package that he'd taken from his bag. "Señora Santucci made them for you."

Legrand opened the package and looked inside. "What are they?"

"Brownies," explained Kenyon. "They always make me feel better when I'm sick."

"Thank you. I am sure I will love them." Legrand placed the package down on his bedside table, then turned off the TV.

The sudden silence filled the room. Finally, Legrand cleared his throat. "Jack, there is something I wish to ask you."

"Sure."

"Why did you not leave me to die and save yourself?"

Kenyon stared at his shoes. "It's hard to explain."

"Please, try."

Kenyon continued to stare at the floor. "When I was a little kid, I wondered what my real mother and father were like. I kind of pictured them living in this wonderful house with a big yard, and a dog, and they had this special room for me all made up, waiting for me to come home." Kenyon looked up at Legrand. "Well, it didn't quite work that way."

Legrand stared out the window. "I am sorry."

"Don't be sorry." The agent turned to leave.

"Your mother had a special room for you," said Legrand.

Kenyon turned back. "Really?"

"Yes. But it was not in her home. That would have been too dangerous."

Kenyon advanced to Legrand's bed. "Where was it, then?"

Legrand looked up at his son. "In her heart."

Kenyon paused for a moment, then reached down and placed a hand on his father's shoulder. "Thanks, Raymond."

Legrand eased himself up on his elbows. "I know that I cannot be the father you really wanted, but I would like to try."

"Me, too." Kenyon bent forward and hugged Legrand. "I've got a favor to ask."

"Anything."

"I decided to keep Lydia's home. When you're better, will you stay there and watch it for me?"

Legrand smiled. "Of course. What are your plans for the gallery?"

"I think Zoë Tigger is up to handling it, so I put her in charge." Kenyon slung his bag over his shoulder and hugged his father one last time. "You take care now. I'll be back soon."

Outside, it was a warm, sunny day. Traffic was flowing briskly down Cromwell Road. Kenyon placed the bag down and held his hand up to flag down a cab.

"Need a lift, old boy?" Detective Inspector Humphrey Arundel stood beside his Bentley, his sunglasses tilted back on his forehead. Kenyon had the feeling the other man might have been waiting for him.

Kenyon smiled. "Yeah. I'm heading out to Heathrow."

"I just happen to be going that way. Hop in."

Kenyon placed his bag in the back of the Bentley and climbed into the passenger side while Arundel slid into the driver's seat and merged the car into eastbound traffic.

"How is Legrand?" he asked, as he blithely pulled a U-turn across three lanes and headed west.

"He's not sleeping that well, but he's doing fine," responded Kenyon. "Is Harry okay?"

"Broken ribs and a punctured arm, but the surgeons expect a full recovery."

"He's a brave man."

"Yes, he is. I suspect Her Majesty has some special trinket in store for Commander Harold Twiggley."

Kenyon laughed. "No wonder he prefers Happy Harry. What about Garbajian and his gang?"

"They are supplying Her Majesty's government with some very interesting information that we will be more than happy to share with our American cousins," said Arundel. "I am constrained from saying anything further."

The traffic slowed for some roadwork, and they sat quietly for a few minutes.

Finally, Arundel turned to Kenyon. "I understand if you don't want to talk, but I would be eternally grateful if you were to explain to me why Ilsa did what she did."

Kenyon stared out the front window for a moment. "Revenge, pure and simple. She hated Lydia for stealing her man, and she hated her even worse for stealing the son she never had. When Ilsa learned that Lydia was going to reveal the truth, she snapped."

"Exactly what did she do?"

"She used Lydia's gallery to plant the bug in her own boardroom so that she could record the encryption code. She enlisted deWolfe and sent him to San Francisco to steal the Cyberworm virus from under my nose. If it hadn't been for the fact that Lydia stumbled across the fake, she would have framed us both and gotten away with it clean."

"Did you ever resolve who killed Lydia?" asked Arundel

"Yeah. Ilsa did it."

Arundel looked over at Kenyon, surprised. "How did she manage that while hosting a charity auction?"

"It wasn't tough," said the agent. "She left the auction near the end of the evening on the excuse she had to look in on Sir Rupert. Once she saw Lydia leave, Ilsa snuck down the back stairs, changed into her riding clothes in the stables, and rode up the bridle path to the Abbey Road. Then she waited in ambush until Lydia passed by, and shone the laser light in her eyes."

"Well, it does sound plausible, but I'm still concerned that the real killer remains at large," said Arundel. "Are you certain it was her?"

Kenyon patted the letter Ilsa had tucked in his pocket. "I'm sure."

They reached Heathrow, and Arundel turned into the exit lane.

"Well, I'm glad of that. I'd hate to think you had plans to continue investigating."

"What do you mean?" asked Kenyon.

Arundel placed his tongue firmly in his cheek. "For starters, you seem to leave an appalling pile of corpses wherever you go."

"Hey, without me, you guys wouldn't have had a case."

"Would you believe me if I told you the authorities are eternally grateful for the invaluable contributions you have made to the protection of Her Majesty's realm?"

Kenyon laughed. "No."

They pulled up in front of the terminal. Kenyon got out of the Bentley and removed his luggage from the trunk, then returned to the driver's side and stuck his hand through the window.

"Thanks for the lift, Humphrey."

Arundel shook his hand. "You're welcome, Jack. And, do hurry back, old boy."

"Why?"

Arundel put the car in gear. "It's so frightfully dull around here without you."

Kenyon watched him pull away, then turned and headed for the entrance.

It took the agent several minutes to find the check-in for his flight, but his first-class ticket meant he didn't have to stand in line very long. The agent flashed his FBI badge at security, and they waived him through the metal detectors into the departure area.

Kenyon ordered a coffee from a cappuccino stand and took his drink to a small table adjacent to the walkway. He watched as passengers streamed by, their arms full of duty free goods, heading for their homes and families, to the people they loved.

He finished his coffee and glanced up at the departures information. The flight for San Francisco was leaving from gate 32. Kenyon gathered up his jacket and bag and headed down a long corridor.

Gate 32 was packed with tourists heading home to the States. Everyone from bleached blond backpackers to grannies in support stockings. Kenyon spotted Gonelli, her big handbag clutched in her arms, a soggy cigar clenched in her teeth. She was sitting by herself, knitting a scarf. Kenyon sat down beside her. "Hi, Marge."

"Hey, kiddo."

Kenyon just sat and smiled at Marge for a moment. Finally, he spoke. "Did you know Lydia was my mom?"

Gonelli stopped knitting. "Yeah. It came up on your background check."

"How come you never told me?"

Gonelli stared down at her knitting. "I don't know."

"Marge, whenever I imagined what my real mom would be like, she always seemed a lot like you."

Gonelli hugged him. "You're a real sweetie, you know that?"

"Yeah, I know. Speaking of sweeties, what happened to our pal Deaver?"

Gonelli laughed. "He was pretty cranky for a few days, but he's okay now."

Kenyon tilted his head to one side. "What kind of deal did you cut?"

Gonelli made a great show of looking offended. "Whatcha talkin' about? Ain't no deal. I just told him he could take the credit for the snatch, is all."

"Is that all?"

Gonelli winked. "Well, I do have a wonderful, glossy photo of him passed out in a wine cellar. I threatened to release it during his run for governor if he ever made any waves."

The overhead PA system crackled. "Last boarding call for flight 445 to Seattle, gate 34," said the announcer.

Kenyon leaned forward and picked up his bag.

"Hey, ain't you coming back to San Francisco with me?" asked Gonelli.

"No, Marge." Kenyon patted his carry-on. "There's something I have to do first."

Gonelli took the cigar out of her mouth and gave Kenyon a kiss on the cheek. "You're a good boy, Jack Kenyon."

The flight took ten hours, and Kenyon was glad to finally get off the plane and stretch his legs when it arrived in SeaTac. He could see the remnants of a rainstorm that had just swept across the airport, drenching the tarmac. By the time Kenyon found a car agency and rented a sedan the clouds had cleared off, and seagulls circled in a brilliant blue sky.

Kenyon headed east, the flatlands around Seattle quickly giving way to the Cascade Range. His car ascended the slopes of the magnificent mountains, the road winding its way upward to a pass into the Columbia basin. Even in the height of summer, snow still clung to Mount Rainier, and the cold, wet winds that whistled down the glacial valleys filling his lungs with clean, sweet air.

Kenyon drove for several hours through the vast plain of scrub and farmland that covered the interior of Washington State, stopping only to fill up the tank at a roadside gas station and buy a burger at a drive-in restaurant.

By mid-afternoon, he had passed through the city of Spokane, and was once again climbing, this time the western slopes of the Bitterroot Range.

By early evening, Kenyon had crossed into Montana. He breathed in the heady forest perfume from the aspen and evergreens covering the eastern foothills.

It was well into the long summer twilight when he reached the turn-off. Kenyon pointed the car north, and the paved highway gave way to a gravel road that wound its way along a broad river valley.

Most of the trees had been cleared for pasture land, and herds of cattle cropped at the summer grass. Every few miles, a pick-up truck driven by a man wearing a ballcap would roll by. Without even thinking, Kenyon would lift the first three fingers of his driving hand, saluting his neighbor.

After driving for fifteen minutes, the road gradually narrowed and began to climb. The pasture gave way to stands of trees, until forest once again loomed over the road. The sun, now low on the horizon, cut horizontally through the trees. Kenyon felt as though he were driving through a long, dusty cathedral.

The road finally dead-ended at the entrance to a ranch. The gate had been built out of pine logs, and was decorated with elk antlers and the skull of a grizzly bear. A wooden plaque had two words carved into it: "Eden Valley." Kenyon opened the gate, drove the car through, and closed the gate behind him.

By the time he reached the ranch house, Cyrus was waiting for him on the porch. Kenyon got out of the car and stood before his grandfather. The deep blue eyes that stared out of Cyrus's wind-worn face were softer than Kenyon ever remembered.

"Welcome home, Jack," said Cyrus. "You want to come in and sit a bit?"

Kenyon looked at the setting sun. "No, I want to do it now."

Cyrus nodded his head, as if he already knew the answer. "I'll go saddle the horses while you change."

Kenyon carried his luggage inside the house. It was just as he remembered it: the potbellied stove, the bear rug on the floor, the guns on the wall. The TV was new; a big Sony flatscreen, but otherwise it was all the same, right down to the smell of pipe smoke and the old, battered enamel coffee pot on the stove.

Kenyon walked back to his room. The bed and dresser seemed so tiny. When had he ever imagined his entire world between these walls? He pulled on his jeans, then dug through the closet. His old cowboy boots were stiff and curled, but they still fit. He took a suede coat off a peg and put it on. It was going to be cool tonight. He removed a package out of his carry-on luggage and tucked it into the wide pocket of the coat.

Outside, Cyrus stood beside the porch with the horses. Kenyon took the reins and climbed up on a tall, roan mare.

"She's just broke last summer, so have a mind," warned Cyrus.

The roan was frisky, but Kenyon kept the reins tight against her neck, and she soon settled down. As they entered a trail behind the ranch, the last of the sun shone against a string of clouds high above the mountains, filling the air with a blaze of orange and gold. A lone eagle circled overhead, a graceful, black dot.

They finally reached the top of a ridge overlooking Eden Valley. Below them, the lights of the farmhouse and barn twinkled in the inky trough of the valley.

They stopped, and both men dismounted. Kenyon stared at the vista for a moment, then turned to Cyrus. "You bring a flashlight?"

The older man dug through his saddlebag while Kenyon pulled the letter Ilsa had given him out of his pocket. The two men stood upon the ridge, Cyrus holding the flashlight, Kenyon reading the letter.

Dear Jack:
When you were one day old, I held you in my arms. You looked at me with your bright blue eyes, and you gripped my finger so hard that when the nurse came for you, I couldn't let you go. I love you now with all my heart, just as I did then.
Lydia

Kenyon took the pouch from his pocket and opened it. The wind was blowing up the slope, and when he scattered Lydia's ashes, they soared skywards, then far and wide over Eden Valley, until you could no longer distinguish them from the stars that danced in the deep, cobalt sky.

Acknowledgments

Over the course of several years, I have had the privilege of consulting many fascinating people from a variety of backgrounds in order to write this book. I would like to thank Herbert Cohrs, assistant legal attaché to the American Embassy in London, and George Grotz, special agent stationed in San Francisco, for their insight and knowledge concerning the FBI, both home and abroad. I would also like to thank London art dealers Harry Blain and Charlie Phillips for their explanation of how the international art sector functions (and, occasionally, doesn't). My gratitude to optometrist Dr. Ken Gellatly for detailing how the eye can be harmed by lasers, and to gun instructor Bill Heyder for showing me how avoid shooting myself in the foot with a Sig Sauer pistol. In addition, many, many thanks to publisher Ruth Linka and all the people at TouchWood for helping Jack Kenyon see the light of day, and to editor Linda Richards for improving my prose immensely.

GORDON COPE is an experienced feature writer and business reporter who has lived in London and Paris and traveled around the world. His travel memoirs include *A Paris Moment* (2005), *So, We Sold Our House and Ran Away to the South Pacific* (2006), and *A Thames Moment* (2010). *Secret Combinations* is Gordon's first novel. He lives in Calgary, Alberta.